Lady Duffus Hardy

Through Cities and Prairie Lands

Sketches of an American Tour

Lady Duffus Hardy

Through Cities and Prairie Lands
Sketches of an American Tour

ISBN/EAN: 9783744681032

Printed in Europe, USA, Canada, Australia, Japan

Cover: Foto ©Andreas Hilbeck / pixelio.de

More available books at **www.hansebooks.com**

THROUGH
CITIES AND PRAIRIE LANDS.

SKETCHES OF AN AMERICAN TOUR.

BY

LADY DUFFUS HARDY.

LONDON:

CHAPMAN AND HALL, LIMITED,

HENRIETTA STREET, COVENT GARDEN.

1881.

TO

MRS. WILLIAM HAYWOOD,

IN TOKEN

OF MY AFFECTIONATE REGARD,

I DEDICATE

THESE PAGES.

CONTENTS.

THROUGH CITIES AND PRAIRIE LANDS.

CHAPTER I.

ACROSS THE ATLANTIC.

Our Good Ship *Sardinian*—At Sea—Our Companions—Their
Amusements—The Theorist—The Phantom Ship—Our Last
Night on Board.

IT is the grey dawn of a July day ; we are up with the
sun, nay, before the sun, eager to start on our first
Atlantic voyage. In order to avoid the hurry and
bustle of a crowded Liverpool hotel, I and my companion, for we are two, had resolved to start by the
first train, and go direct on board. Therefore, at six
o'clock on this bright July morning, we arrive at
Euston Square station, and there find a host of friends,
who, in spite of the early hour, have gathered to bid us
" God Speed." They are all gift-laden ; one brings
books and bonbons, another a basket of rich ripe strawberries, then a patent corkscrew and telescope is thrust
into my hand, and last, though not least, just as the
train is moving out of the station, one late arrival
breathlessly gasps " Good-bye " and flings a packet of
pins, a box of matches, and a cake of scented soap in
at the window.

B

At Liverpool the little steam-tug was in waiting to convey us to the vessel, which lay a short distance from the landing stage. It was a lovely July day; the sun was blooming, like a flower of light, in the bright blue skies, the tiny waves danced and murmured joyously as they ran rippling along the shore, and the soft balmy air, laden " with the briny kisses of the great sweet mother," greeted us with invigorating breath as we steamed across and stepped on board the good ship *Sardinian*, ready to face the fearful ten days which we had so often anticipated with shivering and shudderings at our cosy fireside.

There was a hurried hand-shaking. " Good-byes " and parting words resounded on all sides of us, uttered in varied shades of feeling, some with a choking sob as of friends who would never meet again, others with hearty cheerful voices, as though they were bound for young life's first holiday. Presently stentorian lungs shouted " all for the shore," departing friends and relatives swarmed down the steep wooden wall of the vessel; we all rushed to the side, nods and smiles " that were half tears " were freely exchanged, last words were shouted from one to the other, and amid the waving of handkerchiefs and echoing voices, the little steam-tug which had brought the passengers on board went shrieking and snorting back to the shore, and our great ship steamed majestically up the Mersey, out towards the obnoxious Irish Channel; some weak-minded mortals started with a hazy idea that if the Channel treated them too roughly, they could, if they pleased, land at Moville, and so bid " adieu " to the horrors of the sea for ever; but that was a cowardly idea which I never encouraged for a moment.

My first idea was to take a survey of my fellow-passengers. There were plenty of them; as a rule they were mere commonplace specimens of humanity, such as nature turns out by thousands, with no distinctive mark, but merely labelled "men" and "women." There were exceptions of course. One was an elderly hard-featured man, bronzed and weather-beaten, with keen gray eyes, which looked as though they could detect a spot on the face of the sun without the aid of glasses, and so searching that, like the east wind, they could reach the marrow at a single blow. But my attention was most attracted by a very young and very beautiful widow; beautiful, so far as grace of form, regularity of feature, and soft colouring was concerned, but the beauty of her face was utterly destroyed by its expression, which may be briefly catalogued as "evil." She looked like a woman who had got a story, and not a pleasant one. No accompanying friends had bid her "good-bye," or "good speed." She was alone, but she did not seem lonely. She carried a child about a year old in her arms, and marched up and down the deck, looking neither to the right nor to the left, till the gong sounded and we all went down to dinner; but before the table could be satisfactorily arranged the question arose, "What was to become of the baby?" At last a young Scotchman volunteered to immolate himself on the altar of beauty, and held out his arms for the child; she gave it without a word, and he disappeared up the companion-way, holding it upside down, which awkwardness may perhaps be excused, considering that was the first time he had officiated in the capacity of dry-nurse.

The gilded glories of the saloon were a surprise to

me, as this was the first time I had been on an Atlantic steamer. Of course, in common with the world generally, I had *heard* of the luxurious arrangements and admirably served table on board those magnificent vessels; but I had yet to learn how luxury and comfort combined could make that floating world a pleasant ten days' home. The dreaded voyage turned out delightfully. The Irish Channel behaved beautifully, literally "it broke into dimples and laughed in the sun," as its rippling waves ran dancing round the prow and along the black sides of our vessel, gurgling and murmuring in smothered tones as though they were enjoying a joke, exulting in their hidden strength, knowing that their pleasant playful mood might pass and their tiny wavelets grow into mountains and uplift us in their giant arms and toss us up to the moon, or crush our huge iron-hearted home like an eggshell, and swallow us all up. On we went, cutting a rapid way through the calm waters; the daylight and the land together faded from our sight, the stars came out, and as the silent night closed slowly around us, merry laughing voices sank into quiet sober tones. We seemed to realize the fact that we were alone on the wide world of waters—the same living restless waters whereon Christ had walked, and whose waves he had bidden "Peace, be still." We retired to our cosy little stateroom early, and slept as we had never dreamed we could sleep on our first night at sea, our slumbers soothed, not broken, by the musical "Yo, heave, ho!" of the sailors; and the steady monotonous "thud, thud" of the engine had a by no means unpleasant effect on our drowsily unaccustomed ears. When we awoke in the morning we found ourselves, not tossing, but gliding calmly over the "wild Atlantic waves," which were rolling round us on all sides as far as the eye could reach, a world of palpitating waters, unruffled and smooth as the bosom of a lake. For three days this calm continued. The masculine element grew turbulent and rebelled against this unnatural state of things; there was something wrong about it altogether; even the "rolling forties," from whom some show of spirit was expected, forgot to do their duty, and allowed us to ride over them without a protesting blow; their wild white horses were stabled in the caves below, and with all sails set; a brisk breeze following in our wake, and the briny kisses of the "great sweet mother" on our faces, we scudded along at the rate of fifteen knots an hour. We female passengers thoroughly appreciated the stormless sea, and paced up and down the deck chatting and exchanging harmless confidences; the gentlemen tried to beguile the time with ring-toss and shovel-board. When they grew tired of such harmless occupations they got up a walking match, or ran half-mile races round the deck, and, indeed, in every way did their best to scare away ennui, and make the monotonous days and hours pass pleasantly; for after the first novelty of the scene is over, skies of eternal changeless blue and calm summer seas are apt to grow monotonous, and a thunderstorm or a howling hurricane, "warranted harmless," would have created a pleasant diversion. However, on the whole, time passed pleasantly enough; we were all sociably inclined, and lived on strictly communistic principles, in a general exchange of civilities. Everybody was welcome to the belongings of everybody else; we used each other's chairs, rugs, wraps, and even made occasional walking sticks of one another's husbands, and when we had nothing else to do indulged in a game of speculation concerning the " widow," who held herself aloof, in a state of as complete isolation as though she had been on a desert island; she accepted courtesies without a word of thanks, or refused them with an impatient gesture, till the chivalrous spirit of the gentlemen flickered and died out, and as she resented any offer of assistance, she was left to stagger about the deck at her pleasure.   The child was the pet and plaything of everybody on board; the mother seemed willing to ignore its existence, and gave it only a kind of wooden automatic attention at best.   Nothing attracted or interested her, and the beautiful dark face became a weird strange mystery to us.   We grew accustomed to see the tall lithe figure pacing silently to and fro like a shadowy ghost in the gloaming; for long after the daylight faded and the evening closed in she continued her monotonous round, like a perturbed spirit that could know no rest.

We had a theorist on board, too, who by a sheer habit of aggravation kept us lively.   His theory was *starvation*.   Nobody ought to be sick, nobody ought to be hungry; he pounced upon everybody with an appetite of even the most moderate dimensions.

" My dear madam," he said in deprecating tones, addressing an elderly lady who was modestly picking a chicken-bone, " you are committing an outrage upon nature; she doesn't require that chicken-bone."

" I must eat to support life," said the lady apologetically.

" Bah ! you can support life on the backbone of a bloater; as I say, you are outraging nature, forcing things upon her that she doesn't want, and she will revenge herself by disturbing your digestion and depressing your spirits."

"My spirits are always depressed; I don't know what it is to be cheerful *now*," she answered in a lachrymose tone.

"Of course not. An overloaded stomach acts like a weight to keep the spirits down. Look at me," he added, slapping his ample chest and outstretching his brawny arm, "*I'm* strong and healthy; I nourish myself upon—next to nothing, and I'm never hungry— never depressed."

"Ah, sir!" she answered, shaking her head with a tear in her eye, "if you were in my place you'd never be anything else; but you don't know what it is to lose your life's partner."

"Don't I? Why, I've buried two! This is my third venture." He jerked his head towards a fair pale little woman, whose appetite was evidently under his control. "Why, when I first married my little wife there," he added, regarding her affectionately, "she used to eat three meals a day; now she is reduced to one."

"By the time you have reduced her to half a meal, perhaps, she'll give you a chance of experimenting on a fourth," suggested my companion; which observation our theorist did not choose to hear, but sauntered on, threatening one with apoplexy, scaring another with visions of sudden death; investing everybody with the "ills that flesh is heir to," the one inheritance that nobody is in a hurry to possess. Lobster salad was alive with horrible nightmares, and delirium tremens bubbled in the glass of sparkling

Moet and Chandon.   On all sides his theory was greeted with goodhumoured derision, and occasioned much merriment, and though there was little wit, there was much laughter among us.   At last a living contradiction to his theory stepped out from the companion-way in the person of a fair-complexioned young Englishman, a perfect athlete, broad-chested, strong-limbed, a "crisp and curled Antony," brimming over with the healthful vigour and vitality of young manhood; he could run, row, leap, ride, and in every manly sport had kept to the fore.

"Look at me," he said, "*I* eat four square meals a day, and, perhaps, put more roast beef out of sight than anybody here; but do *I* look like a wreck?   Just feel my biceps."

"My good fellow," said our theorist, regarding him with grave compassionate interest, "you have a good constitution; you are doing your best—but—you have not had time to ruin it yet."

Our vessel carried a hundred and fifty steerage passengers, with whom we had many a pleasant chat on the forecastle deck; some hoped to ply their trade in the cities, some were going up the country.   "We can get plenty of land there, and never a stiver to pay for it," said one burly man, with a large family of small children.   Somebody suggested that the United States offered a wider field and less difficulties.   "That may be," he answered, " but I don't want to cut myself adrift from the old country; I mean my children and their children after 'em, please God, to grow up under the British flag.   The stars and stripes are very well in their way, but the Union Jack's good enough for me."
That was the general feeling among the emigrant

classes; the vast uncultivated lands of the United States might offer better fortune, but, they would not cut themselves adrift from the "old country."

Our captain read prayers in the steerage night and morning, but we first-class sinners had a religious service on Sundays only. Every evening such sailors as were not on duty gathered in the forecastle, and the captain gave them an extemporaneous sermon, in forcible homely language best suited to their comprehension, and allowed them to indulge in a goodly sprinkling of Moody and Sankey's hymns. It was a strange and rather a weird scene, that narrow forecastle, with bunks all round, the long oak table, lit with tiny oil lamps, flickering up in the swart grimy faces of the men, as they united their voices—and with all their hearts, or at least with all their lungs—in praises or thanksgiving, as they tramped on their "March to Canaan's Land" or lingered round the gates of "Jerusalem the Golden."

In a pleasant desultory fashion the eventful days passed on, the smallest thing affording us great diversion; once a shoal of porpoises gambolled beside the vessel, tumbling and rolling over one another in their fishlike frolics; then a school of whales passed within a quarter of a mile of us, uplifting their huge heads, and creating a series of waterspouts by the way. Our route was so far north that no other vessel had hitherto crossed our path; we seemed to have the sea all to ourselves. One morning the exclamation went round, "A sail in sight;" we flew to the bulwarks, but nothing was visible to our unaccustomed eyes; we watched, eagerly straining our eyes in the direction indicated; by degrees a kind of phantom ship, with all sails set, loomed upon our sight; it seemed to hang suspended on the very edge of the world between sea and sky. We watched it breathlessly; but it came no nearer, no clearer. Shrouded in mist, like a spectral illusion, it remained a few moments in sight, and then disappeared as mysteriously as it came, and once more we were alone on the wide desolate sea. That evening we had a splendid sunset; the whole of the western skies were draped with crimson, lighted up with flames of gold. We watched its kaleidoscopic glories change; one brilliant colour fading into and amalgamating with another, till the whole horizon was a gorgeous mass of rose-tinted purple and green and gold, which presently broke up, and drifted, and re-formed till the pale dim skies were filled with floating islands of fire. We literally felt as though we were sailing " into the land beyond the sunset seas, the islands of the blest."

On the evening of the eighth day we sighted Father Point, and sent up a rocket to summon a pilot from the shore; three rockets, red, white, and blue, went whizzing through the air in answer—" coming." In another moment a white light, like a gigantic glow-worm came creeping along the face of the water, nearer and nearer, till the plish-plashing of oars brought a cockleshell of a boat alongside, and the pilot, with the agility of a cat, climbed up the huge black side of the vessel and leapt over the bulwarks on to the deck.

Our pilot embarked, we were soon on our way again. After the long uneventful days and nights, the slightest occurrence amused and interested us, and that day, to our unoccupied minds, seemed crammed with adventures. As we paced the deck chatting and laughing, some warbling or singing snatches of old songs, we were startled by the appearance of a huge black mass, which seemed to grow mysteriously out of the darkness, with many-coloured lights swinging in the empty air. It was the steam-tug which had come off from Rimouski for mails and such passengers as desired to go on to Lower Canada; the lights swung from the shrouds and rigging of the vessel, and shone down with a weird effect upon the bustling scene below. There was a general commotion; impatient friends had come on board to meet their relatives; one after another eager faces swarmed over the bulwarks, and welcoming exclamations and hearty handshakings and embraces followed their appearance; the pleasant greetings of the genial happy voices cast a momentary cloud over our spirits; our thoughts flew homeward; we knew it would be long before familiar faces and friendly voices could give *us* greeting, and we half envied our fellow-passengers their welcome to what to us was an unknown land. But in the unknown there is always a mysterious attraction, and before the little steam-tug was well out of sight we were again buoyantly pacing the deck, with never a thought or care beyond the present. It was a lovely night; the stars, such big blazing stars, shone down like angels' eyes through the dark-blue sky; the waves sparkled and danced beneath the light of the planet Jupiter, which shone like a baby moon upon the dark face of the water. We were all too nervously excited to care for rest that night. We lingered long upon the deck, and at last disappeared one by one down the companion-way, our captain's cheery voice assuring us "we should sight Quebec in the morning."

CHAPTER II.

QUEBEC.

Land again—A Quaint Announcement—A Gastronomical Exhibition—A Pleasant Fireside—The Convent—The Heights of Abraham—Wolfe's Monument—French and English Canadians.

THE next day we were up early, and went on deck in time to see the first rosy flush break from the east, and creep over the cool gray dawn. It deepened, and widened, and spread, till the golden sun rose slowly, and took possession of the pale blue skies, casting his lance-like beams to the right and to the left, tinging all things above and below with his heavenly alchemy, but concentrating his light, like a crown of glory, on the beautiful city which loomed slowly upon our sight out of the shadowy distance.

With straining eyes we watched to catch the first view of Quebec. We had heard of it, read of it, knew of all the vicissitudes it had undergone, had looked upon its pictured beauty scores of times; but now the reality was before us, and the picturesque beauty of its appearance fully realized, if it did not exceed, our expectations. How few things in this world ever do that! Something was no doubt owing to the extreme beauty of the morning, the clearness of the atmosphere, and the glowing sunlight that gilded the tall spires, flecked the sloping housetops, till the china roofs sparkled and flashed like a world of broken diamonds. Slowly we steamed up the St. Lawrence towards our goal. It was good to see land at last. The soft, picturesque river scenery spread like a panoramic view on either side of us — luxuriant, grassy mounds and meadows came down to the water's edge, pretty villages were dotted about here and there, with a background of swelling hills, which rose higher and higher till they were lost in the pine forests beyond. The distant jingle of the church bells broke pleasantly on our ears after the long monotonous plish-plashing of the waves. On our left rose Pont Levis, a busy place or collection of houses, churches and manufactories, creeping up a lofty hill almost as imposing to look at as Quebec itself, and with a tolerable amount of historical associations too, though they have been swallowed up in the more prominent facts of its more beautiful and picturesque neighbour. It was at Pont Levis that the military authorities bided their time, and held their discussions, and arranged their manœuvres before carrying them into effect; and it was there that General Wolfe waited and chafed impatiently for the gray dawn which gave him victory and death.

We disembarked at Pont Levis, and were ferried across the river to Quebec. There our pleasant party drifted away in different directions, some going north, some going south; there was much handshaking, many good wishes, and hopes to meet again. We were very sorry to part with our theorist, who, with his delicate young wife, went on his homeward way to Maine, where we promised to pay them a visit before our tour was ended. At the landing-stage, a forlorn-looking place in a most dilapidated condition, we were surrounded by a clamorous crowd of Irish and French, who made a raid upon our small baggage, and struggled manfully as to who should bear it off. However, while we were looking helplessly around, we were rescued by the timely advent of the hotel proprietor, who, through the thoughtful kindness of our captain, had been notified of our arrival, and had come down on the look-out for us. He thrust the rabble to the right and to the left, handed us into a *calêche* which he had in waiting, and in another moment we were bowling along through the lower market-place, on our way to the St. Louis Hotel. With reckless speed we rattled up the steep, stony streets, the breath almost jostled out of our bodies, and clutching one another wildly in our endeavour to keep steady,—on across the upper and more aristocratic market-square, which is surrounded by large handsome shops, past the puritanical-looking Cathedral, a plain, barnlike building with a tall tapering spire, and were at length deposited safely at the door of the St. Louis Hotel, a commodious and comfortable place enough for a temporary resting-place. We were at once shown into a room on an upper floor, having a beautiful view of the town and river. We looked down upon a congregation of towers, turrets, steeples, and housetops, with the Laval Museum standing out the chief feature below, and the Convent of Gray Nùns standing square and gloomy on the hill above. Having taken a brief look around, we inquired :

"When does the dinner-bell ring ? "

"Sure thin, there's no dinner-bell at all!" answered a stout Irish lass.

" How shall we know when it is dinner-time ? "

" Oh, yez'll know ; 'e 'ollers."

She disappeared, leaving us slightly puzzled as to who would 'oller. We waited a few minutes, and then sure enough, he did "'oller." A pair of stentorian lungs shouted through all the corridors, " Dinner! dinner!" The voice dwindled away, and went wandering in ghostly echoes to remote corners and distant chambers, circulating the fact in this most primitive fashion that dinner was served. Having eaten and drank for the last ten days under difficulties, never being quite sure that our soup would not find its way into our pockets, or our chicken fly into our faces, and obstinately refuse to be driven into our mouths, it was pleasant to find ourselves comfortably seated at a table that wouldn't turn a somersault on its own account, or send the crockery flying about our ears. There were specimens of many nationalities at table, with a fair sprinkling of the gentle Canadians themselves ; and here began a gastronomical exhibition. As a rule (of course there are exceptions) people did not eat, they *bolted*; flung their food into their mouths, and sent their knives after it to see that it was all right. Seated opposite to me was a round, bullet-headed man, like a monk, " all shaven and shorn," with large ears, which seemed to grow out of his head, not on it, and a large loose mouth, that looked as though it could never tighten, and had no idea of ever shutting itself firmly ; but oh! so much went into it! He surrounded himself with the whole bill of fare, and then " fell to," demolishing one thing after another, till I fancied he must have a fit of apoplexy or—burst. He handled his eating utensils with such marvellous dexterity, that

when his knife flashed in the air and disappeared down
his throat, I watched for it to come out at the back of
his head; but no! it always came back. Well, they
are used to playing with edged tools this side of the
water, and provided they do not compel me to join the
game I am content.

The next morning we received a visit from the
Sanitary Inspector (who had been introduced to us
when he boarded our vessel for our bill of health).
He came accompanied by his wife and daughters on
hospitable thoughts intent. We were quite at home
with one another in half an hour, nay in ten minutes,
and in their pleasant home we spent many evening
hours. It was a musical household; the young daughters, with fine contralto and mezzo-soprano voices,
warmed our hearts with some of the sweet home songs
which we thought we had left behind us. Our captain,
too, while he was on shore, occasionally dropped in and
enlivened us with the patriotic ditties in which our
souls delighted. Our mutual favourite was the thrilling ballad of the "Slave Ship." He would bring his
hand down with a crash upon the ivory keys, and
send a shrieking shiver through the chords as he
triumphantly announced :

> "There's always death to slavery
> When British bunting's spread."

His face beamed as though his individual hand was
striking slavery dead. When not patriotic he was intensely moral, and the lesson of "Mrs. Lofty's jewels"
was so vigorously driven into our brain, we ought to
have been dead to the dazzle of diamonds evermore.

On the first day of our arrival we sallied forth to

see the town. The picturesque fascination of its first
appearance, which took us captive as we first steamed
up the St. Lawrence, lessened on a closer acquaintance.
" Distance lends enchantment to the view " in this as
in many other cases. It is a delightfully old historic
city, full of incongruities, and marvellous in its general
aspect of griminess and decay. The ancient buildings
do not seem to be enjoying a hale and strong old age.
They have a gray, worn look, as though they felt their
mournful position, and grieved that no hand was outstretched to save them from the ruin into which they
are fast falling. It seems as though time had robed
and crowned this quaint old town with historic fame
and interest, and then turned away and left it forlorn
and half forgotten ; for it has all the appearance of a
bankrupt estate, with little life or money left in it.
Its glory has departed, there is no doubt of that, and
the good folk are trying to destroy its picturesqueness
as fast as they can. We feel this as we stroll through
the long straggling up and down streets, their china
or slate roofs glistening in the sunshine. The houses,
some old, some new, represent every style of architecture or non-architecture under the sun ; no uniformity,
no regularity anywhere. Some are built of red brick,
some of gray stone, with odd little latticed windows
breaking out in unexpected places. Some modern
occupants of ancient homes have discarded the tiny
twinkling panes, and replaced them with huge squares
of plate glass and other " modern improvements," marring as much as possible the quaint picturesqueness of
the old, without imparting the imposing aspect of the
new. The wooden pavements are in a generally rotten
condition, and the roads when they are not cobble

stones are full of ruts, holes, and pitfalls, which makes us sigh for Macadam and all his host.

We pass through the Governor's garden, where a huge placard warns "not to pick the flowers." But never a flower is in sight; only a growth of dank, long grass, and a thick undergrowth of weeds of the wildest; *they* flourish luxuriantly enough. We pick our way over the stony pathway, and reach Dufferin Terrace, a splendid promenade, which is and will remain for centuries a noble record written in stone of Lord Dufferin's administration in Canada. It is fifty feet wide and a quarter of a mile long. It runs from the fort of the citadel, on the edge of the quaint old town, on the one side, and has a wide extensive land and river view on the other, perhaps one of the loveliest views in all Canada, for as far as the eye can see on all sides there is a well-wooded landscape of undulating hills and valleys dotted with toy villages and tiny towns, with the beautiful river lying like a sheet of silver below, winding and widening till it seems to fade in the far horizon, and is lost in the vast ocean beyond. Leaning over the fanciful iron railing we look sheer down a hundred and twenty feet into Champlain Street, the St. Giles of Quebec, and out over the lower town. Here on this splendid terrace the Quebeckers take their evening promenade when the sultry day is over, for if there is the slightest breeze stirring, it is sure to be found here. Standing back, at about the centre of the terrace, is the monument to "Wolfe and Montcalm," situated in a small square plat, "which is a garden called," but which in reality is like the rest of the public gardens here, a mass of tangled weeds and briars. The renowned general himself looks as though he was rather tired of standing there, and would gladly descend to that oblivion into which all men great and small must sink at last. It is only a question of time. He is doing his best to get away from men's eyes, and is crumbling to pieces as fast as he can. Already he has no features to speak of, and his clothes are crumbling from his back. He has stood there so long that few people care to look at him now except strangers, and they make such scornful remarks upon his generally dilapidated appearance as would make his stony brow blush for shame if the stony heart could feel! Would not all great men prefer to live in the memory of their countrymen till their names become household words in every home rather than be libelled in stone and left to the gaze of unborn generations, to whom their deeds or their works are as a tale that is told,— long past, half forgotten in the greater mass of great works which have succeeded them?

We are not sorry to turn our backs upon the dismal effigy of our hero and get into one of those delightful waggons which are the pride of Quebec, easy, light, well hung; while they serve all the purposes of an open carriage, they shield you most effectually from the sun or the rain, being open all round, and provided with stout waterproof curtains, which can be drawn or left undrawn at pleasure. In the course of half an hour we find ourselves on the Plains of Abraham, where we can indulge in a little poetic dreaming of our hero, and the days that are dead and gone. Standing there and looking round on that historic spot it is easy to send our imagination travelling back to the gray dawn of that misty morning long ago. There are Montcalm's troops encamped around, sleeping securely on that lofty and seemingly inaccessible height, their dusky Huron and Iroquois allies hanging like a ragged fringe upon their rear. Noiselessly and with muffled oars Wolfe and his gallant soldiers cross the river from Pont Levis, and with catlike silence and agility climb the steep sides of the cliff, gaining a foothold wherever they can, hanging on by straggling bushes or jagged edges ; one after another in stealthy silence they creep, they swarm upward ; no clink of sword nor clang of armour warns the sleeping adversary of their approach, till in the gray dawn of the morning they gather, a grim and silent army, on the Heights of Abraham in the midst of the enemy, who are startled from their sleep. We fancy we hear the bugles ring out, and the hurrying to and fro, as the dust and fury of the battle begins. It does not last long, not very long ; a few hours decides the fate of the picturesque old town. Wolfe is wounded ; a gray mass is seen flying eastward. "They run, they run!" a voice is heard exclaiming. "Who, who run?" asks the wounded general. "The French, sir." "Thank God!" he cries, and falls back dead. An obelisk marks the spot where he fell.

Having admired the splendid view from those lofty plains, we turn on our way back to the town. The suburbs of Quebec are very beautiful, being studded with elegant villas, surrounded by gardens all abloom with bright, sweet-scented flowers, that fill the air with perfume. The Foye Road is especially remarkable for its collection of palatial residences. Every man appears to be his own architect, for each house differs from the other, and all are built with more or less originality of design, some highly ornamented, others remarkable for

their elegant simplicity. It would be difficult to classify
these dwellings with any recognized style of architecture. It is strange to observe how entirely the French
and English Canadians keep apart. There is no intercourse between the two. On the side of the French,
at least, there seems to be an undercurrent of the
old hostility still flowing, though it is never brought
actively to the surface, for they are a law-abiding,
peaceful people; in their collisions with the Irish, it is
generally the Irish who make the first hostile move.
They will not learn English nor allow it to be taught in
their schools. You may walk for miles through this
British colony and never hear the sound of your native
language; if you venture to inquire your way you will
be answered in a kind of French that is not spoken
in the France of to-day. They cling to the ancient
French of their forefathers, with no innovations or
modern improvements. The upper classes of both
nations keep as much aloof from each other as the
lower. It is seldom you meet a French family in an
English drawing-room, or an English family at a
French reception; for those little social dissipations do
occasionally take place, though, as a rule, life seems to
flow on in a dull, sluggish fashion in this quaint,
historic town. Religion is the only thing that seems
to keep itself lively, for the air bristles with church
spires, like drawn swords flashing in a holy battle,
pointing upwards. Week days and Sundays, and, as
it seems to us, at all times and hours, the bells ring out
their musical, rhythmical chimes. The Cathedral has
a splendid peal of bells, which play " The last Rose of
Summer" and some other English melodies with exquisite sweetness and precision. It was pleasant to

hear the old home tunes clang out beneath the blue
Canadian skies.

Through the kind interest of our new friends
we gained entrance to the Convent of Gray Nuns.
By a low arched doorway we entered a small stone
hall, with a staircase on one side and a narrow aper-
ture on the other, where the face of an aged nun
appeared as she received or gave messages. We received instructions to go upstairs, and went ; we
passed locked doors and chambers barren of furniture,
except, perhaps, a few bare benches ; we could find our
way nowhere, and after lingering for awhile in these
empty chambers, haunted by the ghostly echo of our
own footsteps, a door opened and a voice bade us enter.
In another moment we had the pleasure of presenting
ourselves to the reverend mother, who was seated in a
light, airy room, the first of a semicircle of nuns, who
were saved from contact with us worldly folk by a partition of wooden railings, which reached from the floor
to the ceiling. There was no space through which
we could even shake their saintly hands. Conversation
under these circumstances was difficult, originality was
impossible; we could make no semi-confidential inquiry
or insinuating remark with those twenty pairs of
smiling eyes upon us, each keeping guard over herself
and her neighbour, and all being under the "right
eye" of their "Mother Commander." Any idea we
might have entertained of digging below the surface
and getting a glimpse of conventual life perished on
the spot. They had evidently no intention of extending their favours further. A view of their bare-
benched chambers and of themselves was considered
privilege enough. " The secrets of their prison-house "

were closed from our unhallowed eyes. Once only in living memory had the convent been unreservedly thrown open to the eyes of the outer world, and that was on the occasion of the visit of the Princess Louise a few weeks previously. Even the simple event of our coming must have created some little excitement, for we were advised that many of the nuns then present had not seen a face from the outer world for forty years until the Princess came amongst them.

In reply to our few commonplace inquiries or remarks, they tried eagerly (speaking all at once or echoing one another) to assure us of their perfect happiness and content, so earnestly indeed as to make us doubt the fact. Yet they certainly had a look of peace and content; not the content that is born of the fulness of joy, or is the result of a happy, busy, useful life, but the peace that is born of sorrow, or of inward struggles and battles, fought out in loneliness and silence; for human nature robbed of her rights will chafe, and struggle, and rebel, till she is broken down and taught to waive her rights in this world that she may grasp a higher right in the next. For that she waits.

The luxurious comfort and bright, sunny aspect of the Father Confessor's chamber (he is the only male allowed upon the premises) was a striking contrast to the nuns' bare chambers. He was a small, wizened old man, with the simplicity of a child. Whether he possessed the "wisdom of the serpent," I query—though how that interesting reptile has proved its claim to wisdom I fail to comprehend. He showed us his photographs and his sample curiosities with as much pride as a child shows its prize picture-book, and attached as much importance to the most trifling things. He was the proud possessor of the skull of Montcalm, and all that is left of that heroic general grinned at us with socketless eyes from beneath a glass case where it reposed on a velvet cushion. "Alas! poor Yorick." He pointed out where some teeth had been extracted without the aid of dentistry; they had been stolen by some British tourists to whom he had exhibited his treasures. He had been spiritual adviser to that world of lonely womanhood for forty-five years, and very rarely went abroad. Well, we took our last look of him, of our friends, the Dufferin Terrace, and the quaint old town, with much regret. We had taken our berths on board one of those palatial river steamers, which are indeed like four-story houses afloat, replete with the most luxurious accommodation, with balconies running round every story, elegant drawing-rooms for the ladies, smoking and billiard-rooms for the gentlemen, and a capital cuisine for everybody's benefit. Slowly we steamed up the St. Lawrence, keeping our eyes fixed upon the gilded spires and steeples of Quebec till the haze of distance shrouded them from our view.

CHAPTER III.

MONTREAL.

The Stolid Indian—Mount Royal—Sir Hugh Allan's Home—The
Banks—The Windsor Hotel.

WE were roused at a most unearthly hour in the
morning, the bells were ringing, the engine shrieking,
panting, and struggling like a refractory steed who
rebels against the will of his rider; but it was brought
to a standstill at the landing-stage at Montreal, and we
were turned out only half awake among droves of bellowing cattle, bleating sheep, and generations of grunting
pigs, from the huge sow, half a ton weight, to the tiny
squeakers a month old. We dodged the horns of the
cattle and scrambled into the hotel omnibus as best we
could. Then we took breath and scanned the scene
around us. All was or seemed to be in a state of
"confusion worse confounded," men and cattle seeming
to be inextricably mixed together. The shouts of the
one and the bellowing of the other shook the air, and
filled our ears with discord. A posse of Indian squaws
and "bucks" stood leaning along the wharf, watching
us with expressionless eyes and immovable stolidity of
countenance. They might have been statues of bronze
for any signs they gave of life. If the playful earth-

quake had paid a sudden visit to the shore and swallowed us up, I doubt if they would have moved a finger or quivered an eyelid. They all wore ragged red shawls or striped blankets wrapped round them, their dark faces and black beady eyes looming out from a mass of thick unkempt hair. This was the first time the untamed savage on his native soil had crossed our path, and I must say they were the most revolting specimens of the human race. It is simply impossible to regard them as "men and brothers," and the more we study the nature, character, and capabilities of these people, the more firmly are we convinced of that fact. Civilization, with its humanizing principles, may struggle with the difficulties, but it will never overcome the inborn blindness of the savage race. They have not the power to comprehend our codes, nor to feel as we feel. Much has been said of their treachery and cruelty, but oppression creates treachery, and that they have been oppressed and hardly used, driven from their native hills and plains to a strange world, which is as a sealed book to them, of which they neither know the letters nor the language, nobody can deny. Regarding their cruelty, it is a quality native born, and directed not against the white race especially; they are cruel to themselves, to one another, and delight in lacerating and torturing their own flesh, regarding (as did the Spartans of old) the endurance of bodily pain as a virtue, courting it as a good rather than avoiding it as an evil, as we more civilized folk are apt to do. This is not meant as an extenuation of the Indian's malpractice, who in reality only carries out the instincts of his nature. The dog, poor brute, cannot help being mad, but it must be got rid of.

Looking on these people, with their low brows and the animal expression on their expressionless faces, we felt there might be some truth in Darwin's theory after all.

Our Jehu cracked his whip, and his bony steeds began to move slowly through the noisy throng. The wharf was swarming with a busy population loading and unloading the many trading vessels which were drawn up by the river side. We passed under a crank of squeaking pigs, which were being swung through the air and lowered on to the deck of the vessel, protesting with all their swinish lungs against such unnatural elevation.

There is a slight rise in the ground as we wind our way from the waterside, but on the whole the city is built on a flat, level plain, lying where the St. Lawrence and Ottawa rivers meet, stretching away, and widening through handsome squares and streets till it reaches the "mountain." It runs round it, covers its feet with pretty villa residences, but never attempts to climb or disfigure its green sides with bricks and mortar. There are no building-plots to let there, for Montreal is proud of its Mount Royal, and keeps it for the pure pride and glory of it. Sir Hugh Allan, the head of that splendid line of steamships bearing his name, has built an elegant and palatial residence there at the foot of the mountain. I am by no means sure that he has not encroached upon it, and planted his greenhouses in its arms, and sent his garden creeping up its soft velvet sides. But Sir Hugh is a benefactor to the city, a pleasant gentleman, and a great favourite with every class of people; no doubt if he even wanted a slice of the mountain he might have it, especially if he was willing to pay handsomely for it. This beautiful " Mount Royal " is much more than its name indicates. It is a perfect sylvan retreat, full of shady groves and bosky dells, luxuriant in its growth of wild fruits and flowers. Fine trees, with gnarled bark and wide-spreading, leafy branches, stand here and there in shady groups, while whole colonies of birds are singing the summer day through. There are whole battalions of nut trees and straggling blackberry bushes skir-mishing round, each struggling to get a sight of the sun, eager to be the first to ripen and fall into the hands of the young children who come " a black-berrying " in the golden autumn days. There is not a single barren spot on the whole mountain ; it is one garden of green, with tiny rivulets of living water, laughing and gurgling as they fall from its grassy crown to its moss-covered feet, which stand on the fringe of the city.

This is not one of the mountains which taxes your energies from the beginning, and makes you pay ever-lasting toll in the shape of aching limbs and weari-ness of spirit, using the sun's rays as a kind of airy razor to scrape the skin off your face and peel your hands till you can scarcely prod its rugged sides with your alpenstock. After much trouble and tribulation, with your clothes dragged off your back, the result of the hauling process common to your guides, you reach the top at last, and stand blowing like a gram-pus on its bald, white head, while you look round upon the wonderfully wide and extensive prospect you have risked so much to see. The sun laughs in your face, withdraws his forces into cloudland, and

flings a white misty veil over the world below. You
see nothing but mist, mist everywhere; your very
brain seems to get frozen and foggy; but what does
that matter? you come down exulting that you have
scaled the precipitous mountain. But you will not
own, like Sir Charles Coldstream, that you found
"nothing in it." Well, Mount Royal is not one of
these. Like a vain and beautiful woman it likes to
show itself off to the best advantage, and has a capital
smooth road, where you can either drive in cosy carriages or walk on foot through a pleasant winding
way, through leafy shade and blooming flowers, till
you reach the top. You can return by another road,
which lands you about three miles from the town.

The city is never out of sight during the whole
progress up the mountain. But from one special point,
which is always indicated to the traveller, there is a
remarkably fine view of the entire city and its surroundings. There is the broad river, studded with
green islets, spanned by the famous Victoria Bridge,
certainly one of the handsomest, and they say the
longest and costliest, in the world; beyond it the
opposite shore stretches away, breaking into small
towns or villages till it is lost in the distance; while
beneath our feet the city itself lies clearly defined
under the deep-blue skies. The white, gray, or red
tiled roofs of the houses, church spires, convents,—
square and ugly in massive gray stone,—public buildings, and Cathedral towers rise out of a forest of
green, for the houses generally are surrounded by
gardens, and the wide streets are bordered on each side
by grand old trees, the relics of the ancient forest, on
whose hoary head the city now stands and holds its

place among the first cities of this Western world. The trading portion of the town, where commerce in every imaginable form is briskly carried on, is lined with handsome shops, hotels, and banking-houses. As we passed by one of the most important of these latter we were stopped by a vast crowd, which thronged the doorway and surged and overflowed across the street, and effectually blocked all progress. A placard was on the door, "Stopped payment," and a sea of human faces, waves of excited, desperate passions sweeping over them, surged round us. On every side we read signs of wrecked hopes and ruined lives. Some, with sullen, despairing faces, went silently on their way; others gesticulated fiercely, with threats and curses "not loud but deep." Some hysterical women were in tears; others crept out of the crowd with white, wan faces, broken down and crushed utterly; they had no voice even to complain or bemoan. Gradually we made our way through this mass of miserable people, and went on through the populous streets, across fine squares, past handsome monuments, all of which are kept in perfect order and neatness. Wherever there is room for a statue, there stands Victoria robed and crowned.

Everywhere in this beautiful city there are delightful promenades; on either side of the spacious streets are elegant villa residences, with tastefully arranged gardens, a light, fanciful railing only separating them from the footway, and sometimes not even that. You may enjoy a perfect feast of the beauty and perfume of flowers as you saunter beneath the trees which border the footway, their overhanging branches forming a perfect shade and bower of green.

Here, as in many other Canadian cities, three-fourths of the population are Catholics, and their churches and Cathedral are among the finest architectural buildings in the city, where churches of all denominations abound. Christ Church Cathedral (Episcopal) is, they say, the finest specimen of English Gothic architecture in America. It is built of Caen and Montreal stone. From the centre of the cross rises a spire 224 feet high; the choir stalls are splendidly carved, and the nave is supported by columns carved in imitation of Canadian plants; but an adequate description of the churches, convents, or museums, here and elsewhere, would each require a volume to itself, and those who require that special kind of information will find it in every local guidebook. Going the general round of these places forms no part of my programme. Such special descriptions are only needed for special objects, and in nine cases out of ten are both wearisome and uninteresting. In their Continental experiences people rush through miles of picture galleries, and visit scores of churches, believing it to be their duty so to do, but at the end of the day few have a distinct impression of any perfect thing. The mind reflects only a confused mass of gorgeous colouring, stained glass windows, groined roofs and arches, all mixed up together, and when they sit down to think things over it is with the greatest difficulty they summon one distinct picture before their mind's eye.

Last though not least among the attractions of Montreal, is the number of its commodious hotels, among which the Windsor stands pre-eminent. It is built at the highest point of the city, under the shadow of the mountains, and for comfort and luxurious ap-

pointments is second to none, either on this side of the
Continent or on the other. The charges here, as in all
other first-class hotels, vary from two and a half to five
dollars per day, inclusive, according to location of
rooms. This is most moderate when compared with
our home charges, where the extras and sundries
swell the bill till it is ready to burst with its own
extortions.

CHAPTER IV.

THE CAPITAL OF THE DOMINION.

River Travelling—Trail of the Fire King—Ottawa—Parliament
Buildings—The City—The Home of our Princess.

THE journey from Montreal to Ottawa is for the most
part dull and uninteresting. We have half an hour's
train, through a rough ragged country, laden with
straggling bushes, rank grass, and charred tree stumps ;
then we take the boat and steam along the river, a
broiling sun overhead and flat barren country on either
side. There being nothing attractive or interesting in
the surrounding scenery, I betake myself to the general
saloon, which is a perfect bazaar, with knickknackeries
of all kinds, and books and newspapers for sale. I
invest a dollar in literature of the lightest kind and
ensconce myself on the most comfortable lounge I can
find, and in rather a limp drowsy state try to keep
myself awake.

My companion, aglow with the delights of travelling, rejoices in the inconveniences thereof, and sits
broiling in the sun, which seems inclined to have no
mercy upon anybody. It glares down with its fierce
fiery eye, breathing a hot sultry breath over everything everywhere. The land on either side is a plain

D

of brown dried-up grass; a few lean hungry cattle are
straying hither and thither, browsing on the dry
breast of mother earth. Brown bare-legged children
wade into the river; some cast off their rags and leap
in, splashing about, laughing as they play at "catch-
who-can." When they are tired they come out and
lay themselves out to dry in the sun. The water has
a sultry sleepy look. It is as clear and still as a glass
mirror, but we wake it into fury as our iron steed
tramps through it; it hisses and runs after us, snarling
with its white foam lips as it closes in our wake, and
under the blazing sun our vessel steams on. The deck
blossoms with umbrellas, which look like gigantic toad-
stools growing out of scores of human heads. Some
put cabbage-leaves in their hats and hang silk handkerchiefs down their backs, as a kind of protection
from the sun's keen rays; but they will not sit down;
they wander in and out of the saloon, like evil spirits
that can know no rest; they like to get bronzed with
the sun and sultry air, and as a rule are not satisfied
till the skin peels off their faces and the tips of their
noses require a bag for protection. I lean back on my
luxurious lounge in a rather sleepy state, and am fast
drifting away into a land of dreams when I am roused
by the loud prolonged sound of the dinner-gong, and
we all crowd down, helter-skelter, to the dining saloon,
where our captain, a big burly man, sits at the head of
the table, with sundry roasts and fancy dishes smoking
before him. We speedily spoil our appetites, and leave
but a mere wreck of bare bones and skeletons. One
dish contains Indian corn cobs about a quarter of a
yard long, looking white and tempting with their
granulated covering. Believing they are some stuffed

delicacies I ask for a small piece.   A smile goes round, and I receive a whole one on my plate.   What am I to do with it?   I glance at my neighbours.   Every one is holding a cob with his two hands, and, beginning at one end, nibbles along as though he were playing a flute till he gets to the other, repeating the process till the cob is stripped of its pearly corn.   I don't think it is worth the trouble of eating, though it is considered a great dainty on this side of the Atlantic.

About two o'clock we reach Carrillon.   The rapids bar our progress up the river; a train runs alongside the vessel; we are soon seated in a comfortable car, and have a two hours' railway journey through what was once a magnificent forest, but is now wild waste land, a terrible fire having swept over it some few years ago, destroying and devouring all before it— farm-houses, flocks, all animate and inanimate things —leaving here and there groups of tall spectral trees, standing weird and ghostly in the summer sun.   Here it had feasted greedily and left nothing but charred roots and fantastic tree stumps straggling over the ground.   One spot on the line of that terrible fire was pointed out to me as having once been a flourishing farm; but the fire fiend swept down upon it in the night, when the inhabitants were all in their beds asleep.   The man rushed out with his wife and child and crouched down in a potato field, trusting that the storm of fire might pass over them; but the red-tongued flames came leaping along and drove them into the river, and all night long he stood up to his neck in water, supporting his wife and child.   The great white moon shone out serene and peaceful in the calm blue skies.   Not a breath of air was stirring, not a sound was heard but the tramp of the fire king as he roared on his blazing way. In the morning they were saved, but the terrible flames had licked the life out of all wayfarers who had barred its progress and left their blackened skeletons grinning in the sun. After a rush of two hours through this weird wild scene we reach Grenville. There we take boat again and steam on till we find ourselves at Ottawa, about six o'clock in the evening.

The approach to this city, the capital of the Dominion of Canada, is by no means imposing; the face of the river is covered and its mouth filled with sawdust; it is stifled, and has scarcely strength to flow, it could not burst into a smile, or ripple under the most tempting of summer suns. Immense booms of timber, which have been floated down from the "forest primeval" hundreds of miles away, float still on the river surface till they are hauled up to feed the hungry mills, mechanical giants, whose rasping jaws work day and night crushing these sturdy "sons of the forest," cutting them in slices and casting them forth to be stacked in huge piles along the river-banks miles before we reach the town. There is no bustle or confusion on our arrival there. On the quiet little landing-stage two or three lumbering vehicles are waiting; we are escorted to one of these by our chivalrous captain, who carries our hand baggage, and superintends the removal of the rest. A little girl, about ten years old, follows us, with a dog almost as big as herself, and looks up at us shyly.

"My little lass, ladies," observes our captain, his face wrinkling and his eyes twinkling with smiles; "she comes down every evening to 'meet father.' It wouldn't seem like coming home if I didn't find Nellie here."

With a proud fatherly air he takes the child's hand, the dog trotting behind them as they ascend the stony hill towards a gray cottage of rough-hewn slate, which he has pointed out to me as "home." We turn on towards our destination in Nepean Street, where we find ourselves so comfortably located, that instead of staying a few days, as we originally intended, we resolve to remain some weeks.

Through the good offices of Mr. Leggo, a popular and most enthusiastic Canadian, we made the acquaintance of Lieutenant-Colonel Dennis, one of the oldest pioneers of the state. Those gentlemen were like animated encyclopædias on all matters regarding Canada; from them we received more information in a few weeks than we could have gained on our own account in a year.

Our first day in Ottawa was spent in visiting the Parliament buildings, which occupy a plateau of about thirty acres on the loftiest point of the city and nearly two hundred feet above the Ottawa River; they are surrounded by beautifully laid out gardens, and seem to be growing out of a bed of soft greensward of velvet smoothness. They are composed of cream-coloured Potsdam stone, the ornamental part being of Ohio and Arupois marbles; they are built in the Italian Gothic style of the thirteenth century, and I am told they are the most beautiful specimens thereof in all America, perhaps in the world. Their elevated position, with their long lines of pointed windows, massive buttresses, and numerous pinnacles and towers, silhouetted against the bright blue sky, are objects of imposing and majestic beauty for miles around. In the front centre stands the Victoria Tower, one hundred and eighty feet high, and surmounted by an iron crown. The chief entrance to the building is through the broad-pointed arches beneath this tower; the royal arms are above the doorway; in the grand Senate Hall there is a very beautiful statue of the Queen, and the vice-regal throne is flanked by busts of the Prince of Wales and the Princess Alexandra. In the most remote, as well as in the most populous districts, the features of the royal family are duly represented. The Canadians are the most loyal of all British subjects; they lower their voices with solemn reverence when they speak of "Her Majesty, the Queen," to whom they never refer as "the Queen," pure and simple; they give her a whole string of titles and adjectives, like the tail of a paper kite, and set her sailing in the heaven of their imagination, as though she were beyond the range of humanity altogether. They seem to regard royalty, not as an upper branch of the human family, but as a higher and holier species; any adverse or quizzical criticism of them or their doings would be met with severe reprimand, if not positive maltreatment. We cannot help wondering how the loyalty of the Canadian people manages to exist, for it has been half-starved, or fed only upon the crumbs flung from the state table. It must have lived on its own robust strength or the clinging patriotic spirit of the Canadian nature, rather than from any consideration or care it has received from the home government. It is certainly the most beautiful, the most fertile of the British colonies, and lies nearest to the mother land, though it seems farthest from her care.

Much has been said, much has been written on the subject of Canada ; we have learned its geographical position, the length and breadth of its lakes and rivers, the extent of its vast forest lands, the height of its mountains, etc., but the figures dazzle the mind, and bring no realization of the fact. Nothing less than a personal visit will enable us to comprehend the wonders of this luxuriant land, which is surrounded and encompassed with its own loveliness. The primeval forest still holds its own in the vast solitudes, sacred as yet from the increasing encroachments of man, its immense inland seas, and fruitful rivers winding through scenery the most picturesque, the most sublime ; to say nothing of its vast unexplored lands and mineral resources, and the wide tracts of rich uncultivated country, watered by springs and rivulets which have been flowing in their living liquid beauty since the days of Paradise. We hear sad tales of poverty and misery in the old land, of scanty crops, wasted labour, and ruined farmers, who, after all, are only tenants on the land they live on ; the small farmer who labours there, on another man's land, may here become a land-owner. There is no room for great farming operations or agricultural enterprise in the limited cultivated land of the old country, every rood of which is occupied ; there is no room for new comers, —the great tide of human life, which is rising every hour, must roll on towards the great cities, and perhaps starve there, for each city is filled with its own people, who work at their different trades, and in their turn overflow into the country, drifting, heaven knows where. There is small chance of rural folks gaining their bread in the old land. Here in the New World there are, not thousands, but millions of acres of rich fertile soil waiting for the magic pick and the plough-share to turn it to a veritable " Tom Tidler's ground ; " only scatter the seed on its broad fair breast, and it will pulsate with a new life and swell the seeds with its own fulness till they burst and blossom into a wealth of golden grain, and " the hand of the sower gathereth a rich harvest."

The Governing powers, in their desire to get the country well populated, are willing to make most liberal terms to forward this object. They are ready to give a grant in perpetuity of one hundred and sixty acres to all or any who are willing to make a home there, with the power, of course, of extending their possessions as their means increase. There is an abundance of wood for building purposes, the rivers and lakes teem with fish in great variety, and the earth gives forth such a variety of wild fruits, strawberries, raspberries, grapes, gooseberries, and huge trees of red luscious plums, and butternuts, we feel that in summer-time, at least, we could live as the birds do, on sunshine and sweet fruits.

We had heard much of the extremes of temperature, of heat and cold, especially in Ottawa, and prepared ourselves for broiling ; well, it was warm, the sun blazed, the hot winds blew, and the dust of this most dusty city whirled and swirled around us, got into our eyes, our ears, crept insidiously down our throats, and seemed struggling to turn us inside out ; but we clutched our mantles around us, and butted against the wind, screening ourselves from the sun's fierce rays as best we could. It is not often that the sun and the wind have such a tussle together. However we reached home at last in an uncooked state, feeling not much warmer than we should do on a summer day at home, though the temperature is much higher, and the hours are marching to the tune of 90° in the shade. We had spent the whole day in wandering and driving about the streets of Ottawa, till we gained a very good idea of its external appearance. It has numerous fine churches, and its town hall, post office, and all the municipal buildings are substantially and massively built in an attractive and fanciful style of architecture. As for the rest of the city, it is in a perfectly unfinished state ; it is as yet only a thing of promise, though it has the making of a very fine town in the future ; but however fast it marches, it will have to keep growing, and work hard too, for another century at least, before it reaches the level of its magnificent Parliament buildings. The streets are wide and long, stretching away out of sight ; they are cobble-stoned and roughly wood-paved for the most part. After passing the principal lines of shops in Sparkes Street, the houses seem to have been built for temporary convenience only, and crop up here and there in a direct line, leaving wide spaces of waste land between, as though they were in a hurry to see which should reach the end of the long street first, the end that seems to be creeping back to the primeval forest, which civilization and time has left far behind.

Ottawa itself is neither picturesque nor attractive, being built on perfectly flat ground. It looks like a timber yard, and smells of sawdust. The Ottawa river has as many long thin arms as an octopus, and they run meandering inland by a hundred different ways ; here, they meet in a vast tumbling mass, falling over huge boulders and broken stony ground till they are dignified by the name of the "Chaudière Falls;" lower down, their headlong course is stopped, and they are utilized and made to turn a huge sawmill where a thousand steel teeth are biting through the grand old trees, tearing them into slips, digesting and disgorging them on the other side; in vain the water foams and groans, crashing its rebellious waves together—man is its master, and will have his way. Just over the bridge is an extensive match factory, employing six hundred children from six to twelve years old, swarming on all sides like busy little ants, measuring, cutting, dipping, and filling the boxes as fast as their tiny hands can move. There is on the opposite side a pail and tub factory, all for exportation; long galleries, filled with tubs and pails from floor to ceiling, enough to scrub the world clean, and turn it inside out and begin again on the other side.

Rideau Hall, the home of our Princess, lies on the outskirts of the town, and is by no means a regal-looking mansion; it is a long low building of grey-stone, standing on rather elevated ground, and has a pleasant view of the town and river from the lawn and flower garden, which enclose two sides of it; the approach is through tolerably well timbered grounds, not of sufficient importance to be called a "park." The Governor and Princess Louise were away, and the house was undergoing repair—it looked as though it needed it. There was nothing to distinguish this from any second or third-rate country house at home, except the one solitary and rather seedy-looking sentinel who paraded before the door. The people of Ottawa speak most enthusiastically of our Princess; everyone has some kind memory or pleasant anecdote to tell of her. It is said that when Her Royal Highness held her first reception, she appeared in a plain high dress, expecting, perhaps, to find fashion " out of joint" in this far-away place ; but the Canadian ladies came trooping " en grand.toilette," with fans and diamonds, trains and laces, like living importations from Worth himself. At the next reception matters changed, and the royal lady appeared in all the splendour of the British Court receptions.

CHAPTER V.

FROM CITY TO CATARACT.

On the Train—The Thousand Islands—At Kingston—Toronto—
The Government House—Arrival of the Princess Louise—
" We expect the Moon "—Niagara Falls.

FROM Ottawa to Toronto is a tedious journey, in consequence of the many changes, from rail to river, river
to rail again.   The train is waiting for us as we reach
the station ; it is a hot sultry morning, the warm air,
sand-laden, comes in short, fitful gusts, and is stifling
rather than refreshing ; the sun blazes down from a
copper-coloured sky—everything is sun-dried, sunbaked ; the city glows like an oven ; the stony, shade-
less streets reflect the burning rays, and blind the eyes
with their white dazzling light ; one might cook eggs
upon the housetops, and set bacon to frizzle in the sun.
It is an undertaking to cross the blank space from
the omnibus to the platform, many a sunstroke has
been got with less provocation.   In a limp, dusty condition, tired before the day has well begun, we take the
first vacant seats we come to—there is little choice, for
the car is half full already, and more people come
trooping in, till it is filled to overflowing with a miscellaneous mass of humanity of all sorts, sexes, and sizes :
there are women with babies, women with bundles,

and baskets of fruit, crockery, and cabbages; two elderly ladies, in corkscrew curls, carrying a pet cat in a basket and huge bunches of flowers, come timidly in, smiling and giving a recognizing nod to everybody with the information that they "have not been in a train for twenty years, and consequently are a little nervous." Hobbledehoys trample on our skirts, and stumble over our feet, and one young tourist, evidently got up by his tailor in stereotyped tourist fashion, for his first outing, struggles into the car under a weight of walking-sticks and fishing-tackle, and commences operations by fishing my hat off, and in the confusion of disentanglement and blushing apologies, all his belongings come rattling about my ears. The bell rings, the train moves slowly; everything moves slowly in Canada—whether it is that the red tape stretches from the mother country and ties their hands, or public spirit languishes, or private enterprise is sleeping, it is difficult to say. The Canadians are a most loyal, kind, and hospitable people. Conservative too, with the worst kind of conservatism, they are content with things as they are, and so long as matters go smoothly in the old grooves, they will not trouble to make new tracks. They want waking up; if they were once possessed with the restless, ambitious, go-ahead spirit of the United States, they would soon be even with them; at present they are a century behind.

We rattle along through a not especially interesting country; here and there we come upon undulating woodlands, with pretty farmhouses lying amid their cultivated lands; but there are whole acres lying idle of rich land, which has only to be tickled with a ploughshare and fed with a scanty meal of grain, and it is ready to burst into laughing fields of golden corn; meanwhile masses of gaudy weeds flaunt their flags in the sun, and straggling brushwood spring aggressively from the ground, and such a glorious growth of thistles as would delight a race of donkeys —no better could be found anywhere. Meanwhile we amuse ourselves, each according to his or her fancy. One woman sucks oranges all the way, another "clucks" and makes zoological noises to amuse her rebellious offspring; the young tourist looks unutterably bored, and plays the " devil's tattoo " on the window; somebody perfumes the car with the odour of peppermint drops. The old ladies enter into a conversational race, and discuss their private affairs in a most audible voice, taking the whole car into their confidence. We catch snatches of a domestic tragedy, blithely borne by the chief sufferer, who dwells upon every revolting detail with great gusto, as though she revelled in the telling; next to enjoying other people's miseries, some people love to gloat upon their own, the excitement following the tragedy overpowering the tragedy itself. Every time the train stops, as it does with a jerk, they clutch each other wildly, and pelt everybody with questions, "Was it a collision?" or "had the boiler burst?" During their excitement the cat wriggles out of the basket, and a general scrimmage ensues before the poor beast can be recaptured.

At ten o'clock we reach Prescott, and there take the boat for Kingston, hoping to catch the four o'clock train for Toronto. Our luggage is soon aboard, and in the course of a few minutes we are seated under an awning on the deck of a palatial river boat; here the river broadens and joins the lake Ontario. We rejoice at leaving the dusty train and baking city behind, and set ourselves to enjoy the fresh genial breeze, and watch for the first glimpse of the thousand islands. We are soon in their midst. It is like a dream of fairyland—the perfect day, warm sunny atmosphere, and fresh cool breeze dimpling the face of the water; the luxuriant islands, as we thread our way among them, seem to be floating with us—they are everywhere, before, behind, and around; some are large, some small; some are inhabited only by water-fowl, some by men of literary and artistic taste, who make their summer home there; but they are all clothed in a luxuriant growth of green, trailing low down to the water's edge, white willow and silver birch coquetting with their own shadows fluttering on its surface. After a few delicious lotus-eating hours' floating on this romantic world of land and water, we reach Kingston just in time to miss the train—everybody misses that train, it is a delusion and a snare, nobody was ever known to catch it, even by accident. I believe the captains and hotel-keepers are in collusion to keep the tourist in Kingston for the night. The best hotel, The British American, has poor accommodation, the table being ill-served and the viands ill-cooked.

We brought splendid appetites to bear on greasy chops, tough steaks, and soup so weak it had scarcely strength to struggle down our throats. The meals were served at most unearthly hours—dinner at twelve, supper at five o'clock. It is a large, old-fashioned town, with a capital fruit and vegetable market in its centre, and fine houses with walled-in gardens; the tallest and gaudiest flowers sometimes climbed up and took a peep at the world outside: a good old-world city, wrapped up in itself and its people; no doubt comfortable enough to live in, but no attractive features to interest the passing stranger. It seems to be an isolated, self-centred place, with nothing to do with the present and no stirring associations with the past. We were not sorry to find ourselves in the four o'clock train en route for Toronto. The cars were clean, and not overcrowded; boys came along, peddling books, papers, hot cake, rich ripe fruit, and "real English walnuts." We were tired, and lounged back in our seats, watching the panoramic landscapes fly past us, and listening to the sweet voices of two young Canadian girls who were singing hymns, nearly all the way. Towards eight o'clock there was a stop of twenty minutes for supper, and a capital supper we got—salmon, trout, cutlets, sausages, fruit, coffee, iced milk, and all for the modest sum of fifty cents!

The sun sets in a glory of crimson, purple, and gold, fading and changing, one colour amalgamating with another, till the western skies are dressed in gorgeous crimson plumes, and the lake is illuminated, glowing red in the reflected light, and the opposite shore seems veiled in the purple mist of dreamland. Slowly the twilight falls, the moon rises, and presently we are speeding by full moonlight along the shores of the Lake Ontario.

It was nearly midnight when the lights of the City of Toronto loomed upon our sight. Our engine bell began its musical ding-dong as we slackened and steamed slowly into the Station, and soon we were on our way to our hotel. Thanks to the delightful baggage system here, as all over the United States, luggage is no trouble to its owner. The arrangement is simple enough : your luggage is taken from your house by the expressman, who checks them to your destination wherever that may be, giving you little brass numbered checks in return ; a similar check is strapped on each of your boxes. About an hour before you reach your journey's end, an express agent boards the train ; you give up your checks, and tell him where to send your luggage. On your arrival, or very soon after, you find it there ; there is a specified charge for each package. The loss of passengers' luggage is unknown ; and by this easy arrangement, much loss of time, trouble, and temper is saved. You may carry as much as you please, and from the time you leave England it is no trouble to you, until you return to Liverpool,—then your vexations begin anew.

We put up at the Queen's Hotel, about three minutes drive from the Station, and facing the lake, though it stands back a few hundred yards from it. We found it a luxurious hotel and perfect home, being an extensive but not a monster hotel, large enough for the most complete arrangements, but not too large to be comfortable. It is three or four stories high, and has a balconied and verandahed front with pretty climbing plants trailing among the lattice work. The Governor, Mr. Macdonald, and his two charming daughters, at that time had a suite of apartments here, having vacated the Government house for the occupation of the Princess Louise and the Marquis of Lorne, who were expected in a day or two to open the Dominion Exhibition. Toronto was much excited on the occasion.

E

The Misses Macdonald took great interest and delight in beautifying their already beautiful home, for the reception of their royal guests. The day before the arrival we accompanied them on a last visit of inspection to see that every arrangement was complete, and add any little finishing touches their refined taste might consider necessary.

The Government house is a massive square stone building, approached by handsome iron gates, and is surrounded by tastefully laid out flower gardens, soft velvety lawn, fanciful conservatories and green-house filled with rare exotics. We get the key from the head gardener, and enter the house : there is no sign of life, not a creature is visible; we saunter through the corridors, up the stairs, and through the vacant chambers, attended only by our own shadows; our tread falls noiselessly on the soft carpet; once or twice a door slams, and an echo wakes up and tries to follow us, but is smothered by the way. The rooms are all in perfect order, prettily arranged, fresh, airy, and beautifully clean, not a speck of dust is to be seen anywhere; everything seems to be in a waiting stage— eider-down beds, spring mattresses all bare, waiting to be made; wardrobes waiting to be filled; fires waiting to be kindled. There is no sign of silver or linen anywhere. We inquire, "Why is this?" and learn, that when the Princess travels, like some visitors to the sea-side at home, she finds her own plate and linen ! The royal servants are expected to take possession every minute; as we are leaving the house, they are beginning to arrive with the baggage in advance. Meanwhile the city is all agog with expectation, people come flocking in from all parts of the dominion. The hotels and refreshment houses are full to overflowing; eager sight-seers throng the streets; we enjoy our gape among the rest. It is a pretty bright town, with long wide straight streets, bordered on either side with fine old trees,—a striking contrast to the blank stony aspect of Ottawa,—and is calculated to show off at the best advantage on such a festive occasion as this. Triumphal arches, covered with a glory of green, bright-coloured flags, and wondrous devices, span the streets on every side; we come upon troops of merry children singing "The Campbells are coming," "Rule Britannia," and "God save the Queen," with all the might of their strong young lungs; great is the excitement of the child-world—they are to muster ten thousand strong to greet the Princess on her arrival to-morrow.

We are roused early in the morning by a general hubbub and a conflicting choir of young voices, and look from our window upon a transformation scene. The whole space between our hotel and the railway, at which point the royal party are to alight, is cleared of lumber, and newly swept and garnished; and on either side, rising one above another, rows of seats have been erected to accommodate ten thousand children, leaving between them a wide avenue for the progress of the vice-regal party. The children are already beginning to assemble; they are all dressed in light colours, generally in white, with broad gay-coloured sashes, worn crosswise from the shoulder, each school wearing a different colour, and having its own special flag fluttering over it. At first the schools seem to be all mixed together in inextricable confusion; teachers and trainers dash franticly about, gathering their wandering flocks together; but long before the slow swinging engine bell heralds the approach of the royal party, each school occupies its proper space and all is in order. From our balcony we watch the train come wriggling like a great black snake into the station. We are not near enough to distinguish faces, but a company of gayly dressed midgets seem to slip out upon the platform, and stand silent in the sunshine. There is a momentary lull. We look down the long lines of children's faces, rising tier upon tier ten thousand strong; they are so arranged that their colours blend harmoniously together, they look like an animated flower garden; a wave of excitement sweeps over them, suddenly ten thousand snowflakes seem fluttering in the air, ten thousand hands are waving tiny white handkerchiefs; the choir of distant voices begin to sing "The Campbells are coming, Hurrah! hurrah!" and soft as the sound of an echo, the old familiar air reaches our ears, swelling louder and louder as it is caught up by one section after another, nearer and nearer, till the whole ten thousand voices fill the air with one great volume of sound. Meanwhile the newly arrived visitors progress slowly along the avenue, and "God save the Queen" and "Rule Britannia" follow in quick succession, the children's voices quickening to a race, so eager are they to finish before the Princess is out of hearing. As she reaches her carriage, there is a clapping of hands and roar of welcome; but she keeps in the background, leaving all the honour and glory to her husband, the Governor-General of the Dominion. Troops of Rifles, and engineers line the streets, and a general festivity takes possession of the city; squibs, crackers and illuminations finish up the day.

The short time we are able to devote to Toronto

passes too quickly; everybody is hospitably inclined, and every day there are luncheons, kettledrums, or dinners to be attended : all are strictly arranged on the "home" principle; in fact the people here are more English than we are ourselves, and scrupulously avoid any peculiarity of the adjoining states,—you may hear Americanisms in London, but never in Canada. The people are lavish in their liberality, but the city carries its economy farther than we care to follow it. On our way to a friend's house one evening, we found the town wrapped in darkness; we could neither see the names of the streets nor the numbers of the houses; we lost ourselves, and at last came upon a dark grey figure carrying a bull's-eye—it was a policeman, who courteously convoyed us to our destination.

"You see, ladies," he said, apologizing for the Cimmeranian darkness of his beloved city, "the moon is expected, and we never light the streets when we expect the moon!" So when the moon is on duty the gasworks have a holiday. Toronto is beautifully situated amid stretches of well-wooded cultivated land, and spreads its wide skirts along the shore of Lake Ontario, where there should be a splendid promenade—but is not; for between the lake and the tall rows of handsome houses, the railway runs close down along the water's edge, marring the prospect with its array of ugly sheds and cattle pens, while heavy goods trains are shunting and shrieking in the face of the town from morning till night : thus the opportunity of making one of the finest promenades in the dominion is lost. From Toronto we steam across the lake to the village of Niagara, where a train is waiting to carry us on to the falls about half an hour further on.

We all watch from the windows, eager to catch our first glimpse of the world's great wonder.

I quote from my companion's note-book on the spot, "There was a break in the wood, a flash of white, a cloud of spray tossed high above the tree-tops; then the dark woods closed again. That glimpse, flashing upon us and passing before we could fully realize that the great tumbling mass was indeed Niagara, can hardly be called our first view of it. . . . It was dark when we reached the Clifton house; the roar of the falls filled our ears, we stepped out upon the balcony, and there was a sight we can never forget. It was a moonless night, and in the dusk we could only obscurely trace the vast vague outline of the two falls, divided by the blurred mass of shapeless shadows which we learned was Goat Island. As we looked upon them silently, and listened to the ceaseless boom like distant thunder, which shook the ground beneath our feet, across the snowy veil of the American Fall, to our left, shot rays of rosy light, which melted into amber, then into emerald. They were illuminating the great waters with coloured calcium lights! In whose benighted mind rose the first thought of dressing Niagara up like a transformation scene in a pantomime? It was like putting a tinsel crown and tarlatan skirts on the Venus of Milo. But these brilliant rays which fell across the American Falls, and which were turned on and off like a dissolving view, did not reach to the Horseshoe Fall away to our right. Vast, solemn, shadowy, we could just distinguish its form in the darkness, could hear the deep murmur of its awful voice. And there, between it and us, what was *that* we saw? Was it some huge pale ghost standing sentinel before Niagara? White, spectral, motionless, it rose up and reached towards the stars—shapeless, dim, vague as a veiled ghost. There was something almost supernatural about it, it was like a colossal spectre, wrapped in a robe of strange dim light.

"'How fine and upright the column of spray is to-night,' said a strange voice beside us. This broke the illusion. But yet it seemed impossible that our ghost should be only a pillar of rising and falling spray! We saw it again, daily and nightly, but seldom again like that. We saw it blown along in clouds; we saw it like a great veil hiding the whole face of the Fall; we saw it one evening at sunset leaping and sparkling like a fountain of liquid gold,—but only once again did we see it rise up in that shape, the dim and ghostly guardian of the night. No mortal eye has ever beheld the base of the great Horseshoe Falls; it is for ever veiled and lost in a wild white chaos of foam, tossed up in the fury of its headlong plunge, and hiding its depths in mystery.

"The Indians hold that Niagara claims its yearly meed of victims. It may be so. Or does Niagara thus avenge itself on the civilization that has trimmed and tamed its forests and dressed it up in tinsel-coloured lights? But the thunder of water thunders on eternally, and before its terrible sublimity we are dumb, as in the mighty diapason our feeble voices are lost." We remain eight days at Niagara; its fascination increases; but we must tear ourselves away, and say good-bye to it, at last; we are bound for the "Golden Gate," and great cities, lakes, mountains and prairie lands are lying between it and us.

CHAPTER VI.

THE EMPIRE CITY.

New York—Fifth Avenue—Madison Square—The Elevated Rail- . way—The Cars—The Shops—The People—West Point.

WE leave Niagara in the early morning, and start on our tedious journey on the long comfortless cars (we learned afterwards, that we might have taken seats in the parlour car). How we long for a lounge in one of our own easy well-cushioned first-class compartments! Here, there are no lounging possibilities, we are forced to sit bolt upright, the back of the seats scarcely rising to our shoulder blades; and the constant passing to and fro of the peddling fraternity, and the slamming and banging of doors as they come and go, is most irritating even to non-delicate nerves. We feel the lack of privacy in these American cars, but in this, as in most other cases, there is some compensation—we are safe from the attacks of lunatics, thieves, or ruffianism of any kind whatever, and we can obtain any quantity of rich ripe fruit, luscious strawberries, bananas and melons, figs, etc.; while there is a tank of iced water in the car for the refreshment, gratis, of thirsty souls. The train rushes through the high streets of busy towns, crossing crowded thoroughfares and public highways, keeping up full speed always, merely ringing the engine bell, to warn people to get out of the way : they have to take care of themselves, and they know it; no precautions are taken for the public safety; the rails are merely laid down in the middle of the streets, and when the trains are not in sight other vehicles use the road. We stop to dine at Syracuse, sup at Utica, and reach New York a little before midnight. A familiar face greets us on the platform, but not until we have engaged a carriage to take us to the Windsor Hotel, which proves to be just two blocks from the station! Our luggage is in the hands of the expressman, and we could have walked to the hotel had we been aware of its nearness in less than five minutes! The rapacious Jehu charged four dollars for our brief occupancy of his dingy vehicle; it was the first and last time we were so beguiled.

It is a starlight night, and we catch a glimpse of the tall dark houses, which seem to be reaching up to the moon. The names of the streets, we notice, are painted on the glass gas lamps at every corner, so that in the darkest weather you may always tell your whereabouts. The carriage stops at the monster hotel—a very mountain of cherry-red bricks and mortar, a huge square building it is, occupying one entire block, built up so many storeys that our eyes can scarcely reach the top; its windows are all shaded by outside linen blinds, which flap and flutter like flags in the dim night. The wide door opens, and swallows us up. We rather dreaded facing the clerk of this magnificent establishment; we had heard so much of the species and the generally cavalier, supercilious manner with which they treated strangers that we preferred our modest request for a double-bedded room in fear and trembling; but our request could not have been more courteously received and answered if we had been engaging the most gorgeous suite in the whole hotel : I believe the supercilious hotel clerk must be classed with extinct animals.   We are politely conducted to the elevator, which carries us up higher—higher, till we fancy we must be approaching the seventh heaven, and at last are deposited in a large handsome apartment on one of the upper storeys.

The next morning we take our first stroll through the " Empire city ; " an enthusiastic and patriotic American friend is with us early, anxious to see the effect the first sight of his beloved city produces on our British constitution.   We step out from the grand entrance of the Windsor Hotel, and with a majestic wave of his arm he introduces us to " Fifth Avenue ! " and watches for the electrifying effect.   Our faces fall, our ideas of the " Glories of the Avenue," which we had often heard sung, fade away.   We look up, we look down ; instead of the wide shady avenue, and brilliant busy scene our fancy had painted, we see only a long, and by no means wide, street, bristling with churches, lifting their lofty spires from amid the rows of tall brown stone houses, which are closely packed on either side, each being approached by a flight of brown stone steps, with ornamental rails, handsome and dreary in their monotonous regularity ; but we catch no glimpse of a green tree anywhere !   The whole street is stamped with aristocratic dulness ; a score or so of well-dressed people are sauntering along the side walk, and clean-looking white " stages," which run from one end of the city to the other, are jolting along over the rough cobble stones

which pave the roadway; the avenue is several miles
long, but it grows less aristocratic, and leaves the even
tenor of its way, when it passes through Madison
Square, which is pretty and quite Parisian in its
appearance, with a splendid growth of fine old trees
and shady nooks and corners, quite an oasis in a desert
of bricks and mortar; streets of stone houses radiate
from all sides of it; and every day, through summer
heat and winter snows, George Francis Train, with
his ruined intellect and shaggy white beard, haunts
the scene; he is generally found seated under one
particular tree, cutting out paper boats and figures
for the troops of children who swarm round him;
and here stands Fifth Avenue Hotel, a stately building
gleaming white in the sunshine. Here the stir of life
begins, and flows in a restless magnetic current the
live-long day. After leaving Madison Square, the
avenue winds and wriggles its way to the lower part
of the city, and mingles with the everyday working
world. Leaving this aristocratic quarter we pass
through one of the cross streets, between lines of the
same brown stone houses, miniature copies of Fifth
Avenue grandeur, and find ourselves in democratic
Sixth Avenue, which is full of the bustle and roar of
life; shops to the right of us, shops to the left of us,
shops everywhere and of every possible kind,—crabs,
eels and oysters, Chinese laundries, fancy toys, barbers,
whisky bars, and fashionable milliners, elbow each
other in true republican fashion. The side walks are
thronged with hurrying crowds of men and women;
along the centre of the road, but raised about forty
feet above it, runs the elevated railway: it looks like a
skeleton gridiron laid on a rack and stretched from one

end of the city to the other, its long arms branching off and running through the intricate labyrinths of the lower part of the town, rounding curves, and turning sharp corners, and, at times, so near to the houses you might shake hands with the inhabitants and see what they have for dinner. This airy mode of locomotion is startling at first, especially at night when the shops are closed, and the streets deserted; you hear the rumbling of the train far off, and it thunders over your head, seeming to swing in mid-air between you and the sky, its green and red fiery eyes staring ahead and plunging into the darkness. Beneath this elevated road, which forms a kind of arcade, run lines of red and yellow cars jingling their bells merrily as they roll rapidly along the iron rails in an almost unbroken line, one following the other in quick succession.

Public conveyances are cheap, and there are plenty of them: cars run from everywhere to everywhere. There are, of course, numerous livery stables, and a limited number of public cabs for hire, but they are very expensive as well as a doubtful luxury, and the drivers are most accomplished extortionists. It is impossible that a drive through the streets of New York could ever be taken for pleasure, in consequence of the rough cobble-stoned roadway; it is a jolting process, you take your drive at the risk of dislocating your neck. The cars are roomy and easy; both driver and conductor are protected from the weather; they stand on a kind of balcony, with an umbrella-like projection sloping over them, effectually shielding them from sun or rain. Everybody rides in the cars, from the lady in costly furs and velvets to the costermonger. You may find yourself sandwiched between a fat negro and lean washerwoman, and facing your jewelled hostess of the night before.

There are some few trifling drawbacks in this land of liberty: the every-man's-as-good-as-his-neighbour feeling, is sometimes unpleasantly obtruded on your notice; especially when you embark on a shopping expedition, there is an absence of that respectful ready attention we are accustomed to meet with in Europe. You enter, say, a draper's shop: the young ladies are engaged in a gossiping match, or a game at flirtation; *you* wait their pleasure, not they *yours*; when they do deign to attend you, it is with a sort of condescending indifference, and even while they are measuring a yard of ribbon, they keep up a fusillade of chatter with their companions. I speak of the rule, of course there are exceptions. Central Park is the only place where you can enjoy a drive—there driving is a delight, the roads are simply perfect, and scores of splendid equipages and beautiful women are on view daily in the grand drives from three till six o'clock; while the bridle paths, winding through sylvan shades beneath full-foliaged trees, are crowded with fair equestrians and their attendant cavaliers: it is a pleasure to watch them at a trot, a canter, or a gallop, for the American women ride well and gracefully. New York is very proud of Central Park; and well it may be so, for it is one of the finest in the world, there is nothing like it this side of the Atlantic. Twenty years ago it was a mere swampy rocky waste, now it is a triumph of engineering skill and a splendid illustration of the genius of landscape gardening: there are smooth green lawns, shady groves, lakes, beautifully wooded dells and vine-covered arbours, whichever way you turn you come upon delicious bits of picturesque scenery blossoming in unexpected nooks and corners. Here and there huge grey rocks stand in their original rugged majesty, their broken lichen-covered boulders tumbling at their base. From the terrace, which is the highest point, you enjoy a view of the entire park with its numerous lakes, fountains, bridges, and statues, spreading like a beautiful panorama round you. Here, too, you fully realize the cosmopolitan character of the city, for here great men of all nations are immortalized or libelled in stone, and their statues stud the park, side by side with the national heroes. Some idea of the extent of these grounds may be gathered from the fact, that there are ten miles of carriage drives, all as a rule wide enough for six to go abreast, about six miles of bridle paths for riding, and twenty-eight for pedestrian exercise; a wide stretch of lawn is set apart for cricket or croquet playing, and a special quarter for children with merry-go-rounds, swings, etc.; there is also a menagerie containing numerous and varied specimens of animals, the nucleus of what is to be, when completed, a fine zoological collection.

The Park is situated in the centre of the upper town. The avenues run lengthwise from one end of the city to another, which are crossed by straight streets in a direct line from the East River, on the one side, to the Hudson on the other; the famous Broadway running diagonally from the upper town, slanting across streets, squares and avenues till it buries itself in the intricate wilds of the lower town, where the streets are closely massed together and densely populated with wanderers from all nations, Polish

Jews, Russians, Italians, Germans, Irish, creating a wild confusion of tongues, all packed in tall tenement houses, in close narrow streets, scores of families living where there is scarcely health-breathing room for one. Castle Garden, where admirable arrangements are made for the reception of emigrants, and the " Battery," once a fashionable promenade, point the lower end of this island city, girdled by the green waters of the Hudson and East River, which meet and mingle here. Wall Street, one of the great financial centres of the world, is situate in the busiest business quarter of the lower town, and runs in a somewhat broken line from Broadway to the East River. The traffic here is enormous, this part of the city is like a human cauldron, with a restless multitude seething and bubbling from morning till night. There must be something in the air which excites the brain and allows to human nature no rest ; every man seems to be rushing for dear life's sake, while life itself is rushing after something else, sometimes hurling itself out of this world into the next to find it. All above Central Park is like a ragged fringe of the great city—long half-finished avenues, straggling sparsely inhabited streets, and skeleton houses ; much of the original swampy ground lies still unclaimed. The Irish squatters in their rickety tumble-down hovels still cling to the land ; the malarial air may wrap them like a shroud, the swamp with its foul unwholesomeness threaten to swallow them up—they will not stir. By slow, very slow degrees, as the Government reclaims the land, they are driven towards the edge, but wherever they can find a footing they squat again.

Although New York is one of the great commercial centres of the world, it is not a beautiful city ; there is

nothing picturesque or attractive about it; take away
Central Park and you have a mere wilderness of bricks
and mortar; streets and houses so closely packed as
scarce to leave breathing room for its inhabitants.
Every one wants to live near the centre, and as its
watery girdle prevents the city spreading, it grows
upwards, piling one story above another till it threatens
to shut out the sky.   It is not a clean city either:
street cleaning is carried on in a slovenly fluctuating
fashion; there are no dust-bins in the backyards, but
ash-barrels stand on the curbstone in front of every
dwelling, and are the receptacles for all household
refuse; dust, ashes, cabbage stumps, fish bones, broken
china, are all poured into the ash-barrel till it overflows
and becomes an unsightly and unsavoury nuisance.

There are several fine libraries, art galleries, and
museums (to give an idea of their valuable and interesting contents would fill a volume), and churches
so numerous that if the piety of the people kept pace
with their churches there would be a scarcity of
sinners.   Their schools are abundant, and their educa-
tional system the most perfect I have seen—every
child may have the advantage of a splendid education
gratis; and the mode of teaching is such that the
veriest dunce must find pleasure in learning.   The
superintendents and teachers are well chosen; with
tact and kindness they lead their pupils, not only to
learn from books, but to think out their own thoughts,
and by suggestive and pertinent questions, cause them
to reflect and comprehend what the lesson teaches, so
making the path of knowledge a path of roses; what
is pleasantly learnt is well learnt and long remembered,
while the learning that is beaten in at one ear often

flies out at the other. In the matter of hospitals, and charitable institutions of all descriptions, the city of New York is second to none ; and all its arrangements are carried out with the large-hearted liberality which characterizes the American people.

Though strongly republican in principle, they do not carry their republican notions into private life. Society is more exclusive than in the old country ; perhaps, not being sure of its own footing, it is afraid of tripping, and watches warily lest any stray free lance should penetrate its interior ; each circle revolves within itself, rarely running one into another. Wholesale and retail mix freely in all commercial matters, are " Hail, fellow ! well met ! " on the cars or in the streets, but on the threshold of home they part. The merchant, who sells a thousand gallons of oil, will not fraternize at home, or be weighed in the social scale with the vendor of a farthing dip. It is always difficult for a stranger to gain admission into the best New York society, but if you are once well introduced, it opens its arms and its heart to you with an hospitality that is genial and thorough. After revolving round its magic circle for a time, you will carry away with you such reminiscences of its brilliant coteries and delightful home gatherings as you will not easily forget.

We are able to take but a casual survey of the Empire City, and enjoy for a brief space the hospitality so freely extended to us. We are on our way to the West, and are anxious to cross the Rocky Mountains before the severe weather set in. Before we start on our long journey, we run up the Hudson, and spend a few days at West Point, celebrated for the great military college; it is a delightful excursion of about three hours, the river winding through a panorama of lovely scenery, the banks on either side wearing their variegated autumn dress of crimson and gold and green; but it is at West Point itself we realize the full glory and effect of the gorgeous autumn colouring. Wonderfully indeed has nature painted the land; the maples are clothed in glowing crimson, and the chestnut and the ash wear their warm-tinted robes beside them, while covering the hundred hills around and overspreading the undulating land are bold patches of purple, orange, browns, gold and greens of many shades, such as an artist would love to dream of. It is one gigantic God-painted mosaic (for such colours could not be manufactured by earthly hands), with a background of cool November sky.

West Point itself is like a bit of an earthly paradise; it stands high above the river, and is surrounded by scenery that is both picturesque and grand. You may lose yourself in its delightful solitudes within sound of the College bells; the river winds in and out about the skirts of West Point like a huge silver serpent; from the terrace of the hotel there is a magnificent view of hill and dale, wood and water, which reminds one strongly of the loveliest, loneliest part of the lake of Lucerne.

There is plenty of gaiety for those who like it: daily parades, military bands, balls, picnics and kettledrums; and during the summer season the hotels—there are but two—are crowded with the rank and fashion of the State.

CHAPTER VII.

TO THE PHŒNIX CITY.

We Start—Our Car—Our Dressing-room—Chicago—Its Park—
The Palmer House.

OF the many routes to San Francisco we chose the
Pennsylvania line of railway, which takes us as far as
Chicago, having been informed by some old tourists
that we should find it by far the most picturesque and
agreeable, besides being the smoothest to run over, the
rails being steel and laid with special care, and the
new carriages being built with all consideration for the
comfort and convenience of their passengers. We had
rather a dread of American railways, having heard so
much of their reckless speed and wilful disregard of
all rules and regulations, that we started on our
journey in some trepidation of spirit, with a nervous
feeling that something *must* happen before the end of
it. But we gained confidence as we discovered the
surprising fact that life is equally dear to its
owners here as at home, and that drivers, engineers,
and other employés are as attentive to their duties here
as in any other quarter of the globe. We settled ourselves comfortably in the seats of our luxurious Pullman car, and prepared to enjoy the scenery.

We fly swiftly through the highly cultivated State
of Pennsylvania; for three or four hundred miles, we
are surrounded by a panorama of picturesque beauty—
sparkling rivers, winding through undulating hills and
verdant plains, with here and there pretty villages
creeping up the green hill-sides or nestling at their
feet.   Presently something that looks like a dark
wriggling worm, with a fierce fiery eye, comes
wickedly towards us.   We are rounding the wonderful
horseshoe curve ; it is our own engine, which seems to
be coming in one direction while we are going in
another ; but it is all right; it drags us round, and
speeds along on level ground once more.   We pass the
Alleghany Mountains, which on this occasion wear a
crown of jewelled flames leaping in lurid fury upon
the dusky night, as though they were trying to regain
the heaven whence they had first descended.   We pass
Pittsburg, with its thousand furnaces glowing in their
own murky atmosphere, flashing their flames, like
threatening fires, in the face of the fair white moon.

As the night closes in, the excitement and novelty
of our day's travel calms down, and we turn our
attention to the internal arrangements of our temporary
home, and are interested in watching our comfortable,
velvet-cushioned section turned into a cosy sleeping-
place ; soft mattresses, snowy sheets, and warm, gaily
striped blankets are extracted from behind the ornamental panels overhead ; the curtains are let down ;
and, lo! we may go to our rest as soon as we please.
But we do not please until we have consulted our conductor, whose sole occupation during the day has been
walking to and fro the cars, punching our tickets till
they resemble a piece of perforated cardboard.   If this

process is to be carried on during the night we think
we shall have small chance of rest. But the matter is
satisfactorily settled; we may sleep in peace. That
punching process is our bugbear throughout the
entire journey. Some are so careful of their tickets
that they never can find them when they are
wanted; and the appearance of the conductor is the
signal for a general hunt. Pockets are ransacked,
portmanteaus are turned out, people nervously feel
themselves all over, plunge under the seats, crawl
over the floor. "It *must* be somewhere." It is found
at last, perhaps wedged in a crack of the window, or it
has dropped into the luncheon-basket and is extracted
from a jelly-jar, strongly impregnated with an odour of
pepper and cheese. I pin mine, as they impale blue-
bottles and butterflies, on the side of the car. Gentlemen, as a rule, dispose of theirs easily enough, and
wear them, like a dustman's badge, stuck in their
hatbands, or like a cavalier's order, pinned upon their
breasts.

This harmless piece of cardboard was the white
elephant of our lives. We never knew what to
do with it. It looked so little and meant so much.
We kept early hours in this our travelling home, and
towards nine o'clock the lights were lowered, and,
soothed by the monotonous movement and rhythmical
rumble of the train, we were soon sleeping as calmly
and pleasantly as in our own beds at home.

Our trial came in the morning, when we marched
to the dressing-room to perform our toilette and found
a whole army of dishevelled females, armed with
tooth-brushes, sponges, etc., besieging the four-foot
space yclept "the ladies' dressing-room," each waiting

for the first sign of surrender to march in and take
possession. This was the miserable epoch in our daily
lives through all the overland journey; in everything
else our car life was delightfully luxurious and pleasant.
Perhaps there were a dozen ladies who every day had
to grapple with the same difficulty and stand shivering,
all more or less *en déshabille* (rather more than less),
biding their time to take temporary possession of the
solitary soap-dish and basin provided for their ablutions. The public are already deeply indebted to
Messrs. Pullman and Co. for an easy and luxurious
mode of travelling, but the debt might be increased a
thousandfold by a small sacrifice on their part. By
devoting a single section to the purpose of a second
dressing-room, they would add considerably to the
accommodation of the ladies, and might fairly issue a
placard of " Travelling made Perfect."

No hotel or dining-cars accompany the morning
train from New York, but eating-stations are erected
at certain portions of the road, where you may get rid
of the most wolfish appetite at an admirably spread
table, and plenty of time allowed for the knife and fork
engagement.

On the second day we found ourselves rushing
along the wide plains of Indiana, a sea of tall, sweet
Indian corn on either side, its beaded cob, like shining
ivory, gleaming from its leaf of tender green. We
reached Chicago that evening, and were most kindly
received at the Palmer House, a palatial hotel built by
Mr. Potter Palmer for the luxurious entertainment of
the travelling public. It is more like an elegantly
appointed home than a mere resting-place for such
birds of passage as ourselves. Each suite of apart-

ments is perfect in itself, with a bath-room and every convenience attached, richly curtained and carpeted, with luxurious lounges and the easiest of easy-chairs; once settled in their soft embrace it is difficult to tear one's self from their downy arms. Being cosily installed beneath this hospitable roof, one feels, like "poor *Joe*," disinclined to "move on." The spacious halls and corridors are furnished in accord with other portions of the house. The walls are lined with *fauteuils*, sofas, and all the appointments of a handsome drawing-room.

As soon as we had enjoyed the luxury of a bath (and, after two days' dusty travel, what a luxury that is!), we went to the dining saloon in search of our dinner, and found an unusually good one, excellently served and abundantly supplied. If we had stayed for a month and eaten *pro rata* as at our first meal, we should have ruined our digestive organs and rejoiced in internal discords for ever afterward. Our *ménu* was illustrated. On one side was depicted a pigstye and a hovel—"Chicago forty years ago." On the other was a wonderful city—"The Chicago of to-day!"

Knowing of the fiery scourge which a few years ago had marred and scarred the beauty of that fair city, we expected to find traces of ugliness and deformity everywhere, crippled buildings, and lame, limping streets running along in a forlorn crooked condition, waiting for time to restore their old vigour and build up their beauty anew. But, Phœnixlike, the city has risen up out of its own ashes, grander and statelier than ever. On the outskirts the line of fire can still be traced; gaunt skeletons of houses still remain to point the way it took, and more than one

ruined church, stripped of its altar and regal signs of
grace, stands blind and helpless in the sunshine;
while in the suburbs picturesque shells of once
beautiful homes greet us here and there. But once
within the boundaries of the city we lose all traces
of the conflagration. The business streets are lined
with handsome massive houses, some six or seven
stories high, substantially built, sometimes of red brick
with stone copings and elaborate carving, while others
are built of that creamy stone which reminds one of
the Paris boulevards. No wooden buildings are
allowed to be erected within a certain distance of the
city. The fashionable trading localities are State and
Clark streets, though there are several others which
are well patronized by a less fashionable multitude.
On either side are large handsome drygoods, millinery,
and other stores of all possible descriptions, the windows being arranged with a tasteful elaboration that
might stand side by side with our fashionable establishments at home, and lose nothing by the comparison.
The different banks, churches, and municipal buildings
which had been destroyed by the great fire-fiend are
all re-erected in a substantial style, though with varying degrees of eccentric architecture. The new waterworks, situated at the northern end of the city, are the
most beautiful illustrations of the vagaries of the architectural brain. It must have wandered into dreamland
and caught up its prevailing idea, for never were so
many cupolas and buttresses, pinnacles and towers,
grouped together on one spot; none but a true artist
could have arranged them into so harmonious a whole,
and produced from a combination of such opposite forms
so imposing an effect.

A painter may indulge in all the eccentricities of his genius, may derive his inspiration from what source he will, there is no restriction to the realms of his art. He may choose his subject, and illustrate it according to his own fancy; he may wander far from the realms of art, and give to the wood a " harmony in blue and gold," or a " study in brass and impudence," and his productions are called " original." But if an architect outruns the bounds prescribed by the five orders of architecture, and dares to give play to his fancy, his work is stigmatized as " bastard art," and he is considered a fit subject for a lunatic asylum. On our drives through and about the city we were struck by the dearth of trees. There were no signs of pleasant green shade anywhere; they had all been destroyed by the great fire. Streets and avenues had been rebuilt, and they were replanting as fast as they could; but nature will not be hurried in her work, her children must have time to grow, and though her fairest fruits are sometimes forced into an unnatural growth, she revenges herself by robbing them of their sweetest flavour.

Along the shore road we drove to the park at the northern end of the city, which gives promise of being a delightful promenade and recreation ground; but it is at present only a park in embryo, though it is growing rapidly. Flowers and shrubs are being planted, grassy knolls built up, and paths and winding ways cut and gravelled. In the course of a few years it will have outgrown its present ragged state, and have bloomed into a delightful pleasure-ground, with the whispering waves of that inland sea, Lake Michigan, kissing with soft foam lips its grassy slopes, while great ships go sailing and steamers ride royally on the breast of the wide waters on one side, and the great city, with its hubbub, bustle, and roar, lies upon the other. Chicago is indeed a great city, full of energy and enterprise. Signs of its hidden strength and powers of progress greet us everywhere; but at present it appears to be wholly devoted to money-making. Art, science (except such science as serves its purpose), and literature are in a languishing state. But it is young yet. Perhaps when it is fully developed, and grown strong in muscle, and bone, and brain, the soul may be born to glorify the commonplace, and stir the latent genius of this city into life and beauty.

With some regret we sit down to our last dinner in this bright, bustling city, and go to bed to dream of to-morrow, for in the morning we begin our journey west, and the magnet which has drawn us across the sea lies at the Golden Gate.

CHAPTER VIII.

WESTWARD HO!

Our Travelling Hotel—The Prairies—The Emigrant Train—Bret
   Harte's Heroes—Reception of General Grant in the Wild
   West—"See, the Conquering Hero Comes"—The Procession.

THE next morning we started, *via* the Chicago and
Northwestern Railway, for Omaha. This is a most
desirable route, over even, well-laid rails, the carriages
easy and luxurious, and we are whirled along over
the illimitable prairie lands with a pleasant, gliding,
almost noiseless motion, which recalled to our minds
the gondola movement on the Grand Canal at Venice;
this we are told is owing to some new invention of
india-rubber or paper wheels which the company have
applied to their carriages, which greatly adds to the
comfort of their travellers. It was here, for the first
time, we enjoyed the luxury of the hotel car. We
were getting hungry, and curious to know what good
things the gods would provide for us. Presently a
good-humoured negro, " God's image carved in ebony,"
clothed all in white, brought us a bill of fare from
which to select our meal. It was an *embarras de
richesses*. There were so many good things that we
held a consultation as to what would form the most

desirable meal. We decided on mulligatawny soup, broiled oysters, lamb cutlets, and peas, and handed the *menu* back to our swarthy attendant. A narrow passage, every inch of which is utilized, separates the kitchen from the rest of the car. How is it that in so many private houses the odour of roast and broil travels from the kitchen and insinuates itself into the remotest corner of the house? It greets you on the doorstep and follows you everywhere. Here the occupants of the car, but a few feet off, have no suggestion of dinner till it is placed before them.

We were curious as to the working of the culinary department, and animated by a noble desire to obtain knowledge we penetrated the sacred precincts of the cook. He gazed sternly at us on our entrance, but we insinuated ourselves into his good graces, and he showed us every nook and corner of his domain. The kitchen was a perfect gem of a place, about eight feet square. A range ran along one side, its dark, shining face breaking out into an eruption of knobs, handles, and hinges of polished brass or steel. Curious little doors were studded all over it. One opened here and there to give us a sniff of its savory secrets, then shut with a laughing clang, so playing "bo-peep" with our appetites. Presently we should enjoy the full revelation of its culinary secrets. Pots, steamers, and "bain Marie" pans were simmering on the top. Every requisite for carrying on the gastronomical operations was there in that tiny space, in the neatest and most compact form. Scrupulous cleanliness reigned supreme over all. There was the pantry, with its polished silver, glass, and china in shining array. The refrigerator, with a plentiful supply of ice, and the larder were side by side. The wine and beer cellar was artfully arranged beneath the car; none but he who possessed the secret of "open sesame" could get access to it. Thus every inch of space was realized to its utmost extent. It was like a dominion in Toyland, inhabited by an ebony giant, who by a species of culinary conjuring produced an epicure's feast from a handful of wood and charcoal. Towards six o'clock every table was spread with dainty linen, and the dinner was exquisitely served according to the previous orders of each traveller. The simplest dish, as well as the most elaborate, was cooked to perfection, and everybody fell to with a will. Early hours were kept here as in our other travelling home, and the same routine was pursued in the morning. Breakfast was served about eight o'clock. The flat prairie land rolled away rapidly beneath our iron tread, and lay in long dusky lines behind us. Imperceptibly the scenery around us changed. We passed a succession of wild, low-lying hills, brown and bare; then more hills growing higher and greener, rising out of the swampy lands, where herds of cattle and wild shaggy ponies were standing knee deep and grazing among the red willows and long green grass. The skies were leaden, the wind began to blow, and the rain to fall. We passed a quiet little lake, dotted all over with wild ducks, and prairie birds flying restlessly over them. Signs of life became stronger. We flew past wooden shanties, and now and then caught sight of a lonely settler's hut high up in the hills. Presently we rolled into a low, flat, straggling village, or rather town, for every group of a dozen houses is so dignified here. This was

Council Bluffs. Here we left our cosy car, and crossed the bleak windy space which yawned between us and the car yclept "the Dummy!" which was to carry us to Omaha.

We were crammed into a long, comfortless, wagon-like car with a host of nondescript folk, some bearing babies, bundles, or baskets of fish or vegetables, some tattered and torn, some unshaven, unshorn, all mixed up *higglety pigglety*. It was stuffy and by no means savory, for the windows were all closed to keep out the wind and the rain, which was now pouring in torrents. For a few moments we looked out shivering on the most desolate prospect. The skies were heavy with huge, black clouds, whose growling thunders went reverberating like a cannonade among the surrounding hills. The wind howled like a shrieking demon, and came creeping in at every crevice, till we shivered in its icy grasp. Dreary without and dreary within!

But we look forward hopefully. In half an hour we shall reach Omaha, where we expect to be well housed and fed. Slowly we begin to move. Our "dummy" finds voice enough to groan and pant painfully with its brazen lungs as it carries us across the bridge which spans the Missouri River and connects Omaha with Council Bluffs. The bridge is a mile long, and we go very slowly over it. The river, which at this point is the colour and consistency of thick pea soup, or a liquefied London fog, winds with a sluggish motion below us, wriggling its way between the iron piers with a sullen, rebellious gurgle, as though it was ashamed of its defiled condition, and hated to be driven from its own bright waters, which were sparkling clear as crystal not so many miles away. But once set floating in a muddy stream in the world of waters, as in the world of men, it is difficult to mingle with the pure living waters again.

At last we creak and rumble into the station at Omaha. Our poor dummy's joints are rusty and want oiling. It seems glad to stop, and so are we. We glance round us, and feel we are on the threshold of a new world. The platform is crowded with a motley assemblage of people, from which the "genteel" element seems to be wholly eliminated. There is a hurrying to and fro of many feet, a general bustle and confusion reigning everywhere. A very babel of voices is ringing round us. The harsh guttural German, the liquid Italian, and the mellifluous Spanish mingles with the Yankee twang and Irish brogue. The emigrant train has just arrived and disgorged its living freight. The platform overflows with them, they are everywhere, all with a more or less travel-stained look. Having been penned up so long in such close quarters they are glad to get out and stretch their legs and rinse the dirt from their grimy faces. Swarthy men, with bare arms, are splashing about in buckets; some are performing their ablutions under the pump, or in anything that comes handy. One sad-eyed German woman, with a child in her arms, is sitting entrenched amongst an army of bags and bundles, and dipping an old handkerchief into a pint cup of water is wiping her child's face and her own, refreshing themselves as they best could there-with. I stop and put a packet of candy into the little one's hand. The mother stares vacantly, and slowly extracting a copper coin from a poor, little, ragged purse, which she drew from her bosom, offers it in payment.

The women as a rule look faded, wan, and anxious; the men energetic and strong, confident and assured, with a bright, never-say-die look upon their faces.

They look as if they meant "work," and were able to do it. There seem to be only a few loafers and loungers scattered among them, weak, indolent creatures, who had not pluck enough to fight their way in their own land, and are journeying in search of a general El Dorado, a sort of "Tom Tidler's ground," where they could go " picking up gold and silver."

They are to wait three hours at the station before they resume their journey west. It is a strange gathering, that flock of varying nationalities, all bound on one adventurous errand—a wave of the Old World breaking on the shores of the New.

The Grand Pacific Hotel having been destroyed by fire, we get into an omnibus which conveys us to the Cosmopolitan, which is a striking contrast to the magnificent hotels which have hitherto lined our route. It is second-rate in style, but also second-rate in price. No lounges; no easy-chairs; no velvet carpets under foot. The floors are sanded; the chairs uncompromisingly hard and upright: but the beds are comfortable enough; meals excellently cooked, though roughly served. We enjoy all the necessities, but none of the luxuries of life. As we only intend to remain in Omaha for a day we walk out to take a view of the town. It is a most dreary, desolate-looking city, with wide, straggling, dusty streets, and next to nobody in them. The shops are numerous enough, such as they are, but seedy-looking and scantily supplied. Nobody is doing anything; there seems to be nothing to do. The shopkeepers lounge in their doorways; they don't appear to have energy enough even to gossip with their neighbours. The very children seem to have no heart for childish roistering; their spirits droop under the atmospheric depression; they come trooping out of school and wend their way homeward in a stolid, orderly fashion. The side-streets are overgrown with dank grass and weeds; in the outskirts of the city little wooden houses, looking exactly as if they had come out of a Noah's Ark, are scattered irregularly about, each standing in its little barren patch of ground. We spend the morning in wandering through these dusty, windblown streets. We return to the hotel, take a hasty lunch, an hour's rest, then sally forth again. By this time something has happened to stir the dead city into life. For the hour it is roused from its normal condition. The shops are closed, the population has turned out into the streets, and people come flocking in from all parts of the country—some on foot, some in ramshackle old vehicles which look as though they had never worn a coat of paint, and so dilapidated we wonder how they manage to keep together; the wheels seem to be struggling to run different ways, but the big, bony steed draws them through dust and mire, till the vantage-point is gained in the streets of Omaha. A few fluttering flags are now flying. The Stars and Stripes are everywhere, and on turning a sharp corner we stand face to face with a triumphal arch built up of egg boxes and old beer barrels, which are partially covered with evergreens and paper flowers, and in big,

G

blazing, though somewhat tumbledown letters across the top is written "Welcome Grant."

So the gallant General is expected to-day, and that is the cause of the commotion. He is to make a royal progress through the streets of Omaha, and all the city turns out to do him honour, though the female part of the population is sparsely represented. Indeed there is scarcely a woman to be seen out of doors. It is here we gain our first view of the Western man precisely as he lives in the pages of Bret Harte & Co., where we have so often seen him in our mind's eye; but here he is a personality before us—dark, hollow-cheeked, stern-visaged, slouch-hatted, top-booted; there are scores of him, hundreds of him; he tramps along the side-walk, he overflows into the stony roadway. The aspect of this swarm of rough, unkempt men is rather alarming to us unprotected females. But "he roars him soft," and respectfully makes way for us to pass. It seems strange to find a silent, well-ordered crowd formed of such rough elements. There is no horse-play, no vulgar "chaff," or foul language, such as would characterize a similar crowd in most of our civilized cities. But, alas! the romance that might cling to this Western hero is spoiled by his personal habits. He has small acquaintance with soap and water, and he chews tobacco. The result which marks his track wherever he wanders is visible and revolting. However, he is stout of limb and true of heart. We feel instinctively that a rude word or discourteous act in our presence is simply impossible, so we lift our unprotected heads and march on triumphant. We feel we must keep moving, though we are disposed to lag and see what is to be seen of the show. We have not

sauntered many steps when the engine bell rings.
" Lo ! the conquering hero comes ! " There is a buzz,
a general stir, and all eyes are turned in one direction. We fall back, and are promoted to a position in
the front rank on the curbstone.

There was a coal-black negress on one side of us,
dressed in a pale-blue dress with white trimmings, a
scarlet shawl, a pink bonnet with red and yellow
roses, and a pea-green parasol. She was evidently
happy, and her white teeth gleamed through a wreath
of smiles. The procession came in sight headed by
a band of music, a huge drum being the chief instrument ; fifes and flutes squeaking their loudest,
each trying to get ahead of the other, running a race
with time rather than trying to keep it. The poor
" Star Spangled Banner " was torn with discords,
tattered in tune, its own creator would not have known
it. Next came the General in an old-fashioned coach
drawn by six horses, evidently promoted from the
ploughshare for this special occasion. Mrs. Grant
followed, with her son and some lady friends, all
looking smiling, good-tempered, and happy, as though
the dreary boredom of a reception awaited them not.
Then came a curious procession of wagons, repre-
senting the different trades of the town. There was
the blacksmith, hammer in hand, labouring at the
anvil, bellows blowing, sparks flying round him as
though he were in his native smithy ; the cutler, the
nailmaker, the carpenter, the cooper, etc., all surrounded by the implements of their trade, and plying
them, too, with a will. Last of this novel procession
came a wagon filled with pretty young girls, all busily
engaged hemming, sewing, and frilling at their

different sewing-machines. This closed the procession, and "The Magnificent Reception of General Grant by the Citizens of Omaha" was duly chronicled. It flashed along the telegraph wires and flamed in the face of the world before the sun had set.

The multitude melted away as quietly as it had collected, and we went on our way to the Pullman car office to secure our section for the morning. The clerk was with the Reception Committee, and we had to wait for his return. We were entertained meanwhile by the rhapsodies of one of the General's wildest admirers, who turned on the tap of conversation and filled us to the brim with voluntary information.

"I fought under the General fourteen years ago. Ah! he's a man, the General is! Talk of him being President! He ought to be emperor. There'd be no disunited States while *he* was around, I warrant. I haven't seen him for years, but he knew me. They stopped at the corner of Tenth; I jumped on the carriage steps: 'Hurrah, General,' says I, 'I fought under you at——'

" 'All right!' says he, and shook hands. Ah! he's a smart fellow. No other general could have done what he did."

A tall aristocratic looking man, who was standing by waiting his turn, moved coolly away from the group.

The face of the General's friend knotted itself into an expression of deep disgust. He evidently deemed that cold water was thrown on his enthusiasm.

"There goes a copperhead," he snarled. "I can smell 'em a mile off. We haven't done with 'em yet: we've only scotched the snake, not killed it; we shall have to thrash 'em again, and I'll be the first to shoulder a musket."

In this strain he continued. We transacted our business and descended the stairs. His voice followed us, growing more fiercely eloquent, till we were out of hearing. I fancy he had been drinking the General's health too freely.

We were not very sorry to leave Omaha next morning, for we had rested little during the night, having made a bad selection of rooms. Our door opened on to the general parlour (all sitting-rooms are called parlours), and a gruff, growling wave of conversation swept over our ears from time to time till long past midnight. Indeed, we were kept lively in more ways than one. Meanwhile a violent rain began to fall, and beat frantically against our window panes, and I dreamt that the whole sky was turned into a dome of whalebone and calico, and this globe of ours was whirling around beneath a gigantic umbrella. I was not sorry when our twenty-four hours at Omaha were over.

CHAPTER IX.

ACROSS THE ROCKY MOUNTAINS.

Our Fellow-passengers—Unprotected Females—Prairie Dog Land
—A Cosy Interior—Cheyenne—The Rocky Mountains—
" Castles not Made by Hands "—Ogden.

WE start once more on our pleasant Pullman car ; we
arrange our tiny packages and make ourselves as much
as possible " at home " in our cosy section. The car is
crowded, as the different lines of railway end here, and
all who are westward bound must come on this one
daily train from Omaha. We look round on our
fellow-passengers. As a rule, they are simply commonplace, such as nature manufactures by millions and
turns out merely labelled men and women, with no
special characteristics except their sex. There are,
however, some exceptions. In the opposite section is
a big, burly fellow in jackboots, a huge sombrero, a
frieze coat, which looks as though it ought to be stuck
full of bowie-knives and pistols, and such a growth
of crisp dark hair, he seems smothered under it ;
a pair of bright eyes gleam out from its bushy
surroundings, full of enterprise, energy, and spirit ;
he is a miner, we learn, going on by stage two
hundred miles from Cheyenne to the Black Hills. The
companion of his section is a tall, delicate-looking

young man, so thin and fragile it seems as though a
gust of wind would blow him out of this world into
the next. He rarely speaks, but sits leaning his head
upon his hand, coughing the terrible, hacking cough
which tells a sad story. He is travelling in search
of health, he tells us; the more eagerly he pursues,
the faster it seems to fly from him. In our mind's
eye we see the phantom Death chasing him from
land to land; it will too surely run him down and
lay him to rest beneath the bright Californian skies,
and hide him from the world's eyes where even his
own mother will never be able to find him. We are
sorry to see this forlorn stranger solitary and alone;
we are anxious to show him some sympathy, but
there is nothing to be done; it hurts him to talk, and
he has all he wants within reach of his own hands.
His rough companion, bound for the Black Hills,
seems to take a tender interest in him, and shows his
sympathy in a silent, unobtrusive way difficult to
specify. In the next section to ours there is a pretty
young girl; she is travelling quite alone from Boston
to Arizona, a journey of twelve days and nights, in
perfect comfort and safety. A lady can do that in this
country without running the slightest risk of annoy-
ance or inconvenience in any way. The conductors
and all the train officials devote themselves most
loyally to her service, and are always at hand to give
her any advice or information she may require. They
pass her on from train to train or from stage to stage
till she arrives at the end of her journey, having
received the same courteous attention throughout.
Indeed, to thoroughly enjoy travelling in perfect comfort and freedom from anxiety, one must be an unpro-

tected female. To her the manly heart yields his
interest in car or stage; gives her the best seat, that
she may be screened and curtained, while he broils in
the sun; for her he fights a way to the front ranks of
refreshment rooms, skirmishes with the coffee-pot, and
bears triumphant ices aloft; for her he battles with
baggage-masters, baffles the hungry-hearted loafer,
scares the barefooted beggar, and, not being her legi-
timate owner, he carries her bandbox, and, should she
be burdened with that doubtful blessing, he even
carries her baby! I have seen him do it. There was
a general demand upon his chivalry on board this car,
but there was plenty of him and only four of *us*.
Besides ourselves and the pretty girl before referred
to, there was a snuff-coloured young lady with snuff-
coloured hair, snuff-coloured eyes, and dress to match,
a greyish complexion, and rather grave, sad expression
of countenance. She was not good-looking, but one
felt an interest in watching her. Her face had a story
in it.

Having so far taken note of our fellow-passengers,
we lean back in our seats and look out upon the vast
prairie-lands, which roll before and around us like a
grey-green, motionless sea. The prospect is wild and
dreary. Occasionally we see a trapper's dug-out or
watch a solitary hunter galloping towards his hut somewhere up in the distant mountains. The scene grows
monotonous; nay, wearisome. Nothing but the grey-
green prairie-land and bright blue sky; the novelty of
it has worn off. Presently we come upon the prairie
dogs' wild domain, and see scores of these funny little
animals scampering along till they reach each his particular hole, where he sits on his hind legs a moment,

glancing curiously round and listening, then, turning a somersault, disappears, head first, down his burrow. They are plump little creatures, like guinea pigs, only much larger, and something the colour of the prairie-grass; they are sociable little animals, and live not only in the companionship of their own kind, for the burrowing owl and even the rattlesnake seem to form part of the family. The owl may often be seen solemnly sitting at the mouth of the hole, and the bones of the rattlesnake have not unfrequently been found therein. Once we catch a glimpse of a herd of antelopes flying, like the wind, across the plain. They have come and gone like a flash; nothing more breaks the monotony of that day's journey.

The blinding sunlight dazzles our eyes; we withdraw them from the scene without and glance round upon the cheerful prospect within. Some are indulging in reminiscences of old times, when it had taken them six weary months of toil, privation, and danger to cross these plains, which they are now doing luxuriously in seven days. In one section a rubber of whist is in progress in sociable but solemn silence; in another a pair of travellers bound for the Black Hills are engaged in the game of poker, and cut, deal, shuffle, and play with such rapidity that we can catch no idea of the game; some lounge over the whist-table watching the players; the snuff-colored girl leans back in her seat with folded hands lying idly in her lap, gazing with vacant eyes, not on the desolation round her, but possibly on her own invisible life, which may be a more dismal prospect still; the pretty girl gets out her tatting, and we have a pleasant chat and exchange small confidences together: her parents are dead, she tells me, and she has not a relation in the world except her brother, who is settled in Arizona, and she is now going to make her home with him.

"I haven't seen him since I was three years old," she added, showing his portrait; "he is sixteen years older than I am."

"You are quite sure of a welcome?"

"Oh yes; I know he'll be glad to see me. He wanted me to come, and he is such a good brother," she added, confidently. "He'll come to meet me in San Francisco, if he can."

So time passes till we reach Cheyenne. There we all turn out in anticipation of having a thoroughly good meal, and are not disappointed. We enjoy a capital dinner, a very necessary thing in these mountain regions. The hot soup is excellent; then we have broiled trout and a roast of black-tailed deer, the most delicious-flavoured, tender meat conceivable; fresh vegetables and fruits are plentifully supplied; and, as a crowning bliss, we enjoy the luxury of black coffee; and, in a perfectly happy, contented frame of mind, we re-enter our Pullman home.

Everybody is content, and everybody has a good word for Cheyenne. Why is it that things are not equally well managed throughout this well-travelled route? As a rule, the eating-stations are wretchedly supplied. We have thrown away many a noble appetite on a tough, tasteless steak and watery soup, that had scarcely strength to run down our throats. Indeed, Cheyenne, Humboldt, and Laramie are the only stations where a thoroughly good, comfortable meal may be relied on. A well-filled luncheon-basket is a necessity, a comfort, as well as an economy, for the charges at these places are a dollar for anything, unless you crowd to the emigrants' refreshment bar, where cooking is by no means studied as a high art.

Leaving Cheyenne we charge gallantly forward, climbing higher and higher, till we are in the regions of snow and ice, and at last reach Sherman, the highest point of these Rocky Mountains, eight thousand two hundred feet above the level of the sea. The rarefied air affects the breathing of some of our party, and one gallant officer, who has gone through the smoke and fire of many battles unharmed, is seized with an ignominious bleeding at the nose. For us, we suffer not the slightest inconvenience. We have left the rolling prairies behind us, and now, by imperceptible grades, begin to descend this wide range of Rocky Mountains. Vast, rugged, and bare in their stony strength they lie before us ; a bright blue sky bends bell-like over us, bathes us in a kind of spiritual sunshine, and shuts us in from the troublous world beyond. We feel we are intruders in this wondrous solitude ; it seems as though Nature should have it all to herself here, and hurl us poor pigmies out of it. But in these days Nature is allowed to hold nothing sacredly her own ; as she retreats we follow her even to her farthest fastnesses,— in time we shall reach her even there. Our living street dashes on through this world of the olden gods. We fancy that in some far-distant ages this must have been a wide overwhelming sea, lashed to fury and then turned to stone. As we descend the scene changes ; the rocks assume strange, fantastic forms, weird, solemn, or grotesque. On every side we are surrounded by some new wonder. There is something in the grandeur

of this silent world which makes us feel small and sad;
we cease talking, and are borne through this sublime
region in awe-struck silence.

Ruined castles, not made by hands, with buttress
and battlements falling to decay, frown darkly over us.
The remains of some ancient cathedrals, where we can
fancy the olden gods held solemn service, cling to the
grey rock beside us. But tower and buttress, castled
crag and battlemented ruins fade from our sight, and
we come upon new scenes of equal wonder. We pass
through serried swords of rock, which look as though
they had been lifted there by some dead Hercules at
war with the mightier gods. We whistle and shriek as
we rush past the giant's jaws, whose jagged teeth seem
set ready to grind us to powder, but they are fixed
immovable till the judgment day. We pass the Pulpit
Rock, where the stony preacher has stood silent looking southward since the world began. There is a
tradition that the Prophet of the Lord, the leader of
the Latter Day Saints, whose province we are fast
approaching, once preached there to his people during
their early perilous journey, while they were ignorant
of the marvellous Salt Lake and valleys beyond, where
they have since made their home. There are numerous
small towns and villages hidden away among those
mountainous regions, which are intersected by fertile
valleys, and where beautiful rivers are eternally flowing; but we see nothing of them, we are only told
that they are there. We are now entering the famous
Echo and Weber Cañons, of which we had heard so
much. Here the grandeur of the whole rugged range
seems to have reached its highest point. We are in a
narrow gorge between rocks of colossal and majestic

dimensions, rising perpendicularly on either side of us, so high and so near that our eyes have to climb steadily till they reach the topmost peak. We, with our petty passions and frail human life, the last, and, as we are told, the best of all God's works, feel dwarfed and insignificant beside these gigantic memorials, which stand through all ages the insignia of His immortal honour and glory. We steam for miles through this rocky world of wonders, amid a stillness so profound that the whistle of our engine echoes, re-echoes, and is flung back upon our ears multiplied and sounding like the shrieks of invisible demons giving us a mocking welcome to their silent land. We are nearing the narrows, where the cañon is drawing its rocky sides together, closing us in as it were. There seems to be no escape for us ; we feel as though we must be dashed down the precipice which yawns below. But we round a sharp curve, and the scene widens. On our right is a wide ledge of rugged, grey rocks, where, we are told, the Mormons made a stand in 1857, and erected a fort close by, the ruins of which are still visible. There they piled up masses of rock and stones to hurl down upon the United States Army, which it was found expedient to send against them. The Nauvoo regiments, we are told, encamped here close beneath the prow of the " Great Eastern," a huge red rock, so called from the resemblance it bears to that portion of a gigantic vessel ; a small cedar-tree waves like a green flag over it, and the deck and other parts of the stony vessel slope away and are swallowed up and lost in the shapeless mass of grey rocks surrounding. A little farther on, sombre and weird, stand The Three Witches, as though whispering together, plotting mischief, manufacturing and sending forth storms, hurricanes, and cyclones to devastate the world of man below. Now we are fast approaching what is perhaps the most marvellous of all these strange formations, "The Devil's Slide," whither his Satanic Majesty is supposed to retire for gymnastic exercises when he has nothing else to do, which is not often, though the "City of the Saints" is so near at hand. It is formed of two slanting walls about a foot thick, which stand out with their ragged, jagged edges about fifty feet, and slope down the face of the huge body of rock nearly close together, but leaving room for a whole company of fiends to amuse themselves by sliding down between them. We flash past The Thousand Mile Tree, the solitary green thing which flourishes in the precipitous wilds, and which tells us we are a thousand miles from Omaha, and within an hour's ride of Ogden. The night closes in very suddenly in these regions, and even as we are looking on the wonders round us they grow indistinct, and are soon lost in the gloomy shadow which comes stealing stealthily down as soon as the sun has set.

It is quite dark when we steam into the station; the gong is sounding (with that whirring, muffled, deafening sound which only a Chinese gong can make) an invitation to dinner, of which we are glad enough to avail ourselves. Porters are dashing about with lighted lanterns, luggage is lifted, and stacked, and wheeled across the platform to the other train, for there is a general change at this point; and all passengers are shifted from the Union, which ends here, to the Central Pacific, which takes up the journey and progresses westward. An hour is allowed for dinner,

and amid the clatter of knives and forks, a hurrying
to and fro of many feet, the sound of genial voices,
chatter and laughter, we dine.   Soon, too soon, it
seems, the now familiar cry "All aboard! all aboard!"
greets our ears.   A few hurried good-byes and the
westward bound speed on their way.   We watch the
red fiery eye of the engine light fade from our sight,
as it winks and blinks away in the darkness.   We
re-enter the house, where we have decided to remain
for the night.   All is silent and deserted now that the
guests of an hour have departed; the lights are out,
and the few dusky servants flit to and fro in a noiseless
way.   We have got the place all to ourselves, and
have plenty of time to look about us.   It is a most
comfortable resting-place, more like a cosy English inn
than the more pretentious-sounding hotel.   There are
no houses near it, the town of Ogden proper being
some little distance off, though still within sight of the
depôt.   Our resting-place is sandwiched between the
two lines of railway, the Union and Central Pacific.
It is a long, narrow, wooden building, only one story
high, the lower part being devoted to railway business
purposes, Pullman-car office, etc., and a large dining-
room, where, as the train steams in with its freight of
hungry travellers, an excellent, well-cooked meal awaits
them.   The upper part consists of about ten or twelve
cosy white-curtained sleeping-rooms.   We should
advise every one to rest here for a night on their way
westward; it forms a delightful break in their journey.
Except for the passing trains this is a most lonely,
isolated spot, weird and still, lying in the heart of the
mountains.   In the evening a blinding snowstorm
came on, and the wind, howling fearfully with a rush-

ing mighty sound, shook the doors and rattled at the
windows as though it wanted to come in and warm
itself at our blazing wood fire. As I said before, we
were the only guests in the house, and the landlady
came in, bringing her work. The shaded lamps were
lighted, the wood crackled and blazed, and cast a
pleasant glow to our very hearts as we drew our chairs
round the fire.

Our landlady had lived in this locality five and
twenty years, and her mind was well stocked with
anecdotes, and filled with the legendary lore of these
wild regions. She opened her stores to us, and, as she
sat sewing, kept our interest alive till nearly midnight,
telling us of stormy times, interspersed with many
romantic incidents during the early days when the
Mormons first crossed the plains, previous to making
their home among the mountains, when the railway·
was unplanned, unthought of, and wagon trains of
adventurous men and women made their slow and
hazardous pilgrimage to the Western World.

The next morning we took the train to Salt Lake
City, and found ourselves plunged at once in the world
of Mormonland.

CHAPTER X.

THE CITY OF THE SAINTS.

Salt Lake — Our Mormon Conductor — Mormon Wives — Their
Daughters—Their Recruits—Their Agricultural Population.

THERE are few passengers on board the train as we
steam through the suburban districts of Mormonland.
The magnificent chain of the Wahsatch Mountains
rising in the east, and the great Salt Lake stretching
away toward the west, the rest of the scene made up
of fertile lands, green meadows, fields of yellow corn,
and purple clover, form an enchanting panorama as we
fly past them; we are full of an undefined curiosity
and anxious to see this City of the Saints of which we
have heard so much. We soon discover that none but
the "Saints" are employed on board this train, none but
Mormon faces gather round us, they check our baggage,
punch our tickets, and render us every necessary
courtesy, which would do credit to the gentlest of
Gentiles. Our conductor seems disposed to make himself quite at home; he takes a seat beside us, and
commences a pleasant conversation; he knows we are
from England, and proceeds to give us all kinds of
miscellaneous and useful information. He points out
the different features in the landscape, and tells us of
thrifty villages and thriving farms which are scattered

among the mountains. He talks freely of the flourishing condition of the City of the Saints; but he avoids any special allusion to the peculiarities of the saints themselves. During our two hours' run from Ogden to Salt Lake City he grows more and more sociably disposed. We try to guide the conversation into the channel where we desire it should go. We wonder whether he is a Mormon or one of the Gentile sect, which is now numerously represented in that once exclusive land. We ask the question pointblank.

"Yes, ma'am, I'm proud to say I am," he answers, swelling with invisible glory; it is now he informs us that the whole line of railway was built by the Mormon people, and is exclusively run by them, no other labour being employed.

"I came here," he adds, "when I was six years old, when our people were forced to leave Nauvoo. I remember trotting along by my mother's side as we were driven out of the city at the point of the bayonet, the soldiers pricking and goading us like cattle. I shall never forget that time,—never, if I live to be a hundred years old; but we pulled through, and here we are in the most beautiful and flourishing valley in the whole wide world."

"And—I am afraid my question may seem impertinent—but may I ask how many wives you have?" I ask, growing bolder. He laughs, pulls off his cap, and exhibits a remarkably fine mass of bright brown curls.

"See my head of hair!" he exclaims. "Well, I have only got one wife; if I took home another, this head of mine would be sand-papered! There are scores of us," he added, "who never dream of taking more than one wife."

"Then polygamy is not imposed on you as a part of your religion?" I inquire.

"Certainly not; but it is our right if we choose to adopt it. It is different now from the early days, when it was necessary, for our good God's sake, that his people of Zion should increase and multiply, so as to fill the kingdom of heaven." I felt disposed to suggest that the kingdom of heaven might perhaps be able to get along without the aid of Brigham Young's progeny, but as that observation might appear irreverent I withheld it, and he continued: "For my part I've found that one wife is quite as much as I can manage. I've never felt inclined to increase my family that way, and I don't believe there is a happier man in all Salt Lake than I am."

We reach the City of the Saints at last, and find it as fair and beautiful as we had expected. It is in truth an oasis in a desert, a blooming garden in a wilderness of green. We can scarcely conceive how this flowery world has lifted itself from the heart of desolation; it is only one more proof that the intellect and industry of man can master the mysteries of nature, and force her in her most harsh uncompromising moods to bring forth fair fruits. It lies in a deep wide valley, bounded on the east by the mighty range of the Wahsatch Mountains, which lift their lonely ice-crowned heads far into the skies, their rugged stony feet stretching away and reaching towards the west, where the great Salt Lake unrolls its dark waters, and widens and wanders away until it is lost in the distance. The streets are wide, the houses of all sorts and sizes, some one storey high, some two or even three, all built in different styles, or no style of architecture;

each man having built his dwelling in accordance with his own taste or convenience. The streets are all arranged in long straight rows, and stretch away till they seem to crawl up the mountain-sides and then are lost. On either side of the roadways are magnificent forest-trees, which in summer-time must form a most delightful shade, though now it is autumn and the leaves are falling fast. Streams of water with their pleasant gurgling music flow on either side, through a deep cutting (which we should irreverently call the gutter), rushing along as though they were in a hurry to reach some everlasting sea. The women come out with their buckets and help themselves, while the children sail their toy boats, clapping their hands glee-fully as the tiny craft is tossed, and tumbled, and borne along on the face of the bubbling water. Street-cars come crawling along the straight streets, crossing and recrossing each other at different points; but a private cab or carriage is rarely to be seen. Every house, be it only composed of a single room, is surrounded by a plot of garden ground, where fruits, flowers, and vegetables all grow together in loving companionship. Everything seems flourishing, and everybody seems well-to-do; there are no signs of poverty anywhere; no bare-footed whining beggars fill the streets; tramps there may be, passing from one part of the State to another, but these are all decently dressed and well fed, for at whatever door they knock they are sure to find food and shelter, charity to those in need being a part of the reigning religion.

The children who swarm on all sides are the healthiest, rosiest, happiest looking urchins conceiv-able; some perfectly beautiful specimens of young humanity. One felt sorry to think they must develop into the bewhiskered man or befrizzled woman; there was not a pale or sickly face in all the multitude. There are no signs of rank or fashion anywhere; there are no drones lounging about in this community, they are all busy bees; every man and every woman, too, does his or her share in the labour market, all according to their special abilities; and here is the only true republic in all America, elsewhere it is the name and not the thing. Here republicanism exists in its genuine form; it is not a commune, and encourages no communistic principles. Here every one must work, uniting therein for the common good of all. Wealth, represented by gold or other possessions, is unequally distributed as in other large cities. Some live in large houses, some in small, some wear broadcloth, some wear frieze; but the man who labours with his hands and the man who works with his brain, those who plan and those who execute, live together in a common brotherhood—for they are equally well educated, and have grown up in or helped to make the world they live in. The idle or the dissolute are speedily hunted out of the community. There is an equality in tone and manner among all conditions of people which strikes rather discordantly upon our ideas of the harmony of things, but we soon get used to it. We meet with a general pleasant courtesy, which is never vulgar, never over-free; there is a sense of equality, a sort of "one man as good as another," which is always felt though never obtrusively asserted. The woman who washes your linen, and the man who wheels your baggage, do it with a sort of courteous friendliness, considering that you

are as much obliged to them as they to you; no
kind of manual labour is looked upon as discreditable
or below the dignity of any man. I have seen a
Mormon bishop, in his shirt sleeves and corduroys,
working hard in a timber-yard or carpentering at a
bench.   Schools and churches of all denominations and
creeds abound; every child has a right to an equal
education at the expense of the State of Utah.   The
Mormon city is now by no means held sacred to the
Mormons, for people of all nations come flocking
thither, erecting their own places of worship, and
following their own faith.   A plot of land has been
lately set apart for a Jewish *synagogue*; but woe upon
any one of them who shall attempt to interfere or win
a single proselyte from the Mormon fold.   While liberal
(with a forced liberality, perhaps) towards other
religions, they are devoted to their own; and in all
social and domestic matters, they keep as much apart
from the opposing forces as though they lived in
different kingdoms.   In all business relations they mix
freely enough and have extensive trading transactions
with all nations, and carry on their operations with a
shrewdness and tact which is popularly supposed to be
the reigning characteristic of the " Jewish persuasion."
There is no exclusion where the " almighty dollar " is
concerned.   They allow no chance of money-making
to flow past them.   Signs of prosperity and plenty are
everywhere; to the mere passer-by or transient traveller, who can judge from outward appearances only,
the State of Utah is the most flourishing in the Union.
With its mines, its metals, its marvellous agricultural
productions, its wealth of fruits and flowers, it seems
as though the horn of plenty emptied itself in the lap

of this favoured land. Out of doors in the streets the brisk, bustling population are crowding to and fro, all is gay and bright; the sun shines, the genial air stirs and invigorates the spirit, the pulse beats to healthful music, while the surrounding scene of swelling hills and glorious mountains is beautiful to behold. It is only on the threshold of *home* that the shadow falls; indeed, there is no such thing as home, regarding it from our point of view, as the centre of domestic happiness, of affectionate intercourse, and mutual confidence; it simply does not and cannot exist. When the interests and the affections are subdivided into so many different channels, they flow in a weak, sluggish spirit through all. I have had the good fortune to get an insight into the inner lives of the Mormon women, and have seen the skeleton grinning on their hearthstones. They are well cared for so far as creature comforts are concerned. The wives of the wealthier classes have handsome, well-furnished houses, and devote themselves to the care and education of their children; but there is a gloom and emptiness at their firesides, a vacant place, which is filled only with a mockery, an unreal shadow. He who is the head of one household to-day hangs up his hat in another home to-morrow. The ladies of refined, cultivated minds, and there are many of them, have a patient-waiting look upon their faces painful to behold; it seems as though the cross they carry is sometimes heavier than they can bear, and they long to lay it down and be at rest. My remarks do not apply indiscriminately to all, for there are many wives who are perfectly happy in the polygamic state; women to whom the children are more than the husband, whose maternal instincts are much stronger than their conjugal affections. This type of womanhood is not specially restricted to Mormonland; but to women of a more delicate spiritual organization, who feel the necessity of loving and being loved in the divinest, purest sense, this life of divided affections is torture. They live a life of daily crucifixion of spirit. They suffer doubly, as they are imbued with a strong sense of religion and believe that polygamy is right; indeed, one of God's holy ordinances. They are constantly engaged in a spiritual warfare, struggling with and against themselves. The voice of nature rebelling against her enforced bondage is regarded as the voice of the evil one, to be stilled only by prayers and self-mortification. The Mormon ladies are not the light-minded, sensuous race they are popularly supposed to be; on the contrary, they are grave, earnest women, strong in the faith they have been brought up in; their minds are completely under the control of their bishops and elders, whose words are to them as the written law of the Lord. It is impossible for any legislation from the outer world to remedy this evil; it lies in the spirit of the people beyond the reach of human hands. It is easy enough to strike the chains from the body, but it is impossible to free the mind from the bondage of a superstitious faith. Polygamy is an ulcer at the root of their religion; it may be dispersed by time and careful treatment, but can never be torn out.

The greater number of the present generation of Mormon women were born there, or from their infancy have drank in with their mothers' milk the teaching of their elders, until it has grown into the essence of their lives; how could it be otherwise? Until late years there had been no communication between Salt Lake City and the outer world. They knew nothing but what they were taught by those whose interest it was to keep them in a state of spiritual bondage. Their parents, in a frenzy of religious fervour, had traversed the wilderness, struggled through famine, and fire, and sword, had gone through the valley of the shadow of death in search of this modern Zion, shut in by inaccessible mountains; their children were bred and born in a whirl of enthusiasm, and naturally inherited the spirit as well as the life of their parents. So much for the present generation of matrons; but they are passing away, and things are looking brighter for the rising population, since the railway has brought civilization with its train of worldly vanities into their midst, and the voice of their sister women has reached their ears, to say nothing of the Gentiles who swarm around them, and whose very presence must have a subtle influence over them. A change has come over the irreverent spirit of youth. The girls are rather shy of entering into polygamous marriages; they have seen enough, and seem to have no desire to enact their mothers' lives over again. Their suitors sigh in vain. The Mormon girls, as a rule, are very beautiful, with fine eyes, and soft, rich complexions like a peach-blossom, and seem disposed to join the general march onwards. In one of our saunters through the city we met two bright, blooming young girls, about seventeen, two of the many granddaughters of Brigham Young, gay, happy-looking creatures. It would be terrible to think they would ever sink into the faded, woe-worn Mormon wife.

I admired their city, and inquired if they would be content to live always at Salt Lake?

"Oh dear, no!" said the youngest and prettiest. "I want to go to Paris to study music; then, if I like, I can come back here and teach, you know," she added with a roguish laugh.

"And I should like to go to Europe to study medicine. I shall never rest here," said her cousin; "and I think I am going next spring."

This is a tolerable sample of the spirit which now animates the young people. The Church has to send its elders across the sea in search of recruits for the matrimonial market, and they rarely fail to return with a good supply as regards quantity; for the quality I would not vouch. During our stay at Salt Lake some half-dozen elders returned from one of these foraging expeditions, and brought back a few score of emigrants, both men and women, some with large families, but all of a most unpromising appearance. It seemed as though they had raked the social gutter, and brought thither the scum of all nations; for a more stolid, stupid-looking set of people I never saw. Well, insomuch as they rescue these poor creatures from stifling courts and alleys, the regions of poverty, ignorance, and dirt, where they have scarcely air to breathe or food to eat, they are doing a good work. Immediately on their arrival at Salt Lake these people are sent off to the agricultural districts, where so many acres of fertile land is awarded to each family, together with wood and all necessary materials for running up a house, and they commence to farm on a small scale, raising stock or grain as may be most expedient. If a man be intelligent and industrious he may speedily become a thriving farmer and landowner in one of the most beautiful valleys in the world. So far, if the

Mormons let them alone, all would be well, but they don't; they teach them their religion, and the men are apt scholars. The seeds of polygamy once sown in the agricultural mind, it grows and flourishes like the rank weeds among their golden grain, and it is universally adopted. If a man wants a dairymaid, a cook, or even a scarecrow—he marries one. A large amount of field labour is done by women, and they, in most cases, are the wives of their employers. Polygamy seems to work well enough in the rural districts; quite different from its manifestations in the large cities, where the women have more time to brood and to feel; besides, the people are of a different calibre, and are drawn from a lower rank in life. I once drank tea at a farmhouse, far removed from the noisy city; there were four or five of the farmer's wives, all busily engaged in their several duties; one was looking after the washing and ironing, another was making up and packing butter and eggs for market, others were passing to and fro, while the children swarmed like bees on all sides of us, their chattering voices and merry laughter making the only music that is ever heard in that solitary homestead. The farmer took us round the farmyard to show us his pigs, poultry, and cattle; we seized an opportunity to remark upon his feminine household, and expressed a wonder that so many wives managed to get along without jarring.

"They've got too much work to do to think of quarrelling; besides, they're all in one boat, you know—no one has got a pull over the other; and so long as folks don't come spying around, putting rubbish into their heads, they will be content to live—for the glory of God."

CHAPTER XI.

AMONG THE MORMONS.

Society—A Mormon Wife's View—The Shops—Amelia Palace—
The Tabernacle—The Organ—Endowment House—A Mor-
mon Widow—Currency in the Old Days—The Elders Hold
Forth.

DURING our stay in Salt Lake City we found the
Mormons most friendly and genial in their disposition
towards us; but they do not like to talk of their
religion; to the ladies especially the subject is dis-
tasteful; neither do they care to receive into their
houses visitors from the Gentile world. They have
been so vexed and annoyed by the indiscreet questions
of curious tourists that they are disposed to shut their
doors upon the whole race. Through the influence of
some friends in England I made the acquaintance of
a Mormon wife, who admitted me within her family
circle, where I received advantages which are accorded
to few strangers. She has travelled a great deal in
Europe, but is now permanently settled in a beautiful
house in the centre of the city; her mind has been
enlarged and enlightened during her sojourn abroad,
and, though still a good Mormon, she has withdrawn
from polygamy and left her husband in the full possession of three other wives; perhaps they suffice to

absorb his conjugal affections. At her house I met some pleasant Mormon families. Gentlemen do not escort a battalion of wives to these social gatherings, but each accompanies the particular wife to whom he is for the time devoted. No favour must be shown; his affections must be weighed to a fraction, and divided equally between the several claimants thereto. The ladies were refined and pleasant enough; I cannot say much for the gentlemen. The Mormon men are genial and good-natured, but as a rule are coarse and sensual-looking, full of the physical strength and energies of healthy life; one cannot imagine a bad digestion or ill-regulated liver among them.

Everybody asked us "how we liked Salt Lake." That question being satisfactorily answered at least fifty times in the course of an hour, we talked and chatted in much the same fashion as the rest of the world would have done under similar circumstances. Knowing that the typical state of society here was utterly different to that in any other part of the world, we were in a vague state of expectation and excitement, and watched for some indication of it to come to the surface; we watched in vain. It was the same here as elsewhere. In general society all the world over, there is a frothy bubble of conversation carried on; little is said that is worth repeating, indeed that is worth saying. I received a good deal of local information, and was both amused and interested in the gossip that gradually grew into circulation. Late in the evening, while chatting more confidentially to a coterie of ladies, I tried to seize the helm, and without any actual breach of good breeding to steer the conversation towards matrimonial matters, but on that subject

they were scrupulously silent. They were delighted
to talk of their children; some, and they were young-
looking matrons too, told me they had "fourteen
blessings;" others who had not had time to produce
such a growth of humanity seemed, however, to be
doing their best to increase the population as fast as
they could.

A woman is appreciated and respected according to
the number of her children; those who have no family
are merely tolerated or set aside as "no account." As
a rule the childless wives live together under one roof,
while those "more highly favoured of the Lord" have
separate houses, and are more honourably regarded.

I visited one lady, the wife of a wealthy merchant,
an English gentleman, who had outraged his family
connections and nailed his colours to the Mormon
mast, though he had at no time indulged in the luxury
of more than two wives, and at present has only one.
Their residence is extremely beautiful; it is built in
the fashion of an old-fashioned country house, with
gabled roof and pointed windows, and stands in a large
garden, beautifully laid out with rare shrubs and
luxuriant flowers, a lovely home; the mistress thereof
is a stately, noble-looking woman, with a grave earnest
face, and eyes that seemed to be looking far away from
this world into the next. There were two or three
young children playing with their toys on the hearthrug; some others were playing hide and seek, "whoop-
ing" in the garden. It seemed to me that a whole
school had been let loose to enjoy a holiday.

"Sure," I exclaimed, "these children cannot *all*
be yours?"

"They are, and they are not," she answered. "I

have fourteen children; some are still in the nursery, some are out in the world. Those," she added, indicating a pair of toddlers on the hearthrug, " belong to my sister wife, who died about a year ago; but they are the same as mine; they know no difference. Our children were all born under one roof, and we have mothered them in turn."

" This must be an unusual state of affairs," I ventured to remark, " even in Salt Lake. I should hardly have thought it possible that two ladies could have lived happily together under such circumstances."

" Nevertheless it is true," she answered.

" But do you mean to say," I urged, " that you *never* feel any petty jealousies ? "

" I do not say that," she said somewhat sharply. " We are none of us perfect, and are all liable to the evil influence of earthly passions; but when we feel weak and failing we pray to God to help us, and He does."

" You are a strange people," I could not help observing. " In no other place in the world could such a state of things exist."

" Because nowhere else would you have the same faith to support you."

" But would you desire your daughters to enter into a polygamous marriage ? " I persisted.

" If I could choose," she answered gravely, " they should each be the one wife to a good husband; but that must be as God pleases. Whatever their destiny may be their religion will help them to bear it."

Evidently desiring to end the conversation, she invited us into the garden, showed us her greenhouse, and gathered us some flowers, and we took our leave, having spent a delightful afternoon.

"I am afraid I have been more inquisitorial than good breeding sanctions," I said apologetically; "but how can I gain any information unless I ask for it?"

"I am very glad to have seen you," she replied, with a cordial hand-shake, "though as a rule I do not care to receive strangers—so many come with no introductions and intrude upon our privacy, and ask us questions, and then circulate false reports about us. They seem to regard us as zoological curiosities; quite forgetting that our homes are as sacred to us as theirs are to them. We used to be very hospitable," she added, "but now we receive no one unless they are introduced to us as you have been."

The Mormons are very fond of theatricals and great patrons of the drama. A good company there is sure to draw a good audience. The patriarchal days, when Brigham's large family formed the greater part of audience and actors too, are past; they have a commodious theatre, so far as size is concerned, but it is a square brick barnlike building to look at. The business streets are lined with shops, which are amply stocked with all necessary and some superfluous articles, but the windows are not what we call "dressed" to attract the passer-by, but are exhibited in a higgledy-piggledy sort of fashion; the owners sit behind their counters or lounge in the doorways reading the news, and think nothing of keeping you waiting while they finish reading a paragraph, and seem supremely indifferent whether you buy or not. A spirit of piety inspires their business transactions, a godly text being placed over the doorway, and sometimes being woven into the mat at your feet. They have a large co-operative store in the main street, with an inscription in large gold letters running along the top : "Holiness to the Lord." There is very little in the city that is architecturally worth looking at, with the exception, perhaps, of the Amelia Palace, which is a large and very elegant mansion, built in the modern villa style, with a great deal of ornamentation. It is reported that Brigham Young erected and presented this beautiful residence to his youngest and prettiest wife, favouring her so much above the rest ; but this is indignantly denied by the Saints generally.

"Brigham" (whose name is held in great reverence among them) "had no favourite," they say. "The Amelia Palace, so called because she once stayed in it for a few days, was built expressly for the reception and entertainment of strangers and visitors of distinction, and for no other purpose." Unfortunately its promoter died a short time after its completion, and it seems to be a bone of contention among the Mormons, and looks as lonely and deserted as though it had been thrown into chancery. They are also building a new tabernacle for winter use, which has been some years in the course of erection, but will be finished now within a few months. It is built of white granite hewn from quarries in the State of Utah, and is being constructed in a highly ornamental and imposing style ; it is to be used for all general services during the cold weather, owing to the great difficulty of warming the larger tabernacle, which stands a few hundred feet off. This far-famed structure strikes one as a huge monstrosity, a tumour of bricks and mortar rising on the face of the earth. It is a perfectly plain egg-shaped building, studded with heavy entrance doors all around ; there is not the slightest attempt at

I

ornamentation of any kind ; it is a mass of ugliness ; the inside is vast, dreary, and strikes one with a chill, as though entering a vault ; it is 250 feet long and 80 feet high ; its acoustic properties are wonderful—the voice of him who occupies the rostrum can be distinctly heard in the remotest corner of the building. If you whisper at one end your words are repeated aloud at the other, without being caught up and hunted through every crevice by ghostly mocking echoes. A gallery runs all around, supported by rows of thin, helpless-looking pillars. The seats in the body of the building are raised on sloping ground, like the pit of a theatre,—a wide expanse of empty benches, dreary and depressing to the wandering eye, which finds no pleasant spot to dwell upon. In the centre stands a fountain with four plaster-of-Paris lions *couchant*, poor, mangy-looking beasts at best. From the white plastered ceiling or dome, being concave perhaps it may be called so, hangs a gigantic star, hung round with artificial flowers and evergreen pendants, something like a monstrous jack-in-the-green turned upside down. The whole interior is gloomy and dark ; I doubt if people could ever see to read their prayers. At one end of this huge barnlike building hangs an immense blue banner emblazoned with a golden beehive, which flaunts over the heads of the faithful. At the other end stands an organ, the largest in the world they say, and it may be so, for it is certainly immense. They are justly proud of it, for it is of home manufacture entirely, and was built precisely where it stands, under the supervision of an English convert named Ridges, and contains upwards of a thousand pipes, some of such a circumference you feel as though you could wander up and down them, and be lost in a world of music. Notwithstanding its immense size, it has not a single harsh or metallic sound ; on the contrary, it is marvellously soft-toned ; from the low flutelike wailing voice of the *vox humana* to the deep bass roll which stirs the air like a wave of melodious thunder, it has all the delicacy of the Æolian harp, with the strength and power of its thousand brazen voices. The case is of polished pine of elegant and simple design. All the wood, metal, and other material used was brought from the forests or mines of Utah. Sloping down from the organ towards the auditorium are semicircular rows of seats, for the elders and dignitaries of the Church. In the centre is a desk with a shabby blue sofa behind it ; this was used by Brigham Young and his two chief councillors. Below this are the seats for the twelve apostles and for the choir, and benches where the elders may congregate to consult together. In front of all this combination stands a long narrow table, an altar perhaps it may be called, covered with a red cloth, whereon is arranged a gorgeous array of silver cups, of all shapes and sizes, as though prepared for an unlimited christening party or an everlasting service libation to some heathen deity rather than to a Christian God. Passing out from the tabernacle we glanced at the Endowment House, where many of their religious ceremonies are performed, and where, if rumour speaks truly, gross licentiousness is carried on under the sanction of the Church—where some ugly secrets and mysteries lie hidden, of which no one can speak and live. Across the road stands the president's office, and next to that the " Beehive House " of Brigham Young notoriety. It is a long, low-roofed, adobe building, railed in, a desolate-looking place where, in old days, some dozen of his wives were domiciled; it is now occupied by his widows—some of them. A high stone wall filled in with adobe incloses the president's residence and many other buildings, with arched gateways and heavy wooden gates; there is a double archway leading to some factories and stables, surmounted by a beehive in the grip of a monstrous eagle—an illustration of the Mormon faith in the cruel clutch of the Stars and Stripes. Close by is the school-house, first erected for the sole education of Brigham Young's family, which was large enough to fill it; it is now devoted to the benefit of the masses. The whole of these buildings are crowded together, and are generally surrounded by a high wall, which gives them a gloomy appearance, suggestive of an Eastern harem. There is, however, a wide difference between the Mohammedan and the Mormon—the two polygamic nations. Whereas the former keep their women in a state of slavery, idleness, and ignorance, the Mormons give their women every possible advantage of education, and permit, nay encourage, them to take their part in the world's work and in the management of affairs generally.

The Mormon marriage-vow reads "for time and eternity!" There are, however, forms of matrimony "for time" and "for eternity" alone, and the one may be contracted independently of the other. Thus, a man may, and frequently does, marry a widow "for time," under the obligation to hand her back to her deceased lord "for eternity." A woman may, by gracious permission of the head of the Church, seal herself in "celestial marriage" to any deceased saint she may elect to honour with her preference. Also, a marriage may be arranged by the living for the dead. I heard of a case wherein a widow, anxious lest her lord should feel lonely in the celestial spheres, shortly after her bereavement hastened to the Endowment House to seal to the beloved lost, not *one*, but *two* dear friends of hers. I inquired whether the two brides would not consider it a wasteful proceeding to bestow themselves on the dead? "Oh no," answered my informant gravely, "of course they were dead too."

This presented rather a ludicrous picture to my mind's eye; there is evidently no escape for the Mormon from the evils of this world, even though he flies into the next, where good Christians hope to find peace. I imagined the seraph's surprise, perhaps dismay, at finding two cherubs in full chase accredited claimants to his eternal affections, whether he would or not.

We paid a visit to President Taylor at his office, with an *arrière pensée* that he might present us to his wives, but he did not. He received us most courteously, and we spent a pleasant half-hour in the exchange of polite nothings; he pointed out to us the portraits of the brothers Smith, the founders of their faith, which hung upon the walls, but when we tried to bring about a discussion upon the Mormon faith, or the working of that faith upon the Mormon people, we ignominiously failed. He is a remarkably fine-looking man, about seventy, with a rather large loose mouth and cunning gray eyes, which look as though they would never let you see what was going on behind them.

In the old days before the railway reached them, when the city was first settled, indeed for long afterwards, there was no money in circulation, and the Mormons lived on a general exchange system. A facetious record of the time says : " A farmer wishes for a pair of shoes, gives a load of wood in exchange, and is straightway shod ; he gives a calf for a pair of pantaloons ; seven water-melons are paid for admission to the theatre. One man paid seventy-five cabbage per quarter for the teaching of his children. The dressmaker received for her services four squashes per day. The Church dues were settled in molasses. Two loads of pumpkins paid a subscription to the newspaper. A treatise on *Celestial Marriage* was bought for a load of gravel. And the cost of a bottle of soothing syrup for the baby was a bushel of string beans."

All this is changed now ; there is plenty of gold and silver in circulation, and the general exchange system, once universal, is now dead.

The matter of marriage is very simply conducted ; if a man desires to make an addition to his family in the shape of a wife, he makes such desire known to the president of his Church with whose permission he proposes to her, she of course, as in all Christian countries, having the right to refuse or accept him. On the other hand, if a lady has any predilection for a certain gentleman, she is encouraged to make her preference known to him, her tender feeling being considered as a prompting of nature which ought to be obeyed.

We were anxious to hear the holding forth at the Tabernacle on Sunday morning, and went early to secure good seats. Slowly the auditorium, galleries and all, filled to overflowing, with a motley set of

people, who seemed to set worldly fashion at defiance.
There were some elderly heads in corkscrew curls and
poke bonnets, trimmed with sad-coloured ribbons or
faded flowers ; some of the coal-scuttle celebrity projecting till you only got a telescopic view of the faded
face within it. As a rule they wore short scanty
skirts and old-fashioned kerchiefs or shawls pinned
across their breasts. Such a collection of antiquated
millinery and quaint combination of colours it would
have been difficult to find elsewhere. Here and there
a pretty young face bloomed from an artistic arrangement of lace and flowers, as though the hand of a
French milliner had dropped it from the skies. An
occasional parody on the famous Devonshire hat
loomed upon our sight. One or two were got up like
fashion plates direct from press. It was a strange
combination of the Old World and the New. Manhood was represented in a similar fashion. Some in
top-boots, frieze jackets, and stubble head of hair, with
gay-coloured bandannas round their throats. Others
in misfitting suits hanging loosely on their ungainly
limbs. There was a sprinkling of dandyism among
them in frockcoats and flowers in their button-holes ;
but broadcloth and fine linen generally occupied seats
near the organ, and were grouped around where the
elders and priesthood were seated in great solemnity.

I was sorry to learn there was to be no general
service on this Sabbath morning ; four of the elders
had just returned from Europe, and were to stand forth
and give an account of themselves to the community.
The service (for so I must call it for want of a
better word) commenced with a prayer, which seemed
rather to carry an assurance of their own worthiness

to the throne of grace than a supplication for its
mercy; then the organ poured forth its volume of rich
sounds, and the voices of the thousands present united
in a grand old hymn, glorious to hear. That ended,
a young elder, clean shaven and in funereal black, stood
up in the rostrum, in front of the table, and held
forth : " He had travelled under the guidance of a
special providence " (he spoke as though it were a
special train), " and claimed the thanks of the multitude for his safe return." Then commenced a tirade of
self-glorification ; not a word of supplication, of prayer,
or praise fell from his lips; his moral attitude was one
of exultant vanity, as though they had absorbed all
piety, all virtue, and left not a grain for the hungry
world outside. He talked a mass of irreverent twaddle,
as though he were in the secrets of the Almighty
Ruler of men ; he communicated to those present the
private information which he had received direct from
heaven, " that that modern Babylon, that most foul and
evil city of Great Britain, whence he had just returned,
should be destroyed by the fire of God's wrath ! Not
one would be saved, not one, except those few brands
which *he* had plucked from the burning " (those brands
being represented by an awkward squad of ignorant
humanity, who looked as if they had marched in
the rear of civilization, and been covered with the
dust from its trampling feet; indeed, they seem to
have gathered together the scum of all nations to be
cleansed and purified by the process of their patent
piety !). He wound up his edifying discourse with the
surance "that *they*, and they *only*, the saints of the
modern Zion, who were gathered in that sacred valley,
could be saved ! While flames of fury were licking

up the rest of the world, *they* would be in glory singing from harps of gold;" indeed, he dealt out death and damnation to all the rest of the world, but grasped salvation as their special right. This assurance seemed to give general satisfaction, for the poor withered faces round me lighted up with a frenzied faith and rejoicing in their own election.

There was little more to be done in Salt Lake, only the springs to be visited, and they are neither of them a great distance from the city. The sulphur springs are about a mile from our hotel, the Walker House, and can be reached by horse cars by those who dislike walking. At these springs there are baths of all description, Turkish, Russian, hot-air, etc., beside the natural baths, which are lukewarm, and being of a sulphurous nature are very penetrating and delightfully refreshing, providing you do not stay in too long. The hot springs are the greatest wonder in the city; there is a small alcove in the limestone rocks, even with the surface of the ground; the water steams and bubbles up boiling hot, with a temperature of 200°! Eggs can be cooked therein ready for table in three minutes. Close by, beyond the green meadows, is a beautiful sheet of water called "Hot Springs Lake," which is supposed to be fed by other hot springs beneath the surface; and strange to say, in spite of the temperature of the water, some excellent fish are to be found there.

Having conscientiously done our duty, so far as sight-seeing was concerned, we bid adieu to Salt Lake City, the great social problem of to-day.

CHAPTER XII.

ACROSS THE SIERRAS.

Ogden Station—Bustling Bedtime—Boots—An Invasion—A Wedding Aboard—The American Desert—The Glorious Sierras—Cape Horn—Dutch Flats—" Here they are "—A Phantom City.

THE sun is setting. The skies, so beautifully blue an hour ago, are changed by some celestial alchemy to realms of gold. Pale sea-green banners float faintly hither and thither. For a moment we seem to get a glimpse of heaven " through its gates of gold." Slowly the pale yellow changes to a rich red hue, with a rapid mingling of amethyst and royal purple, like the jewelled mantle of some invisible king, with feathery plumes flying, and trains of brilliant cloudlets hurrying across the face of the heavens, as though some gorgeous festival was being held on high. Then the gray sombre clouds come gathering together, like heavy household troops at the close of a grand procession, and the brilliant scene is over. There is no long dreamy twilight in these regions. The sun does not " slowly sink to rest." It drops down in a blinking, lazy sort of way, as though it was tired of shining so long in one place. Its fleecy flock of clouds surround it. We have scarcely time to behold its glory ;

even as we exclaim, "What a gorgeous sunset!" the gates of heaven are closed, and it is night, though a scattered colony of soft gray shadows still linger among the mountains.

We are at Ogden Station, waiting to resume our journey westward. The engine snorts, and spits, and whistles, and clanks its iron harness, in a hurry to be off. Lights are flashing hither and thither. The nervous man, hot, dusty, and with an agonized face, rushes after his baggage. He *will* keep an eye on it; he cannot be persuaded that the baggage-master's certificate is surety for its safety. He watches it swallowed up in the van, then with a sigh of relief returns, to begin a fresh hurry and worry about something else. We feel ourselves quite old, experienced travellers by this time, and have learned to take things easily. Our nervous friend cannot even eat his supper in peace; he rushes out between every mouthful to make sure he is not left behind. Presently the conductor's well-known call, "All aboard, all aboard," greets our ears, and we leisurely walk out upon the platform. There stands the long line of " silver palace cars." (Query : Why " silver," when they are painted bright yellow ?) We have left the rich, brown, sombre-hued Pullman cars of the Union Pacific, and are now about to resume our journey on the " Central Pacific," in cars of gold. An obliging official stands at the entrance of every carriage, and shows you to your special section, as courteously as you would be shown into the reception-room of a friend. The engine bell, which sounds to us like the voice of a friend, sends forth its monotonous "cling clang, cling clang," its brazen clangour grows faint and fainter, and is still.

With a final rattle and a shriek we plunge into
the night, the sparks, like fiery comets, flying from
its smoky throat. We strain our eyes for a parting
glance at the Wahsatch Mountains, glorious in their
grand loveliness, and at the marvellous cañons and
gorges which we know are yawning and opening their
mysterious depths on either side of us. But they are
wrapped in a weird shadowy twilight; we can only
see their dim outline, and are left to imagine their
darker depths as we fly past them. The thin crescent
crown of the baby moon was visible a while ago, but
it has gone now, and the stars come out—celestial
shepherds keeping ·watch over their fleecy flocks on
high. We know we are rushing along by the fishless
waters of the green salt lake, but we look out upon
a world of darkness; we shall see nothing till the
morning, so turn our thoughts bedward.

Our car is still in a state of commotion, some people
are so long settling down. There is a wiry-looking
elderly lady in corkscrew curls, who seems as restless
and lively as a summer flea. She bounces from one
side of her section to the other, rummaging her satchel,
then her valise, for something she can't find, fishes a
vinaigrette from her lunch-basket, and with a grunt of
satisfaction sits sniffing at it for a while; then hops up
as though she had been suddenly pierced with needles,
and begins setting things tidy. Her section overflows
with tiny packages of all shapes and sizes. They will
fall off the seat and roll into somebody else's section;
she scrambles and dives after them, shaking and
patting her property as though she had just rescued a
rat from drowning. She is always losing something,
and shaking herself to find it. Then came a general

stir, the letting down of berths and making of beds. The gentlemen retired to the smoking-room during the preparations for retiring. One by one the ladies disappear behind their curtains. Our restless friend vanishes into her berth with a bounce; her curtains bulge and flutter; at last, with a series of moans and mutterings she is still, but not silent, even in her sleep.

The gentlemen return with a creaking of boots and banging of doors. One by one they too disappear. One who is "fat and scant of breath" laboriously climbs into his berth and rolls into it like a worn-out hippopotamus; another climbs up with the agility of a cat; a third swings himself up as though he were performing an acrobatic exercise, then a pair of pantaloons dangle for a moment in the air and are suddenly drawn up by their owner, and all is peace. There is nothing left of mankind but his boots, standing in solemn array along the floor. Any one with an eye for character might have gained some knowledge from a study of these "boots." The spirit of their numerous owners seemed to cling to the uppers or linger about the soles. Here was a pair of spick and span patent leathers, suggestive of spotless linen and irreproachable character, with not a thought beyond etiquette and broadcloth. Others had a careless philosophical look, with uncompromising soles, tough uppers, with little or no attempt at shining, slightly worn down at the heels, and turned up at the toes. Some bulged out in suspicious places. Some looked as if they had tramped the world through; others as though they had trod on velvet.

We slept soundly, lulled by the monotonous swing of the cars, till about three o'clock in the morning, when there was a slight stir in our car, a gruff rumbling of masculine voices. The young lady in the opposite section was roused from her slumbers.

"Get up, miss, please," said the conductor; "a gentleman has just boarded the train and wants to speak to you."

"It is I, Agnes," said a manly voice; "make haste and dress yourself." There was a rustle and flutter behind the curtains.

"What is the matter? Is there anything wrong?" said the girl's voice in some alarm.

"Oh no; I rather think everything is pretty considerably right," was the assuring answer. "Be quick, there's a dear girl."

She made a hasty toilette, and the pair went out upon the platform to discuss their plans. A whisper flew round with the daylight that there was to be a wedding at the place where we were to stop for breakfast. This startling intelligence created a general interest. There was a whispering and a wondering of the why and the wherefore of this strange proceeding. The lovers were too much occupied with one another to make any communication even had they been disposed to do so. The lady was coy; she hesitated. The idea of a wedding without orange blossoms, bridesmaids, or even a slice of wedding cake! But the bridegroom elect sternly whispered: "Now or never." From the brief scraps of conversation which fell to our ears we gathered the simple fact that the engagement was a clandestine one, and was disapproved of by their mutual friends, who were awaiting the arrival of the lady at "Sacramento." Once under their influence they would contrive to break it off, and put an end to it. . The gentleman got an inkling of this, and prepared to frustrate their diabolical purpose. He had travelled with all speed to ——, secured the services of the judge, and left him waiting there while he came on to meet and prepare the lady. While we were quietly taking our coffee and eggs those two were made one. A great deal of handshaking and good wishes passed round.

"All aboard, all aboard," came the familiar cry. The newly married couple were driven off in an old ramshackle chaise, the best the place afforded, in the direction of the Black Hills. We had no old shoes to throw after them "for luck," but somebody routed out a baby's worsted sock and flung it straight into the bride's lap, and they drove off amid chatter and laughter and a world of good wishes.

We wake up in the morning and find ourselves speeding along the great American desert, a wide expanse of desolation covered with tiny gray-green buffalo grass, only there are no buffaloes now to eat it. It is devoured by meaner animals. Looking through our glasses, we see what looks like an army of animated ant-hills. We are told they are immense herds of cattle, thousands strong, who are sent up there to get their own living some months of the year, and then descend to the valleys as fat as butter, a mine of wealth to their owners. The earth is slightly covered with snow, and looks as though it had been sprinkled with salt and put in pickle. All is blank and bare; there are no more architectural wonders of the great unknown, no more ruined castles and towers standing solemnly in the silent air. Hour after hour the earth flies beneath the hoofs of our iron horse. We are not sorry when the night comes and shuts this desolation from our sight, for the day has been a long and a dreary one, and we retire early to rest.

We go to sleep in the dismal, snow-covered heights of Nevada, and wake in the glorious, pine-clad forests among the foot-hills of the grand Sierras, having passed their summit during the night. There is no more glorious sight in the whole wide world than this which now opens upon our view. We hold our breath, awe-struck and wondering, as we swing round the shoulder of the mountain and plunge down its rugged sides. We feel as though we were rushing through the air. There is nothing but this narrow trestle between us and the boiling caldron a hundred feet below. We lift our heads and look up at the wonderfully wooded heights, where the pointed pines seem to prick the skies, and down to the deep valleys below, winding through sunless gorges till they are lost in narrow cañons where the foot of man has never ventured yet, and where the grizzly still finds his home undisturbed. All the picturesque beauty and solemn grandeur of the wide world seems to be gathered together here in this noble range of the Sierra Nevadas, covered with all the luxuriance of summer's divinest bloom—a kind of spiritual sunshine, falling straight from heaven on lake and river, gorge and cañon, covering and glorifying all. A beautiful purple mist lies in a dreamy softness everywhere. We dash round sudden curves and up grade and down grade, new and picturesque beauties opening on all sides of us. There is a general stir. " We are nearing Cape Horn," cries somebody, and in another moment we are speeding round a sharp curve, rushing along the face of the mountain, clinging to the narrow ledge of rock. Our engine itself seems dizzy as it swings us round with a shriek and a rattle, looking down two thousand feet upon the boiling river below. Soon the scene grows more magnificent still, the views more vast and extensive; the wonderful chasms are frightful to behold; the mountains open into wide galleries of rocks and boulders, stretching out and upward till they are lost in a world of pines and peaks of ice and snow. All the Kohinoors that were ever dug out of the bosom of the earth are poor and pale before these diamond peaks now flashing in the sunlight. We would like to stop the train, and get out and wander up into these forest mountains and down into the glens, and dabble in the sparkling waters, so pure and bright they might be flowing direct from the throne of the Almighty God, but we are, perforce, carried on. We pass the mining districts of Dutch Flats, where hydraulic operations were once extensively carried on, and have broken up and ravaged the country round, damaged its fair face in the greed for gold, and left but bare and ragged mountain-sides, whose gaping wounds are slowly healing and are being gradually covered by nature's tender green. We can still trace where the immense body of water has been hurled against the mountain and torn down hundreds of tons of earth and stone, and sand and gold, which were all flung down and caught in a series of iron sieves or gratings, some charged with quicksilver to attract the smaller grains of gold which escaped the sifting process.

This part of the scenery is interesting from its association with the old, dead days, when the solitude

K

rang with the rush and din of thousands, all hurrying
and jostling one another in their search for gold.
The tumble-down ruins of the miners' huts are still
clinging to the edge of the water or at the foot of
the broken mountain, like a weird memory lingering
in the haunts of old.

We sat silent now, enjoying the genial air. On
our first view of these glorious Sierras we had run the
gamut of our unbounded and rapturous delight; we
had pointed out our phrases with big notes of mental
admiration; we wanted a new coinage of words before
we could express ourselves. We had grown tired of
the old phrases,—for the time, at least,—so we sat in
silence, letting our eyes rest and our thoughts revel on
the scenes we were passing through.

Presently our engine-bell began its monotonous
"cling clang," and we steamed into the station of
Sacramento; and there, on a table running along the
whole length of the platform, an excellent lunch was
served. Tea and coffee, chicken-salad, ham and eggs,
and no end of fruits and flowers, were most temptingly
laid out; and here we gained our first glimpse of the
moon-faced, almond-eyed Chinese officiating as waiters
—clean, quick, and obliging. Having supplied ourselves with all we required, we asked of our attentive
Celestial—

"How much to pay?"

"Two bittee," he answered, smiling.

I inquired again, emphasizing my words. The
same answer, with an additional grin. Then, speaking slowly, severely, in a louder tone, looking sternly
in his face, I repeated, pausing between each word—

"I—want—to—pay."

"Two bittee," he answered, grinning from ear to ear, and looking so pleased with himself that I felt inclined to laugh too.

"Twenty-five cents," explained a gentleman at my elbow. "They count in bits here, and two bits is twenty-five cents."

By this time I had noticed two gentlemen and a lady searching eagerly among the passengers, evidently for somebody they could not find. Having scanned all the faces assembled on the platform, they wandered from one end of the empty cars to the other. Then held a brief consultation together.

"So very strange," I heard one say. "She certainly started from Chicago. We'd better telegraph."

I fancy they are searching for the bride. They will search long before they find her. She is far away, up in the Black Hills by this time. But nobody attempts to put the clue in the hands of the seekers.

After a stop of twenty minutes we resumed our way in very jubilant spirits. We knew we were nearing our journey's end. We passed through the beautiful Valley of Sacramento, all abloom with fruits and flowers and aglow with the glorious sunshine. We took in every feature of the landscape, though we were watching eagerly the while, and looking forward to the first glimpse of the Golden City. We gathered our things together, then commenced to smarten ourselves up to make a decent appearance in the face of the New World. In another hour we shall be there. We make a few minutes' halt at San Pablo, and are just putting a few finishing touches to our toilette, when "Here they are!" cries a familiar voice. We look up, and there is the well-known

face of an old friend, come out from the strange
world to greet us. And how glad we are to be so
greeted! There is a good deal of laughter, an exchange of gossip from the Old World to the New.
We speed through the streets of Oakland, our bell
" ding-donging " to warn people out of our way.
There are shops and houses on either side ; people are
flocking to and fro on the sidewalks, buying and sell-
ing, some lounging lazily, gossiping over the garden
gates among the tall hollyhocks and big tuberose
trees. They glance indifferently at us as we rush
along, as though it was quite a common thing for
people to come three thousand miles over desert and
mountain to visit their wonderland. We pull up at
Oakland Ferry, having been for the last ten minutes
skimming over the face of the water on an invisible
trestlework. Here again, familiar faces, with their
hands full of flowers and their hearts with welcome,
were there to meet us and escort us across the bay in
loyal numbers. It is eight miles across the bay to
San Francisco, and the ferry-boats are like floating
palaces, with velvet lounges, gorgeous in carving and
gilding, with a painted ceiling, giving views of the
surrounding neighbourhood, and mirrors on all sides,
reflecting and multiplying you in such numbers that
you cannot get away from yourself. You come face
to face with your own ghost whichever way you turn.
The sea-breeze coming to us, salt laden, through the
Golden Gate, is delicious, and stirs our blood, and
sends it leaping madly through our veins. Sister
boats pass and repass us on the way, and more important vessels, with the Stars and Stripes or flags of
many nations fluttering from their mastheads, are

gathered in crowds in the beautiful bay, and, as they
are riding at anchor, dip and courtesy as we pass.
Thousands of shrieking sea-gulls swoop down, throw
up their heads, and, dipping their white breasts in the
water, float upon its surface as proudly and almost as
gracefully as baby swans. We all crowd up to the
bow of the vessel. In vain our friends point out the
different rocks and islands which stud the bay, and
the long, curving line of the distant shore. We have
no eyes, no thought for anything but San Francisco.
That is our Mecca—the shrine whereon we are prepared to lay our heart's devotion.

The sun is setting, and the whole of the Western
hemisphere is draped with crimson clouds slashed with
flames of purple light, and, slowly looming from their
midst, the Golden City breaks upon our sight. We
cannot distinctly distinguish a single feature. The
palace-houses which crown the hill-top, church steeples
and spires, are all hidden and shrouded in purple mist,
which rolls down the steep streets, spreads everywhere,
and covers everything with a soft, sweet mystery, and
we only see, or seem to see, a wide, extensive range
of buttressed, battlemented castles—a ruined castellated
world. And so we catch our first view of San Francisco, like a phantom city lying in the arms of the
sunset.

CHAPTER XIII.

THE GOLDEN CITY.

The Streets—Kaleidoscopic Scenes—The Stock Boards—Wild Cat
—Bulls and Bears—The Markets—The "Dummy"—Lone
Mountain.

WE pass through a deafening crowd of hackmen, who
are ranged on either side of the landing-stage, and a
posse of hotel porters, each in a monotonous sing-song
calling the name of his hotel.   To all insinuating invi-
tations we sternly answer "Occidental," and are allowed
to pass without further let or hindrance.   We find our
comfortable hotel coach waiting, and jolt and rumble
through the stony Market Street.   We see nothing but
throngs of people, flaring gas-jets, and lighted shop-
windows, and in a few minutes are deposited at the
door of the Occidental, a strange sound to us then,
but soon to become familiar as a household word.

A cosy suite of rooms had been prepared for us, and
here again friendly hands had filled our room with
flowers, giving us a most sweet floral welcome to
California.

On this, our very first evening in San Francisco,
friends we have not seen for years come rallying
round us; their bright, familiar faces and pleasant
voices ringing out a kindly welcome, bring back a

glimpse of the old land and the old scenes wherein we had all played our part in the dear long ago. For a moment I only see their faces through a mist, but the mist is in my own eyes. Everybody is anxious to come to the fore and escort us on our first tour round their Golden City.

The next morning early we sallied forth to get our first general view of San Francisco, as we like to familiarize ourselves with the face of a friend before we criticise his features or attempt to discuss his character. Our hotel is situated in—or, as we may say here, *on*—Montgomery Street, one of the busiest portions of the city. There are some notably handsome jeweller's and other shops; but by far the greater number, both there and on the lower part of California Street, are public notaries, bill-brokers, stock-brokers, attorneys, and mining agents; in fact, every facility for financial ruin yawns on all sides of you. There is a tempting restaurant sandwiched in here and there, or you may descend into a kind of cellar and take your refreshments comfortably underground. There are, besides, numerous barbers' shops, as no American, East or West, will shave an inch of his own chin; and open spaces where gentlemen lounge on velvet chairs and read the news while their boots are having " a shine for five cents," for here, as in other parts of America, you must clean your own boots and shoes or go out and have a public " shine for five cents." The shoeblack's being a strictly outdoor industry, forms no part of anybody's domestic duty.

There is a general rush and flow of mankind through this busy street, the Exchange being situated hereon. The moment its doors are open everybody seems to be flocking up or hurrying down the steps. There is an endless stir and passing to and fro. They gather in crowds upon the sidewalks, swarm at the street corners, and surge into the roadways. Curbstone brokers, the ragged fringe of the stockboards, lie in wait everywhere, like spiders, waiting to catch some silly, inexperienced fly in their financial web of fine promises. There are men of all kinds and all nations, a kaleidoscopic company of Jews and Christians, Orientals of divers degrees, even South Sea Islanders washed up from the shores of the Pacific, the grim-visaged Tartar chief, and foreigners from all parts of the civilized world make up the incongruous gathering, all babbling together, creating a very Babel and confusion of tongues. You may hear men grumble in guttural German ; swear in high Dutch ; insinuate in soft, mellifluous Italian or musical Greek ; and, indeed, bargain, wrangle, and chat in every language under the sun. The spirit of speculation is in the air ; its subtle influence stirs the very centre of life ; everybody speculates ; everybody has " something in stocks ; " the poorest servant-girl, the hard-working mechanic, with the rest of the labouring population, invest their little all in stocks. You may see their eager faces crowding round the windows where the rise and fall in stocks is exhibited every hour. Millions of dollars are floating about in investments in worthless mines, which will never yield an ounce of gold. Well, the stocks are up to-day, down to-morrow ; the fever is in the blood of the people ; they will drain their pockets, sell their clothes off their back, the home that shelters them, the very land they live by, all in the race for wealth. So long as they have a cent or " wild cat " is to be got in the market, they'll have it. Well, somebody grows rich. Somebody rides on the great third wave, though thousands sink beneath it and are lost.

I, like the rest of the world, fell into the gilded snare, and with one of my too confiding friends, was induced to take a hand at this game of speculation. Silently and secretly we matrons laid our plans, letting not our right hand know what our left was doing. We had reason to believe that a certain mine would disgorge heaps of gold within the next two weeks; shares were low at the present time, but as soon as gold came to the surface, they would double, treble, nay quadruple, in a single day—perhaps rise from five to a hundred dollars per share! In a frenzy of gold fever we rushed off to a stockbroker's office, and invested all our ready cash, even to our last dollar, in that promising stock. We turned our faces homeward, beggars in the present, millionaires in the future. We seemed to tread on air, and sent our thoughts flying through the realms of imagination, building castles in the air, and making glorious plans for the future; we felt as though we already held that El Dorado in our pockets, and disposed of it, each in our own fashion. My friend chose a lovely spot, over-looking the bay, and the green hills beyond, and announced her intention of building a house there, and presenting it to her liege lord on the next anniversary of their wedding day; she decided on the kind of wall-paper, the particular dado, and even on the style of furniture, which was to be selected on purely Art principles. My ideas were equally magnificent, though my plans were more indefinite, and certainly did not run in the house-building line. For two weeks the one golden idea possessed our minds; every morning we watched eagerly for news. At last it came. The miners had reached the expected spot, and struck—not gold, but water! Our hopes were washed away, our expectations drowned in a sea of repentance.

But this is a digression. To return to our first day's experience. While we were jostling our way through the bustling streets of San Francisco's business quarter, staring on all sides with all our eyes, and, like *Chowder*, seeming "to want another pair," some one of our party proposed a visit to the Stock Boards, it being just about the time when the financial hounds would be in full cry, and the "bulls" and "bears" tossing and tumbling among the stocks, sending them up or pulling them down in the wildest fashion. To "bull" is to send up the stocks; to "bear" is to pull them down.

We were ushered into a gallery overlooking the scene of operations; directly in front of us was a platform; two or three men were writing at different tables, and, at one in the centre of the platform, stood a stout, stolid-looking individual with a small bell beside him; below, seated in circular rows rising from the floor of the building, were the shareholders in the different mines, watching, with anxious faces, the financial fight. In the railed-in centre, which was something like the old gladiatorial arena, the stock-brokers themselves held the floor. There was a momentary lull as we entered; it was the close of the first session. Every face was turned towards the platform, waiting till the sphinx should speak. A few hurriedly uttered words from the stolid individual above alluded to—and such a commotion! A deafening roar of voices, pitched in a hundred different keys, clattering and clanging one against the other ! A sea of excited faces, eyes flashing, arms tossing wildly, fingers flung out and snapping in each other's faces, a struggle, a rush, a swaying to and fro of the crowd, which seemed wedged into a solid mass ! It seemed as though a sudden, go-as-you-please free fight was going on. We fancied they never could emerge whole from the conflict; their clothes must be torn from their backs, their limbs from their sockets. One stroke on the bell, and, as though by a magic touch, all is still—all silent. In that few minutes' commotion fortunes have been lost and won.

The clerk, in a monotonous, sing-song tone and rapid utterance, goes over the amount of business transacted. Strange it seemed to us, that out of that "confusion worse confounded," that tangled skein of words and babel of sounds, he extracted the clear argument, drew out each particular thread, and reiterated the quotations of stocks and by whom they had been bought or sold, never in a single instance making a mistake. Through all that din and confusion of tongues it had been plain sailing to him. The "bulls" had it to-day, the "bears" would have their turn to-morrow. So the world goes round.

Next we strolled up Kearney, the Bond or Regent Street of San Francisco. It is a very handsome street in the most fashionable quarter of the town, with elegant, tastefully arranged shops on either side. It is quite the fashionable promenade on Saturday afternoons. All the *élite* of the city, elegantly dressed women (the San Francisco ladies do dress elegantly, though sometimes with a daring combination of colours

that are somewhat disconcerting to the æsthetic taste),
and men in broadcloth and beaver, turn out like
soldiers on parade, and lounge up and down. Friends
and acquaintances congregate together and hold their
receptions on Kearney Street. It is quite a kaleidoscopic scene of bright dresses and pretty, smiling
faces. The dusty business men, in their cutaway coats
and slouch hats, keep to their own quarters in Montgomery Street, hard by, and seldom venture to intrude
on dainty Kearney Street. But, alas! there is a blot
on this bright picture. There are sundry open alcoves,
cigar and tobacco stores, pretty and pleasant enough to
look at, for they are gay with gilding and mirrors and
bright with flowers, but there is generally a crowd of
the tobacco-chewing population congregated here, and
the sidewalk is in such a disgusting condition from
this chewing and smoking that it is impossible for
a lady to pass without gathering up her skirts, and
even then she runs the risk of having a quid squirted
over her as she passes along. All over America,
more or less, this evil habit obtains, and everywhere with the same revolting effect. It is, however, much worse in the Western cities than in the
Eastern States. In New York, especially, they seem to
be awakening to the error of their way, and expectorate
less frequently in the presence of ladies. It is even
possible to ride for an hour in a car without being
disgusted once. But here in the West the vice rides
rampant. It is impossible to escape from it. In the
streets, in the cars, on the railway trains—it follows
you everywhere, wherever men (I was going to say
gentlemen, and some are so as far as the tailor can
make them) are travelling to and fro. This state of

things would not be allowed in any other city in the civilized world, and it might be easily remedied if the authorities would take the matter in hand as they do in the case of other nuisances, which may be more serious, but are far less disgusting. On all the ferry-boats there is a placard: "Gentlemen are requested not to spit about the deck; it is used by ladies." And they don't. The floor of the deck is as clean as a drawing-room. Why should not the same rule hold elsewhere?

We stroll through the markets, and wonder where the mountains of fruit and beautiful flowers have come from, and where they are going to. Such heaps of luscious peaches, plums, and nectarines, bushels of rich, ripe strawberries, raspberries, blue and green grapes, melons, and oranges, and red and gold bananas, and vegetables of every possible description in tons and scores of tons piled on all sides. Nothing wilted or stale; all fresh, and crisp, and green. Everything is in such royal profusion it seems as though nature had opened her heart and showered her best and fairest flowers throughout this Golden State. Pro-visions of every kind are to be found in these markets, of which there are several, and all in populous places, easy of access. Dairy farmers send their golden butter, plump chickens, and boxes of white, fresh eggs; and long-legged fowls, prairie hens, and a whole tribe of feathered favourites hang like malefactors suspended overhead; and dainty white pigs, with lemons in their mouths, tails curled up and tied with pink ribbons, and pigs that had outgrown the lemon period, and were waiting to be turned to bacon, and silver trout and salmon,—such rich, luscious-looking salmon,—with their scaly armour glittering in the light, and big-whiskered lobsters, prawns, and crawling crabs, all opening their formidable mouths and stirring their hundred feelers in protest against their unnatural usage. Every crustaceous delicacy the sea affords is there, all ready to tempt the appetite of omnivorous man. Everything was refreshing and pleasant to the eye, and so artistically arranged that we looked round on a perfect mosaic of beauty, a kind of poem, not made up of similes, rhymes, and rhythms, but of fruits and flowers.

The streets of San Francisco are a wonder and a marvel. On every side there is an ever-changing, animated scene, unenlivened by organ-grinders, dancing dogs, or Punch and Judys. The industrious fleas or the intelligent canaries are all equally unknown here. The attraction of the streets is entirely due to the polyglot gatherings of people from all lands, and the variegated tide is eternally flowing to and fro. Strange vehicles of all indescribable descriptions are dashing about the up-and-down stony streets at a breakneck pace. Clattering milk carts, travelling soda fountains, brewers' drays, sociable rockaways, and solitary "sulkies," their owners perched up between the spidery wheels, seemingly seated on nothing, are all rushing along pell-mell, helter-skelter. The streets are a perfect network of rails, and huge red cars, blue cars, and yellow cars, with their jingling bells, cross and recross at every turn. We look out for a collision, but none comes, and we elbow our way on. We are jostled on one side by a Polish Israelite, in whom there " is no guile," with a long beard and high peaked hat. A moon-faced Mexican, with long hair, golden earrings, and red serape, walks in his shadow. A slipshod woman, in a grimy, Oriental dress, flits past and disappears in a dark alley. A South Sea islander, a New Zealand chief, and a Mongolian merchant catch our eyes among the surging mass of European faces, and the blue-bloused, pig-tailed Chinaman, with his gliding, silent tread, swarms everywhere. He is always busy, always at work, carrying such weights as would set a donkey staggering. He has a long, hickory pole across one shoulder, and balancing at either end are huge, round baskets filled with goods of all descriptions, enough to fill a waggon, but John carries the weight easily enough. At the corner of California Street we come to a dead stop. There stands a kind of double vehicle, the foremost part being open, with a canopied top, seats running all round, and a man in the middle keeping solemn guard over a huge lever or crank. On the benches on either side were seated some half-dozen people, facing outwards, their feet dangling or resting on a narrow plank at their pleasure. We took our places on the front seat, faces set forward; a pretty balcony or wire lace-work ran in front of us breast high. The hind part was a common omnibus car, such as we are used to see all the world over. What magic would set the whole in motion? Of course we were going somewhere. There were no horses, no engine, no visible means of propelling us forward. A newly arrived Mongolian, seeing this strange vehicle for the first time, eyed it curiously, " No pushee, no pullee, no horsee, no steamee ; Melican man heap smart." At the sound of a bell the man turns the crank and off we go, flying in the face of the wind at the rate of ten miles an hour. We charge up one steep hill, then dash down, and up another, and so on for about four miles. Never was such a delicious breeze, such a flow of fresh,

invigorating air. Long lines of elegant houses, some
of distinguished architectural grandeur, with stately
palms lifting their grand, green heads like sentinels on
either side of the entrance doors, or rising from the
smooth-shaven lawns embroidered with flowers of
brilliant hues, fly past us on either side, their peaks
and gables silhouetted against the bright blue skies.
Streets and alleys, some wide, some narrow, diverge
and radiate from either side of us. And through this
vista of quaint habitations, of all sorts and sizes, we
get such delicious bits of harbour and river scenery as
would have delighted an artist's soul. On we go,
till we lose sight of sea and river, and the whole
city unrolls itself beneath our feet, sliding down from
its hundred hills, spreading in picturesque and panoramic beauty on all sides of us, till it is lost in the
amethyst haze beyond. Whirled through the air by
our invisible steeds, we look down upon church spires
and steeples, massive towers and palace houses, on
miles of streets, green squares, and blooming gardens,
which Eve herself might have revelled in and dreamed
of her paradise regained. With cheeks aglow, and
spirits buoyant with the delight of our magic journey,
we reached the foot of Lone Mountain. Before we
left our strange vehicle, called by the natives " the
dummy," we ascertained something of its mysterious
engineering. It is of similar construction to that in
use for a time on the old Blackwall railway at home,
being propelled by an underground cable, which runs
along the centre of the road between the regular track
rails, and the hidden underground force is controlled
by the crank, deftly handled by the official who stands
in the middle of our " dummy."

We are at the foot of Lone Mountain, towering high among the surrounding hills, with the holy cross planted on the top. It is the loveliest grave-garden in the world; not an echo reaches it from the busy, bustling city below. Surrounded by wild, widespreading uplands and undulating sandhills, barren, and soft, and gray, with the boom of the Pacific waves thundering among the low foothills, it stands in isolated solitude, this beautiful city of the dead. There are no grim head and footstones, no tons of monumental marble crushing down upon the helpless dead, enough to give a ghost the nightmare to think of its poor body being buried under it. Here the dead are really laid to rest in a veritable flower-garden. The ground is arranged in plots, varying from twelve to thirty feet square, and each plot is owned by one family, who decorate it according to their own fancy. Every family grave-garden is surrounded by a low, light fence, and is entered through a rustic gate, and is laid out with narrow, neatly gravelled paths, a foot wide, and borders and flower-beds, some filled with beautiful roses, some a mass of purple and white violets, others with different kinds of sweet-smelling flowers of bright and variegated hues. Everything is kept in perfect order; not a weed is to be seen. Opposite the entrance-gate is a small slab chronicling the name of the dead below. It is sometimes so hidden by the luxuriant growth of evergreens and flowers that you have to search to find it.

Here, in the fragrant and peaceful shade of this fair garden, the old pioneers, the heroes of the strange days of '49, the storm of their turbulent lives over, the battle fought, the victory won—or lost! lie at rest.

L

CHAPTER XIV.

THE OLD MISSION.

The Windmills—The Golden Gate Park—The Seal Rock—The
Cliff House—The Mission Dolores.

ALEXANDER wanted more worlds to conquer. If Don
Quixote had sought for more windmills on a general
tilting-ground, he would have found them here. They
are everywhere. We wonder what they are all doing.
It is so unusual to see such a world of windmills in
a large city. Looking round from California Street
hills we see scores of them; they come upon us, one
after the other, till we forget to count them. They
are of all sorts and all sizes; some short and stumpy,
with fat arms, wheezing laboriously as the wind sends
them around, as though they were working against
their will; others are tall and lanky, their long, gaunt
arms whizzing and whirring through the air, always
hard at work except when the wind is still, and that is
not often; they are painted all the colours of the rainbow, and look quite gay flashing round in the sunshine.
Every house of the slightest pretensions has a well
and waterworks on its own premises; the windmill
stands sentinel above them, and sends the fresh cool
stream through the leaden arteries of the household,
and irrigates and refreshes the land when no rain is

falling and the summer sun tries to burn the green
verdure to tinder, for this is a rainless land for six
months of the year. During summer not a drop falls
to moisten the parched face of the earth. Everything
is done by artificial irrigation.

We soon leave the city and its windmills behind
us, and enter the Golden Gate Park, where, a few
years ago, the Pacific waves were rolling; but these
hundreds of acres have been reclaimed from the
sea, and are planted with rare shrubs, young trees,
evergreens, and blooming flowers. It is tastefully
laid out, a landscape garden and park in one;
there are picturesque winding paths and shady nooks
and corners where you can hide from the sun's
searching rays, and, while you listen to the singing birds overhead, hear the boom of the breakers
on the shore below. We pass through this paradise
of green and reach a silent sea of yellow sandhills,
smooth and soft as velvet, billowing round in graceful,
undulating waves as far as the eye can reach; there
is a sudden curve, and the wide Pacific Sea, in all its
glory, lies before us clothed in the sunshine, its white
foam lips kissing the golden shore; its long, level line
stretched against the distant skies. We drove down
to it; nay, drove into it, and watched its tiny waves
dimpling into a thousand welcomes beneath our wheels.
The sun and the sea conspired together to fill the air
with bright beams and balmy breezes. We felt the
soft spray blowing in our faces, stirring our blood, and
setting our cheeks aglow, and, as we breathed the
crisp, soft air, laden with three thousand miles of
iodine, we seemed to be taking a draught of the elixir
of life. The full fascination of the sea seized our

senses ; we could not tear ourselves away. Presently, mingling with the monotonous moaning of the waves, we heard a sound like the barking of a kennel of dogs. Before us, rising out of the sea about a hundred yards from the shore, was a picturesque mass of broken crags known as the famous Seal Rocks, whereon thousands of those sensible creatures, from the soft seal baby to the barnacled old patriarch, lay basking in the sunshine, barking their satisfaction aloud, floundering about, rollicking and rolling one over the other, and splashing into the sea, while some stood solemnly on end watching the fun. Standing just above, on a steep, rocky eminence which rises abruptly from the shore, stands the Cliff House, where an excellent table is always spread for those who choose to partake of the good things thereon. It is a favourite resort of the good folk of San Francisco ; they turn their backs upon the noise and bustle of the city and enjoy here perfect solitude ; they can descend from the piazza some fifty rugged steps, and stroll along the wild seashore, undisturbed except by the shriek of the sea-gull and the barking of the seal colony mingling with the soughing of the wind, and the low, sullen roar of the waves ; or saunter up and down the piazza, sipping their coffee or smoking the beloved weed, and watch the great, red sun sink like a ball of fire, and drown itself in the Pacific Sea.

On our way home we passed the old Mission ; at least, all that is left of it, which is not much—the mere remnants of some redwood houses and the ancient church, a quaint-looking, low-roofed home of desolation, with its adobe walls of sunbaked clay about four feet thick, which promise to withstand the encroaches of time a century longer. A chime of three bells still hangs in three square portholes; their long tongues, red with rust, droop dumb and motionless from their silent mouths. Only a hundred years ago they were brought from Castile, blessed by the holy fathers, and brought here to the edge of the wild Western world to ring out and summon the heathen and the wanderer to worship the one true God. You enter the ruined church through a low, arched doorway. The broken font is still there, but the last drop of holy water was spilled from it long ago. The mullioned windows are of a quaint, fanlike shape, and the genial sun tries to pierce through the grime and dust and send its beams dancing over the crumbling ruin within. The painted wooden shrines of St. Joseph and St. Francis (who gave the settlement of Yerba Buena the name of San Francisco) are still there. Near by are the Madonna and Child, but the paint has worn off, and they are all discoloured and stained with the damp wind and the rain which drips, in the rainy season, from the dilapidated roof. The crumbling decorations, though they are of a rough, rude workmanship, still bear the stamp of artistic design, though crudely executed by unaccustomed hands, who laboured for the love of God. It is about a hundred feet from the threshold to the altar. Give reins to your imagination, set it galloping back a hundred years, and see the priests, the white nuns, and hooded friars clustered round the empty altar busy in the service of the Lord; the aisles filled with kneeling Indians, who know little of the faith they have adopted except that there is an unknown God somewhere who makes their corn grow, watches over their lives here, with a promise of a life hereafter; men from Mexico,

Peru, and Spain, and wanderers from all along the wild Pacific coast are standing reverently round; censers are swinging, lights are burning, and a choir of voices chant the Ave Marias. A Christian host gathered in that wilderness by the sea. Where are they all now? Vanished like the children of a dream.

A mouldy, funereal odour clings about the ruined walls, and we are glad to step out into the little grave-yard outside, where the English hawthorn and white winter roses are blooming and the grass growing rich and luxuriant above the moss-grown graves. Whole tribes of Indians lie buried in the dust beneath our feet. There is no more desolate spot in the world than a dis-used graveyard. We read strange unfamiliar names upon the broken, half-buried stones, and crumbling urns, dilapidated angels, and crippled cherubs are tottering round us. Here and there we decipher an English name, and, beneath, the information: "Died by the hands of the V. C.;" "In mercy we slay the enemies of the Lord." The V. C. means the Vigilance Com-mittee, who, in the early, lawless days, executed justice swift and sure upon proven criminals. The strict justice of their decisions was never called in question. A certain number of men of known integrity were in-vested with supreme power of life or death, and the guilt of a man being once fully assured he had a brief trial and swift execution. There was no legal quibbling, which often lets loose some atrocious criminal to prey upon the world again until, at the end, he is launched out of it. Near the low, arched gateway stands the di-lapidated figure of a woman, her sightless eyes and lifted hands pointing upwards—mute significance of one hope for all the miscellaneous dead.

A fresh breeze was blowing outside, but here it seemed to hang heavy and still, laden with the damp odour of mouldering graves, which mingled with and destroyed the sweet scent of the flowers that are flourishing so luxuriantly above the dead. This was the first we had seen of the many remnants of the old mission days, when the Spanish fathers first came to the wilderness to sow the good seed and reap the harvest in their Lord's name. About the year 1820 the missions began to decay, the soldiers were recalled from the Presidio, where they had been stationed for the protection of the friars and their property, and from that time the missions dwindled, till the fathers were recalled to Spain. They carried with them all their cattle and movable goods, and left their buildings to decay. These are scattered throughout the State of California, wherever the fathers held temporary sway. Still, though they and their labours have passed away, and are well-nigh forgotten, they have left their traces behind them : throughout the country we find the old Spanish names still clinging to the soil, such as Santa Clara, Santa Rosa, Santa Barbara, San Rafael, San Jose, Los Angeles, Monterey, Carmelo, etc. Mr. John S. Hittell, in his "History of California," has given a most interesting and graphic account of these missions, their people, their work, and their effect upon the country from their first establishment to their decline.

The city has grown out of the wilderness, and crowded so close to the crumbling walls of the ruined mission that as we leave the gloomy precincts we step out into the populous streets, which are full of hurry, bustle, and vigorous young life. It is like stepping from the old century into the new. Gaily painted cars and omnibuses are dashing up and down the wide Mission Street, each following the other so quickly that before you can step into one another is on its heels.

As we rattle up one street and down another we cannot help noticing the scarcity of shady trees in all parts of San Francisco. People take great pride in their beautiful flowers, their smooth velvet lawns, and stately palms, which lift their crowned heads on high, their broad leaves drooping like blessing hands over the household ; but never a shady tree is planted anywhere.

Although the blissful shade, so highly prized and so eagerly sought for in other lands, may not be desirable here, where people literally live in the sunshine, yet we feel that the planting of rows of leafy, green trees on either side of the streets would turn them at once into magnificent boulevards. They could still walk in the sunshine, but the luxuriant green would be refreshing to the eye. The long range of California street hills so planted would be a paradise for the gods to stroll in.

CHAPTER XV.

Street Architecture—Curiosities of Climate—Brummagem Baronets
—The Sand Lot—The Forty-niners—" Society Ladies."

ROME stands on her seven hills ; San Francisco sits
enthroned upon a hundred. The one is enjoying
her centuries of rest after her triumphant onward
march of a thousand years; the other is just awakening, like a royal babe in swaddling-clothes, her
infant hands outstretched to seize the sceptre she
will one day wield as Empress of the West. She
looks down upon scenes of surpassing beauty—wide-
spreading hills and valleys, wooded dells, and dark
pine forests reaching away till they are lost in the
purple hills beyond. She is more than half surrounded by water. Along the east runs the beautiful
blue bay, sixty miles long, studded by green or rocky
islets, and honeycombed by smaller bays, wherein lay
shady villages and thriving towns. To the north lies
the Golden Gate, opening out to the glorious Pacific
Sea, whose white-crested waves break and boom like
muffled thunder along the sandy shore, rushing onward
and bounding with its bright waters the western part
of the city, which has scarcely a level square in the

whole of it. It is built in an up-and-down, zigzag fashion, some of the streets creeping up the hill sideways like a crab; some, such as California, Clay, and Sutter, dashing straight up, as though they were in a hurry to get out of the city and be lost in the great beyond; while one end of Montgomery Street rushes up the steep slope of Telegraph Hill so precipitately and abruptly that the basement windows of one house have an excellent view of the chimney-pots of the next.

The houses are all built of wood, to which the cunning builder gives all the massive appearance of substantial stone buildings. They are generally painted white, sometimes picked out with drab or gray. The fronts are always elaborately carved, and sometimes bordered round the windows with the natural red wood left unpainted. This mass of dazzling white houses gives the city a wonderfully brilliant appearance, especially when seen from the street hills. On California Street hill are some really palatial residences, the homes of the railway and bonanza kings. Some are built in the most ornamental style of a kind of mongrel Gothic, with as many peaks, spires, and gables as could be crowded into one spot, oddly shaped windows—oval, oblong, diamond-shaped, or square—breaking out in unexpected places, variety of form being in every way more considered than the strict adherence to any special form of architecture. If we could make a twelfth cake as large as an island, and stick one of these special mansions on the top, its airy elegance would be the admiration of the world. General Colton has here a really splendid residence. A "villa" he modestly calls it; we style it a mansion. It is built in the pure Italian style of architecture, elegant and

graceful, yet stately and imposing in its grand simplicity.   It stands out in striking contrast to the
decorated dwellings on the other side.   Every man
who builds a house lays "a trap to catch a sunbeam"
in the form of a bay window.   They are everywhere,
in every street, and on both sides of it.   The Palace
Hotel seems built entirely of bay windows from its
base .to the height of its seven floors.   This immense
caravansera is honeycombed with them, and it has the
appearance of a straight square mountain covered with
bird-cages.   The sun in other cities is a luxury of life,
here it is a necessity.   "Sunny suites" are advertised
and sought for everywhere.   In other places people
usually avoid the sun, and seek the shady side of the
road. ·Here they bask like lizards in the sunshine ; it
is only dire necessity that drives them into the shade.
There is no scarcity of sunshine either ; the land is
flooded with it.   Nowhere is the sun so bright, so
genial, and strong, always looking down with warm
friendly eyes, never sending its fierce, fiery lances
down to smite and slay with their cruel stroke.   The
heat is tempered by a cool, invigorating breeze, and
while the sun inclines you to throw off your seal-
skin, the wind warns you to cling to it.   Some never
leave off their furs, others never put them on.   The
variations of temperature during summer and winter
are so slight that one style of clothing serves for the
whole year.   Your wardrobe never suffers from an
irruption.   You may meet a lady promenading in lace
and muslin in December, and in velvet and furs in
June ; or in a single walk through the city you may
meet one lady in the airiest of costumes, another
cloaked and muffled up to the chin ; one gentleman in

a linen duster, another in a top-coat. Nobody is ever
too warm, nobody is ever too cold. It seems like a
riddle, but you must come here to read it. Everything seems *bouleversé*, even to the climate. There
is no settled rule anywhere or in anything; it is a
sort of "go-as-you-please" city. There is a general
rush and hurry everywhere, a kind of picturesque
lawlessness, which is most refreshing to those who
come from the other side of the world, where propriety always wears her best bib and tucker, and
etiquette in her regulation dress, tied with the reddest
of red tape, reigns supreme, and natural impulse is
bound down in the straitest of strait-waistcoats.
Fashion is the only tyrant, the spoilt pet and ruler
among the ladies, for if a San Francisco lady is not in
the fashion she is nowhere. In their desire to attain
to the utmost height of that fickle goddess they sometimes "o'erleap the selle, and fall on the other side;"
but as a rule they are well and tastefully dressed.
The gentlemen are supremely indifferent on the subject; each dresses to please himself, and consults only
his own individual comfort and convenience, whereas
in most large cities, where the sacred "chimney-pot"
prevails, one man is as like another as two peas,
faultlessly attired in the same fashion, from the crown
of his head to the sole of his feet. Here it is altogether
different; here are hats with high crowns, low crowns,
or no crowns, straw, felt, willow, or wide Panama;
gray suits, white suits, and blue suits. But the Californian proper is very particular in his choice of a
necktie, which is always of the most brilliant hue.
Even in Eastern or Continental cities, where black
ties are the rule, he will burst out in gorgeous colours.

In the evening, however, when he presents himself before the ladies, the swallow-tail coat is strictly *de rigueur*.

Social life flows on in an easy, pleasant, *sans souci* fashion, for the San Franciscans are a most hospitable people, and are disposed to open their hearts as well as their doors to their visitors from the outside world, and do all in their power to make their beautiful city a home to the passing stranger. This open-hearted hospitality is sometimes imposed upon by an influx of British baronets, whose names are unknown in their native land, and pseudo lords, made up by their tailors, whose names have never figured in the peerage. Occasionally these Brummagem gentry dip their fingers into the purse of the open-handed Californian, and sometimes make themselves too fatally agreeable to the ladies ; but as a rule their false pretensions are discovered, and they are quietly driven from the city, before the damage done is irreparable. The inhabitants are apt to give too easy credence to a self-asserting class, who swagger about the hotels as true gentlefolk never do, and whose brassy impudence for a time passes as pure gold. But perhaps it is better to be sometimes deceived than always distrustful.

There is no settled " society " here, regarding the subject from our point of view. It is impossible there should be in a country which is in a constant state of fermentation, fluctuating from one extreme to the other, where the game of speculation is being played on all sides, and everybody takes a hand. The cauldron is for ever bubbling and boiling over, and somebody goes to the bad. Men and women who have held their place in brilliant circles one year drop out of it the next, and sink down and are lost, no one knows how or where. The circle closes, and the dance of life goes on.

Of course there are many people of wealth and position who have played a winning game, and are satisfied now to settle down and watch the growth of the beloved city they have helped to make. Most of the families of culture, intellect, and refinement are those who came there thirty years ago, when the gold fever first broke out and drew some of the best blood from every land towards itself. And those men and women, too, who came out in the old, rough days, have grown purer, stronger, and better from mingling with the new life in a new land. There has been no effete civilization here. Every man has depended on his own brains, his own hand for his well-doing. It may truly be said, in this land above all others, that every man is the architect of his own fortunes. Of course much of the coarse, vulgar element of mankind has swarmed and is still swarming into this Golden State. Some regard it as a sort of Tom Tiddler's ground, where they can run about picking up gold and silver. When they find their mistake, and learn that here, as elsewhere, men must bring labour of hand or brain to the market and pay in full for every crust they eat, they enrol themselves in the noble army of the unemployed, parade the streets in lazy battalions, hold mass meetings, and howl over their misfortunes, shake their fists in the face of calamity: "Why can't they drink the wine of life and revel in champagne and roses?" They will do anything, everything, but work for it. These people, who are not native born, but are the mere refuse of other nations, which has rolled across the sea and been flung

upon the shores of the Western World, have won for
themselves the title of Sand-lotters.   They have their
meetings on a vacant sand-heap on the edge of the town,
which is held entirely sacred to them, and here they
bluster, and storm, and loudly assert their " rights."
They decide who is fit to live and who is fit to die.
Figuratively, they hang the capitalist on his own
threshold and divide his wealth among their worthier
selves.   If the general atmosphere were more com-
bustible their incendiary speeches would set the land
in flames.   These people, though contemptible in themselves, create a general agitation and confusion, drive
capital away from the city, and have given rise to
a general sense of insecurity.   As a grain of sand will
set all the delicate working of a watch awry, so they
have disturbed the peace for a while ; but it is a storm
in a tea-cup, that will soon be over.   The party of
law and order is firmly knit together, and dignified
in its silent strength.   So long as the dronish population confines itself to buzzing and burring around,
carrying on a boisterous war of words only, they keep
a dignified silence ; but at the first attempt to sting,
it will be crushed like a wasp.   In no other country
would a foreign element be allowed to create so much
disorder.   The native population are a peaceful, law-
abiding race.   " This is a land of liberty," they say ;
but when liberty becomes license to the vicious, alas
for poor liberty !

America is willing to stretch a welcoming hand
to all comers without regard to creed or nationality,
to give land to such as desire to make a home among
them, and a free liberal education to their children,
to throw open its offices of State and General Govern-

ment to all candidates who are fit to fill them. It is large in generosity as mighty in strength, and it is a small thing to ask that its laws be kept and its institutions respected by the stranger who benefits by the national hospitality.

Young children must go through certain physical disturbances before they arrive at a state of healthy maturity, and I suppose young States must go through similar mental distractions before they settle down into a dignified calm. The adolescent State of California is no exception to the rule, but it is cutting its wisdom teeth and learning to comport itself with a dignity befitting the great Union of which it is a part.

Men no longer carry their lives in their hands, as in the old days of lawless, romantic adventure, but I am afraid a few still secretly carry arms in their pockets, and use them, perhaps, upon small provocation. But things are improving and changing rapidly; the people are prospering, and, the essentials of life being secured, their thoughts and ambitions are soaring into higher regions. Civilization, which, for years past, has been marching westward, subduing prairies, cutting down forests, piercing mountains, and spanning rivers, seems to have ended her grand progress and, for a time, sat down to rest here; resting, though working still, establishing rule and order. There are no stagnant ideas, no stereotyped monotony here; everything is full of electrical life; people think, move, and act quickly; they are not content with what *is*, but look forward to what *shall be*. This beautiful California—land of the sun, of the palm and pine—has only one chapter in its past, but it is creating for itself a glorious future.

Things happen here that we cannot conceive happening in any other city in the world. Walking through the streets one day, we met a strange figure carrying a parti-coloured umbrella—red, white, and blue. He was a gray-haired, elderly man, dressed in a faded military uniform, with tarnished epaulets, and a scarlet feather in his cap. He may be seen wandering through the streets of the city in all weathers. He has been so wandering for the last twenty years or more. He labours under the delusion that he is " Emperor of all the Americas." The people humour him, and allow him to indulge in that delusion. He issues proclamations, which are printed in the newspapers, and posted at street corners. Sometimes, being in want of twenty dollars, he levies a tax upon his "loyal subjects." Some wealthy citizen answers the demand at once; he is never denied. He dines where he pleases, free; patronizes such places of entertainment as he chooses, free; rides on the cars or on the trams, free; indeed, he has the freedom of the city in the truest sense of the word. On inquiry we learn the reason of this general indulgence. He was a mason and a forty-niner, they say; and was ruined by the great fire, when his wits were shaken, and this royal delusion rose on the wreck of his reason, and the kindly people, in the spirit of true *camaraderie,* will never let the old man want.

Here is another anecdote characteristic of San Francisco kindliness, being the history in brief of Bummer and Lazarus (the names being descriptive of the habits of one dog, and the appearance of the other, on his first entrance into public life). " Bummer " was a big dog, a vagabond much beloved

M

of the town, who could not be coaxed into civilized ways. He disdained to live in a house, or to serve one master. He was a kind of canine tramp, who lived by his wits. Like the Emperor, he too enjoyed the hospitality of the city. Lazarus was a little mangy cur, thin, sickly, and half-starved. One day some other dogs attacked poor, miserable little Lazarus. Bummer, perhaps moved by kindred feelings—the assailants being household property, and Lazarus a tramp like himself—plunged into the fray to the rescue of Lazarus.

From that day the two wanderers were a canine Damon and Pythias. They became well known in the city. Lazarus looked starved and sickly no longer. Bummer introduced him to his own chosen haunts. They went together to such restaurants as they chose to honour, and dined gratis. Messrs. Bummer and Lazarus were always welcome, and never sent hungry away. It was observed that the big dog always gave his small companion a full share of the delicacies of the season. When an Act was passed commanding all dogs in the city of San Francisco to be muzzled, a clause was made exempting " Bummer and Lazarus." However, their time came. Bummer died one day; Lazarus was found dead by his side on the next. An old resident of the city who knew the dogs well, and had fed them many a time, told me this story. They are stuffed now, and have their place among the many mementoes of "old days"—old in the space of thirty years.

Only the healthy and the strong keep their grip on the land, and these, the early pioneers of the State, form the most delightful society in San Francisco.

Their homes are the abode of elegance and refinement.
We are sometimes disposed to wonder how all this
culture has reached this far-away land,—the " Wild
West " we call it,—wild now in nothing but its natural
attractions ; in no country in the world are there more
luxurious, happy homes than here in San Francisco.
Those who are in a position and have the power to
entertain their friends, do so with genial cordiality.
Some have one evening in the week, some another ;
there is no set formality ; but we meet with the
gracious courtesy of the Old World warmed by the
hearty whole-souled welcome of the New.   Those who
have the power to indulge their æsthetic fancies gather
about them all that is beautiful in the way of art that
can attract and satisfy the most artistic taste.

The home of one lady is at this moment present to
my mind's eye.   She has travelled over the world, and
brought back with her some perfect gems in the way
of bric-à-brac, paintings, and sculpture.   There are
among them two exquisite marble statues, both unique
in conception and excellent in execution.   The one is
" Delilah," a grand, grim piece of workmanship ; the
other, the more poetical and sympathetic " Lost
Pleiad ; " the yearning, searching look upon her face
reaches the heart, and we wish we could help her find
her way home.   Here it has been our good fortune to
fall in with some of the " Forty-niners," as all who came
over in that year are called.   Many may have come
over adventuring earlier or later.; no matter, they
have no distinguishing title to chronicle their advent.
Only the " Forty-niners " are regarded as the original
pioneers.   Their numbers are lessening day by day ;
but a few are now remaining, and they are all a fine,

stalwart race of men, with no signs of age or decay,
some with delicate poetical faces, which it is difficult to
associate with the rude times we know they have
passed through; they have grown gray with the
passing years, but not old; they look as though they
could brace themselves together and do their work
over again.   In this electric air age seems chary of
advancing; youth blooms long after it would have
perished elsewhere.   The perennial springtime in
earth and air seems to have communicated itself to the
lives of men.   They are full of anecdote, and brimming
over with the romance and stirring adventure of
bygone days, and proud of their beautiful city, too; as
well they may be.   They have watched it grow stone
by stone, street by street, and have helped to make
it what it is.   They found it a heap of hovels and
sandhills, and when they are carried to their graves
in Lone Mountain, they will leave it the fairest and
loveliest city in the world.

In addition to these pleasant gatherings, San Francisco frequently breaks out into grander gaieties, and
entertains her hundreds in the most magnificent
fashion.   Society sounds her trumpet, and her armies
gather round her in gorgeous array, when frivolity and
fashion hold high revels for a season.   There is no
genial sociability then; it is all gaslight, music, roses,
and champagne.   Gentlefolk are divided into two
classes, "society ladies," and ladies pure and simple.
The "society lady" has her dresses chronicled in all
the public papers; whole columns are devoted to the
description of dresses.   To all the Pacific coast is made
known the important fact that the young and beautiful
Miss So-and-so wore pink silk trimmed with point-

lace, while the lovely Miss Such-a-one wore pea-green
and apple blossoms, her stately mamma appearing in
imperial velvet and rubies. And so on. Woe be to
the audacious damsel who dares to appear in the same
dress twice running! Everybody knows all about it,
and the cost of every yard of satin or inch of lace
is catalogued in the feminine mind. And woe be to
the simple toilet which will not do credit to the
reporter's pen! The girls all wonder how their dresses
will look in print, and to that end select them. Here
a noble course of ruin begins—so far, at least, as an
extravagant woman can ruin a man, and we all know
how much she can do towards it. There are sometimes more dollars on a woman's back than remain
in her husband's pocket.

It is a pernicious habit, this advertising business,
and brings to the surface the smaller, meaner passions
of the female nature. There are numbers who would
gladly break from this iron rule of custom, but they
either have not the courage to strike the first blow
or are borne down by the great majority on the other
side. But things here, as elsewhere, will right themselves in time.

CHAPTER XVI.

THE FLOWERY KINGDOM.

A Visit to Chinatown—Its General Aspect—A Tempting Display
—Barbers' Shops—A Chinese Restaurant—Their Joss House
—Their Gods.

It is nine o'clock in the evening when we start for an
investigating ramble through Chinatown. Time was
when men went over "the sea in ships" when they
desired to visit the celestial land; now they can go
there and back in an hour, and not travel on telegraph
wires either. The mountain has come to Mahomet,
and deposited its load in the very heart of the "Golden
City."

Kearney Street is brilliantly lighted, the shops are
temptingly arrayed in their best wares, and a well-
dressed world of men and women are strolling up and
down, chatting, laughing, bargaining, and buying.
We watch the California Street dummy charge up the
hill with its last load of passengers, its red fiery eye
blazing boldly on us as it drops down the other side
of the hill, and is lost to sight. We feel quite at home
here, though we are eight thousand miles away from
our native shores. A sudden turn out of the bustling
thoroughfare, a few steps forward, and we know we are

in a foreign land. We are escorted by a private friend
and a police detective, without whose protective presence it would not be safe to venture into those dingy
courts and alleys which lie festering in the very heart
of the " Flowery Kingdom." We keep close to our
escorts ; we feel that we have stepped beyond the
bounds of civilization, and are surrounded by a subtle
element utterly foreign and inimical to our own. We
are in the city of the idolatrous heathen, in whose
sight our Christian civilization is an abomination and
a snare. Pig-tailed, blue-bloused Celestials swarm in
the roadway and on the sidewalks. They surge round
us with their silent, stealthy tread. At the sight of
our escort's face, or the sound of his voice, they slink
away and are gone like shadows. The streets are
dimly lighted ; the gas does not blaze, it blinks behind
its glasses, but the big white moon gives light enough
for us to see the cheap gaudy magnificence around us.
We are passing the Joss house. It flaunts its scarlet
streamers overhead, and flanks its doors with legends
in saffron and gold. Within is a glitter of tinsel, a
subdued light, and the flicker of a tiny lamp before
some figure of barbaric ugliness. The air floats out
loaded with the fumes of smoking sandal-wood and
strange odours from the East. The doors are open,
but we do not enter yet. We stroll up the street,
taking an exterior view before we penetrate to the
interior. Coloured lanterns are strung along some of
the balconies, or hang from the windows. Red and
black signs in crooked characters are everywhere, and
from all sides resounds the echo, it seems, of a hundred
unknown tongues. The slant-eyed pagans leer at us
curiously as they pass to and fro. They bear us

"white devils" no good will, if we read their looks aright. Lights stream from cellar flaps, creep through open doors and window chinks, but the shops are only lighted by a succession of dingy oil lamps. Discordant noises of rasping fiddles, gongs, and sundry unknown tuneless instruments mingle with the clatter of strange tongues. The very laughter comes to us jangled and out of tune, and the air is filled with odours the reverse of sweet. Mouldy fruits, wilted vegetables, stale fish, too long divorced from its native element, all mingle in one common and most unsavoury scent.

The Chinese shops make no endeavour to attract the eye or tempt the appetite of the Celestial horde. But, perhaps, what seems to us a disgusting display may seem to them a tempting sight. The butcher, who is a general merchant as well, sells Joss sticks, teapots, tobacco, and scores of other things. He flanks his door on either side with the carcass of huge slaughtered hogs. They are not quartered and jointed in Christian fashion, but are hacked, and hewn, and torn asunder just as the meat is wanted, and present a mangled, shapeless mass, sickening to look at. Split chickens and fowls are flattened out like sheets of paper, and nailed against the wall. Delicate titbits, steeped in oil and dried, are strung up and hung like cherry bob across the windows, and scores of oily cakes, like lumps of yellow soap, are laid on benches. Lumps of delight they are in Celestial eyes, judging by the lingering glances they cast thereon. The shops are very dingy and dark inside, and those which are not devoted to the sale of eatables have a spicy, pungent odour everywhere, no matter what

articles of merchandise they sell. We went into two
or three shops in search of some special article which
we might carry away as a souvenir of our visit, but
could find nothing but cheap, tawdry trash, beryl
bracelets, bead necklaces, tiny cups and saucers, etc.
There was no brilliant display of gold embroideries,
vases, and Oriental magnificence, which characterizes
our Chinese shops at home. The Chinese merchant
sits in silent state behind his counter, watching our
every moment with his stealthy almond eyes. He
makes no attempt to force his wares upon us; indeed,
he seems sublimely indifferent whether we buy or not.
His long, shapely hands are folded before him as he
sits on his high stool serene and dignified, while we
peer curiously about, examining anything that catches
our eye. We see nothing we care to purchase, so
make a smiling apology for our intrusion, and he bows
us out with courteous but most majestic silence.

We pass on our way, look down the cellar flaps,
and see the barbers at work in their underground
shops. Within a radius of half a mile there are no
less than fifty of these places, devoted to the cleansing
and decoration of the Mongolian head. You may
glance down these steps at any hour of the day or
night and you will see the operators busy at their
tonsorial labour. Never was such clean shaving, such
delicate cleansing of eyes, ears, and nostrils, such trim-
ming and pencilling of brows and lashes, such a
scraping and polishing of oily faces, such a plaiting
of the beloved and sacred pigtail, and the Celestial
pagan issues from the hands of the barber a proud and
happy man, the perfect ideal of a Chinese beau; every
inch above his shoulders is scraped and polished to

perfection. This luxurious treatment which he receives at the hands of his barber is a law among the followers of Confucius. The Chinaman feels the necessity of frequent rejuvenation under the razors, probes, and pencils of the barber, who is one of the best employed and most important persons in the community. The almond-eyed pagan is never seen without his pigtail; the loss of it is considered the greatest calamity that can befall him. When he is engaged in his household work he winds his pigtail round his head in the fashion of a Grecian knot.

Our next visit was to a Chinese restaurant, which is patronized by the wealthier as well as the lower order of that peculiar people. The ground-floor is a kind of general utility store for the sale of miscellaneous comestibles. Bright, blue-bloused little China boys, their pigtails just sprouting, are squatting on the floors, cutting and chopping up meat and vegetables. In the kitchen, a few steps above, the cooks are busily at work preparing the unsavoury savoury feast for the hungry horde who are presently expected to supper. Beef or mutton is rarely if ever used in their culinary operations. Pork, rats, rabbits, geese, or fowls form the staple part of their substantial food, but these are never eaten in their natural simplicity; they are disguised and minced, and mixed with spices, vegetables, entrails, oil, and rancid butter, sometimes stewed, and sometimes being rolled in a thin wafery crust of paste. We saw plenty of these arranged for frying, like sausages in disguise. There is a greasy oleaginous look about everything, a smell like rusty bacon everywhere. A culinary war was being carried on in the kitchen, the pots and pans were specially clean and bright, the cooks went clattering round lifting lids and stirring one thing after another, and handing us a long iron spoon hospitably invited us to dip in and taste, assuring us it was "velly good," which invitation I need not say we courteously refused. A few steps higher on the first floor is the dining-room or grand saloon, which is only used by the wealthy merchants. It is furnished with very dark walnut, with quaint ebony carvings of birds, curious beasts, and flowers, all beautifully executed, and worthy of a better place. The tables and chairs were of the same heavy dark material. The room was divided in two by a wide archway. There was an alcove on one side for musicians, and all kinds of queer, quaint musical instruments, some twisted like serpents, some like grotesque, misshapen guitars, were hung against the wall. Lacquered cabinets and tea-trays, with tiny covered cups and saucers, and hideous bronze ornaments, were scattered around. Rich tapestried hangings were draped across the windows, and the wide balcony was filled with flowers, and a string of lighted lanterns were hung over the outside railings. On one side of the room, about two feet from the ground, was a raised platform covered with matting and cushions, a block of wood in the centre to hold a lamp. Thither the luxurious Mongolian retires to smoke the inevitable opium when the feast is over. At the entrance-door of all eating-rooms stands a bowl of chop-sticks; each guest as he enters supplies himself with a pair. The floor above is arranged in a simpler, rougher fashion for an inferior class of visitors. The floor above that is simpler and rougher still. And so the grade goes upward, and so does the tea. The real, fine, aromatic herb, in all perfection, is served on the first floor; water is added to the leaves (for they are an economical race), and served on the second; more water for the third. And so on, till a decoction of damaged water is served to the lowest, albeit the highest class of guests, for the poorer class here mount heavenward so far as this earth is concerned.

Laundries abound, though they are by no means confined to Chinatown. They are found in all quarters of San Francisco. Sometimes the Chinese laundry is a mere wooden shed, wedged in between tall houses, or standing in some out-of-the-way nook, where you would hardly think of pitching a pigsty. We passed some of these rickety places, the white linen drying on the roofs, flapping to and fro in a weird, ghastly fashion in the moonlight. The work is carried on by night as well as by day, for these moon-eyed Mongolians are a most industrious race, and in their economy of time and space a double set of workmen occupy a single room, and labour in relays. When the day-labourer retires to his shelf the night-worker rises from it, and carries on the business till the morning; so the fire is never out, and the starching, ironing, plaiting, and pleating is always going on. Passing through the streets of San Francisco at any hour of the night you see the faint glimmer of the laundry-lamp flickering through the dingy window-panes.

We next turned into one of their many Joss houses, where the worship of their hideous idols was in full swing. We ascended a dingy, dirty staircase and entered a large room on the first floor, which was furnished with gods and altars of all descriptions. Crowds of worshippers were passing to and fro, now in

single file, now in battalions; some were smoking,
some were conversing in their low, liquid language
one with another. One jerked his head with a kind of
familiar nod, which was meant for a reverential
obeisance to a specially ugly deity. Another threw
a stick into the air in front of the altar, and according
to the way it pointed as it fell his prayer would be
granted or not. I do not know whether Joss was
propitious, but his worshipper picked up the stick and
retreated downstairs. There was certainly no estab-
lished set form in this religious business; but I suppose
there must on occasions be some special ceremonials
when priests are needed, for two or three of them,
dressed in the fashion of stage heralds, came out from a
little back room, stared at us, and retreated, closing
the door behind them. The worshippers passed in and
out, and to and fro among their gods with perfect non-
chalance. There was neither reverence, nor superstitious awe, nor fanatical devotion visible among them.
What seemed to be their favourite, judging from the
number of his worshippers, was a huge monster like an
immense painted wooden doll, with flaming vermilion
cheeks, and round black eyes starting from his head.
He was dressed in wooden robes of the gaudiest, strongly
contrasted colours, and surrounded by all kinds of
tinselled magnificence, in the way of gilt paper, artificial wreaths, and wax roses as large as cabbages,
while standing before him on the altar was a bowl of
ashes stuck full of Joss sticks, some burnt out, some still
smouldering, the offering of later worshippers.

The altar is of ivory, and is exquisitely carved and
gilt. It illustrates the history of some great battle which
was fought two thousand years ago. It is protected,

and so partly hidden, by a wire network. There are
sundry other smaller altars and idols in the same room.
Some are distorted libels on the human form divine;
others are grotesque representations of birds, beasts, or
reptiles held sacred by the Chinese; some are of
bronze, or of brass, and some of painted wood. There
are no seats, and the floor is thickly sprinkled with
sawdust. The walls are hung with scarlet and blue
paper prayers and gilt thanksgivings. Among these
was an advertisement, which our guide translated to
us. It was the offer of a reward, not for the discovery
of a murderer, but a reward for the committal of a
murder. Ah Fooh and Wong Ah had roused the
anger of the great Joss, who promises to grant the
prayers and take into special favour him who will put
the obnoxious Ah Fooh and Wong Ah out of the way;
viz. the gods will favour him who commits the crimes,
which are no crimes when the gods command their
committal. Our guide informed us that the objection-
able parties would assuredly " disappear," no one
would know how, or when, or where. Such murders
are never discovered. The Celestials hold their secrets
close, and it rarely happens that one will bear evidence
against another in our courts of law. If he does, well,
it is likely enough he " disappears " too. They care
nothing for our laws and customs, and have a supreme
contempt for our legal institutions. They have their
exits and their entrances, their lotteries, their imports,
exports, diversions, secret tribunals, and punishments
of which we know nothing. They are under the
surveillance and rule of the Six Companies, who hold
supreme authority over them. They have laws within
our laws, which are to us as a sealed book. They

rarely, if ever, appeal to the United States authorities for the settlement of their difficulties. If they do the judgment is sure to be reversed in their own courts, the prosecutor is tried and punished by the secret tribunal, and the whole affair is shrouded in a mystery that the outside world can never penetrate.

We passed from this large and most important chamber through a nest of dingy, dirty rooms, each presided over by a god or goddess more or less hideously grotesque, and lighted only by a tiny glass lamp, which hangs before every shrine, and is kept burning night and day. Each has a bronze bowl of Joss sticks burning in his or her honour, filling the air with smoky, stifling incense. Lying about on sundry small tables are miniature copies of their ugly idols, and tiny curiosities in the shape of birds, beasts, and fishes, all part and parcel of Chinese mythology. There were some superb china vases (which would make the eyes of the collector twinkle), filled with tawdry paper flowers, standing here and there among Joss sticks and split bamboos, sometimes used in the interpretation or divination of the will of the gods. Brummagem decorations and tinselled magnificence abound everywhere. In one room was a curious adobe oven. We wondered whether it was used to bake Christians or purify the heathen, but we learned that it was used at certain seasons of the year when Satan is symbolically burned, he being represented on the occasion by torn strips of red paper, which have been appropriately cursed and sentenced by the priesthood. The smaller gods had fewer worshippers, and it was strange to observe there was not a single woman among them. Perhaps, having no souls to be saved in the next world, they have grown weary of praying for the good things of this. In every room, great and small, there is a rough wooden structure like a very tall stool. Within it hangs a bell, and above it either a gong or a big drum. These are used to rouse the drowsy gods from their slumbers, or to attract their attention when they have been too long forgetful of the desires of their devotees. Wherever we went a crowd of these olive-skinned, pig-tailed figures gathered silently as shadows about us, staring at us with their melancholy, expressionless eyes. The Chinese seem all to be made on one pattern. They have all the same serenity of face, of gait, and manner; their features never stir, their eyes never vary, they never gesticulate, are never excited: only the meaningless smile that is " childlike and bland" occasionally creeps over their faces. The more we see of these strange, passionless people, the stranger they seem to us, and we more fully recognize that they are an utterly alien race, whom we can never comprehend. Looking on their sphinxlike faces we wonder what feelings, what human passions, what emotions, lie hidden beneath them. We might as well try to solve the riddle of the Sphinx's self. But in spite of their impassibility we feel that the barbarous element is there, steady, strong, and cruel. The Chinese are a puzzle, which the subtlest minds have failed to piece together. California has a hard nut to crack, and I fear it will break its teeth before it gets to the kernel.

CHAPTER XVII.

The Pawnbroker's Shop—The Opium Dens—The Smokers—A
World within a World—The Women's Quarters.

WE were rather tired of our night's wandering, but as
we did not desire to encroach upon the kindness of our
guide by occupying his time on another evening, we
resolved to see all that was to be seen at once; we
therefore retired to a restaurant for a temporary rest
and refreshed ourselves with tiny cups of tea. Neither
milk nor sugar is served with this refreshment; only a
grape or raisin is swimming in the liquid amber, which
has a delicious flavour, quite different from the finest
Chinese tea imported for European consumption. Our
escort endeavoured to dissuade us from farther pene-
tration into the mysteries of Chinatown, as he feared
we might be shocked at the sights and scenes there;
but we had left our nerves at home, so girding on our
mental armour, we sallied forth again.

We turned into Sacramento Street, and descended
one of those cellar flaps, where the barber was still busy
with his tonsorial operations. We passed through his
pigtailed congregation of customers, some of whom
looked as though they sorely needed combing, and

N

found ourselves in a dingy pawnbroker's shop, lighted by a single oil lamp, and certainly not more than twelve feet square; but every nook and corner, hole and crevice, from floor to ceiling, was crammed with a miscellaneous collection of unredeemed pledges. There were clocks, caps, quaint Chinese ornaments in great variety, which the collector might search the civilized world for in vain; firearms and pistols of all patterns and all ages (most of them, we were informed, were loaded); daggers and knives without end; among them was the curious fan-shaped stiletto, which may be carried in the hand by a lady without rousing a suspicion as to its real use, for when sheathed it represents a closed fan; some of the knives, their favourite weapons in social and street warfare, are short and broad, some long and narrow; the most formidable are about a foot long and six inches wide; these are used in pairs, one in each hand. Our escort informed us that with these implements he had known one belligerent Chinaman slash another into an unrecognizable mass in less than five minutes. Besides these there were beds, bedding, divers articles of clothing, cooking pots and brass pans; in fact, everything except the sacred pigtail, without which a Chinaman can hope for no honour in this world nor any glory in the next.

Through this, we stooped our heads and passed under a low doorway into a black hole—I can describe it in no other way—where there was a bin for ashes or kitchen refuse and a heap of battered pots and pans; a wooden bench or stool, black with grime, a few wooden bowls and chopsticks, while sundry bits of rag hung on a line over our heads. A coolie was crouch-

ing over the fire in one corner, stirring some horrible
compound with a long wooden spoon. The fire
sputtered and sent forth feeble flame flashes and dense
volumes of smoke, through which the swarthy form of
the crouching coolie loomed upon our sight like the
evil genie of some Arabian tale. This was a kitchen!
There was no chimney, no window, no drainage. And
in this foul den scores of hungry Celestials would come
presently to feed. From this we entered a labyrinth
of galleries, running in all directions. On either
side were rows of small chambers, honeycombed with
an economy of space that outwits the invention of the
white man altogether. The majority of these are just
long enough to lie down in, and broad enough for a
narrow door to open between the two beds of straw,
each of which contains two sleepers. On reaching the
end of this gallery, we were informed that it was a
hundred and twenty feet long. There is no ventilation,
and not a breath of air enters, except from the cellar
through which we entered, and even that comes filtered
through the barber's and pawnbroker's shops before
alluded to.

We gladly return to the fresh air, but only for a
moment's breathing-space before descending to still
deeper depths. The very bowels of the earth, it seems,
are riddled and honeycombed by these human moles,
who, like the ghost of the murdered Dane, can " work
in the dark.". We light a candle, which burns but
feebly in the subterranean darkness of this double
night. We thread our way single file, keeping always
within an inch of our escort's coat-tail, and descend
into these lower regions. Here in the heart of a city
filled with light and beauty, we find ourselves groping

our way two storeys underground by the light of a
tallow candle! Through dingy courts and alleys, up
steps and down steps, round corners, and up or down
zigzag stairways, we explore the mysteries of Chinatown. It is as dark as Erebus; only the light of our
one solitary dip flickers in our eyes; we feel as though
there is something weird and ghastly clinging to ourselves, for our voices have a smothered, hollow sound,
even to our own ears. No one really knows how far
these human gophers have burrowed underground;
they wander, it seems, from one living grave to another; perhaps to avoid taxation, the assassin, or the
grip of the law. It is a dismal city of refuge for lost
souls.

If Dante could have cast his sorrowful eyes into
these dark regions, he would have found here an
appalling reality which outstrips the imaginary horrors
with which he has illustrated his *Inferno*. We gather
up our skirts and pick our way slowly, for the ground
is slippery with Heaven knows what, and the walls
are reeking with black slime, the odour is horrible,
and everywhere there is an accumulation of filth which
ought to breed fever and death, but does not. We
suddenly turn into another of these narrow galleries;
on either side are mangy-looking curtains, some partially closed, some open; the ceiling is so low we can
almost touch it standing on tiptoe, yet on either side
there are two tiers of hard wooden boards, divided by
a slight partition into sections, each being large enough
for two occupants, and every bunk is full. This is one
of the numerous opium dens. Some are preparing the
enchanting poison—a tedious process, which reminds
one of an incantation scene; the two lie face to face,

chatting in low voices, a look of delicious anticipation glowing in every feature; they recline at full length, their heads reposing upon blocks of wood or roughly improvised straw pillows; a small lamp flickers between them; their long pipes are of bamboo cane; at the lower end of the stem is an earthen bowl; a jar of opium, a kind of thick, black paste, stands close to the lamp; the smokers dip a wire into this paste and then hold it in the flame till the particles of paste which cling to it fizzes and bubbles; it is then deposited on the rim of the pipe-bowl, and the smoker at once inhales three or four whiffs, which empties the pipe, and the process of refilling is renewed. It is evidently a labour of love with them, for their eyes glisten and gloat upon the bubbling drug. They take no heed of us; we are mere mortals, *they* are far on the road to paradise. Their talk grows gradually less and less, feebler and feebler; their low laughter has a delirious sound; their eyes are filled with a dreamy light, but their lips are glued to that magic tube; they are rapidly floating away to a land we know not of; their fingers relax their hold; they sink back upon their pillows and are suddenly silent; their dusky faces ashen pale, having the look of some plague-stricken corpse: this one pair of opium-smokers represents the many. We drop the curtain and pass on, making our observations as we go. Some have had their delirious dream and are sluggishly stirring, slowly awakening back to life, and with wan, haggard faces stagger out of the dingy den into open day; some flit past us like ghostly shadows, wandering through the shades of Hades; they glide along shrinking against the wall, and stare at us with lack-lustre eyes, mere spectres of humanity, not humanity itself. But when such men as William Blair, Richard Baxter, De Quincey, Coleridge, and others become victims to the habit of opium-eating, what wonder is it that an enslaved and degraded race should rush into a temporary world of dreams and enjoy its delirious delights, little heeding of the thraldom eternal and immutable which will follow their awakening?

This terrible drug (which, for a time, fills the brain with feverish dreams of ecstatic delight, but is the sure forerunner of unimaginable horrors and agonizing death) lies within the reach of all. One of the most celebrated opium-eaters tells us that "happiness may be bought for a penny and carried in the waistcoat pocket, portable ecstasies may be had corked up in a pint bottle, and peace of mind may be sent out in gallons by the mail-coach." In some parts of India opium is taken by the criminal condemned to death. If he can only get his brain filled with opium fumes he may be said to die happy. We grope our way through this Inferno, obscured by the dense smoke of the poisonous drug, and are glad to breathe the fresh air of heaven once more.

Then we pass on to the women's quarter. The Chinese rarely, very rarely bring their wives or families across the water; but they import large numbers of female slaves of the most degraded class, and for the most immoral purposes. These poor creatures have no sense of degradation, no knowledge of morality, they but fulfil the condition they are born to. So loosely, indeed, are social and domestic ties held by these people, that if a wife displeases her husband, or a child her parent, they have the right, and frequently exercise it, too, to sell either one or other to some trafficker in human kind, and take the profits as in any other mercantile transaction. A sense of dignity or family pride prevents the higher class of Chinese from entering into this sale or barter business. They have other ways of disposing of their surplus womankind.

We entered a long narrow court with tall, dark houses on either side, so tall they seemed to shut out the skies; but in this confined space are domiciled twelve hundred of these females slaves, for slaves they are still, though sojourning in a free land, and by the law free agents, but the law is powerless to reach them. They are held in bondage by their own people and by the laws of their own nation, which no good Celestial, especially a woman, would dare to call in question. They have no thought of any higher state. If, by chance, as sometimes, though rarely happens, a creditor appeals to the United States law to settle his affairs, no matter what decision is given it is sure to be set aside by their own tribunal, and the prosecutor has reason to bewail his temerity in daring to appeal to any other. In all cases, whether of murder or lesser criminalities among themselves, they are examined, tried, condemned, and their punishment, be it torture or death, is carried out by their own secret tribunal, whose laws are to us a sealed book, and whose councils here are held in some hidden underground spot that we know not of.

We picked our way through the dingy, deserted court, for though it was the women's quarter, there was not a woman to be seen. Some were evidently indulging in social festivities, for the sound of the gong, rasping fiddles, and screeching voices broke upon the silence of the night. Shadowy forms, like creatures from another world, stole by us with their noiseless tread and disappeared in the doorways on either side. We grope our way along by the light of our one solitary dip, and become suddenly aware of a dim light falling across our pathway. We look round and observe an open grating about a foot square, and framed therein is the face of a Chinese belle. There she is precisely as we see her on our fans and tea-trays, her hair dressed in wings or fancy rolls and pinned with gilt pins, and profusely decorated with paper flowers of various colours, one half of her face being painted a bright vermilion in one blotch, beginning from the chin, covering the eyebrows, and reaching back to the ear. On either side were the same gratings, with the same painted beauties behind them.

We went our way through the silent moonlight with a strange, weird feeling falling over us, as though we had been wandering in dreamland, or living through the misty pages of the " Arabian Nights."

CHAPTER XVIII.

CHINESE AMUSEMENTS.

Gambling Dens—Theatres—An Acrobatic Performance—New Year's Visits—The Bride—The Hoodlum—A Scare—The Matron's Pretty Feet.

GAMBLING is another of the favourite vices of the Chinese, and is popularly indulged in by all classes, though it is strictly forbidden by the United States laws; but the evasion of legal authority is mere child's play to them. These numerous gambling dens are so carefully guarded that only the private police (some of whom, I am told, are in the pay of the Celestial authorities, and when gold dust is thrown in the eyes who can help blinking?) can ferret them out, and only then on rare occasions and with great difficulty.

So great is their passion for games of chance that they will sell or pledge anything to obtain the means to indulge in it. Not only are cards, dice, and dominoes used, but straws, sticks, brass rings, etc., are thrown upon a table, or on a mat upon the ground, while silent, eager faces crowd round, and the fate of the players literally hangs upon a breath. There are a hundred of these establishments under the eyes of the police. Some of them employ private spies to warn them in case of danger; but these places are seldom raided by the police, for they know it is almost impossible to storm the barriers in time to catch delinquents in the act. On the first sign of danger a warning signal is sounded throughout the building, and a sudden change seems to take place in the ground plan; passages are shut off; the pursuer, rushing along the winding ways he thought he knew, finds himself in a blind alley; a mysterious sliding-panel takes the place of a door, or he rushes into the suspected chamber,—he is fooled again! He finds nothing there, only a harmless Celestial, smiling and bland, most innocently employed making a cup of tea! Every sign of guilt is swept away. The arch hypocrite knew the enemy was coming long before he had time to appear.

Dramatic performances, too, are a passion with the Chinese. In a space of half a mile there are no less than four theatres, though there is nothing to distinguish these places of amusement from the general run of houses except the scarlet hieroglyphics which are pasted on the doorposts and a row of paper lanterns over the doorway; sometimes a flag flutters from the balcony. A discordant din of gongs, tin trumpets, and squeaking fiddles wanders out into the street. Celestial economy of space follows us even here. Within a few feet of the entrance door a moon-faced Mongolian sits receiving custom, fifty cents for admission the beginning of the evening, the charge dwindling down to five cents as the hours roll on. A paper curtain was lifted aside, we ascended a flight of dirty stairs, and were at once ushered into our box, which had been previously secured for us; once seated therein, we proceeded to survey the scene at our leisure. The house was crowded from floor to rafter. It is divided into two parts, the pit or parquette, which slopes upward from the footlights to the back of the house; above that is a gallery, which extends over and seems ready to fall on the heads of those below, and rises steadily backwards till the last row of Mongolian heads seems to touch the ceiling. On one side are three private boxes, if they can be called private, for they are simply partitioned off, breast high, from the rest of the gallery; these are reserved for the use of the more distinguished visitors. On the opposite side a similar portion of the gallery is partitioned off for the use of the women, for even in this (the only recreation the poor creatures seem to have) they are not allowed to participate with their lords and masters. The partitions in all cases are so low that every one is in full view of the rest of the house. There is no attempt at ornamentation anywhere; the walls are whitewashed; benches, etc., are all of the roughest description. The stage is merely a raised platform, with a few wooden steps on either side, up and down which actors and audience are constantly passing; there is no scenery, no decoration of any kind. The musicians are seated at the back of the stage, and on either side is a curtained doorway, through which the entrances and exits are made. No drop-scene falls between the acts, and there is no attempt at realization anywhere; no regard is paid to the fitness of things. Say there is a wedding, a battle, and a death; the priestly cortége walks out at one door, the warriors enter at another, each whirling one leg as he leaps from an imaginary horse; there is a tremendous uproar and they dash at once into the fray. The musicians in the background are pounding away at their discordant instruments, each making as much noise as he can with no regard whatever to rule or rhythm, while one invincible hero with a pasteboard sword keeps a whole army at bay. He slays them by scores, but as fast as they are slain they get up, run round to the back, and begin the fight over again. At last the hero is overpowered; a hundred swords pierce him to the heart, he is trampled on, and he goes through all the contortions of a horrible death; then gets up, smiles, nods at the audience, and conquerors and conquered crowd off the stage together.

At the moment we entered a battle royal was going on; the noise was deafening; we had been warned of this, and plugged our ears with cotton-wool, but that was slight protection; the waves of sound struck upon the drums of our ears till our brains seemed to feel the blows, and our heads ached distractedly.

It was a strange sight—that mass of shaven faces, their slant eyes fixed with intense earnestness on the stage, revelling with solemn delight in the ludicrous performance. They never applaud, they never condemn; but sit stolidly smoking. The women, too, indulge in the fragrant weed, and largely patronize the seller of sugar-cane and sweetmeats, who stalks about the house with a basketful of these dainties on his head, but makes no sound, utters no invitation to buy. The battle was succeeded by a domestic disturbance of the most uncelestial character; the wife ran about the stage screeching like a wild cat, her indignant lord pursuing her with furious threats and grimaces, leaping over invisible chairs and tables. At last a window was brought in; she rushed behind it, and so made an imaginary escape from his fury;

being so far safe, she leant out, Juliet-fashion, he
making frantic attempts to get at her ; and they
rehearsed their difficulties with an accompaniment of
gongs and fiddles, their screeching voices reminding
us forcibly of a wrangling duet between two irate tom-
cats on the back tiles. This was succeeded by a half-
military, half-acrobatic performance. First a warrior
entered with a wild moustache and grey-green beard,
marvellous to behold ; his nose and ears were painted
white, with black rolling eyes, and altogether a most
ferocious aspect. He flung his sword up in the air,
whirled round on oné leg, shook his fist menacingly,
as though defying some one to mortal combat. His
challenge was accepted. A score of warriors entered,
surrounded him, shook their swords, and rushed about
as though in the fury of battle. Soon their arms were
flung aside. They had evidently changed their minds,
and the warfare resolved itself into an acrobatic display.
They twirled round like dancing dervishes, leapt into
the air, made two or three somersaults, rolled themselves
into balls, fell and rebounded from the floor like india-
rubber. They turned like wheels upon the ground, or
spun like tops in the air. So rapid were their movements the eye could scarcely follow them. One weird,
half-naked figure, with his face and body painted in
stripes of different colours, went through the most wonderful contortions. He tied his legs round his neck,
leaped high in the air and came down upon his elbows,
walked on his head without the use of arms or legs,
rolled himself into a knot and flung himself into the
air. Having gone through sundry other evolutions
too complicated to mention—indeed, having done
everything but turn himself inside out—he left off.

These performances are supposed to lighten and vary the dramatic representation, which generally lasts six or eight weeks, giving two or three acts every night.

On the occasion of the Chinese New Year, which fell in early February, we accompanied a friend to pay a ceremonious visit to some wealthy Chinese merchants, with whom he had been in the habit of transacting business. It was a general visiting day, when everybody belonging to the flowery kingdom called on everybody else. All the streets in Chinatown were gaily decorated with flowers, flags, and paper lanterns; gongs were beating, cymbals clashing, and fiddles scraping in every direction; the streets were thronged with moon-faced Celestials in gala dress, all pricked out and polished fresh from the hands of the barber.

Our first visit was to Ki Chow, one of the leading merchants of San Francisco. We descended from the street, as usual, and found ourselves in a large cellar filled with benches and forms; a fire was burning in one corner, where cooking was being carried on. This was where Ki Chow's *employés* fed. Leading out of this was his private apartment, which contained a few rough wooden seats, a worm-eaten desk, and two tables, furnished on this occasion with an elaborately chased silver service, goblets, tankards, etc., and a display of cut glass of rare antique shapes, ornamented with gold and crimson; decanters filled with choice wines, trays and filigree baskets with cakes and sweetmeats. On one table was a hideous figure of a favourite Joss, before whom a light was burning. Sweets, wines, and other good things were placed before him for his godship's special entertainment. The liberal and dainty display on the other non-illuminated table was for our mortal gratification. We were compelled by Chinese etiquette to take a tiny toy glass of wine, which we cautiously sipped, it being a foreign production, and as our host informed us, " velly stlong " ; it was rich, luscious, and of a peculiar flavour. " It velly good, it made of lice," said Ki Chow, the loss of the unpronounceable " r " in this case giving the announcement a peculiar character. He next passed round tiny blue willow-patterned plates, containing cake covered with red cabalistic characters, dried fruits, nuts, candied watermelon, and numerous unknown uninviting compounds of a gelatinous nature. The fruits and candies were very good ; the oily cakes we could not bring ourselves to touch. Ki Chow invited us into the cellar adjoining, which was his bedroom ; it contained a bed with silken hangings, chairs, and a table decorated with a vase of blooming flowers, which seemed sorely out of place in this dingy stifling nook, lighted only, like a prison, from a grating along the top. Ki's wardrobe was strung up on a line overhead. He was evidently proud of his bachelor quarters. He nodded, smiled, and volunteered the information—

" Me have tlee wives, all gone back to China ; when they here, me have big house."

On our expressing a desire to see a Chinese lady, he offered to present us to a friend who had lately married and brought his wife to San Francisco. We accepted the invitation, and accompanied him to Wong How's forthwith. It was a large roomy house in Sacramento Street ; the entrance-door was on the latch as usual, and we ascended a flight of cleanly swept stairs to the first floor ; one tap at the door and it was opened by a most majestic-looking Chinese gentleman, very handsomely dressed in blue silk and gold embroidery.

He received us with high-bred courtesy, with a layer of formality on the top of his politeness; he spoke in the purest English we had heard from Mongolian lips. This apartment was very handsomely furnished, with quaintly carved ebony chairs, and lounges and tables beautifully inlaid in the finest style of Chinese art, some with gold filigree, others with ivory or tortoise-shell, and the windows were draped with curtains of gorgeously embroidered silk. Here, too, were tables spread, one for the god, one for the visitors.

We had scarcely seated ourselves when other visitors began to arrive in quick succession, one after the other, and host and guests salaamed and saluted each other in true Oriental fashion, lifting the two hands to their foreheads, and bending lower and lower till their heads almost touched the ground; then followed handshaking, and a babble of soft, liquid tongues, evidently exchanging cordial good wishes. We inquired for the lady.

"Oh! she come plesently; she flightened; me only mallied tlee months, and she never seen no more man but me; to-day she bling coffee and sweets for evelybody; it is our custom fol a wife to wait on her husband's fliends once in evely year; she never see man other times."

In a few minutes the poor little bride entered, bearing a silver tray filled with little cups of the national beverage. She was gorgeously dressed in pink silk, trimmed with silver embroidery, interspersed with pearls, her hair bowed and puffed, and decorated with pins and flowers, according to the fashion of her people. She was leaning on two waiting-maids, who had much ado to support her tottering steps between them. She was painfully shy, and trembled, so that the cups and saucers rattled on the tray, and kept her eyes fixed upon the ground, trying to screen her face with a large feather fan; but we could see her lips quiver, and the deep blushes that dyed her face and neck contrasted with the red paint upon her cheeks. We compassionated her distress too much to keep her long under our gaze, and having received our empty cups upon the tray, she was scurrying off in a great hurry to get out of sight, but was somewhat harshly recalled by her lord, and more dead than alive, blushing and trembling more than before, she dragged herself across the room to serve her master's friends as any other slave would have done.

"She velly pletty," remarked Wong How confidentially to me, as the poor creature shuffled off the scene. Of course we contributed our share of admiration, and her owner coolly said: "Me got two more like that in China."

We were the only Europeans present, and while we were gathering scraps of information from our host, the door opened and some rakish-looking young hoodlums, the special production of San Francisco, being a cross between the French gamin and the English rough, half entered the room, exclaiming with a jaunty, patronizing air—

"How are you, John? We've come to pay you a morning call; hope you're glad to see us." Our host stepped forward with much dignity, saying—

"Excuse me, I have ladies here." The intruders at this moment caught sight of us, snatched off their

caps, and with some half-uttered apology beat a hasty
retreat. A number of cigars and a quantity of sweets,
which they had no doubt purloined from some other
"John," rolled out of their hats upon the floor, and
they never stopped to pick them up. Wong How
secured the door from further intrusion.

We were listening to the chatter and watching the
collection of dark expressionless faces, when Ki Chow's
countenance suddenly changed; an unearthly pallor
overspread his face; he lifted his finger with a rapid
motion. " Come! " he exclaimed, as he flew to the door
and descended the stairs, we following as fast as our
feet could carry us. Arrived in the street, we hurried
after Ki Chow and inquired " What was the matter?
What had occasioned his sudden flight? He had not
even given us time to exchange parting civilities with
his friends! " By this time Ki had recovered his usual
equanimity; he turned upon us a face smiling and
bland; innocent and unconscious as a child he exclaimed—

" Me no understand. Me takee see other lady."

What it was that caused our sudden retreat we shall
never know. It must have been something serious,
for I shall never forget the horror-struck expression
of Ki Chow's face. Until that moment he had most
deferentially made way for us to precede him; then,
he had flown down the stairs, his blouse and pigtail
flying behind him, merely calling to us " Come! "

The " other lady," to whom he now introduced us,
was a matron of five years' standing; a relative of
his, I believe. We found her in a similarly handsome
apartment to that we had just left, attended by two
maids, who stood behind her and only moved to assist

her in rising or walking. At her feet was a quaint
little bit of living China, a miniature man, pigtail
included, frolicking among his toy-gods and tin soldiers.
He stared at us with his beady black eyes and retreated
behind his mamma, who rose up saying—

"How you do? Me velly well." She shook hands
and invited us to be seated. She spoke a little English,
giggled a good deal, seemed pleased with our admiration of her clothes and of herself (for she was as
gorgeously apparelled as the other), and appeared
ready and willing to gratify our curiosity so far as
she was able. We examined the gold ornaments she
wore upon her arms and neck, and the huge hoops in
her ears. Her outer dress was of light blue, artistically
and richly embroidered with silk, the colours beautifully blended together. We picked up her long loose
sleeve and counted six dresses which she wore one over
the other, all of different-coloured silks ; they were so
soft that the whole together did not seem much thicker
than half a dozen layers of tissue-paper! We examined her complicated head-dress, which was quite
an architectural trophy, so greased and waxed and
strained, such wings on one side, such plastered puffs
on the other. We inquired how much time was daily
spent in the arrangement.

"Me no dless evely day. Me takee down in tlee
or four days, and doee up again."

"How do you lie down ? how do you sleep ? " we
inquired. She despatched a maid for her pillow—a
round block of wood, covered with silk—which she
placed at the back of her neck.

"Me sleep so, allee same so." A novel way of
taking rest.

We showed her our big feet; she showed us her little feet, *i.e.* a small misshapen hoof. We had always believed that the Chinese ladies really had small baby-feet, which had never been allowed to grow; but Ki Chow informed us that they never meddle with the feet till the child is from *six* to *eight* years old, when they gather the toes together and twist them under the foot, then bind them with strong ligatures, which on no pretence whatever are loosened or taken off for two years, the whole of which time the child is, of course, undergoing great torture.

"Me have two little girls in China," said Ki Chow, coolly. "My wife lite me word she makee tlem pletty feet now, and they cly, cly, all night, all day, allee same, till two years gone."

It would be curious to inquire how this barbarous custom first obtained, and how long, in these days when enlightenment is creeping into the heart of China, it will be permitted to endure.

CHAPTER XIX.

CHRISTMAS ON A CALIFORNIAN RANCHE.

Old Friends—The Ranche—Christmas Day—Salinas Valley—
A Magic City—A Californian Sunset.

CHRISTMAS has come. So the almanac tells us, but we can scarcely accept the fact, Christmas being associated, in our minds, with frost and snow, fogs and rain, which seem so far away now we feel as though the damp, chill atmosphere could never enfold us again. Here we look from our windows on a bright, sunlit scene, where the tall, green palms stand fair and stately in the city gardens, and calla lilies lift their fair faces to be kissed by the sun. The skies are intensely blue, and the breeze clear, cool, and invigorating as the breath of our own spring mornings. Every day we say, " This is the finest we have ever seen," but the morrow comes and brings with it another as lovely as the last. Our thoughts fly homeward, as, indeed, they often do. We know that the sleet is beating against the windows, the bleak wind tearing through the streets, whistling through every crevice, chilling the marrow of those who are shivering at the fireside, while the world without is lying stiff and rigid in its shroud of winter snow. We think of the friends who

have been so long and so dearly associated with this
season. The charmed circle was broken " A year and
more agone ! " Since then link by link has dropped,
familiar faces have faded into shadowy memories. One
after another, they have followed rapidly "into the
silent land," "the land of the great departed," till this
world seems to be growing empty and the next filling
so fast we feel we shall scarcely be sorry when the
order comes for us to " move on " and join them.

But here the sun is shining, and somehow, in spite
of the leaden weight upon our spirits, there is something in this health-laden air that stirs the spirit and
sets the pulse of life flowing as in its first springtide;
and, though we know the autumn of life is upon us
and the winter may not be far off, ready to sprinkle its
last snows upon our heads and write *finis* to our life's
history, yet our hearts grow lighter and rise, as though
inflated with this brilliant atmosphere, till we feel like
floating away in the sunshine. After all, the living
must march ever onward, and leave the dead days
mouldering behind them.

We loved the city which our new friends had made
so pleasant to us, but we were not sorry to pack up
and leave it for a while. We were going to spend the
Christmas on a Californian ranche with some old
friends who were closely connected with the " days
that are bygone," but who had been living in the wild
part of this Western world for the last five-and-twenty
years. No doubt we each expected the other to be
changed past recognition; for my part, I thought to
find the dashing young officer, who had borne himself
so bravely during the Russian campaign, developed,
through agricultural association and pursuits, into a

Californian farmer, somewhat lanky about the lower limbs, hollow-cheeked, and with the soft and by no means unpleasant drawl of the native Californian.   I do not know why I was so strongly impressed with this imaginary portrait, for, since my advent into the State, my preconceived opinions concerning it had undergone a rapid transition ; things were so different from what I had expected ; even the Californian drawl had dwindled into a thing more imaginary than real.

We leave San Francisco on Christmas Eve, a brilliant, sunshiny day, and take our seats in the cars of the South Pacific Railway, with a protest against the heat, for, December being a winter month according to the division of time, the stoves are lighted at either end of the car ; the blinds are closed to keep out the burning rays of the sun, but they keep in the stifling hot air of the stoves till the crowded car becomes uncomfortably close and warm.   The rest of the passengers sit and bake in uncomplaining calm ; to us the suffocating air grows unendurable ; we get out and sit upon the steps of the rear platform, and are whirled along through pretty home scenery at the not especially rapid rate of twenty miles an hour.   We have not long been in possession of this position when a polite brakesman taps me on the shoulder.

" Sorry to interrupt you, ma'am, but you see what's written there," he said, pointing to a warning above the car door.

. I look up and shake my head with the blank ignorance of the " heathen Chinee."   " I can't read," I say.

He translates the sentence :   " Passengers are strictly forbidden to stand on the platforms."

" Ah! but we are not standing," I exclaim, exult-
ingly, " and there is no prohibition against *sitting*."

He smiles, vanquished, and leaves us in possession of
the field.

After a run of about four hours, we steam into
Salinas station. But few passengers alight. The
generality are going to places beyond. We had
scarcely time to step out upon the platform and
glance round, when the only occupant thereof—a tall,
stately gentleman—came hurriedly towards us, and,
in unmistakable British accents, welcomed us most
cordially. The tones of the well-remembered voice
came back to me like the melody of an old song that
has slept in the memory for years and is awakened
suddenly by a new singer in a new land. A bridge
seemed to be flung over the gap of time, and we old
friends met as though we had parted but yesterday.
Yes; we had both changed. I had developed from a
mere thread paper to—but no man (or woman either)
is bound to criminate him or herself. He had grown
from a rather languid, delicate young fellow to a
strong, stalwart man, broad-chested, with muscles and
biceps which warranted him to come off only second
best in a tussle with a grizzly; the fine-featured face
was bronzed and full, but the smile and the kind
brown eyes were still the same. He pointed out to
us the ranche as we bowled over the rough, uneven
road. It is about three miles distant from Salinas,
and, being situated in the flat, extensive valley, it was
visible from the moment we left the station behind us.
The tall, substantial windmill which surmounts the
waterworks, and the numerous white adobe buildings
gathered round the main dwelling-house, give it the

appearance of a pretty rural village lying sleepily in the sunshine.

The Valley of Salinas itself is neither pretty nor interesting. It is about twenty miles long and proportionately wide. The land is rich and productive, and every rood is well under cultivation; but we miss the beautiful green hedges which divide the fields and border the pleasant country lanes in the old country. Here there is no such luxuriant landmark; not a bush, not a tree to be seen; nothing but the wide, level plain surrounded by a perfect amphitheatre of hills and mountains covered with dark pine or sombre fir trees. Occasionally, we are told, their bald heads are covered with snow, which is rarely known to reach the valley below.

The ranche stands some distance from the roadway, and is approached by a long, wide avenue. On either side are planted rows of trees, which don't seem inclined to grow; they look weird and sickly, and, though they have been coaxed and nursed in the best agricultural fashion, they will not put on their dress of luxuriant green; they look dismal and melancholy, as though they wanted to expand into respectable, shady trees, but have not the heart to do it; they seem to feel the cruel gopher feeding on their roots and sending the poisoned sap through their tender veins. This is the third year this experiment has been tried and failed, as it is failing now.

We drive through this avenue and through an old-fashioned, arched, adobe gateway into an open court-yard. On one side is a collection of adobe buildings, the dwelling-places of former inhabitants, but which are now used as barns or lumber-sheds, and are the sleeping-places for the farm labourers. On another side is a low range of adobe rooms or houses, comfortably fitted up, where some of the male members of the family sleep. On the left-hand side is the family residence, a comfortable frame house, two storeys high, which was sent out from England years ago, and, after travelling half the world over, was planted in that far-away corner of the Western world. It is arranged and furnished in every way according to the requirements of a refined and cultivated English family. A large hall has been added to the main building, forty feet long by twenty wide, with a great, old-fashioned bay-window at one end, looking out in a sweet, wild wilderness of a flower-garden. A wide chimney, with andirons, whereon pine logs are plentifully laid, ready for kindling, is on one side, a piano stands opposite, cosy rocking chairs, and other signs of a comfortable home life are scattered round the hearth; a long table runs down the centre of the hall, which is generally used as a dining-room when the family is increased by guests who, like ourselves, find always a welcome at the ranche, and come not in "single spies, but in battalions." The laundry stands in a corner of the courtyard, opposite the gateway, and the dairy in a field beyond. We received a cordial welcome from the ladies of the family. A collection of pretty girls and fine, manly young fellows, the sons and daughters of the house, came out into the courtyard to meet us. It was a pleasant sight, that father and mother, still in the prime of life, with their unbroken circle of blooming girls and sturdy boys around them—children of the Old World taking root in the soil of the New. I found my host was more British than ever. So far from his interests and sympathies with the Old World languishing or lessening from his long sojourn in this far-away land, they were keener than ever ; he marches side by side with us in all social questions, and is more thoroughly conversant with political matters, both at home and abroad, than many who are in our midst. Papers, magazines, pamphlets find their way from the heart of London to the core of the Western world. We found the daughters of the house purely English in thought, tone, and feeling, all their aspirations rising towards the old land, and their longings turning thitherward, while the sons seemed as purely American in theirs.

Behind the ranche, and as it were keeping guard over it, rises Gapilan Peak, the highest and loveliest of all that mountain range. It seemed so near to us that I proposed a morning scramble and luncheon on the top, but I was speedily informed that it would take a long day, of pretty rough travelling too, to climb the rugged mountain sides, and would necessitate spending a night on the summit, from which, however, could be seen a most glorious sunrise. This sounded romantic, but I had no desire to taste the doubtful delight. We occupied the principal guest chamber, which had no actual communication with the house, but opened on to a wide verandah, which led down through a deliciously wild garden direct to the woods. As we lay in our beds at night we could hear the coyotes come howling down from the wilderness, but the deep bay of our good watch-dogs speedily chased them off the premises. We had no fear of tramps or stragglers, for we had gallant defenders near, with guns and rifles loaded.

On Christmas Day there was a frost, and the ponds

were covered with a coating of ice. They said we had brought an English Christmas into the midst of the sunlands. Such a thing as frost and snow had not been known there for twenty years. A clear, cold, frosty air, blue skies, and a blazing sun roused us early in the morning, and on descending to the breakfast-room we found pretty souvenirs of Aballone jewelry, peculiar to California, beside our plates, and the Chinese servants had presented the members of the family with some native toy., according to their custom.

At dinner the large family circle was increased by the advent of some solitary friends and neighbours. We were merry and sad and glad together. We thought of those who were gone, but we talked of those who remained. Our host proposed "The Old Country." I think there was a tug at our hearts, and our voices were scarcely steady as we rose with one accord and accepted it. I presently whispered a name which was caught up and echoed from one end of the table to the other—" With love and greetings across the sea." Then somebody suggested that " Rule Britannia " would be appropriate for an after-dinner melody as we gathered round the blazing pine fire. Forthwith that lady commenced ruling " the waves," and I don't think she ever performed that ceremony with more true and loyal hearts around her. We were all feeling ridiculously patriotic. We grumble when we are at home, and are severe on the faults and failings of our Motherland; we pick holes in her best coat, and find flaws in her finest policy. But when we are away, and thousands of miles of land and sea divide us from her,—well, she might beat us with her trident and we'd forgive her !

We passed a delightful time with this interesting family. We all had our own opinions, and strong ones too. We drove about the country, or roamed through the woods all day, and in the evening gathered round the fire (for it was cooler here than in the city), and discussed ourselves and our American cousins. We picked one another to pieces, and put ourselves together again, amid much fun and laughter, and a tolerable amount of fairness on both sides.

We had often heard our host alluded to in the local papers as "the Big Bug of Salinas;" a strange phrase, which sounded to us of the offensively facetious order, but it was not so held by the inhabitants of the place; by them it is employed quite as a title of honour, and applied to one whom all the towns-folk held in the highest esteem. It is no wonder that the people of Salinas paid this tribute of respect to our host, for he was the founder of their city, and it is entirely owing to his enterprise and judicious management that it has grown to be the important place it is. Twelve years ago the Salinas Valley was a vast uncultivated plain, with two wretched tumble-down Spanish villages—Natividad and Santa Rita,—both of the most miserable description, which are settled in one corner of it. He chanced to be passing through this lovely tract of country, where a winding river trailed its silver waters; numbers of waggon trains and other traffic passed along this valley on the way to Monterey and other settlements on the coast, and he thought it would be an admirable site for a halting-place. To think was to act. He bought an extensive tract of land, consisting of many thousand acres, selected an appropriate spot, and staked out lots

for streets, churches, public buildings, etc., and advertised them for sale in all the Californian and many other
papers.   His venture met with entire success ; the lots
were bought up and building commenced with great
rapidity, and the place has now developed into a city
of between three and four thousand inhabitants, with
numerous aids to religion in the way of churches,
a bank, a town hall, and even a prison, which was
occupied on the occasion of our visit by a handsome
horse-stealer and a predatory Chinaman.   The former
was stretched upon his straw pallet reading a recent
copy of the *Atlantic Monthly*.   The city of Salinas is in
a most flourishing condition ; building is still going
on, and as the wind blows fresh faces thitherward
it promises to double its present numbers before many
years are past.   The whole of the valley, as I have
said before, is in a state of high cultivation.   There are
several flourishing farms and extensive fields of grain.
Opposite our entrance gate is a cornfield more than
two miles long.

We soon exhausted the beauty of Salinas Valley,
but could not so easily exhaust the hospitality of our
friends, who resolved to escort us on a tour to
Monterey, one of the oldest Spanish settlements along
the coast, where there are still the remains of a most
interesting mission built a century ago.   We are to
start in the morning, and we go out to take a last
evening stroll, escorted by all the young folk of the
family, one of whom, a young gentleman aged seven,
proves an heroic acquisition.   He marches in front
of us, runs after the squirrels, chases the gophers into
their holes, pelts the pigs out of our path, and at last
compels an advancing corps of cattle to turn tail and

run, while we take shelter from their crumpled horns behind a gatepost.

The sun sinks rapidly behind the hills, and leaves the Western hemisphere aglow with golden light, with feathery plumes of crimson, isles of amber, and pale amethyst cloudlets floating therein, changing and amalgamating their gorgeous hues, till they form one brilliant cavalcade of coloured glory. Long after the sun has departed the skies retain their brightest blue ; slowly the trailing skirts of the twilight cover them, and we take a last look at the mountains shrouded in the purple mist peculiar to the Californian climate, which for the time gives them a mysterious airy appearance, as though they were growing in cloudland rather than on this solid earth of ours. In the glowing daylight this airy drapery is invisible ; it is only seen when the shades of evening begin to fall.

CHAPTER XX.

IN THE VALLEY OF CARMELO.

Monterey—The Ruins of the Mission—The Spanish Inhabitants
of the Old Town—The Moss Beach—The Lighthouse—The
Pebbly Pescadero—Good-bye.

WE reach Monterey in the cool of the evening. A
queer, tumble-down Spanish town lying close along
the sea-shore. One or two fishermen are trailing their
nets on the face of the water, and some fishing-smacks,
with their brown, patched sails, are anchored in the
bay, and are rocked so gently by the waves they seem
to be coquetting with their own shadows. Not much
more·than a century ago a host of Spanish vessels
sailed into this now lonely and deserted harbour, their
colours flying, their decks crowded with soldiers,
sailors, priests, and nuns. Here they landed in search
of a good site whereon to found a mission for their
priestly labours. They stationed themselves on an
elevated point about two miles from the sea ; there the
labour of love began. They built a *presidio* for the
soldiers to protect the fathers from the native Indians.
Every man who had hands to work devoted himself to
the cause, and laboured till the church and mission
buildings were completed. All that part of the

country was taken possession of in the name of the King of Spain, and the work of conversion began. The ceremony was performed with a blare of trumpets, beating of drums, and salvos of artillery, calling out an army of echoes from the surrounding hills and mountains. The poor Indians were at first dazed with the display of tawdry magnificence and frightened at the · thundering sounds which shook the air and seemed to make the solid earth tremble beneath their feet; but by degrees they approached, and then learned that this wonderful expedition was organized expressly for their benefit. Peace in this world and glory in the next was freely promised them. The gates of Paradise were opened before them; they had nothing to do but walk in and take possession. Scores were converted every day; they bowed down before the altar. The acolytes swung the incense, the fathers preached and chanted in an unknown tongue, the nuns, from behind their grated gallery, lifted their songs of adoration and praise, and the poor heathen souls were caught up in the great mystery and won to God.

From Mexico and Spain settlers soon came flocking into the beautiful valley, establishing themselves upon the sea-shore, building dwellings, grazing cattle, and growing fruits and flowers, increasing and multiplying themselves and their houses till the city grew and, for a time, flourished in peace and plenty, carrying on a thriving trade not only with Spain and Mexico, but with the inhabitants along the coast. The descendants of the first settlers, to a great extent, still occupy the now half-deserted, dilapidated town. The mission church, presidio, and other buildings appertaining thereto are on an elevated spot some two miles distant

P

from the town, overlooking the lovely and extensive Carmel Valley.

Only a century ago the church was filled with priests and converts, the presidio. with soldiers, their clanking arms and breastplates glittering in the sun; vessels rode at anchor in the harbour, and crowds of Dutch and Spanish traders, with their bales of merchandise, swarmed upon the silver-sanded beach below. Now all is gone, like painted shadows fading from the sunshine.

The church, crowning the hilltop and dominating the landscape for miles round, is one of the most beautiful, picturesque, and perfect ruins upon the coast. Its exterior is complete, even to the rusty bell which still hangs in the belfry tower, and creaks with a ghostly clang when the wind blows through; and we are surprised to find so much of the decorative masonry still intact. Dilapidated saints and cherubs, with broken trumpets and mouldering wings, still hold their places, while all around is slowly but surely crumbling to decay; and, though in places you may see the daylight streaming through the roof, you can still ramble through the nuns' gallery and look down upon the altar, where the broken font still clings to the wall.

On the occasion of our visit, a small side chapel or vestry was decorated with ivy, evergreens, and paper flowers, and tin sconces, with the remains of guttering candles, were left upon the walls. It had been evidently used very lately—by the villagers, perhaps, for some festive gathering. The extensive range of adobe buildings which surround the church and were occupied by the converts and day labourers, are still in a state of semi-preservation; the roofs are gone, but the walls are still standing. The whole of these sacred possessions were enclosed, and entered then as now by a massive gateway at the foot of the southern slope.

The town of Monterey is only interesting from its association with the past. It is dirty, it is dusty, it is utterly void of all modern improvements. Streets! there are none to speak of, except, perhaps, a row of slovenly shops which have been run up by some demented genius the last few years. The old adobe houses—and they are all made of that species of sun-dried clay—straggle about in the most bewildering fashion; it is much easier to lose your way than to find it. The people are all strongly characteristic of their Spanish origin; they are a dark, swarthy, lazy-looking race, and scarcely seem to have energy enough to keep themselves awake. Their houses have no pretension to architecture of any kind; there is no attempt at pretty cottage-building or rural decoration; not even a creeping plant is trained to hide the bare walls; they have low doorways—a tall man must stoop to enter them — and small, square windows set in the thick clay walls. I suppose the men *do* work some-times, but I have seen them at all hours, shouldering the doorposts, smoking in sombre, majestic silence, while the wives sit on stools beside them, generally with bright-coloured handkerchiefs pinned across their breasts, huge gold hoops in their ears, and often thick bracelets on their arms. In her barbaric love of dis-play the woman forms a picturesque and striking figure in the shadow of her majestic lord; she is a piece of brilliant colouring, from the full, red lips, rich-hued complexion, to the sparkling black eyes which illuminate the whole.

In the heart of the town there is a long, low range of deserted buildings formerly occupied by the military; the windows are all broken, the worm-eaten doors hang, like helpless cripples, on their hinges, and only the ghostly echoes of the wind goes wandering through the empty chambers. In all quarters of the town you may come upon houses with windows patched or broken and padlocked doors, the owners having died or wandered away, and no one (but the rats) cares to take possession of bare walls. Nobody heeds them; they are left to natural decay. We passed some lonely, barnlike dwellings, with curtained windows and large gardens behind, where we could see the orchard trees, and flowering shrubs, and white winter roses growing; these were shrouded with almost monastic quietude. We go to the primitive Catholic Church on Sunday, and wonder where all the beautiful women dressed in their picturesque national costume have come from. They have a proud, haughty look upon their faces, and seem to resent our intrusion. These, we were told, are the aristocratic remains of the ancient dwellers in the city, who form a small, exclusive society among themselves, and live in the secluded barnlike buildings above alluded to. Some are in the midst of the town; some scattered on the outskirts. The music was good and the service reverently conducted.

There are two or three old-established hotels, all of a more or less indifferent kind. We went to the best, which is of quite a second-rate character, but it serves well enough as a resting-place for passing tourists. The inhabitants are strictly conservative—not with the true spirit of conservatism, which retains the best and improves or lops off what is bad in its constitution, but they carry out the conservatism of ignorance; they will not advance with the age; "what was good enough for their forefathers," they argue, "is good enough for them; as they were in the old days, so they are now; they plod along in the old groove, and keep to their old customs, and nurse their old superstitions with undeviating blind persistency. Why should they trouble about improving?"

There is not a drop of water fit to drink in the whole city. The bright sparkling springs may be bubbling beneath their feet, but they will not dig for it. The tourist must drink aerated water, lager beer, or a poisonous decoction called *wine*. Even the visitors have hitherto been content with the meagre accommodation afforded them. The United States, which, as a rule, is quick to perceive and put its progressive ideas in motion, seems to have forgotten Monterey and left it, so far, to govern itself. But things are changing now. People are awakening to a sense of the importance of Monterey, which might, and most probably will, become one of the most delightful seaside resorts in the State; it has every requisite to make it most attractive. It has excellent facilities for bathing, a magnificent sea view, and the walks and drives about the surrounding country are beautiful in the extreme; there are wooded bosky dells, luxuriant green valleys, and undulating hills on every side, and it is in close proximity to points of great interest; the roads are pleasant and easy to drive along; in fact, the only want at Monterey is accommodation for visitors, and that want is being rapidly supplied. A monster hotel of quaint Swiss architecture is in course of erection within a short distance of the town; it is partially surrounded by a wood of scented pine and grand old forest trees, and a wide, magnificent sea view stretches before it; its appointments are to be. of the most luxurious description ; hundreds of busy workmen are employed upon it, and a promise is held out that it will be opened for this summer season.*

One clear, cool morning we pack a luncheon basket and start for a " cruise on wheels." We drive first past the old mission buildings to the Moss Beach, lying along the shores of the Pacific Ocean, and so called from the peculiar mossy .character and beauty of the seaweed it flings so liberally along the pure, white sand, for the beach here is like powdered snow, and stretches far into the wild inland, its still, billowy waves sparkling like diamonds in the sunshine. A few miles farther on, and after a pleasant drive through pretty home scenery, we pass a Chinese fishing village, it being a mere collection of miserable hovels, and, as an Indian decorates his wigwam with scalps, these are hung inside and out with rows of dried and dying bodies of fish. The beach is covered with their bony skeletons and fishy remains in different stages of decomposition, and the whole air is redolent with an " ancient and fishlike smell." We are satisfied with an outside view, and have no desire to explore, but drive on as fast as we can till we reach the " pebbly beach of Pescadero," which is quite a celebrated spot. People come from miles round to visit it, and spend many hours in hunting for moss agates ; for these, and many others of a beautiful and rare description, may be found in great numbers there. But apart from the chance of

---

* Since these lines were written the Hotel Del Monte has been completed and is now opened.

finding these treasures, the pebbly beach is in itself a great attraction for its rarity, as all along that portion of the coast there is only a sandy shore.

Thence we drive on to the lighthouse, which stands on a rocky eminence jutting out into the sea. We climbed the narrow stairway to the top, and enjoyed an extensive panoramic view of the wild sea and wilder land surrounding. A lonely, desolate place it was, and to some folk would be maddening in its monotonous dreariness, with the waves for ever beating round its rocky base, varied only by the screech of the sea-birds or howling of the wandering wind. Yet even in this bleak spot the keeper has coaxed flowers into growing, and hollyhocks, scarlet geraniums, dahlias, and other hardy plants are blooming round the lonely dwelling.

We are to take our lunch at Cypress Point, which we reach about three o'clock in the afternoon. This interesting and romantic spot which we had selected for our temporary festivity is an extensive grove, a miniature forest of cypress trees, covering and growing to the very verge of a lofty cliff which rises about two hundred feet perpendicularly from the sea. Their sombre forms, still and motionless, though a stiff breeze is blowing, turn oceanwards like dark-plumed, dusky sentinels keeping watch and ward over the rock-bound land. How many centuries have they stood there? Their age is beyond our ken. We feel the strange fascination of this gloomy spot. The ancient trees have grown into strange, fantastic forms. Some lie prone upon the ground, gnarled and twisted as though they had wrestled in their death-agony ages ago, and left their skeletons bleaching in the sunshine, for like the whitening bones of a dead man they crumble at the touch. Some have twined their stiff branches inextricably together, apparently engaged in an everlasting wrestling match. Here, like a half-clothed wizard, stands a skeleton tree with withered arms outstretched, and crooked fingers pointing menacingly at its invisible destroyer. On every side the weird, strange forms strike the imagination, and though the sea is laughing and sparkling in the sun, and the soft wind fanning us with its cool, invigorating breath, the grim, silent congregation gives us an uncanny feeling, though we gather under their shade and eat, drink, and are merry. We shiver as we think what a spectral scene this cypress grove must be in the moonlight.

We drive through the beautiful Carmel Valley, with its wealth of picturesque beauty spread in rich luxuriance for miles round us. Wood and water, undulating hills and grassy slopes succeed each other, making a natural panorama, as we drive slowly on, taking in the dainty scene with unwearying eyes. Occasionally we passed a lonely farmhouse in the valley, or a chicken ranche half hidden among the trees on the hillside. These, we were told, are many of them occupied by English gentlemen of culture and education. Indeed, not only in this part of the country, but all over California and in Colorado, in corners farthest away from the sight and sound of their fellow-men, we find our countrymen have settled down as tillers of the land and cultivators of the soil. We are sometimes disposed to wonder what has driven them to these far corners of the earth. With some, perhaps, a love of adventure ; a desire to form a part of the electric life of a new land. One gentleman informed us that he had been plucked at college; another had failed in a public examination. They had generally been crowded out of the Old World by failure of one kind or another, and wandered away to the New, where there is room for men to build up another life, and every facility for striking out " into fresh fields and pastures new." They appear prosperous, happy, and contented, but one and all seem to encourage a desire to return to the old land " when the children have grown up."

Our pleasant visit came to an end. I don't think any of us cared to say " good-bye," but we went through the ceremony with dignified calm. The wonder rose in our hearts, though it never reached our lips, " shall we ever stand face to face in this world again ? " " Perhaps," whispers hope softly. We shake hands. " Good-bye," " Good-bye." With a shriek and a whistle our train steams onward. We carry away with us, and I hope leave behind, many pleasant memories of our Christmas in California.

CHAPTER XXI.

ON THE BANKS OF THE BAY.

Now Year's Visits—The Gentleman's Day—Local Attractions—
Berkeley College—Saucelito—In Arcadia—Among the Woods
and Flowers—A Fairy Festival.

THE streets of San Francisco are empty—that is, empty
as regards the female population.   Not a petticoat is to
be seen ; Kearney is deserted, and masculine humanity
is left in full possession of California and Montgomery.
Rank, beauty, and fashion is " receiving " to-day.
Buggies, sulkies, rockaways, and every conceivable kind
of vehicle, filled with gentlemen in evening costumes,
are dashing frantically along the streets; hospitable
doors are open, and a constant stream of the nobler
sex flows in and out ; they come and go in such quick
succession it seems as though they were shot out of
a catapult one moment and shot back the next.   It
is a sort of " go-as-you-please " visiting race, and he
who pays most calls between midday and midnight
rises to an imaginary place of honour.   The 1st of
January is essentially the " gentleman's day."   Every
lady—that is, everybody who is anybody, and many
who are " nobodies," who hold neutral ground, and
cling, like a ragged fringe, to the skirts of society—

stays at home to receive New Year's calls and friendly greetings from her gentleman friends. The advent of a lady on this occasion would be considered an outrage of all propriety. Sometimes ladies unite, two or three together, and hold their mutual receptions under one roof, generally choosing the most important and most central position, so as to simplify as much as possible the labours of their admirers. Their decision is generally announced to the world in this fashion : " The lovely Miss A. and the accomplished Miss B. will assist Mrs. So-and-so in receiving to-day." Although the sun is shining brilliantly without, the windows are closed, the gas lighted, the rooms beautifully decorated with choice flowers, and the ladies descend in their full accoutrement of charms and enter into this artificial night to receive the greetings of their several admirers. This custom obtains in all the great cities of America, but in San Francisco it is held in the fullest splendour and maintained with the greatest tenacity. The next day the press teems with a thrilling account of the day's proceedings. Whole columns of the *Chronicle* are devoted to details of the ladies' dresses; the number of their visitors are duly chronicled, and woe be to the delinquent *he* who has failed in his duty; the rest—well, I fancy there is a good deal of uncharitableness working behind a masked battery of smiles·in the exchange of female confidences on the next day's meeting.

The time flies so fast in this beautiful, hospitable land that we are anxious to make the most of it, and, having fulfilled our engagements in the city, we decided to pay flying visits to some of the lovely resorts lying along the banks of the bay, which,

as I have said before, is large enough for all the
navies of the world to play hide-and-seek in. Oakland, perhaps, takes precedence, it being the most
extensive, the most important, and certainly among
the loveliest of these rural suburbs. It has a railway
of its own dashing through the crowded public
thoroughfares from one end of the town to the other,
its engine bell cling-clanging, warning everybody out
of the way as it charges onward. There are plenty of
handsome shops, some very fine churches, banks, and
a free mercantile library, presided over by an accomplished and efficient lady librarian, for female intellect is held at a higher premium, and is utilized
to a greater extent in the New World than in the
Old. Branching off from the populous highway are
picturesque grassy streets, with quaint or fanciful
dwellings on either side, all detached and surrounded
by blooming gardens, stretching away on all sides, till
the busy, bright little town, with a series of coquettish
manœuvres, touches the green slopes of Berkeley, the
seat of learning, the fount of knowledge, whence the
youth of California draw their mental sustenance.
There stands Berkeley College, presided over by Professor John Le Conte, one of the most eminent classical
scholars of the day, of European reputation. The pro-
fessors are all chosen from the foremost rank of whatever branch of study they adopt. The college is formed
upon the principles of similar institutions in England,
and, if they take proper advantage of the benefits to be
acquired there, the Californian youth should be second
to none. The building itself is of handsome red brick,
massive and simple in its architecture. It lies at the
base of the foothills, surrounded by a luxurious growth

of green, and it forms a principal feature in the landscape for miles round. Oakland and Berkeley seem to run hand in hand till they are lost and buried in the green hillsides. Many of the citizens of San Francisco make their homes in those attractive suburbs, which lie about eight miles across the bay. Magnificent ferryboats, decorated with mirrors, carving, and gilding, with luxurious lounges and velvet carpets, ply to and fro every half-hour during the day. Alameda, St. Quentin, and many other sylvan retreats are settled down in cosy nooks scattered round the bay, all being equally attractive and easy of access.

One bright February morning, when the bay is as smooth as glass and a score or two of vessels with sails all set to catch what little breeze is stirring are floating like white birds on the face of the water, and the sky wears its Californian livery of intense blue, we start to spend a long day at Saucelito, which lies in quite an opposite direction across the bay. We watch the steep streets of the city (the people passing to and fro, the vehicles crawling up and down are dwarfed to the size of dolls and toy carriages) recede from our view. We pass by "the silent guns of Alcatras"; they are muzzled, masked, and silent now, like lions couchant and asleep, but should danger threaten that city of the sunland they would rouse up and roar as loudly as in days gone by. Small green islets, some sparsely inhabited, others the solitary home of the waterfowl, are scattered round the fortified island. These, with the richly wooded hills surrounding this part of the bay give a picturesque beauty to the scene. The briny breeze, laden with three thousand miles of iodine, sweeps through the Golden Gate, and as we breathe this health-giving air our pulse quickens and we feel we are taking a lease of a new life, and as though lassitude of limb or weariness of heart could afflict us never any more. There is a glorious sunshine over-head, and we look out through the Golden Gate at the silvery Pacific stretching away and lying like a bar across the distant sky, while behind us a chain of soft green and purple hills embrace the peaceful Bay. The fresh invigorating wind sets our cheeks aglow, and our spirits seem to rise on invisible wings. We feel it is a glorious thing to live. Life *is* worth the living while there are such days and hours to enjoy, and our hearts sing their voiceless song of thanksgiving, which only God can hear.

The boat slackens speed. We have been so occu-pied by the extensive land and sea views that we have failed to cast our eyes towards the sheltered nook we are now fast approaching. We seem to have come suddenly upon a delicious bit of Italian scenery trans-planted to this far corner of the Western World. The richly wooded land rises before us, clothed in its glory of luxuriant green. A few tiny cottages are strewn along the bay shore, and we catch glimmerings of white-faced, red-tiled dwellings, hidden here and there among the trees on the sloping hillsides. Two or three drowsy officials are lounging about the landing-stage, and a shabby-looking vehicle, with a skeleton steed, stands baking in the hot sun, waiting for pas-sengers. But there is no one else about, no sign of humanity abroad, everything is quiet and peaceful everywhere; it seems as though nature had taken all her living children in her arms and lulled them to sleep in the sunshine.

We climb into the vehicle aforesaid, and begin slowly ascending the undulating hillside. It is a lovely, winding road, with luxuriant trees, flowering shrubs, and sweet-smelling wild flowers sloping away from us on the one side, and climbing up the gradual ascent on the other. The brisk breeze which had swept so keen and invigorating through the Golden Gate dies away here into a murmuring soft and low, making music in the tall tree-tops, stirring the leafy branches, and coquetting with the wealth of wild roses. Here and there we come upon some quaint, fanciful dwelling peeping out from a bower of green, the gardens running out in unconfined loveliness, as though they were proud to show their blooming progeny to the passing world outside.

There is no such thing in America as hedging and walling in private grounds for the solitary gratification of the owner only. Everything is liberally and lavishly thrown open for all the world to see, and in so much, the poorest tramp trudging along the road, or the poorest labourer in the field, shares his more fortunate neighbour's wealth, and may enjoy the luxury of the rich man's pleasure-gardens, even as the rich man shares with him the sunshine God freely gives to all. Although, according to the division of time, it is early spring, it might be blooming summer-time, for here it is the very carnival of flowers; they are everywhere growing in such glorious profusion, too. The dainty plants, such as geraniums, fuchsias, myrtles, roses, etc., which we are accustomed to see flowering in pots or perhaps growing two or three feet from the ground, here expand into monstrous bushes or tall graceful trees. We have stood under a geranium tree and looked up, through its wealth of scarlet blossoms, at the blue sky beyond. Camelias, orchids, and other delicate plants and shrubs bloom out in the open air, laden with a gorgeous display of dainty flowers. We counted one hundred and ten waxen white camelias on one tree alone, and were lost in admiration of the California Acacia, which flung out its golden banners on every side, its soft fluffy blossoms, like plumes of fairy feathers, hiding every trace of the green leaves which gave them such fostering shelter only a few weeks ago. We wound our way slowly through this romantic Arcadian scenery; there were no wanderers, no tourists, no tramps astir; the narrow winding road was solitary enough, except for once or twice, when we overtook a batch of women, in short petticoats and sun-bonnets, trotting along singing, in not unmusical voices, to beguile the way. Our skeleton steed, jingling his bells as though to advertise to the world how much work he was doing, suddenly pulled up at the foot of a rugged green bank, broken with rustic steps, leading up to a kind of "Glen Eyrie" or eagle's nest, half hidden in the rugged hillside. This was our destination; we climbed up the rough-hewn steps and found ourselves at the entrance-gate of a pretty white cottage with a verandah literally covered with creeping plants running along in front of it.

Our hostess came out to greet us—a sweet, grave-looking woman, whose smiling eyes had a shade of something in them, as though, in some invisible part of her nature, there was

> " A feeling of sadness and longing
> That is not akin to pain;
> Which resembles sorrow only
> As the mist resembles rain."

She formed a pretty picture, standing there beneath her trailing vines to welcome us wanderers from the Old World. We followed her into a long, low-roofed, comfortable room, with chairs and lounges covered with the skins of animals; cases of rare birds, and butterflies, and natural curiosities of all descriptions were arranged on all sides; gatherings of great rarity from the bowels of the earth, realms of the air, and the depths of the sea, spoils from the very heart of nature were arranged in every nook and corner. Both within and without the house everything was quaint, picturesque, and suggestive of Old World fancies.

Our hostess was one of those women to whom Pope alludes as

" Mistress of herself though china fall."

It appears we had mistaken our day. We should have put in an appearance the day before, when all preparations had been made for our entertainment. Now the lady was alone, absolutely alone in the house. Her Chinese servants (they all employ Chinamen here) had gone to participate in some national festivity, and the sudden irruption of half a dozen unexpected guests must have been trying to the nerves of our solitary hostess. We ought to have grovelled in the dust, but didn't. She was equal to the occasion, and, in a genial, pleasant way, made us feel quite at home—as though, indeed, we could not have come at a better season. We all enjoyed the idea of a general picnic, improvised on the spot, and, amid much chatter, laughter, and the mildest of mild jokes, there was a stampede towards the larder; but the idle drones and butterflies of the party (whose offers of assistance in the culinary department were wisely declined) went

Q

wandering about the wilderness of a garden and strayed out into the sweet-scented woods beyond, looking down through the tangled branches upon the shining bay below. A perfect paradise this Saucelito seemed to us, made up of flowers, and peace, and sunshine; a fitting birthplace for romance; the cradle of poetry, where fine thoughts are nursed till they burst out into full-fledged phrases, and fly abroad, and stir the soul of the world with their wise philosophy or tender song. Presently the melancholy voice of the horn came moaning through the woods, calling us to return. We knew what that meant, and were not slow in obeying the summons, taking with us such healthy appetites as would have digested the sole of an old shoe if dressed to taste.

We found our way into the kitchen, where the feast was spread. It was not a commonplace kitchen, where the whole culinary battery is unmasked and its mysteries are carried on before your very eyes, and clatter of pans and frizzle and frying take away your appetite without opposition on your part. This was a poetical kitchen, with no signs of prose about it; coppers bright as mirrors reflected you from the walls, multiplied you by scores, till the room seemed full of your shadows. Quaint old china decorated the dressers; bunches of the beautiful pampas grass and vases of wild flowers were ranged upon the shelves. The most useful articles were of an ornamental character. Standing in one corner was a shining black, quaintly designed stove, with bright brass knobs and decorated scrolls, polished to the highest point of polishing, like a black prince with " gilded honours thick upon him." His fiery eye was closed; he had done his work

and was at rest. From the bowels of this gnome had
been conjured the dainty repast which awaited our
attack. A table spread with fine linen, rare glass,
and quaint old china, such as would have made a
collector's mouth water, was ranged along one side of
the room. As for the repast, it was a *recherché* thing,
that might have tickled the palate of an epicure.
There were broiled chickens, crisp salad, mayonaise,
and such rich, luscious fruit and cream, with lovely
flowers and trailing smilax nestled among them. The
very wine, as it was poured out into the Venetian
vine-stemmed glasses, seemed to bubble and sparkle
and cream over, as though it quite enjoyed being
drank out of such rare prettiness. We kept the door
which led into the garden wide open. The tall calla
lilies bent their fair heads, and the saucy red roses,
blushing at their own beauty, sent their perfumed
breath wandering towards us, fluttering their tender
leaves as though to frighten away the droning bees,
who would rifle their sweets before our eyes. A whole
squadron of familiar shrubs and flowers were gathered
thickly round them, and they shook out their rustling
leaves, nodded their fragile heads, and stared in at us
with their white and violet eyes. We stared back and
thought how lovely and refreshing it all was.

Our day in this modern Arcadia passed quickly,
too quickly; we would fain have put on the drag and
kept it for awhile. The purple mist began to fall
over the mountain-sides as we started on our way
homeward through a beautiful wide cañon, fringed
with graceful ferns and tall stately trees, screening
from our sight the light of the setting sun; a poor
little wandering stream crept in and out among the

broken boulders, as though it was tired and wanted to rest somewhere, and was trying to find its way to the great sea; once absorbed in the everlasting waters there would be peace, or it might chance to filter its way down to the hearts of the dead men who lie there shrouded in weeds waiting for eternity. We were late in reaching the boat, for we had been tempted to linger by the way; the bell was ringing and we had scarcely stepped on board the boat, when the engine gave a great satisfactory snort, swung round and started.

The sun had already sunk behind the hills, and the shades of twilight were rapidly closing around us, but the red clouds were still floating in the west, and ragged banners and broken bars of gold still streamed through the darkening skies. It was quite dark when we reached San Francisco; we saw the lights in her steep streets, and the fiery eye of the dummy dashing up and down, and the red and white car lights flashing hither and thither like fireflies; truly she looked like a queen gorgeously arrayed, flashing her diamonds of living light in the face of the sombre night.

CHAPTER XXII.

IN THE FOREST PRIMEVAL.

Pleasant Retreats—Californian Trees—Cañon and Forest Scenery—
Duncan Mills—A Stormy Evening—The Redwoods—Farewell
to the "Golden City."

THERE is so much that is beautiful, and of a most
varied kind of beauty, from the magnificent and sublime to the pretty and picturesque, all along the wonderful Pacific Coast, and reaching inland to rivers and
mountains, you might spend many months there and
not have time to exhaust, nor even to thoroughly
enjoy, them all, but to those whose time is limited it
is difficult to know what to do with it; but there are
some places which must be visited, some things which
must be seen. There are the orange groves of Los
Angeles, where you wander for miles through forests
of golden fruit, which, in this month of February,
have just reached perfection, and are ready for the
gathering. Men, women, and children are busy at
their work, piling the dainty fruit in bushel baskets,
with such delicate handling that not a bruise shall
fleck the smooth gold skin, while the air is literally
laden with the pungent perfume. Some of the fruit
grows to an immense size, as large as melons, but

what they gain in size they lose in flavour; in fact, it is so with the generality of Californian fruits, which are magnificent to look at, both as to size, form, and colour, but they seem to have outgrown their strength and weakened their flavour, for it is very inferior to that of the same kind of fruit which is grown in the Eastern States. Of course there are exceptions, but I refer to the rule.

San Joaquin and San José are the most wonderfully prolific wheat-growing countries, perhaps, in the world. The grain grows so tall, so heavy and full, that the tasselled ears droop and seem toppling over from their own weight. These miles of fair fruitful lands lay rolling out from the foot of the mountains, catching every gleam of sunshine, absorbing every breeze that blows. Thriving farms are scattered throughout these valleys; on all sides there are vineyards, grain fields, orchards, and extensive cattle ranches; signs of thrift and prosperity are evident everywhere. It is very pleasant to pass through these highly cultivated lands, where civilization has left her mark in such unmistakable characters; but Nature in her wilder stages, amid her kingly rivers, her lakes, her unapproachable mountains and untrodden forests, is more sublimely impressive.

We were anxious to visit Yosemite Valley and the Mariposa Grove of big trees, but that was impossible, the valley being still snowed up, and the roads leading thereto rough and almost impassable. In order to be thoroughly enjoyable a pleasure excursion to the Yosemite Valley should be taken from early June until late October; during these months the magnificent scenery of this wonderful valley is seen in the highest perfection. Of course there are many adventurous spirits who make the tour at all seasons of the year, and force their way into the valley when it is clothed with icicles and crowned with snow. As we must, perforce, miss the Yosemite for this year at least, we decide on a visit to the Redwood Forest in Sonoma County. Once more we cross the bay, pass on the other side of Alcatraz, and thread our way through the green islets surrounding it till we are landed at St. Quentin; thence we take our tickets for Duncan Mills—the railway station is close to the landing stage. It is a narrow-gauge line; the carriages or cars are long and narrow; we can only sit three abreast. It looks like a train of tiny toy carriages, but our bright little engine is up to its work, and carries us on in a swift, spirited way, as though it was taking a holiday on its own account, not at all on ours. It looks like a serpent winding its way through a paradise of luxuriant green. We run alongside of Tomales Bay, nay, run into it, and cross its long arms more than once. Scores of wild ducks and geese are skimming along the face of the water. On one side of the bay is a range of low-lying hills, while our little train is puffing along on the other close under the shadow of massive gray rocks, with skeleton trees and stumpy bushes growing out of their broken sides. We pass the pretty fishing village of Tomales, and some few queer-looking hovels, on the edge of the bay, inhabited by Indians, for the squaws and little brown children are grouped under the eaves mending nets or making willow-baskets. We soon leave the bay behind us, and pass by picturesque villages nestling peacefully among the foothills, and here and there a

half-ruined deserted dwelling at the mouth of a deep
cañon, which leads hundreds of miles away into the
wilds where the brown bear feels safe from the hunter
and the young wolves bay the moon at night. We
cross deep ravines upon narrow trellis-work which
would have made us shudder in the old days. Presently we find ourselves running along the base of
thickly wooded hills, with their wealth of strangely
beautiful trees, which were new to our eyes. Here
are a group of Madroño trees, with their orange-
coloured bark, sometimes deepening to crimson, but
always shining and smooth as polished ivory, their red
veins running like graceful lacework through their
leaves of tender green. These lovely trees will flourish
nowhere but in their native woods. All known
methods have been tried to raise them in ornamental
grounds, but they obstinately refuse to take root; in
spite of the tenderest care they droop and die. Then
comes the Manzanita, with its pale-green leaves and
delicate pink blossoms, drooping in bunches so close
to us we could reach out our hands and pluck them
as we pass. We are going now at only the rate of
ten miles an hour, and the conductor occasionally gets
off the train and runs alongside, gathering flowers or
specimen leaves for us till we are overladen. Higher
up the hillsides stand whole families of ash and poplar,
looking as fresh and green as the hand of spring could
paint them. Here, grim and hoary, rise a company
of live oaks, their ragged mossy robes scarce covering
their long straggling limbs, but hanging all over them
like a jagged fringe or gray beard matted and falling
from its bald head, twisting and writhing round it as
though to strangle the little life that lingered in its

gnarled and knotted trunk. The scene changes, and, glancing across on the other side of the bed of the Russian River, we see the fir and pine trees growing in dense dark masses, with here and there a clump of golden trees, like yellow islands in a sombre sea of green. Presently we reach the forest, drive into it and through it for many miles; the dark trees, grown so straight and tall and strong in their native solitudes, close round us on every side. Looking upward we can scarcely see the sky, and the sun tries hard to fight its way down through the branches, but only succeeds in sending a bright lance here and there to smite the ground we are rolling over. Then the forest, on one side at least, falls back and climbs the sloping hills on our left. On our right lies the Russian River, which has followed us all along, winding its way through the dense forest, playing hide-and-seek with the sun; sometimes with silent, secret persistency forcing its way through broken boulders and other natural impediments which hinder its progress; then, dividing its forces, creeping stealthily through narrow crevices till it unites again with double strength, and storms its way onward till it reaches a low-lying rocky ledge, and sweeps over with a thunderous roar and falls into its bed below. It is all right now, and its swirling waters roll on, leaping and laughing in the sunshine, on their smooth and pleasant journey towards the sea. Here and there we pass a wooden house lying upon its side in the bed of the river. Some of these capsized cottages are entire, as though they had merely toppled over; some are dilapidated and broken like match-boxes. We wonder how they got there, and are told that a few months ago the river rose fifty-four feet,

overflowing its banks, and, rushing in its mad, headlong course through the country, swept all before it,
leaving the *débris* where it still remained, some lodging
on the banks and some lying in the bed of the river.
The wreckage of homes and lands are strewn for miles
along the river's course. We had but one fellow-
passenger through all this journey, and he was
shrouded in self-complacency and a linen-duster. He
sat with his hat pulled over his eyes, and his nose
buried in a book ; he never once looked out on the
grand scenery we were passing through ; but that was
Nature's book, perhaps he couldn't understand the
language. He had been a candidate for Congress, we
were told, and failed ; if he had been a candidate for
Napa Asylum, I think he'd have got it.

Duncan Mills is the terminus ; the train goes no
farther ; it lies in the very heart of the forest. It is
a mere station ; it cannot by any stretch of fancy be
called a village. It consists of one handsome residence, the home of Mr. Duncan, the owner of the great
lumber mill, whence the station takes its name. The
wood, cut down some miles away, where they are
clearing the ground, is floated down the Russian River
to its destination here. There are also some half-dozen
cottages for the lumbermen, a livery stable, where
excellent horses and carriages may be had for excursions in the surrounding country. Of course wherever
a train stops there must be a hotel ; here is one, a
pretty rural-looking place, two storeys high, with a
verandah running all round it, externally most pleasant
to look at, and the interior arrangements render it a
most delightful place for a temporary residence. In
summer it is crowded with tourists, who are sometimes

so charmed with the picturesqueness of the place as to settle there for many weeks, and season after season visit it again. Its surroundings are lovely and romantic in the extreme, mountain, river, and forest scenery lying close round you. It was the off season, the tourists had not yet began to arrive, consequently we had this charming primitive hotel all to ourselves; there were no chambermaids, no Chinamen.

"We arrange things on a different plan when the real season begins," said our hostess, a pleasant-mannered, sensible-looking woman. "We have plenty of waiters and that kind of thing, but till then my daughter and I manage the work between us."

We were glad to have arrived at a season when there were no "waiters or that sort of thing;" it was pleasanter to be waited upon by our landlady and her charming young daughter than by a pig-tailed "Chinee" or the supercilious white, who looks as though he was doing you a favour every time he hands you your soup. A violent storm arose on the evening of our arrival. There was a kind of haze over the sky, and the sun set with a heavy mist circling round it. We looked out and watched the gathering shades of evening creep down the sable-skirted pine forest, and were struck by the intense silence; the invisible insect world seemed suddenly to have sank to rest; there was not a sound on the earth nor a tremulous motion in the air. A black darkness by degrees overspread the heavens, and big raindrops began to fall faster and faster, splashing on the verandah outside. The wind, from a low sullen murmur, swelled to a perfect gale; we heard it sweeping down the defiles and hurrying along the hillsides, shrieking like a company of fiends, surging round and battling with the big trees till they groaned and reeled and shivered beneath the assaults of its fierce, strong breath. The rain increased to a perfect avalanche of water, as though it would drown us and send us floating down the Russian River. A dimly lighted room in a strange hotel was not a comfortable location for a stormy night. Our landlady invited us into the family sitting-room, where there was a big blazing wood fire; we drew our chairs round it and sat rocking in a lazy, listless way, listening to the storm without and enjoying the comfortable scene within. The mistress of the house sat sewing by the light of a softly shaded lamp, while her daughter was busily engaged arranging some dried ferns and flowers. Presently the door opened, and a tall brown-bearded man, a perfect type of the strong stout-hearted frontiersman, with top-boots, frieze coat, and leather breeches, strode into the room. He glanced at us with a pair of sharp bright eyes. Mrs. W——, with a half-introductory smile, said, " Mr. G——, our express agent; he lives here all the year round." He drew his chair to the fire, " hoped he didn't intrude." *He* apologized for his presence, *we* apologized for ours, and in the course of a few minutes found ourselves engaged in an interesting conversation. They knew we had come from England, and were deeply interested in all concerning it. We would rather have gathered information of this wild Western world, teeming as it is with new interests, new life; but their thoughts were directed to the grave Old World across the sea. Their lives were saturated, filled to overflowing, with the adventurous, restless spirit that permeates their beautiful land; they seemed to enjoy the distant con-

templation of the settled dignity and steadfast institutions of the mother country. They talked of the
political aspect of to-day contrasted with that of the
past, and argued that one had grown out of the other.
In the course of conversation there were allusions to
the repeal of the corn laws, the passing of the Reform
Bill, and such bygone matters, with all of which they
were perfectly conversant. They discussed Lord
Palmerston's foreign policy as contrasted with that of
the present, and were strong upon the ministerial
difficulties of to-day, insisting that the then Conservative Government would go out, having made so many
and such disastrous mistakes, and the parliamentary
ribbons must fall into Mr. Gladstone's hands. They
watch our political movements at home with as much
interest as their own elections. We are not petticoat
politicians, and occasionally found ourselves floundering out of our depths; it is as much as we can do to
swim on the surface of the smoothest political waters,
and were not sorry when politics went down and
literature came up. They were familiar, the handsome
express agent especially so, with our old dramatists
and popular prose writers, and discussed their works
with a propriety of expression, appreciation of subject,
and judicious criticism that one could scarcely expect
to find in these latitudes. There was a strength and
originality in his thoughts and expressions, which we
seldom find in what is called "cultivated society,"
where originality of any kind rarely comes to the
surface. Towards the end of the evening our host
entered the room quietly and gingerly, as though he
were treading on eggs; he seated himself on the very
edge of his chair, clasped his hands stiffly on his knees,

and was dumb; if anything struck him as "funny" he
opened his mouth, let a laugh escape, and shut it
again with a snap. Long before we parted for the
night the storm was over.

The morning broke calm and fair; no sign of the
last night's tempest lingered on earth, in air, or sky,
and we started on an excursion to Austin Creek, a
beautiful romantic spot, about four miles on the other
side of the forest.

On first starting from Duncan Mills we had to
ford the Russian River, which was somewhat swollen
owing to the heavy rains of the previous night. The
horses plunged in, and before they had taken many
steps the water was up to their bellies and surged over
the axletrees of the carriage. Instead of crossing the
river direct, our driver turned and drove towards the
sea. I say "drove," but he merely let the reins lie on
the horses' necks and allowed them to follow their
own devices. To our eyes, looking over the sides of
the carriage, it seemed as though we were being
carried away by the strong tide that was flowing
seawards. We glanced at our driver's face; it was
perfectly serene; he was evidently master of the situation. In answer to our anxious eyes he said, "There's
no danger, ladies; these horses have swum this river
when it was sixteen feet deep."

"All very well for the horses," I replied, "but the
carriage couldn't swim too." After going about a
hundred yards down the river, he turned the horses'
heads, and we were thankful to be once more on
dry land. Almost immediately we plunged into the
narrow forest paths, which are rough and uneven, and
by no means pleasant to travel over, especially when

we come to a piece of corduroy road, which consists of the felled trunks of trees, laid across, and partially sinking into a muddy Slough of Despond.

We are so bumped and bruised, and jolted from one side to the other, we can scarcely breathe,—we clutch the carriage sides,—we cling to each other, and when we are safe over, we feel our limbs to see if there is not a case of dislocation somewhere. For nearly two hours we drive through the solemn redwood forest, the tall straight trees growing like an army around us; there is no gentle swaying or fluttering of branches here; they rise high above our heads, and twist and turn their dark masses together, shutting out the light of the sun. We presently come to a part of the forest more densely populated with its silent multitude, where the trees grow larger, taller, and their gnarled roots force their way upward, and lie, like writhing serpents, petrified on the ground. The sound of the woodman's axe has never echoed through this solitude; it is a wild, virgin forest, vast, and in parts almost impenetrable. The roughness of the roads detracts somewhat from the pleasure of this excursion, though on arriving at Austin Creek you are well repaid for your trouble. It is a most delightful spot, dreamy and romantic; you feel inclined to sit there by the bubbling water, and dream the long day through. An old backwoodsman,—quite a character in his way,—lives in a pretty rustic cottage near the creek, and is always ready to refresh his visitors with a good supply of lager beer, tea, coffee, the whitest of bread, and yellowest of butter; and, perhaps a salmon trout, fresh from the stream, to add flavour to the simple meal.

We made sundry other excursions in the beautiful

neighbourhood of Duncan Mills, and left on the third day. The household turned out to walk with us across to the station, which is not fifty yards from the hotel door; the women with bright-coloured kerchiefs thrown over their heads; our solemn, silent host carrying our valise; a fat sow, with a young litter of grunters; two huge setters, with whom we had made great friends, and a pig-tailed Chinaman bringing up the rear. Our kind hostess handed us a dainty basket of fruit and sandwiches as we shook hands all round, and said "good-bye." Our gallant expressman, too, put in an appearance at the last moment; he had just time to wave his sombrero and wish us "God speed," when our smart little engine gave a snort, a jerk, and started on her way.

Beautiful as the redwoods are in this locality, they are not so fine as the redwoods in the neighbourhood of Santa Cruz, which is one of the loveliest seaside resorts on that part of the coast. The road to these redwoods is a most attractive one, through cañons filled with trees, all stretching their long arms upwards ready to clutch you as you pass by; sparkling streams, whose waters are ever flowing round spurs of timbered hills, broken with gorges and deep ravines, scars of an earthquake or sabre-cuts of time; then we wind along the steep mountain-side, looking down upon the boiling river, which is rushing among the broken boulders below. At last there is a sharp turn, and rapid descent into the forest, where there are some magnificent redwoods, second only to the world-famous "big trees" of the Calaveras and Mariposa groves. We are soon in the midst of them; they grow so smooth, so straight, and high, like the columns of some great cathedral, outspreading and uniting .their leafy crowns like a groined green roof, more than a hundred feet above our heads. We wander through these symmetrical, silent aisles, — the triumph of nature's architectural grandeur,—and feel inclined to bow our heads and lift our hearts heavenward.

It is difficult at first to realize the dimensions of these giants of the forest, all being of an immense size and height. There is no contrast; but when some of our party went to measure one we speedily realized its magnitude, for the men and women looked like animated dolls parading slowly round the huge trunk. They measured it about four feet from the ground, and ascertained that it was more than seventy-five feet in circumference. This was considered one of the largest. We entered into one hollow trunk where General Fremont had taken a fortnight's rest during his arduous expedition westwards. After he had vacated this sylvan retreat a man with a wife and two children took possession and lived there for two years, while they were gathering together money and materials to build themselves a home on the fringe of the forest about three miles eastward. On one side they had inserted a glass window, which is still there, and, strange to say, unbroken; in another place they had cut a huge round hole, evidently for a stovepipe to carry off the smoke. One very fine symmetrical tree was clothed to the height of six feet with visiting cards, stuck on with tin-tacks! We wandered for some hours through this sacred solitude, and left it with much regret, feeling it was perhaps the last excursion we should make on this side of the Rocky Mountains.

We return to San Francisco, and somewhat dolefully make preparations for our departure from this glorious sunland; but our time is up, and the longer we stay the greater will grow our regrets. We spend our last few days in paying farewell visits, and go through that melancholy ceremony with satisfactory calm. We keep our lugubrious feeling deep down in our hearts, and say " good-bye " with smiling faces. We had entered San Francisco at sunset; we leave it in the rosy morning, when the sun is shining and flooding the beautiful city and its purple hills with golden light. A host of our kind friends escort us across the bay. Our hearts are too full to talk much, so with eloquent hand-clasps and brief " good-byes " we part.

The huge ferryboat bears them back to their Golden City, which fades from our sight in a mist, a mist that blurs it in our eyes only; then the great yellow cars of the Central Pacific bear us eastward. We pass through the Sacramento Valley, climb once more the grand Sierras, and California fades from our sight, and is fast becoming only a memory and a dream.

To all those who are in search of health, of novelty, and who are able to enjoy the noblest, grandest, and most varied scenery this world can boast, I would say, " Go Westward," go over the sea, across the Rocky Mountains, the glorious Sierras, and sit down at the Golden Gate and rest.

CHAPTER XXIII.

THE SILVER STATE.

Snowed in—Indians—Journey to Denver—A Forage for a Supper
—" Crazed "—Domestic Difficulties—Colorado Springs—Chey-
enne Cañon—The " Garden of the Gods "—Ute Pass—Glen
Eyrie.

ONCE more we are travelling eastward. It is early
April, and in the land we have left the earth is
wearing her gorgeous spring robes, embroidered with
the loveliest and brightest of wild flowers; they are
everywhere, they cover her like a jewelled mosaic of
crimson, violet, white, and gold. Nowhere is there
such a luxuriant growth of wild flowers as in California. We soon begin to feel that we have left the
land of the sun behind us. The weather grows cool,
and the blue skies are filled with floating islands of
leaden clouds. At Colfax, which we reach about six
o'clock in the evening, there is a general bustle and
confusion. There is something wrong ahead; everybody worries everybody·with inquiries "What is the
matter?" and we learn, to our chagrin, that the
weight of snow has broken in a thousand feet of snow
sheds on the summit of the Sierras. We are shunted
on to a siding where we are to remain for the night,

while fifty men are told off to clear the road. They come swinging down upon the platform, a crowd of strong, weather-beaten fellows, while the moon, shining like a white ghost amid the thunder-clouds above, lights up their swarthy faces. An engine and truck is soon prepared. They swarm into it, loaded with pick-axes and shovels; they overflow and cling wherever they can find a foothold; and the engine, with a huge snow-plough as big as a house, goes snorting and shrieking on its way, the men shouting and hurrahing as it bears them out of sight. We go to bed some-what disconsolately; the idea of being "snowed in" at the foot of the mountains is not pleasant, and we look forward anxiously to what may await us at the top. At six in the morning it is telegraphed "All clear," and we recommence our journey. A gray mist has rolled over the Sierras, and shrouded the magni-ficent forest in a gray cloud mantle; we look down on a weird world of shadows; here and there a gleam of sunlight breaks out from the gloomy skies and is gone in a moment. It is dreary travelling for a while—a gray sky above, a gray world below, and a gray cloud mist falling over us on all sides; but our living street moves slowly with slackened speed through all. We settle down in a comfortable palace car, and with a chosen few of our fellow-passengers form quite a pleasant coterie. We visit each other's sections, passing freely from one car to another; we read, chat, tell anecdotes (some of us had quite a gift that way), and keep the ball of conversation rolling pretty briskly; when our wits are exhausted we take refuge in the inevitable fifteen puzzle.

In the evening we had our section lighted, and played

a solemn game of whist, or were initiated into the mysteries of euchre, or watched the rollicking game of poker being carried on by a merry party in the opposite section.

The weather changed, the clouds lifted, and the next morning we found ourselves once more ascending the Rocky Mountains, which struck us with an idea of even greater sublimity, now that the novelty of our first view had worn off. The sun shone brilliantly, and an intense blue sky bent over us as we slowly wound our way through the lovely God-created world of stone where no man dwells. At Elko, and sundry other mountain stations, the Indians came down to see the trains pass. There were braves of all ages, with their squaws and pappoose staring in silent stolidity at the bustling scene. They were evidently got up for effect. The women wore striped blankets pinned round their bodies, and bright handkerchiefs or shawls over their heads. Their long matted hair streamed over their shoulders, sometimes over their eyes; and they had added to their natural attractions by blotches of coarse red paint daubed on the dark faces. The men were, on the whole, more gaily dressed and painted than the women. One especially attracted our attention. He was evidently a " buck " of the first water. He wore a blue blanket wrapped round him, and on his head a broad-brimmed ragged felt hat, with a mass of blue feathers drooping on his shoulders. The men stood in groups, solemnly regarding us with their big black eyes, still as statues; the women squatted on the platform or peeped at us from round corners. It was not exactly pleasant, but very interesting to find ourselves amid a score or two of this savage race, the men all armed with guns and knives. Some of them got on to the train (all Indians are allowed to ride free, getting on and off as they please : they never ride in cars with the other passengers, but on the steps or in the baggage van) and went with us to the next station.

After a run of five days we reach Denver City, capital of the Silver State of Colorado. It is near midnight as we roll through the silent streets and stop at the Grand Central Hotel, whose doors are hospitably open to receive us. We are tired and hungry. We had reserved a good appetite, intending to dine at Cheyenne, where we knew we should get a luxurious meal; but as we desired to push on to Denver that night, and there was no connecting train at Cheyenne proper, we turned off at the junction, and having missed our dinner reach Denver in a semi-exhausted state. A solitary black porter, all smiles, relieves us of our hand-baggage, and shows us to a clean comfortable room on the third floor, the only unoccupied room in the house. It was fortunate we telegraphed, or we should not have had that. The house is crowded, the town is crowded ; people are pouring in and out every day on their way to and from " Leadville," a city that has grown up in two years, and has churches, banks, waterworks, stage roads cut out of a wilderness, and thirty thousand inhabitants. Mines are open, shafts sunken, and thousands of workers are digging in the bowels of the earth, searching for gold and silver—finding it, too. We ask for supper. We cannot have anything till the morning. The cook has gone ; the larder is locked up. We stand aghast, but not cast down. We insist that we shall die of exhaustion before the morning, and we " *must* have something—anything, we don't care what." He grins, shows his white teeth, scratches his woolly head, and shakes it in the teeth of our distress. At last, by dint of prayers and entreaties, we induce him to go on a foraging expedition into the town. He returns presently—I believe he knocked up the doctor —with some roughly cut sandwiches of rancid butter and tough leathery beef in one hand, and a bottle of lager beer in the other. With this we are forced to be satisfied, if not content.

The next morning we have a capital breakfast, and are most anxious to go on a reconnoitring expedition through the town, but a blinding snowstorm confines us to the house. Still it is not cold; although there is a stove in the room we do not need a fire. It clears up in the afternoon; we wrap ourselves in our warmest clothing and prepare to sally forth. As we cross the hall we hear our name uttered in a familiar tone, and we encounter an old friend whom we had last seen in a London drawing-room. He recognized *us*; we should never have recognized *him*, in his frontier dress, with top-boots, broad sombrero hat, and clean-shaven face, bronzed and brown with the " bright sun's kiss." He had just returned from a seven-hundred-mile ride through the Indian territory, and still had his knives and pistols in his belt. These he now deposited in a huge box, which the office-clerk proudly opened for our inspection.

" See here, ladies ; " he said ; " when the gentlemen come down from the hills they leave their arms here. Ours is a peaceable town now ; there is no need to go armed. A dozen years ago every man carried his life in his hand—the air was full of pistol-shots ; in foul

weather it rained bullets. *Now* it is altogether different.
You are as safe in the streets as in your own houses."
He slammed the lid down with a clang.

Our Chicago friend volunteered to escort us about
the town if we would give him time "to refresh himself." He was a long time refreshing, and when he
made his reappearance he was refreshed out of all knowledge. He had discarded his top-boots, frieze jacket,
and broad sombrero, and now appeared, white-shirted
and frock-coated, fit for a lounge in Bond Street. He
had dug out the insignia of civilization from the
depths of a huge trunk which travelled ahead of him
"in case of being wanted." He had destroyed his
picturesqueness, but looked respectable. With this
renovated being we paraded the streets of Denver. Its
ancient rowdyism is dead ; its bowie-knived, swaggering, swearing population of ten years ago has departed ; it is now a peaceful, law-abiding city, with
long streets or boulevards planted with fine trees,
which in summer-time must form a delightful shade,
but in consequence of the great altitude, I suppose the
summer is very backward here, for at present there is
not a single green leaf to be seen. There are numbers
of handsome dwelling-houses, mostly occupied by
families who have flocked from all parts of the world,
and settled here in consideration of the beautiful
climate, which is genial and pleasant at all seasons,
and especially beneficial to those who are in the least
affected with any chest or lung disease. I have met
here many hale, strong, hearty men, who the moment
they leave the city and descend to the valleys below
become suffering invalids. It is the same throughout
the entire State of Colorado ; the pure rarefied air has

a surprisingly healing effect upon the lungs, and the asthmatic sufferers breathe like healthy men; they only recognize their afflictions when they leave these mountain heights. There are numbers of very handsome shops of all descriptions, the jewellers making a specially brilliant display; they are the best patronized, perhaps, of any here, for the miners, when they have made their "pile," come down from the hills and invest their gold in diamonds and jewellery for their wives or sweethearts. There are substantial banks; plenty of churches and chapels for all denominations and creeds; very fine public buildings—town hall, library, police courts, etc. The inhabitants are especially tetchy, and take seriously to heart any observation concerning the respectability of their city, and are greatly scandalized by any allusion to its former delinquencies. It is like a reformed rake in broadcloth and fine linen, and resents any allusion to its days of bowie-knives and buckskins. There is very good, though not exactly luxurious, accommodation for travellers in the way of hotéls; but there is a monster hotel now in the course of building, which promises a combination of luxuries and comforts to tourists of the future.

The city is built on a wide plateau five thousand feet above the sea-level. A few streets and houses cover a wide area; there is plenty of room to build and breathe in. Some of the streets, two miles long, have scarcely fifty houses in them, but these are surrounded by gardens and pleasure-grounds; they are very wide, and planted with rows of cotton trees. The roads in all directions are beautifully smooth; it is a delight to drive over them. It is now the 12th of

April; there is a bright blue sky, warm balmy sunshine, and a crisp invigorating air, but there is not a flower to be seen, not the twitter of a spring bird to be heard anywhere. Ranges of hills and mountains arise on all sides of it, some far away over the plains, some near, but mostly covered with eternal snows, their icy peaks flashing in the sunshine in striking contrast to the blue foothills below. Glancing on one side we see a wide endless plain; it seems bounded by the horizon. This, by mild gradations, unbroken by hills or mountains, leads through towns, forests, and cultivated prairie lands to the Mississippi river six hundred miles.

Having promenaded the streets of Denver for some hours we return to our Grand Central Hotel. On our way up to our rooms we meet a young, pretty-looking girl with an intensely preoccupied look upon her face. She hurries past us. We are inclined to ask " if anything is the matter?" but before we have time to think she is gone. We meet her several times during the after part of the day, running up and down the stairs, or roaming along the passages, still with the same strange, intent look upon her face. Late in the evening, while we are sitting chatting previous to retiring to rest, the handle of our door is very quietly turned. We step forward and throw it open. There is no one there, but this girl is hurrying along the corridor, wringing her hands and moaning pitifully, " I've lost a pair of little baby's shoes!" and throughout the long night she was wandering about the house, along the passages, and up and down the stairs, uttering the same pathetic cry.

The next morning we were roused by a succession of piercing shrieks, and on our hurrying out to learn the cause, found the poor girl being dragged through the corridor by two sturdy, rough-looking men, who certainly did not " do their spiriting gently." All the visitors had turned out of their rooms, alarmed at the tragic disturbance, and though every one deplored what seemed to be the unnecessary violence of these petty officers " dressed in their brief authority," no one spoke to prevent it, well knowing that any interference with the " police " is dangerous, and followed by dangerous consequences. In spite of her heartrending shrieks, and appeals for help, the unfortunate creature was dragged down the stairs uttering the one piteous cry—

" I've done no harm. I was only looking for my little baby's shoes."

" She's crazy," volunteered the head waiter. " It is very sad. She's a stranger, too, in these parts ; nobody knows anything about her. She drove up here yesterday morning in the station fly, and engaged a room, but she behaved queer, roaming about the house all day and all night. We were forced to send for the police to take her away ; we could not have crazy folk hanging round here."

We returned silently to our rooms, all of us, I think, sad at heart—the men looking especially downcast, evidently feeling that they might have done *something* for this solitary distressed woman. But what? They all knew that authority once acknowledged in these mountain cities must be held unquestioned and supreme.

It is quite a common thing in Denver for families to take up their residence entirely at hotels. Only two classes of people can enjoy the luxury of a home : viz. those who possess great wealth, and are able to keep large establishments, and pay princely wages for very indifferent service ; and those who are able and willing to do their own housework, cooking, etc., without any extraneous help whatever. People of modest means, who in the old country might enjoy a cosy home and neat-handed maidservant, must not look for it here. An English lady resident in the hotel gave me her experience in the matter. She took a pretty house, furnished it, engaged a " help," and prepared once more to enjoy the luxury of home : the "help" had laid down the law what she *would* do, and what she would *not* do. All preliminaries being satisfactorily arranged, she entered on her duties. The dinner-hour came ; the table was laid for three.

" There will be only the Captain and myself to dinner to-day ; we seldom have company," said the mistress.

" But there's *me !* I'm to dine with you, I suppose ? " replies the " help."

Upon its being mildly suggested that their conversation would not be particularly interesting to her— besides " they preferred dining alone"—she flounced out of the room. An hour afterwards the mistress ventured into the kitchen to learn the cause of the dinner's delay, and discovered that savoury meal flung into the scullery sink, the fire raked out, and the irate " help " departed !

Household labour is at a premium. The social aspect of affairs seems to be turned upside down ; it is the *employée* who dictates terms, not the employer. There exists a kind of female domestic guild, whose members seem eternally " on strike." They decide who shall be served and who shall not be served ; the scale

of wages, and the rules to be observed by the household they condescend to enter. Woe be to the mistress ·
who rebels against her maid!—she shall be maidless
ever after. In spite, however, of this trifling drawback
to domestic bliss, many ladies are brave enough to face
the difficulties, and accompany their lords to the fields
of gold, as in the old days they did to the field of battle.
Denver is, and will long continue to be, crowded with
adventurers from all parts of the world, for it is a
place where fortunes are easily made,—perhaps as
easily lost. It is a paradise, they say, for men, dogs,
and horses, but no heaven for women.

The next day we bid adieu to our friend, who is
starting for Leadville, while we take the train for
" Colorado Springs," about four hours' run from Denver
City. We reach the depôt early, and take our seats in
an empty car ; throngs of people begin to arrive, some
on foot, some in ramshackle vehicles of all descriptions ; ·
the hotel omnibuses dash up one after the other and
empty their living freight upon the platform, which is
speedily crowded with an array of masculine humanity ;
but there is not a woman to be seen—not one !

A dark, swarthy, rough-looking set of men they
are, with stern, impassive faces; they are mostly
armed, and are evidently bound for the hills hundreds
of miles up the country. One after another they
swarm into the cars, exchange silent salutations; a nod,
a smile, perhaps a few low-voiced words, and that is
all. There is no laughing, no handshaking, no jesting,
no geniality ; they are thoughtful, energetic men, and
all seem bent on the world's most serious business;
each bearing the weight of his own concerns. Some
read the *Denver News*. Nobody seems to be sociably

inclined towards his neighbour; occasional scraps of
conversation are floated to our ears; but they are
mostly silent and preoccupied.   We are the only ladies
on board the cars, but that is not an embarrassing
fact.   No one takes any notice of us; they don't even
seem to glance our way, though the fact of two ladies
travelling in these regions without an escort must have
been a novelty.   Occasionally, if the sun incommoded
us, a. hand belonging to an invisible body arranged
our blinds comfortably: by this token only was our
presence recognized.

We reach Colorado Springs about midday, and as
the train stops, a bearded giant in top-boots addressed
us in lamb-like tones—

"You get out here?   Strangers, I guess?"

We admitted both facts.

"Know what hotel you're going to?   No?   Well,
I guess you'll find the National about the thing."

In another moment we find ourselves and our hand-
baggage deposited in the omnibus of the National
Hotel, and our depositor, with a profound obeisance,
stands bareheaded as we drive away.

Colorado Springs (so called, I suppose, because the
nearest spring is five miles off) stands on a sandy
plain, six thousand feet above the sea-level; the Rio
Grande Railway has a station here, where there is
clean, comfortable, though not luxurious accommodation
for tourists desiring to explore the attractions of this
wonderful State, with its boundless plains, ice-crowned
mountains, and great rolling uplands, sweeping away
till they are broken up by the low, rugged foothills, or
lost among eternal snows.   Colorado Springs is a
bright, lively little town, which, during the last five

years, has risen from the wild prairie land, and has now a population of three thousand residents. There are two other delightful resorts in the neighbourhood—the old Colorado city, sedate, solemn, and picturesque, but much neglected by tourists generally, who prefer the brisk, bustling "Springs," or the more aristocratic "Manitou," about six miles off, which is most romantically situated, and has luxurious hotel accommodation. In the immediate vicinity are several soda and iron springs, at which any passing traveller may stop and drink. Any one who tastes, as we did (we did more than taste, we drank draughts of it), the sparkling soda water bubbling up from its natural source, will forswear the manufactured article ever after.

On the afternoon of our arrival we start on an expedition to Cheyenne Cañon, some half-dozen miles from the "Springs." We feel the full magnetism of this rarefied mountain air as we speed over the wide, rolling plain, which spreads in billowy waves of short gray-green grass on all sides of us. The skies are intensely blue, the air flooded with sunshine. Not the twitter of a bird is to be heard, not a tree is in leaf, not a flower in blossom, and it is late in April. The white bare branches of the cotton tree stand out like silvery lacework, traced in fantastic patterns upon the bright blue sky. There is nothing of soft, pretty picturesqueness here ; it is all grand, wild, and bare.

"You should have come here in June," says our driver; "there will be plenty of greenery and flowers then. Of course everything is looking dry and thirsty now ; we haven't had a drop of rain since last August. It's due now, though; we're expecting showers every day."

We get out of the carriage at the mouth of the cañon, and make our way through this wonderful chasm on foot as best we can, climbing over the rough, broken boulders crossing and recrossing the creek, now on felled tree-trunks, balancing ourselves on stones or stumps, climbing up slippery banks, beneath the shadow of the great gray rocks which lift their rugged heights five hundred feet above our head. Looking up we see a band of blue sky. We are wandering through a twilight world; not a gleam of sunshine ever strays into these mysterious depths. We are surrounded on all sides by these dark, jagged rocks—above, below, everywhere—as though they would crowd round and crush us. Here and there a gnarled skeleton tree starts from some deep fissure, as though it had wasted its life trying to get out; and the gurgling waterfalls, gliding down from their home in the mountains to join the brawling stream below, makes a pleasant plashing music to our ears. We spend two hours amid the gloomy grandeur of Cheyenne Cañon, and return to the hotel in time for dinner.

The next morning early we start for the "Garden of the Gods," which is no paradise of shady groves and blooming flowers, but a collection of bright red rocks of most curious formations, covering an area of about fifty acres. At the entrance to the garden stand two tall red sandstone cliffs, rising sheer up from the ground to a height of three hundred feet. Glancing through these gigantic gates, and framed as it were within them, we see "Pike's Peak" flashing its icy crown in the face of the sun. It is seventy-five miles away, but it is so clearly outlined it seems quite near. We fancy we can distinguish the cattle grazing among the blue foothills below. We enter between these gates and find ourselves amid what might even be the ruins of some grand God-created cathedral, created and ruined before the age of man; the tall straight columns still stand crumbling in the deserted aisles, and the "garden" is spread like a panorama before us; the bright red sandy ground, rising and undulating in all directions, is embroidered with silvery sage brush and tufts of gray-green prairie grass; here and there the straggling evergreen trees struggle into a dwarfed, half-barren life. Their scanty verdure is, however, a relief to the eyes, for the intense blue skies and the golden sunlight, shining on the red rocky world round us, form a mass of brilliant colouring that is dazzling to the sight, and contrasts strongly with the massive white rocks which stand outside the garden gates. Weird, strange figures and half-formed fantastic shapes are on all sides of us, sometimes grotesque, like things seen in a dream, but always realistic and impressive. Local genius has classified these wonderful formations, and given to them familiar names; but the glib guide's chatter is wearisome. We prefer to wander at our leisure through this marvellous locality, and let our imagination run riot amid this warm glow of brilliant colouring and world of petrified wonders. It is easy to fancy that this must have been the playground or workshop of some athletic gods of old, who were disturbed in their work or in their play when the thunder of the Almighty Voice rolled down the mountain-side and called them home. The laggards were turned to stone; the warrior, with his broken club, is half-buried in the ground; and the tall figure of a veiled nun and hooded friar are rooted to the earth, where they are doomed to stand for all the world's wonder till the judgment day.

We cast many a long, lingering look behind us as we leave this fascinating spot, this veritable region of enchantment, which holds our thoughts chained long after it has passed from our sight. We drive on to Glen Eyrie, where there are some curious rocky formations of various colours—green, purple, and a dull dead gold; and, rising amid a very wilderness of cottonwood and fir-trees, stands a group of gigantic needle-rocks—tall, straight-pointed shafts, which might be used to sew a broken world together. There are various other grotesque formations, grouped in harmonious confusion amid a luxuriant growth of evergreens, which flourish here in greater perfection than in the wide open plains above. A stream of sparkling water runs gurgling through the glen. Clinging, as it seems, like an eyrie's nest to the face of the cliff on the opposite side, is a lovely villa, the residence of General Palmer, the owner of the glen; from this spot the view of the surrounding scenery is unequalled for its extent and picturesqueness.

On our return journey we drive to the Ute pass, which, for the grandeur and sublimity of its scenery, is second to none. Not the ghost of an Indian is to be seen now on this their once favourite hunting-ground; its narrow winding paths—with steep precipice and brawling river running below on the one side, and the tall gray cliff rising on the other, sometimes overhanging above as though they might fall and crush us —are crowded now with waggon-trains, cattle, lumber-carts, and squadrons of men, women, and children all plodding their way to the Leadville mines near a hundred miles away. We could not abandon ourselves wholly to the beauty of the scenery, for we were occasionally diverted by the cries and shouts of the men as they extricated some little staggering calf from between our horses' hoofs or carriage wheels, while the poor mother lowed piteously in at the window, her horns in unpleasant proximity to our faces. We went as far as the Rainbow Falls, and then drove back through the pass, and thence to Manitou, where we pulled up for a few minutes and drank some delicious draughts from the sparkling soda springs. During the whole of this route our attention was constantly directed to some lovely homes, built sometimes on the hillsides, sometimes nestling at their feet, but always on some choice picturesque spot. These, we were told, are generally inhabited by English gentlemen, and one or two exceedingly pretty villas were pointed out to us as the residences of some American ladies of literary and artistic distinction.

It was late in the afternoon as we rattled over the breezy uplands and across the bleak, bare plains, back to Colorado Springs. We caught many a glimpse of the gigantic gates, which guard the bright red garden of the gods ; in fact, they form the chief point in the landscape for many miles round. We regretted bitterly the compulsory shortness of our stay in this wonderful region ; but we must " move on," leaving the utmost grandeur unseen. We had heard so much of the beautiful valleys, verdure-clad ravines, gloomy gorges, and almost inaccessible mountains, rugged and icebound with eternal snows. Among the most regretted of these unseen wonders is the mountain of the " Holy

Cross." This most remarkable mountain is nearly fifteen thousand feet high, and the ascent is so difficult that few attempt it. A contemporary describes it thus :—

" The characteristic which gives it its name, is the vertical face, nearly three thousand feet in depth, with a cross at the upper portion, the entire fissures being filled with snow. The cross is of such remarkable size, and distinct contrast with the dark granite rock, that it can be seen nearly eighty miles away, and easily distinguished from all other mountain-peaks. The snow seems to have been caught in the fissure, which is formed of a succession of steps, and here, becoming well lodged, it remains all the year. Late in the summer the cross is very much diminished in size by the melting of the snow. A beautiful green lake lies at the base of the peak, which forms a reservoir for the waters falling from the high peaks. The perpendicular arm of the cross is fifteen hundred feet in length, and fully fifty feet in breadth, the snow lying in the crevice from fifty to one hundred feet in depth ; the horizontal arm of the cross averages seven hundred feet."

Although Colorado is a rainless land, water is plentiful, rivers and streams are abundant enough, and the system of irrigation is perfect. In no other part of this vast continent are there more fertile, flourishing farms, or such a production of gigantic fruits and vegetables ; they tell of cabbages weighing forty pounds—potatoes, apples, grapes, in fact, fruits and vegetables of all kinds, in similar proportions.

July and August are the best months for a tour in Colorado ; then the mountain-passes are open, the snow has almost disappeared from the higher regions, and

the beautiful parks and valleys lying among the
mountains are easy of access, while the gloomy gorges
and marvellous cañons, inaccessible at other seasons of
the year, may be fully explored. There are some
curious laws in Colorado. Any man who may be found
spending his time in public-houses, saloons, gambling-
houses, etc., and who is without any visible means of
support, is liable to be arrested as a " vagrant," and
upon being convicted by a justice of the peace, he is
handed over to the sheriff's officer, to be sold at public
auction to the highest bidder, for his services, for a
term not exceeding three months. The proceeds of the
sale to be given to his family, or, if he has no family,
the money is added to the city treasury. I have just
read a case in a Leadville paper : " Charles Green,
having been convicted of vagrancy, was ordered to be
sold at auction, and was placed on sale in front of
Justice MacDowall's court yesterday forenoon, and
auctioned off by Marshall Watson. Either his services
were not considered valuable, or the principle of buying
at auction was not favourably entertained, for the vag
only fetched two dollars. Mr. Wyman was the successful bidder."

CHAPTER XXIV.

BRICKS AND MORTAR.

The Road to St. Louis—The Kansas Brigands' Exploit—Picturesque Population—Mississippi River—Washington—The Capitol—Public Buildings—Society—A Monument to a Lost Cause—Mount Vernon.

WE rest one more night in Denver, and start early next morning for St. Louis, *viâ* Kansas City. We soon feel as though we have left all the beauty and brightness of the world behind; for anything more dreary than the road thither cannot well be imagined. The whole day long, from morning till night, we look out upon the dull, uninteresting prairie land; the icy peaks, snow-clad mountains, and verdant valley have all disappeared, as though the magic plains had collapsed with all their wonders. We see nothing but the dreary dead level covered with short tufts of buffalo grass, so much beloved and so nutritious to the beasts of the plains. The road is strewn with the bones and bodies of dead cattle, some seeming to have dropped but yesterday, others bare skeletons, their bones bleached dry and white in the crisp rarefied air. No loathsome flies or birds of prey are hovering in the air; for the bodies do not decay, they simply dry up, and in time the bones

crumble into atoms, like pulverized stone. It is a
pitiful scene. The poor brutes have wandered from the
herded numbers, to freeze and starve on these bleak
plains. It is dull gray weather, the blue has faded
from the skies, and for the greater part of the time a
drizzling rain is falling. We buy a paper of the
perambulating newsboy, and read the startling intelligence, that only yesterday, on this very journey,
two swaggering ruffians, armed to the teeth, had
boarded the train at a small wayside station; the conductor recognized them at once as the two notorious
brigands, Jesse and Henry James, whose illustrated
" Lives and Exploits " were at that time, by a strange
coincidence, being sold on the cars for twenty-five cents.

" For God's sake, keep quiet—take no notice, whatever they do," whispered the anxious conductor to the
rather alarmed passengers; but they were evidently
" off duty," neither robbery nor murder were on the
cards that day. They swaggered about the cars,
talking and laughing loudly, their very aspect creating
alarm, as no one knew what might come next. They
presently selected a table, ordered " supper and a
bucket of champagne—quick as greased lightning, too."

Their order was obeyed promptly as might be;
they flung their six-shooters on the table before them,
enjoyed a hearty meal, becoming quite hilarious
towards the end; then readjusted their arms, stopped
the train in the middle of the wilderness, stepped off
the platform, saying—

" Charge two more suppers to the Government."

No such adventure befalls us; we have a mere
commonplace journey, with no genial companionship to
brighten the way. So, for nearly eight hundred miles,

we journey through this interminable desert land.
During the last hundred miles, however, signs of cultivation begin to appear. The first sight of green fields
is blessed and refreshing to our eyes. Herds of cattle,
thousands strong, are feeding on these wide Kansas
plains, and presently homesteads and farmhouses are
dotted here and there, lying in the laps of their own
cultivated lands. Soon, among the gathering twilight
shadows, there looms upon our sight a wide-spreading
city, rising from the level plains. This is Kansas
City. We steam into the station; there is a general
hubbub and confusion on the platform, which is
crowded with a heterogeneous mass of humanity. There
is the half-breed, clothed in a flour-sack or blanket; the
cattle-dealer, in his quaint-cut fustian; and a scanty
few western tourists going eastward. There is a great
pushing and struggling, everybody rushing in search
of the right train, often getting into the wrong one;
engines are whistling and dashing in and out of the
station, going to or coming from all points of the
States. We wait here half an hour for refreshments;
there is a capital buffet, where you may get anything
you require at a moderate price. For any one who is
not professionally interested in agricultural progress,
there is no temptation to stay in Kansas City. We
change carriages, having secured our sleeping-car, and
proceed on our way. Next morning about eight o'clock
we reach St. Louis.

Once more we are in a land of bricks and mortar; the
air is close, warm, the atmosphere what is best under-
stood by " muggy." We breathe the air with a sense
of depression, both physically and mentally, and in the
course of twenty-four hours our energies had left us so

completely, we thought they would never come back.
The city is a fine, large, substantial one, with long
streets and fine houses, with the usual amount of public
buildings, churches, theatres, and other places of
amusement. It is full of bright, bustling life, flourishing trade, and thriving manufactories ; there is a look
of settled solidity about it that contrasts strongly with
the Western cities we have been lately passing through.
In some respects we might almost fancy ourselves
transported back to London. Here are the omnibuses,
tramcars, the gas-lamps, the long rows of tall houses,
the hazy atmosphere, and the suffocating air of a damp
July day ; a gray, cloudy sky above, and the glorious
Mississippi rolling sluggishly through the town in a
state of far more muddy impurity than our own much-
maligned Thames. An extremely light and elegant
bridge, both for foot-passengers or carriages, spans the
river and connects one part of the city with the other.
There are pretty little parks or pleasure-grounds breaking out in all parts of the crowded town for the people's
benefit. On the outskirts there are two very beautiful
and extensive pleasure-grounds—Tower Grove and
Forest Park ; the former having been presented to the
city by an English gentleman who has been a resident
there for many years. It is beautifully laid out in
shady walks and drives ; great taste has been used in
the arrangement of the rare shrubs, trees, and flowers,
which are everywhere displayed to the best advantage.
Forest Park is farther away from the town, and is on
a wilder, larger scale, and rich in natural beauties.
There are grand old forest trees, bosky dells, green
slopes, and shady nooks and corners, with a rich
luxuriant growth of green everywhere. So far St.

Louis reminds us of our native land; but on closer observation, as we ramble through the streets and round about the town, we realize the fact that we are in a strange country. We explore the markets, and they abound in all quarters of the town, and street stalls, which are likewise plentiful. Here are bushels of cocoanuts, yams, sweet potatoes, egg and oyster plants, rich gold and red bananas a quarter of a yard long, and all kinds of tropical fruits and flowers, and crowds of coloured people everywhere, engaged in every possible kind of business—a bright, busy, industrious population; groups of curly-headed coloured children, slates and satchels in hand, hurrying to or from school, chattering and fluttering round like so many magpies. Little brown babies are paddling about, making mud-pies in the gutter, with a mingling of white babies joining in the fun; women flash about with their short cotton skirts, big gold earrings, and kerchiefs of all the colours of the rainbow pinned across their breasts, or bound turban-like round their heads. The weather had partially cleared, and a lurid red sun looked down through the murky clouds on this semi-tropical city, as we took our last stroll through the busy kaleidoscopic streets.

We stayed just long enough to get a glimpse at the outer aspect of the city, and to test the hospitality of one of its most prominent members, which was characterized by all the hearty cordiality of our friends at home. St. Louis, I believe, is justly proud of its cultivated and refined society, of which Judge H. J—— and his charming wife are most attractive representatives. We spent a brief but pleasant time in their genial society, and only regretted our inability to stay longer and enjoy more of it.

Another two days' railway travelling through the populous Eastern States; through manufacturing towns and agricultural regions, with signs of prosperity and well-doing everywhere; through straggling villages and grassy meadows—no wild, unkempt lands, gloomy cañons, or weird ravines flash past us now—we reach Washington late in the evening, and drive through the brilliantly lighted streets to our hotel, the Ebbitt House, one of the most luxurious and delightful resting-places. In the morning we begin our usual campaign, and issue forth to reconnoitre the city—the finest and fairest of all the modern cities we have ever seen, or I believe we ever shall see (San Francisco excepted : *that* stands unique and alone). Its situation is most picturesque; it stands at the head of the beautiful Potomac river, a chain of low wooded hills forming a kind of amphitheatre, behind and around it. The city was planned by George Washington during his early days at Mount Vernon, and his design has been carried out in every particular, and has resulted in the production of one of the finest residential cities in the world ; for Washington is by no means a busy, money-making, mercantile city. It is one of the most aristocratic quarters—if we may use that term in this republican land. Here is the seat of Government, and thither flock the diplomatic corps with their wives and families. The army and navy, the medical and legal professions, are also largely represented ; for the pulse of the nation seems to require constant regulating, like a Brummagem watch with the mainspring out of order ; and the legal machine is always at hand, well oiled and in good order, ready to right the wrong, or wrong the right, as the case may be. There is society here, too,

which keeps rigidly to its own lines, and allows no
doubtful outsider to set foot within its magic circle.
You must have your credentials ready, and well attested,
for delivery at the doors.   There are gradations of
society here as elsewhere, from the *élite* and fashion
of the White House, to the lowest rung of the social
ladder.   Each forms its own circle; one rarely touches
the other; each keeps distinct and to itself.   The
equality and fraternity system, if indeed it exists anywhere, certainly ends here, and Madam Etiquette holds
sovereign sway.   No fear of meeting a man-milliner in
her domain ; everything is exclusive and select ; everybody as a rule knows " who's who," and if they do not
they take the quickest and surest means to find out.   A
visit to the consul of any special nation is generally
satisfactory in such personal matters.

It is a positive pleasure to walk about the streets of
Washington ; they are all wide, beautifully clean, and
paved with tiles as red as cherries, with rows of shady
trees on either side—a luxuriant regiment keeping guard
over the quaint, old-fashioned-looking brick houses
behind.   There are no ragged edges, or jagged fringe
of squalid homes, clinging to the skirts of the town.
It is all neatly finished up ; there are no dilapidated
sidewalks, or rugged roadways ; it is everywhere
smooth and pleasant, either for driving or walking.
There are wide streets of handsome shops, as well
stocked and tastefully arranged as those on the Paris
Boulevards.

The public buildings are generally of fine white
marble, or of sandstone painted to resemble it, and
most impressive and massive structures they are.   The
Patent Office is really a splendid edifice—a fine specimen

of Doric architecture, most striking for its simple, majestic grandeur; the body is of sandstone painted white, but the wings are of pure marble. The Treasury is also remarkably impressive; it has a colonnaded front 330 feet long, supported by thirty elegant Ionic columns, and is flanked on either side by extensive buildings of massive granite masonry, which breaks the monotony of the long colonnaded front of the chief building; it has several magnificent porticoes, and on either side of the platform or steps leading thereto are masses of beautiful shrubs and flowers. About the centre of the city, and dominating the landscape for miles round, stands the Capitol, high and mighty in its pure architectural glory, crowning a gently swelling hill, and surrounded by a garden of velvet lawns, and shrubs, and flowers, sloping down to the wide park-like streets, which radiate from all sides of it; its white wings spread on either side. Lofty flights of marble steps lead to the colonnaded galleries which encircle the building. The beautiful white dome (which is only four feet lower than St. Paul's, and, standing on a cleared space of elevated ground, appears higher and more imposing), with its graceful spire, is silhouetted against the bright blue sky. The architecture is purely Corinthian, and in every particular it is most elaborately finished. The view from the portico of the Capitol is very fine. The city's self spreads a wide panorama on all sides, melting away into the softly swelling hills and wooded valleys beyond; while the silvery streak of the Potomac seems to creep out from between the distant hills, gliding and wending its serpentine way till it meets and merges into the shining waters of the bay. To give the briefest description of the rest of the public buildings, schools, etc., of this beautiful young city would fill more pages than I dare devote to the subject; they are all specimens of architectural beauty of varied kinds. The Smithsonian Institute is perhaps one of the most striking; it makes no attempt to trench on classic ground, and is of no special style, but a mingling of many. Some, who will accept nothing without a name, call it Romanesque, or Byzantine, or Norman; it is neither, but a fanciful rendering of all, and the result is most striking and effective. The Botanical Gardens, comprising ten acres of land, lies by the West Capitol Park, and the elegant conservatories and beautifully laid out grounds form a prominent feature in the landscape. Rare trees, and shrubs, and flowers of every clime are flourishing here; among them is one of rare significance, the *dumb*-cane of South America. If man or woman taste the sap from the root of this tree, it destroys their powers of speech.

We could not be in Washington without paying a visit to the Senate Chamber and House of Representatives, to which the public have free access, even when the House is sitting. Of course the floor of the house is occupied by members of Congress. A gallery, three or four seats deep, runs round the building for the use of visitors. As we entered, Mr. Thurman was speaking on the Alabama indemnity. He has a fine presence, a good delivery, and spoke most eloquently upon the subject. I don't know whether he was much listened to. A good deal of parliamentary eloquence is flung to the wind. Each member had a desk before him. Some were writing, some were reading the news, some were dozing, others looked extremely bored, while a few were having a genial conversation. The floor was strewn with papers. Boy-messengers were flashing hither and thither, larking by the way as though they were just out of school. The whole scene was wanting in that grave decorum and order which characterize our own parliamentary assemblies. On going from one Chamber to the other—the Senate which represents our House of Lords—we heard loud talking, it seemed of many voices. We glanced through the half-open door at the crowd within, and inquired of the thin, loose-jointed individual who was lounging about on the threshold taking his duty easily, "if there was anything interesting going on?"

"They're doing nothing," he answered, with supreme contempt; "they're always doing nothing—and they take a long time about it. They've been a-filibustering and a-filibustering all day, and I suppose they'll go on all night. I'm sick of 'em."

There are lovely drives all round Washington City, some of historic interest. Our first visit was to Arlington House, the home of General Robert Lee; it is but a short drive from the city, and stands in a most prominent position on Arlington Heights, surrounded by lovely scenery, and in the distance, looming out of the city's midst, stands the Capitol "with white dome lifted." At the close of the war the estate was confiscated, and a great portion of the beautiful grounds was set apart as a burial-ground for the Union soldiers. On every side, stretching away into the dim distance, are graves—graves everywhere; thousands upon thousands of them, not raised in mounds, but under the smooth turfed ground. Each one is marked by a stone about a foot high, setting forth the name and age of the sleeper below. It seems a strange fatality that the home of the grand old rebel soldier should be the resting-place of the federal dead. In one part of the grounds stands a massive granite sarcophagus, which is placed over the bones of two thousand one hundred and eleven unknown soldiers, gathered from the battle-field of "Bull Run" and the route to Rappahannock after the war. The house is dismantled now, and our hollow footsteps echo through the vacant passages and empty chambers. As we wander through the deserted dwelling, we scarcely feel we are alone. The ghost of the dead days seems to be an ever-haunting presence there. Arlington House, in its isolated lonely state, stands there as a most melancholy monument to a lost cause.

Outside, at the back of the house, are the kitchens, stables, and slave quarters—all empty now, dilapidated and falling fast to ruin, like ghastly skeleton homers, scarred with many memories, and mutely eloquent of the days that have been. On our way homeward we drove through the beautifully picturesque grounds of the "Soldiers' Home," which consists of about five hundred acres, tastefully laid out in lawns, meadows, gardens, and lakes, and about seven miles of drives winding now by the lake side, or under the shady trees, or through the blooming "garden of roses."

Our next visit was to the home of Washington, the founder and father of the Union. Mount Vernon is situated about fifteen miles from Washington, down the Potomac river, passing through pretty home scenery, and some highly interesting spots by the way. We have splendid views of the Arsenal grounds which run along the banks of the river, and the Government home for the insane, a magnificent building standing on elevated ground east of the city. Presently we pass Fort Foote and Fort Washington. Every rood of ground on either side of this lovely Potomac is marked by the footprints of the war, and is historied and enriched with its many memories. At length we reach Mount Vernon—a spot dear to American hearts of every degree, however one man may differ from another in social, political, or sectarian matters. Whatever tumult may rack the State, or tear at the spirit of the Union, all unite in their reverence for this one noble dead. When the horrors of war ceased for an hour, thither came men from both armies, with hands red with their brothers' blood ; but here all was peace. The bitter enmity and hatred which convulsed the land was forgotten here ; and the men in blue and the men in gray stood side by side, bared their heads, and bent reverently as before a shrine, by the grave of the father of their country.

General Washington is laid to rest in the grounds of his own home ; we pass his tomb on our way to the house. Everything here is kept in perfect order ; the quaint garden, designed and laid out by Washington himself in the fashion of the old days, with odd-shaped beds, and thick box borders about a foot high, is filled with gay, sweet-scented, rather than rare, flowers ; on the lawn there are several trees, and a hoary old hedge four feet high, and four feet thick, all planted by the beloved General's own hand, nearly a hundred years ago ; and they are all green and flourishing, as though they meant to live another century at least. Here also is a superb magnolia tree, reared from a slip brought by the hand of Lafayette from St. Helena. The slave

T

quarters, gardeners' cottages, laundries, stables, etc.,
are all ranged on the lawn at the back of the house.
These are still occupied by coloured people, the direct
descendants of those slaves who were raised on the
place in the old days; and they are as proud of their
race, and their connection with the Washington family,
as though they had descended from a line of kings.
They are a very superior and obliging class of people,
and provide an excellent lunch for visitors, at a very
moderate price.

Mount Vernon, though very beautifully situated,
and surrounded by fine views, sloping away from all
sides of it, is not so imposing an edifice as Arlington
House. It is built of wood to imitate stone, and has
a long, wide verandah running along the front. The
rooms are small, with the exception of the banqueting
hall, which, in comparison with the rest, is a large,
handsome apartment. Here are some fine old oil paintings, and portraits of Washington and his family, with
some few miscellaneous curiosities; among them, the
key of the Bastile, presented by General Lafayette.

So much loving reverence surrounds the name of
" Washington," that every room in the house is named
after a particular State, which holds it in special
care. The rooms are all furnished after the fashion of
the old time; many still contain the Chippendale furniture that was used by the Washington family; there
is the General's own escritoire, with its numerous
pigeon-holes, and cunning secret drawers, the chair he
sat in, and the bed he died on, in exactly the same
position, and with the same coverlid and fast-fading
hangings as when he left it. There is not a speck of
dust to be seen anywhere. The house and grounds are

the property of the Mount Vernon Ladies' Association, and everything is arranged and carried on under their personal supervision and care. Every relic having the remotest connection with General Washington is gathered together here, and most carefully preserved. A sweet scent of the old dead days lingers everywhere ; even the roses that climb round the verandah have a perfume all their own—different, it seems, from other roses. As we retrace our steps through the quaint garden, down Washington's favourite path, between the thick box hedges, in our mind's eye (which sees so much more than mortal sight) we see him walking before us, in his cocked hat and periwig, with head bent down, and hands clasped behind him, exactly as, we are told, he used to walk there, to and fro, a hundred years ago.

CHAPTER XXV.

THE QUAKER CITY.

Baltimore—Its Stony Streets—Druids' Park—A Stroll through the
City—Aristocratic Quarters—Washington Monument—Philadelphia—General Aspect—Picturesque Market Street—Fairmount Zoological Gardens.

A two hours' drive and we are at Baltimore, one of the
busiest and brightest of Southern cities, with miles of
streets running in all directions, in a state of labyrinthine uncertainty, as though they did not know which
way to turn, or where to go next; some are straight
and wide, some narrow and crooked. The houses are
of many colours; they scorn to be bound to the commonplace rules of mere bricks and mortar; you may see a
pink front blushing near a sombre gray, a creamy
white or chocolate, picked out with amber, elbowing a
bright blue, or olive-tinted green; the side-walks are
paved with cherry-red tiles, and all this varied colouring, together with the quaint style of street architecture, gives the city a gay, picturesque appearance.

The business thoroughfares are overflowing with
the hurry and bustle of life, and at certain hours of the
day the side-walks are crowded with a jostling multitude, fluctuating to and fro, while the roadways are
alive with many-coloured cars, dashing hither and

thither. It is pleasant enough riding on tramways, but you cannot enjoy the luxury of a private carriage—without running the risk of dislocation, at least; for the roads are of the roughest cobble-stones. The vehicles, driven at reckless speed, lurch and plunge from side to side, and bump you up and down. You hold on to the sides breathlessly, feeling they *must* topple over. But they don't; they land you at your destination alive, though with splitting head and aching bones. You are disposed to patronize the humble cars in future; and the cars go everywhere, and one bright morning they landed us at Druids' Park.

You enter through a lofty pair of handsome iron gates, into a wide avenue, flanked on either side by stone vases fifteen feet high, filled with evergreens in winter, and in summer with showy flowers. The Baltimore folk are very proud of their Druids' Park; and well they may be, for it is a most lovely spot, consisting of about five hundred acres of land beautifully laid out, their natural attractions being supplemented, not overwhelmed, by art. There are clumps of grand old forest trees, grassy slopes, and shady dells, filled with evergreen shrubs, feathery ferns, and sweet wild flowers, and a silvery lake, winding like a glittering white serpent through a paradise of green. Groups of coloured folk, with their wives and rollicking little piccaninnies, and young men with their swarthy sweethearts, all sprucely dressed in broadcloth and fine linen, with flowers in their button-holes, light-gloved, and patent-booted, their faces shining, as though they had been extra polished by Nixey's patent, are strolling under the trees, or sit chatting beneath their branches. The women, as a rule, wear less gaudy colours than their sisters at St. Louis, and altogether seem of a better-educated class.

Any lady desiring to enjoy the luxury of shopping, should postpone that pleasure till she gets to Baltimore, where there are plenty of shops, well stocked, and well arranged with every possible kind of fancy articles, as well as the necessary articles for daily use, and at certainly one-third less price than she would pay in most of the Eastern cities; besides this advantage, she will be treated with respect and civility, which does not seem indigenous to the nature of the American shopkeeper or his subordinates.

The residential part of the city, viz. Monument Square (and such-like fashionable localities), has a quiet, dull, deserted appearance, like a country town on Sundays when the shops are shut and the good folk are all at church, undergoing their spiritual ablutions. The houses in these aristocratic quarters of the city are more uniform and monotonous than the busier portions, and yet there is a picturesqueness in the monotony of the long rows of tall brick houses, picked out with white, the white steps projecting on to the red-tiled pavement, while rows of green trees stretch their green arms before them. In every city throughout the United States statues of their beloved founder, George Washington, abound—some execrable, some well enough to look at; but that which occupies the centre of Monument Square is a finely conceived and splendidly executed piece of work. There is no exaggeration, no attempt at ornament or decoration about it—a tall, fluted column rises from a square stone platform, surmounted at the top by an effigy of General George Washington; it is no theatrical figure of an impossible athlete in an attitude of patriotic ardour or military devotion. He stands in the position of a simple gentleman, as he may have stood many times in the flesh, with folded arms, looking out over the city to Chesepeake, where the stars and stripes of the Union he founded are streaming now from scores of vessels in the beautiful bay.

The hotel accommodation is comfortable enough, and no doubt answers all the requirements of the mercantile population who are constantly passing to and fro this busy trading city, for the river is filled with shipping from all parts of the world, and the wharfs swarming with a working population, loading and unloading the vessels; the visitor who runs down for a glimpse at these characteristic localities gets bewildered in the tangled collection of cranks, cattle, and the surging mass of pushing, shouting humankind. The hotels are wanting in some of those luxurious arrangements to which the tourists through the great cities of America have grown so accustomed as to regard them as necessities.

Our next point of attraction was Philadelphia, which delightful city we entered under most favourable auspices; the atmosphere was bright, warm, and cloudless. We caught our first glimpse of it from our car-windows, and beheld it afar off lying in the sunshine, its shining domes and cupolas outlined in the broad blue skies, and its myriad spires lifted lance-like in the air. On arriving there and first driving through the long, stately streets, we were struck by the number of magnificent buildings we passed on our route—marble fronts, marble columns, marble steps, marble everywhere.

The city is clothed with architectural beauty on whichever side you look. The public buildings, academies, churches, etc., are all, without exception, magnificent structures, some most striking from their grand simplicity, others from their varied and fanciful picturesqueness. Mr. Lippincott has published a guide to "Philadelphia and its Environs," profusely and beautifully illustrated with woodcuts of many important private dwellings and all the public buildings, the centennial erections in Fairmount Park, and some of the lovely scenery surrounding it. When you have "done" the city, you will not throw aside your guide, but keep it as a pleasant refresher to your memory in after days. It is a pleasure to walk up and down the clean, pretty streets, with their quaint old houses. Every window has an outside protection from the summer sun; some have the thick wooden shutters rarely seen in these days, others have green venetians, which makes you feel you are in a semi-tropical region.

The streets running one way across the town are named after different trees, which at one time were supposed to have flourished on their site—such as "Chestnut," "Pine," "Spruce," "Filbert," etc.; those running in an opposite direction are simply numbered on the same plan as that followed in New York. Market Street, one of the great trading thoroughfares, runs straight across the city from one river to the other; it is a splendid street, a hundred feet wide. In Penn's time this was the High Street of the city. Some of the houses have gaily striped awnings, stretching across to the roadway; some have flags or banners flying, and adopt other fanciful means of calling attention to their special attractions. A full-length figure of Pocahontas, or some other savage celebrity, generally stands at the door of the retail tobacconists, offering a pinch of snuff to the passer-by. An eagle spreads its wings over one Art Gallery, while a lion in a cocked hat paws the air on the opposite side. Altogether, the streets have always a gay, festive appearance.

The great thoroughfares are crowded with pedestrians and vehicles of all description. Wholesale and retail trading we know is being briskly carried on ; but there is no skurry or confusion anywhere, no pushing and jostling ; the living stream flows evenly to and fro ; business seems to be conducting itself in a quiet, orderly fashion. Taken altogether, Philadelphia is a sedate city ; there is an air of severe respectability and old-world solidity about it, we feel it would take a great deal to stir its substantial self-possession. It lies between the Delaware and Schuylkill rivers, and covers an area of great extent ; it is nearly double the size of New York, with a population considerably less. There are no overcrowded quarters here, no narrow courts or gloomy alleys, no tall tenement houses, like rabbit warrens, swarming with human creatures, sheltering hundreds within its reeking, dilapidated walls, where there is scarcely room for a score to live and breathe in. Everywhere in Philadelphia there is room " to turn round in, to breathe, and be free."

No grim poverty parades the streets, no sickly faces turn to the wall, no wolf-eyed hunger lurks in corners ; the working population looks healthy, strong, and self-respecting, free from that communistic element which is agitating the far Western cities. Every man,

from the lowest rung in the ladder, can rear his family
in a home of his own if he pleases; rent is cheap, and
the smallest cottage has its bath-room, wash-house,
and patch of garden-ground.   The city is confined
within no limits; it has overflowed the river on either
side, where there is plenty of room for it to stretch its
limbs and grow, as it has grown, with its beautiful
suburban branches, Kensington, Southwark, German-
town, etc.   It is growing still; elegant villas, substantial squares, and meandering streets are springing
up as fast as they can, clinging to the skirts of the
great city, which is like a monstrous body, with arms
as long as a gigantic octopus, reaching away on all
sides, seizing all it can, or like a loadstone attracting
all to itself.

Philadelphia is rich, too, in historical associations,
and has preserved many interesting relics of the old
times; for a century acquires the dignity of age in the
New World, and anything that is a hundred years old
is considered worthy of a pilgrimage.   Penn's cottage,
occupied by him in 1701, is still extant; so far it has
escaped the improving mania which has swept so
many of the old landmarks away.   It is a small, un-
pretentious brick building, two storeys high, situated in
Letitia Street, near the market, and quite overshadowed
by the fine buildings which have sprung up round it.
Indeed, many of the old interesting homes of the earlier
settlers have wholly disappeared; others are elbowed
away out of sight, to make way for the elegant villas
and marble palaces of the present generation of wealthy
Philadelphians, who form a nucleus of the most refined
and cultivated society to be found in any quarter of
the world.   The oldest inhabitants of the State have

still their representatives in Pennsylvania, though they congregate mostly in the city. Thither, in early days, came wandering branches from some of the best families in the old countries, and their descendants still occupy the land. We recognize a kindred spirit as we walk through the public streets, and feel the fascination of the Old World mingling with the vigorous strength of the New.

Philadelphia has not the cosmopolitan character of New York, and consequently does not present such varied fluctuating phases of life. It is a sedate matronly city, with nothing fast or frivolous about it, and its inhabitants uphold its dignity in a manner worthy of themselves. The most beautifully picturesque scenery lies round the immediate neighbourhood; few cities contain so many attractions within their grasp. The views on the winding Wissahickon are especially lovely, with a warm glow and romantic loveliness which makes one inclined to "linger long summer days" beside its banks. But Fairmount Park is, however, Philadelphia's greatest pride; its position and its natural beauties are indeed unsurpassed. Lying along the loveliest part of the Schuylkill river, it occupies three thousand acres of land, and is one of the most extensive parks known, being three times larger than the Grand Central Park, New York—and that, with its twelve miles of driving roads, strikes every one with surprise; but Fairmount has double that space set apart for driving and riding exercise.

At certain hours of the day the streams of handsome equipages and regiments of fair equestrians, driving and riding along the wide curving road by the river, presents a kaleidoscopic scene of great brilliancy; it is like a living panorama, which breaks up and fades like a dissolving view, as one by one they turn out of the main drive. Some disappear in groves of shady trees, or are lost among the romantic hills or pleasant winding ways which lead, between banks of blooming flowers, to the more secluded parts of the ground. But to thoroughly enjoy and appreciate the beauties of Fairmount Park, you must go on foot, ramble among its leafy dells and sunny slopes, its placid lakes hidden away in the heart of the woodlands, amid the tangled masses of a luxuriant growth of green, lichen-covered boulders and moss-grown banks, left to flourish in their natural wilfulness and beauty. Magnificent fountains have been erected in different parts of the ground, and marble monuments to deceased statesmen, philanthropists, and heroes are gleaming white on every side. That to Abraham Lincoln is perhaps the finest of them all.

In no country in the world are there such extensive and delightful public parks and pleasure-grounds as in America. Nature, in most cases, has laid so much material ready to hand—rocks, hills, wilderness, forest land, and rivers. Art has but to wave her magic wand, clear away or reject all she does not require, and utilize and lay out the rest according to her tasteful pleasure. Thus, many of the primeval forest trees, rocky mounds, and sparkling rivers of the dead ages beautify the recreation grounds of to-day. The Zoological Gardens, lying along the opposite bank of the river, promise to be second to none; they occupy a vast extent of beautifully laid out ground, and the different buildings already erected there are architecturally pleasant to the eye, and at the same time those best suited to the requirements, and for the exhibition of the remarkably fine collection of animals gathered therein. The society has agents in all parts of the world, being resolved to spare neither pains, labour, nor expense in their endeavour to make their collection the most perfect of its kind in all the civilized world.

CHAPTER XXVI.

SUMMER AMONG THE GOTHAMITES.

A New York Summer—How they meet it—Airy Customs—Coney
Island—Rockaway and Long Branch—A Mountain Village—
Ellenville—View from "Sam's Point."

PHILADELPHIA to New York is a pleasant three hours'
journey, and we were glad to find ourselves settled
down for a few weeks' rest in the "Empire City"—if
rest can be obtained in that electric atmosphere, which
quickens the pulse and fills you with its own restless
life, whether you will or no. We arrived there in the
middle of May. The season was over, their fashionable
season being the reverse of ours, for their gaieties are
at their full flood-tide during the winter months, when
ours are ended—if such things ever do come to an
end in a great city, but it seems to me that the general
mass build up a tolerable palace of pleasure out of the
débris the fashionable world leaves behind it.

Our friends, the few who remained in Gotham to
battle with the fierce summer sun, regretted that we
had come back at the dead season; but they managed to
make it lively enough. What with excursions on the
water, picnics on land, theatres, and social gatherings
at home, the time passed only too quickly. The days

were too short; if we could lengthen them as we do
our skirts, by adding a flouncing of a few hours, we
should have had engagements enough to fill them.
The weather was unusually warm for May, the ther-
mometer sometimes rising as high as 90° in the shade.

As the weeks passed on, the temperature became
almost unendurable. The coolest place in all New
York was the Madison Square Theatre. The ther-
mometer had mounted to 100° when we received
a box for an afternoon miscellaneous performance in
aid of the Edgar Poe Memorial Statue. Among the
many other things selected for the occasion was an
abridged version of " The Taming of the Shrew," when
Edwin Booth consented to play Petruchio. Nothing
less than a desire to see this celebrated actor would
have tempted us to stir. The sun, like a ball of bur-
nished copper, filled the skies with a heat-created mist,
and poured upon the earth a fiery atmosphere that
seemed to burn as it touched you, and the very breeze
might have issued from the mouth of a furnace; but
we gathered ourselves together—all that was left of
us, for we were gradually melting away—and, armed
with fans, smelling-salts and sundry antidotes to faint-
ing fits, panted our way from Forty-fifth Street to a
Sixth Avenue car, which landed us close to the theatre.
Immediately on entering, we felt as though we had
left the hot world to scorch and dry up outside, while
we were enjoying a soft summer breeze within.
Where did it come from ? The house was crowded—
there was not standing-room for a broomstick; but the
air was as cool and refreshing as though it had blown
over a bank of spring violets. We learned the reason
of this. By some simple contrivance the outer air,

circulating through and among tons of ice, is forced
to find its way through a thousand frozen cracks and
crevices before it enters the auditorium; thus a flow
of fresh air is kept in constant circulation, which
renders an afternoon in Madison Square Theatre a
luxury during the hottest of dog-days.

The death-roll is terrible during these hot spells,
sometimes amounting from sun-stroke alone to twenty
in a single day. The New Yorkers, however, know
how to make the best of their semi-tropical summer.
The more sensible portion of the masculine population
go about in their linen suits and panama hats, though
some men cling to their beloved chimney-pot and
swelter under a weight of broadcloth; but no man is
above carrying an umbrella, white, green, or brown,
as the case may be. Rivers of iced lemonade are
flowing at the street corners, at two cents per glass.
You may see a multitude closing round and pouring
in and out of the " drug stores " (chemists' shops).
You think there must have been an accident—somebody run over, somebody killed. No such thing; it
is only the more aristocratic thirsty multitude, who
eschew street corners, crowding in for their iced
drinks. The " drug stores " have, every one, a neat
white marble fountain, with a dozen shining silver
taps, which pour forth streams of fruit-flavoured iced
drinks—pine, cherry, strawberry, raspberry, and lemon
cream soda, the most delicious of all. From early
morning till late in the evening these fountains never
cease playing; small fortunes pour from their silver
mouths into the pockets of their owners.

In the summer evenings the whole indoor population of New York seems to overflow on to the

"stoops" of their house. Walking through some of the best streets, you may glance in at the open windows, and see the elegantly furnished vacant rooms, with their luxurious lounges, paintings, mirrors, and gilded magnificence, mellowed in the low-burning gaslight, while the inhabitants are taking the air on their doorsteps. The white moon, shining down on the yellow gas-lighted streets; the elevated railroad, rushing with its living freight through the air, blinking its green-and-red fiery eyes upon the world below; the tall dark houses, with their dimly lighted, luxurious interiors and family groups, from paterfamilias down to the youngest-born, the ladies, in their pretty, fanciful toilettes, taking the air on the doorsteps;— all combine to form a pretty picture, quite like a theatrical scene on the broad stage of life. Rippling waves of low laughter and scraps of musical chit-chat follow you as you pass along. This is an old knickerbocker custom, which still obtains everywhere except in the sacred Fifth Avenue, which confines itself strictly within doors, shrined from the vulgar gaze; perhaps the *nouveau riche* element (being largely represented) is afraid of compromising its dignity by following old-fashioned customs.

· As the weeks passed on the weather became more and more trying, and we made daily excursions to the numerous watering-places immediately surrounding New York, leaving home early in the morning and returning the same evening, which is easily done. Coney Island, one of the great resorts for the million, is reached from the foot of Twenty-third Street in about an hour. A few years ago it was a mere wide waste of sand, and was bought by a clever speculator for a mere song; it is now worth millions of dollars, and is covered on all sides with a miscellaneous mass of buildings of all descriptions. Restaurants, shooting-galleries, pavilions, and refreshment-rooms to suit all classes, and some monster hotels, of light, airy structure, lift their faces towards the sea. Culver, Brighton, and Manhattan Beaches, the one being a continuation of the other, spread their wide stretch of silver sand along the side of the island and down to the blue Atlantic waves below. There are no pleasant walks or drives, there exists not a tree, there is no shade from the fierce, blinding sun to be found anywhere. No gray rocks or picturesque battlemented cliffs; nothing but the level island, with its wide stretch of silver sand and a world of sea. The hotels are crowded, every nook and corner of the island filled to overflowing during the season; the beach is covered with a lively mass of holiday-makers, all bent on enjoying themselves; gay bunting is flaunting and flying everywhere; musicians are hard at work, beating drums, scraping fiddles, and blowing trumpets, as though their very lives depended on the noise they are making. Altogether, it is a gay, stirring scene. Coney Island is not a place where the fashionable or aristocratic multitude most do congregate; it is a rather fast, jolly, rollicking place, and serves its purpose well, as the health-breathing lungs of a great city.

Rockaway Beach is about half an hour's journey off, and is disposed to set up a race of rivalry with Coney Island. Its general aspect is much the same— flat, level land, and sand, and sea; it is less frequented, less gay, and certainly has not such good accommodation; but a very fine hotel is now in course of erection, which promises very superior accommodation to visitors. Rockaway is scarcely as flat and barren as Coney Island; in its immediate vicinity clumps of trees are making praiseworthy efforts to grow, but at present their long, gaunt branches are but sparsely covered with green. Long Branch and Long Island are both of easy access from the upper part of the city, by ferry and rail; they are equally favourite watering-places with those already mentioned, though of a rather different character; they do not depend for popularity on a floating population, being the resort (Long Branch especially so) of the more fashionable public. There are whole legions of hotels, and squadrons of boarding-houses, together with numerous elegant villas or cottage residences, which are let by the season, to such as prefer the freedom of their own household to establishing themselves in an hotel. Many build their own fanciful dwellings, and migrate thither in early summer, and remain till the chill autumn breezes drive them back to the city; others make it their head-quarters, and reside there all the year round.

Long Branch is a delightful place. You can choose your companionship, and join the coteries of pleasant society, and have as much gaiety or as much social seclusion as you please. Some of the first-class hotels, which are largely patronized by transient travellers, have been erected on the low bluff which rises behind the strip of sandy beach. A fine wide avenue runs between them and the sea. They are none of them grand, imposing-looking buildings, and have no pretensions to architectural beauty, being for the most part long, low, frame-houses, with wide verandahs and

It was decided among us that " Sam's Point," a lofty peak of the Shewangunk, must be visited. We started one bright morning by a narrow winding road which is carried along the face of the mountain, climbing upwards through tangled brushwood, past banks of flowering laurel, their shining leaves half hidden by their luxuriant masses of delicate pink and white blossoms ; up, still up, through forests of pine and fir, over broken masses of lichen-covered boulders, with fantastic rocks looming on every side, and on over sloping stretches of breezy uplands, till we came to a strip of table-land. The horses pricked up their ears and put on a " spurt." Poor, tired brutes ! they had travelled that road often enough, and could find their way to the low-lying shanty, where they know they are to be stabled for the next hour or two, without any of our guidance. At this stage of our journey we came in close view of " Sam's Point," standing out in clear-cut lines against the sky.

Here, according to the general custom, we unpacked our luncheon-basket. It was filled with such good things, and so many of them, we hardly knew which to begin first. We spread our feast under the shadow of a belt of dark trees, the last of their line that can lift their heads and grow on the now barren, flinty soil. With much fun and laughter we got through a luxurious meal ; then our general commanding for the season insisted that we must climb to the very top of " Sam's Point." We obey, and start on a scrambling expedition up the sloping stony path, where straggling thorny bushes caught us viciously at every turn. With the hot sun blazing fiercely upon us, and a high, warm wind almost blowing us off our feet, we struggled on to the top. No, not quite the top : we halted on a rocky platform, just below the extreme point, and looked down from its dizzy, precipitous height upon the lovely landscape below, lying in the peaceful smile of a glorious sunshine, rolling and spreading out hundreds of feet below, as far as the eye can see. Dark belts of forest trees outline the distant horizon, thickets and wild woods sweep down through the hilly defiles, reach out their green arms, and run like a fancy network of nature's cunningest pattern over the valleys, while the silver thread of a river runs round and about, lacing the green meadow lands together. Scores of white villages, dwarfed by distance till they look like collections of dolls' houses, are scattered over the plains or cling to the sloping hillsides. The colouring, and the lights and shadows falling everywhere, give an additional charm to the exquisite picture before us. It holds us like a magnet ; we cannot tear ourselves away from it ; we perch ourselves on the narrow parapet and gaze our fill. There is a mellowness and balm in the atmosphere, and slowly a soft pink mist falls over the landscape like a bridal veil, and covers everything with a tender mystery.

We turn and scramble down the stony path, and are soon winding our way down the mountain road homeward, still feasting our eyes with delicious bits of scenery as we go along. We drive round among the foothills to get a view of the Nopanoc falls, which are only about half an hour from Ellenville. They are not grand or imposing, nor do they fall from any visible height, but they are beautiful from their wild surroundings, and come creaming and foaming down the rugged mountain-sides, till they reach the stony bed

below, and flow on beneath our feet to their far-off
watery home ; they seem arranged by nature for
transfer to an artist's canvas. Tired though we were
with our long day's outing, we enjoyed our homeward
drive through the evening shadows. There was no
moon, and the dusky air was full of fireflies, floating
about, like globes of living light; and the " whip-poor-
will " commenced his melancholy plaint, which he
never utters till the day is done. The bird came to his
curious cognomen something in this wise. A be-
nighted sinner commonly called " Poor Will " was
stumbling home late one night when the bird began
to sing, and to his muddled ears the notes arranged
themselves into the words, " Whip poor Will." He
knew he deserved whipping, and believed that an order
for his future castigation was being despatched
through some mysterious agency to the realms above.
Thenceforth, whipped by the stings of an awakened
conscience, he set to and repented as hard as he had
sinned, and the name stuck to the bird ever afterwards.

The " whip-poor-will's" notes had hardly died away,
when the frogs, huge green goggle-eyed monsters,
commenced their croaking concert, which is by no
means an unpleasant thing to listen to ; it goes with
a rather musical, monotonous swing, quite different
from the harsh croak of their froggy brethren on our
side of the water.

The next morning we returned to New York, to
rest one more night, our last, in that city previous to
our visit to Boston. We left Ellenville with much
regret. I know of no place where one could so delight-

fully dream away the long summer days, as in that
rural little village with its tempting and delightful
surrounding. It is reached by the Erie Railway from
Jersey City, and is about four hours' journey from
New York.

below, and flow on beneath our feet to their far-off watery home ; they seem arranged by nature for transfer to an artist's canvas. Tired though we were with our long day's outing, we enjoyed our homeward drive through the evening shadows. There was no moon, and the dusky air was full of fireflies, floating about, like globes of living light; and the " whip-poor-will " commenced his melancholy plaint, which he never utters till the day is done. The bird came to his curious cognomen something in this wise. A be-nighted sinner commonly called " Poor Will " was stumbling home late one night when the bird began to sing, and to his muddled ears the notes arranged themselves into the words, " Whip poor Will." He knew he deserved whipping, and believed that an order for his future castigation was being despatched through some mysterious agency to the realms above. Thenceforth, whipped by the stings of an awakened conscience, he set to and repented as hard as he had sinned, and the name stuck to the bird ever after-wards.

The " whip-poor-will's " notes had hardly died away, when the frogs, huge green goggle-eyed monsters, commenced their croaking concert, which is by no means an unpleasant thing to listen to ; it goes with a rather musical, monotonous swing, quite different from the harsh croak of their froggy brethren on our side of the water.

The next morning we returned to New York, to rest one more night, our last, in that city previous to our visit to Boston. We left Ellenville with much regret. I know of no place where one could so delightfully dream away the long summer days, as in that rural little village with its tempting and delightful surrounding. It is reached by the Erie Railway from Jersey City, and is about four hours' journey from New York.

CHAPTER XXVII.

THE "AMERICAN ATHENS."

Aboard the *Massachusetts*—A Perambulation—The Electric Machine—An Easy Way of committing Suicide—Boston—The
Cars—The Common—The " Glorious Fourth of July."

THERE had been so many terrible accidents by the
river steamers during the last few weeks, that we were
half inclined to go to Boston by rail; but on reflection
we determined not to yield to an imaginary evil.
Judging by averages, we ought to have a safe passage,
for one of the finest vessels had been destroyed by
fire only two days before, and great disasters are rarely
continuous. Because misfortune had happened to
other people, it was no reason it should tread upon
our heels also.

Accordingly, we started on one of the finest Providence Boats, the *Massachusetts*, for Boston, leaving
New York at five o'clock in the afternoon. We spent
the few remaining hours of daylight in admiring the
river scenery, as our majestic boat steamed towards the
Sound, and enjoying the brisk sea-breezes. Never
had the " briny kisses " of the great sweet mother
seemed so fresh and invigorating. The captain, to
whom we had been previously introduced, invited us

into the wheelhouse, which, contrary to our home custom, is lifted high up above the deck, commanding a clear view of all surrounding objects. There we watched with great interest the steering and working of the vessel. The bell seemed always to be ringing its signal, warning the small craft out of our way, and informing the larger craft which way we would " keep her head."

Afterwards we descended into the engine-room, and found the huge monster well worth seeing—its black body bound in bright bands, and studded with polished decorations of brass and steel, like a grim warrior wearing his coat of mail. We saw him fed with his vast furnace fires. He seemed always hungry, opening his red mouth for more food. We watched its gigantic walking beam rise and fall, in its solemn march across the world of waters. The vessel in all parts is lighted by electricity; and we were allowed to go downstairs to inspect the generating apparatus. In order to reach it we had to go through the machinery-room, where the crashing, groaning, and thudding, the rapid whirling of wheels, and clanking to and fro of countless bars, and the up-and-down stroke of the piston, deafened our ears, dazzled our eyes, and bewildered our senses, while the walking beam above, the great propelling power of all, tramped steadily on.

We passed through this distracting place, crossed a narrow passage, and at the end of it found ourselves in an empty room—empty except for the electric machine, with its invisible wonders working before our eyes. We could not absolutely *see* the machine; its evolutions were so rapid, they might have been impelled by lightning. It was surrounded by scintillating sparks of weird greenish light, playing round it as though some fiery genie was confined therein. There was not much noise, only a whizzing, whirring sound, and the ground shook beneath our feet with a quivering motion like a living thing in mortal pain. Radiating from the machine were sundry thin wires, each conducting the illuminating power to the decks and saloons, both above and below. Two wires ran perpendicularly one on each side of the apparatus, one conducting the negative, the other the positive current. Each one might be handled singly with impunity, but a simultaneous touch of the two together would be fraught with instant death. This easy mode of committing suicide lay within reach of our hands. We shuddered, and beat a hasty retreat, lest a sudden impulse might tempt us to try the experiment. How many unintentional suicides have been hurried into eternity by the uncontrollable impulse of a moment!

About seven o'clock a capital dinner, à la carte, was served, and we had the double delight of enjoying a dainty meal, and watching the sunset from the saloon windows. There was no gorgeous colouring such as sometimes clothes the western skies with the barbaric splendour of crimson, amethyst, green, and gold; but the whole hemisphere where the sun went down was filled with floating islands of golden light, sailing hither and thither in the face of the pale-blue sky. But soon came the twilight, trailing her dusky skirts between land and sea, and shut the heavens from our sight.

After dinner we went on deck, but there was nothing to tempt us to stay there. It was a cool gray evening; there was no moon, and not a star was visible; we therefore went into the grand saloon, which is gorgeously upholstered in crimson velvet, and decorated with much carving and gilding, while mirrors and looking-glasses reflect and multiply you by dozens on every side. A piano stood at the farther end, and there was already a man in possession. He was short, he was fat, he was bald, and wore an immense pair of green goggles, such as are rarely worn except when crossing the ice. He looked as stupid and stolid as an animated jelly-fish, and knew as little about music as an oyster; but he sang, out of tune and out of time, the most lugubrious ditties. He enjoyed them if nobody else did. When he got to the end of one, he began another. He might have seen the expression of disgust on everybody's face, but he was self-absorbed, he never looked; if any one attempted to talk within earshot, he glared round reproachfully and sang louder than before. It is strange, but painfully true: it is precisely those people who can neither play nor sing who attempt to do both for the torture of their fellow-passengers on those river excursions, and perhaps on some other occasions.

We were driven to our state-room early, and the first thing that met our sight was a huge pair of ominous-looking life-preservers. We tried them on, saw that they fitted and fastened correctly, then leisurely proceeded to plait our hair in long pigtails for the convenience of our escort, so that, in case of accidents, he might float us easily. We had passed the wrecked remains of the *Seawanhaka* an hour before; it had been destroyed by fire, and scores of its passengers had met their death within fifty yards of the shore. These river boats are splendid to look

at, luxurious to travel in, but if a fire once seizes on
any part of the vessel, being made of wood, it burns
like a matchbox; there is no hope for it. There was
nothing left of the unfortunate *Seawanhaka* but the
huge boiler and a few ribs of iron, lying like a
mutilated skeleton on the shore. It was not a pleasant
picture to possess our mind the last thing at night;
but we went to bed, and, strange to say, slept soundly
enough until six o'clock in the morning, when we
were served with a comfortable breakfast, and left the
boat at Providence, where the train was waiting, and
in about an hour we reached Boston.

It was one of the loveliest of summer mornings.
A kind of spiritual sunshine lay upon the silent land
as we drove through the empty streets, for at that
early hour few people were astir. We felt as though
we were entering some solemn cathedral town of the
Old World; everything is so different from any other
American city which we have lately been passing
through. There are no long, straight streets, no lines
of tall stone houses, whose sameness wearies the sight;
no dull monotony here. The streets are labyrinthine;
they radiate from all sides and cross at all angles;
they run up and down, round corners, curving or
straight, wide or narrow. There is no irritating
uniformity anywhere.

From the first glance we feel that this city has
a character of its own, and that character is essentially
English. There is a certain undefinable something
in the general aspect of the place and of the people
which makes us feel near home. Familiar names greet
us at street corners, their nomenclature being similar
to our own. No tubs of household refuse stand on the

side-walks, or flow over into the gutter. The streets
are beautifully clean; it is a pleasure to walk in them.
Beacon Street, which is one of the most fashionable
localities, reminds us forcibly of Park Lane; in fact,
it is Park Lane, in miniature, seen through the
wrong end of a telescope. The houses are all in good
taste, though of different sizes and varied forms of
architecture. Some have old-fashioned bay windows,
others are flat fronted, some of white or gray stone,
some of cherry-red bricks. One has its balcony and
window-sills filled with bright-hued and sweet-smelling flowers; another is literally covered with Westeria,
all abloom with rich purple blossoms. It is the pretty
floral decorations and varied style of building which
gives it so quaint and picturesque an appearance. It
stands on gently rising ground. At the top is the
State House, a very handsome colonnaded building,
crowned with a huge bronze cupola shining like bur-
nished gold, dominating the landscape and visible for
miles round.

In front, railed in with light elegant railings, and
running the whole length of Beacon Street, is the
" Common," as the Bostonians modestly call it, though
it is in reality a very beautiful park; but a park without carriage drives, devoted entirely to pedestrian
exercise. There is a fine growth of forest trees, which
for centuries cannot have had an axe among them.
There are fountains, too, and flower-gardens, and comfortable seats arranged under the umbrageous shade of
the spreading walnut trees. On one mound of elevated ground is a handsome memorial in honour of
their dead ancestors; in another part of the common,
on a greater elevation, stands an equestrian statue of

General Washington. No city is complete without a statue of the founder of the United States. The common is a delightful rural promenade and pleasure-ground, and when the band is playing presents a most brilliant and imposing scene.

The absence of the tobacco-chewing process and its disgusting results is another striking feature in Boston. You may walk through the public streets or ride in the cars the whole day long without once being subject to the nuisance to which we ought to have become accustomed. In the streets, on the cars, or among the people, you recognize a familiar Old-World look, and signs of refinement and cultivation everywhere. Even a Boston crowd is a well-behaved, orderly gathering. We were there on the 4th of July. In the morning, escorted by a friend whose name will remain ever green in our memory, we went to an entertainment at the grand opera-house, which we imagined would partake of a national character. We expected to hear martial music and the national airs sang with the enthusiasm of a people who "exulted to be free;" but we didn't. The concert was confined to a few everyday melodies—"The Old Folks at Home" and "Annie Laurie"—all well enough in their way, but hardly suited to such an occasion as the "glorious fourth." Then, for the first time in our lives, we heard the "Act of Independence" read, with great emphasis and distinctness. We felt we ought to have blushed—but didn't.

In the evening there was a grand display of fireworks, an open air orchestral concert, and other amusements. The people swarmed upon the common by hundreds and thousands of all classes, all degrees.

There were no "reserved seats," and no possibility of
enjoying any part of the festivity in "luxurious ease."
Anybody who wished to see or enjoy anything must
go on foot. It is this temporary incorporation of the
refined with the rougher elements of humanity which
makes an American crowd different from any other.
There is no pushing, no horse-play, no practical joking;
nobody hustles or tramples on you. It is essentially
a polite crowd. Of course we never got into one
from choice, but sometimes from necessity found ourselves in the midst of it, and everywhere, in other
cities besides Boston, found the same orderly behaviour.

On the evening of the "glorious fourth" we went
out, with a pleasant titillation of curiosity, mingled
with a nervous notion that brickbats might be flying,
or squibs and crackers be fizzing about too freely, or,
perhaps, some little patriotic pleasantry awkwardly
demonstrated.

An American visiting in England had said on a
previous "fourth," "Ah! in my country every man
will be gloriously drunk to-night; not a single one
will go sober to bed." This perhaps coloured our ideas
of the "glorious fourth;" whereas it might have been
the fourth of any other month. The concerts which
took place on different parts of the common were by
no means of a patriotic or exhilarating nature. The
orchestras were excellent, the music well played, but
ill chosen; that is, ill chosen for such an occasion. It
was chiefly classical. Occasionally it pranced off into
a waltz, and encouraged the idea of frivolity for a
moment, but was speedily recalled under cover of the
big drum, and a more select fugue or fantasia took its
place. Classical music is not fitting for an open-air

x

promenade, when nobody's attention can be wholly absorbed by it, as should be the case when good music is being played. Fancy a running fire of chit-chat, or cannonade of laughter being carried on, while the solemn strains of Handel, the subtle harmonies of Beethoven, or sweet melodies of Joseph Haydn are filling the air! Merry catching tunes or patriotic airs are best suited to these occasions, but never the ghost of one was abroad that night. John Brown's soul might have marched to the end of his journey, and lain down to undisturbed rest; there was no one to "rally round the flag," shouting the battle-cry of freedom. The star-spangled banner was folded away out of sight, but the stars and stripes fluttered faintly from a few windows, and that was all.

The fireworks crackled and fizzed, while the multitude looked solemnly on. Roman candles burnt blue, showers of golden light were falling, Catherine wheels were whirling in circles of brilliant colours, fantastic designs, and fine set pieces blazed on all sides. We made our bow to an illuminated President, and watched the American eagle light himself up with a golden body, bright-green wings, and ruby claws, big enough to clutch the world by the throat. He was a gorgeous bird, and dazzled our sight for a few moments, and then faded from it. We went home to bed with a virtuous feeling that we had assisted at the celebration of the "glorious fourth."

The arrangements for street traffic in Boston are as nearly perfect as they can be. Cars are running everywhere every minute of the day. Most comfortable cars they are—a great improvement upon any similar conveyances we had seen in any other part of the States. Some are closed, some are open ; the seats are placed so that every one sits face forward. They are splendidly horsed, and you can fly in the face of the wind from one end of the city to another for five cents (2½d.). It is well lighted, and the numerous cars, with their coloured bulls'-eyes behind and before, illuminate the streets, like the flashing of monster fireflies.

Here, as elsewhere, are handsome churches, museums, picture-galleries, etc. No one need ever pass a dull day in this intellectual and cultivated city. Like Washington and Philadelphia, Boston is exclusive in the matter of society. Its social laws are many, and strictly kept. Reserved and dignified in its everyday life, it is not overgiven to demonstrative rejoicing, even among its best friends. We have all our little weaknesses, and perhaps Boston may be a *little* vain of its intellect and refinement. " We don't do 'that' in Boston," is a common phrase, and considered strong enough to condemn "that" when it is done elsewhere.

The rural surroundings of Boston are very beautiful ; but the interest of most tourists centres in the city itself, which, besides its many attractions, is the home of two men who have made the genius of America known and honoured in every quarter of the civilized world—I mean of the Poet Longfellow, and the genial philosophical poet and essayist, Oliver Wendell Holmes.

CHAPTER XXVIII.

FAREWELL VISITS.

A Visit to Longfellow—The Poet's Home—Dr. Oliver Wendell
Holmes—Newport—A Fashionable Watering-place—The Old
Town—The "Cottages"—Homeward.

It is not admissible, as a rule, to turn the result of a
private visit into public copy. To be received into
a family circle on terms of social equality, and there
gather up scraps of conversation, and turn the sayings
and doings of the unsuspecting household into public
property, is a most ungracious return for kindly
hospitality; therefore I have hitherto avoided all
mention of my private friends in these pages. But
every rule has an exception, and as the general world
is supposed to be interested in, and are kept fully
informed of, the most trivial circumstances surrounding
the royal rulers of nations, I take it for granted that a
much livelier interest must cling round the monarchs
of mind, whose names are "familiar to our ears as
household words"—whose gentle genius, playful
humour, or tender philosophy has coloured the lives
and gladdened the hearts of thousands, and helped to
make the ignorant wise and the wise happy. Their
thoughts come to us over land and over sea; invisibly

and subtly, as the sweet fresh air we breathe, they permeate our lives, and become a part of us, circulating, with a pure ennobling influence, from the cottage to the palace. These are the only true magicians, god-inspired workers of miracles; shrined in the sanctity of their own peaceful homes, they are working to give light to the blind old world, that it may be better for their lives when the Great Master calls them home.

We should have been sorely disappointed if we had been compelled to leave Boston without paying our affectionate homage to Longfellow, whose name is associated with our earliest awakening thoughts. He had been so often with us in spirit for this many a long year, that we longed to see him in the flesh; it was therefore with great pleasure we received an invitation to pay him a visit at his marine residence, Nahant, where he generally spends the summer months. Nahant lies on the shores of the Atlantic, just outside Boston Harbour. We had a glorious sail, for it was one of summer's loveliest days—earth, air, sea, and sky were all invisibly blended in one perfect harmony. Our brief, bright journey was soon over, and on turning a sudden point of the bay we found ourselves scudding along on the waves of the Atlantic. Nahant was before us. Longfellow's house was pointed out to us from the vessel; it seemed to be lying close on the shore, but in reality it stands on elevated rising ground, open to the sea, but about a quarter of a mile from it. A carriage waited on the landing-stage to convey us to the house—an attention for which we were grateful, as a walk uphill, even for so short a distance, in the face of a blazing sun, was not desirable. After a short breezy drive, the carriage

stopped at a delightfully picturesque villa, or cottage
ornée, though it was more like a Swiss chalet than
either. A child was playing with its toys and dolls
in the verandah which ran round the four sides of the
house, and two gentlemen were seated in rocking-
chairs facing the wide winding road. As we drove
up, one of the gentlemen rose and came down the
steps and across the small front garden to meet us.
There was no mistaking the man—it was our host
himself; we had seen him often gazing at us with
stony photographic eyes from the shop-windows
thousands of miles away, but no more like the poet's
actual self than a stagnant pool is like the living sea.
We observed him well as he came down the steps,
with a gracious dignity born of a benignant spirit.
He is tall, slight, and erect as a soldier on duty, with
refined features, and a pale complexion, with a slight
tinge of colour on his cheeks, almost as delicate as the
blush of a woman, kind blue eyes, and wavy hair, which
is more white than gray; he wears a beard, has long
shapely white hands that any lady might be proud
of; his voice is peculiarly soft, and his manners full of
that gentle courtliness which is fast dying out. He
is in his seventy-fourth year, but looks considerably
younger. There is none of the physical feebleness or
querulous spirit of age about him; he seems now to
be in the full autumn-tide of a hale, healthy life. Time
is dealing very gently with him, leading him imperceptibly (as it is leading us all) down the valley
towards "the silent land" which he has told us of.

After shaking hands and exchanging the usual
greetings, he presented us to his two brothers-in-law,
who reside with him. The household was not entirely

masculine, however; the poet's two daughters were
out in their yacht enjoying a sail: the one is married,
and, with her little child, is only on a visit; the other,
a very charming young lady, lives at home with her
father. We went through the house and sat in the
back verandah. A tempting-looking hammock swung
there, and wild roses climbed up the lattice-work and
nodded their odorous heads at us, and showered their
pink petals at our feet. The poet gathered us a bunch
of the fairest blossoms; they lie faded and scentless
in my album to-day, but the memory of that July
afternoon at Nahant is fresh and green still.

We sat there chatting in a pleasant way of the Old
World and the New; the gray Atlantic, scarcely
wrinkled in the light breeze, lay before us. We
watched the various vessels—light brigs, sloops, and
schooners, all full-rigged to' catch the breeze, and
stately. steamers on their march across the world of
waters, and pretty yachts, some curtsying to their
own shadows, others with their white sails spread, like
gigantic swans skimming over the face of the ocean.
Presently the one particular yacht we awaited came
prancing over the tiny waves, like a steed that knows
he is nearing home. The two ladies sprang ashore,
and speedily made a pleasant addition to our party in
the verandah. The time passed only too quickly. The
pretty, fair-haired little grandchild sat in the lap of its
blooming young mother, playing and prattling its baby
prattle. It was an idyllic picture, with its pleasant
home surroundings—a living illustration of three
stages of life: the dawn, the meridian, and the evening
before the sun sets and the night closes in.

The conversation was never allowed to flag; somehow, the merest everyday chit-chat seemed to gather weight and pungency by the mode of utterance : a pointed word, a look, the turn of a sentence, gave to every commonplace phrase an attraction and a meaning it would not in itself possess. Mr. Longfellow is no egotist; he evidently does not care to talk of himself or his work. He is full of that modesty which generally characterizes great genius, but is lamentably wanting in the many poetical aspirants who are buzzing about the world, trying their wings to see how far they can soar into those ideal realms where true genius sits calmly crowned. Whatever he says it is pleasant to listen to.

During the few brief hours of a first acquaintance, it is rarely we get into a very deep or animated discussion on any subject; we must first get the key to each other's minds, and become *en rapport* with each other's feeling, before the spirit of either can give forth its fullest, freest tones. As a rule, it is enough to skim the surface of the current topics of the day.

We sat down sociably to a *recherché* little dinner, the first course of which was one of the national dishes, to which we were by this time well accustomed—clam chowder. The meal, gastronomically considered, was on strictly international principles ; we sipped the vintage of Champagne, while we enjoyed the pork and beans of Boston, and washed down corn-cobs and hominy with mineral waters of Germany.

We were obliged to leave Nahant early, as the Boston boat was at the pier, and time and tide wait for no woman, even in this chivalrous land. Cordially and regretfully we said " Good-bye." The dear old man, with his delightful family group, stood in the verandah, shading his eyes from the setting sun, watching till we were out of sight. He is photographed on my mind; I shall see him often in days to come, as I looked my last upon him then.

The next day, according to appointment, we paid a visit to another celebrity, Dr. Oliver Wendell Holmes, who has made himself a name in the Old World as well as in the New. He, too, was residing at his country cottage at "Beverly Farms," another of those delightful rural retreats in the vicinity of Boston, being little more than an hour's railway journey from it.

We reached Beverly Farms about noon—the fiercest, hottest part of the day. We had no idea how far the Doctor's residence might be from the station, but trusted to find some conveyance to take us there, feeling that it would be an effort even to walk a hundred yards in the heat of the blazing sun. The train steamed away from the platform, and we looked round in search of some one of whom we might inquire our road, and then looked blankly at one another. We had no idea which way to turn, and there was not a creature in sight to tell us. We walked through the empty station; the ticket office was closed, and not a railway official was in sight. Only a big black dog was lying curled up under one of the benches; every other living thing had mysteriously vanished. Some labourers were working in a field not far from the station, and we noticed a pretty white cottage close to the roadway on the opposite side—scarcely a stone's throw from us. A gentleman in a linen suit, a straw hat, and carrying a green umbrella, came out of the gate and walked quickly towards the station; we advanced to meet him, and inquired if he could tell us where Dr. Holmes lived?

"I am Dr. Holmes," he answered, "and you, I presume, are the ladies I was hurrying to meet?" We acknowledged that we believed we were. He turned back with us, and in another moment we all three entered the garden which we had seen him leave a moment before. It was a pleasant first introduction, and here we scored another delightful day. We found Dr. Holmes a most genial and agreeable companion— exactly, as from reading his books, we had expected he would be. He is neither tall nor short, but of medium height; a thin, wiry man, with iron-gray hair, and eyes twinkling with humour and philosophy. Age has not dimmed their lustre, nor taken the spring from his elastic spirit; he is as brisk in his movements as many a man at five-and-twenty. Mrs. Holmes, a gentle-mannered lady, just the wife necessary for such a man—one who would make his home a harbour of rest and peace—came out to meet and welcome us. It is always pleasant to see a genius and philosopher well matched in his life's companionship; unfortunately, we have so often to look on the reverse picture. The right woman is an inspiration to the one, a study for the other; but the wrong acts like an irritant and blister, his whole life through. We were presently joined by his daughter—a brilliant young widow, a feminine edition of himself. Altogether we made a very pleasant party, and soon floated off into a brisk conversation. I wish I could reproduce his spirited, quaintly-turned phrases and quick repartee, to which the expression of his face gave additional point and high flavour. I think the most dryasdust doctrine would quicken into life if passed through the alembic of his sparkling philosophy.

It is not often that poetry and philosophy go hand in hand together as in this case it does. Dr. Holmes seems surprised to find himself so much more famous in this country for his prose works and philosophical studies than for his poetical productions. Scientific research and semi-philosophical lectures and literature are the occupations of his daily life, but poetry is the darling of his heart, the beloved companion of his holiday hours, the airy architect who builds for his spirit a home we know not of. We retired to luncheon in a pretty parlour looking out into the flower-garden, where the bees were droning and the tall lilies and roses nodding sleepily in the sunshine. He seemed very much interested in our intonation, and frequently called attention to our mode of pronouncing certain words. He afterwards read to us some scraps and snatches of his new poems, which was a great treat to us, for he has a melodious voice, and reads with great emphasis and spirit; indeed, we were so deeply engrossed by his brilliant conversations that we almost lost our train. With much regret we bade him and his family a cordial adieu.

There was one more visit to pay, and that the last. Time, the great " whipper-in," was behind us, bidding us gather our energies together, for we must soon—too soon—bid adieu to the New World, and turn our faces homeward towards the old land. The next day we started to pay a visit to Newport, Rhode Island, whose fame as the most beautiful, select, and fashionable watering-place in America had long been familiar to us. It is only about four hours' rail from Boston. Our host

and hostess met us at the station, and we were too much
occupied in conversing with them to take much notice
of the town as we drove through it; we made closer
acquaintance with it afterwards.   A half-hour's drive
took us through the lower part of the town, the business quarters, and past the " old mill" which stands in
a wide, open square.   Some say it is a relic left by the
Norsemen who once overran the land, and others assert
that it was built by the earliest colonists centuries ago ;
but nobody knows exactly when it was built, nor what
was its use.   It is a massive stone tower, with no
visible means of entrance ; it must have been entered
by scaling-ladders from without.   It is now a ruin, by
no means a picturesque one, but it is the only ancient
relic on the island, and the people are proud of it;
they seem to have a vested interest in its antiquity,
and regard it as a sort of illustration of their history
and of themselves.   Past this ancient monument,
through a pleasant winding road, with charming villa
residences, and shady trees on either side, and we turn
through a pair of handsome iron gates into some beautifully laid out grounds ; a miniature park, indeed, with
clumps of fine old trees of the most rare and varied
descriptions, and evergreens and shrubs of the choicest
kind, all so arranged that the foliage of one should contrast artistically with that of the other.   We roll through
a long, curving drive, and in another moment stop
before an old-fashioned red-brick mansion, with gabled
front and pointed roof, which might have been lifted
bodily up, and transplanted thither from some ancient
English manor.   The house in its general style and
all its arrangements was purely English, and both host
and hostess were simply perfect, and combined the re-

fined courtesy of our country with the lavish liberality and genial hospitality of their own. It is the same in quality and degree in most American houses ; there is no stiffness or formality, but that peculiar kind of good breeding and *bonhommie* which makes the transient guest feel most perfectly at home. There is nothing fast, frivolous, or shoddy about Newport; only the *crème de la crème* of American society congregates there ; the fun-loving, vulgar herd, with their holiday squibs and crackers, hold no orgies on its sacred shores. The floating population is clothed (metaphorically speaking) in broadcloth and fine linen ; it takes up its abode for a night or so at the one solitary and rather gloomy-looking hotel, and passes away.

Newport proper, that is the lower, older portion of the town, is a dull, ragged, out-at-elbows sort of place ; it looks tired and worn out, as though it had had its day, and wanted rest. Indeed, it has been busy and bright enough in its time. A century ago it was a bustling seaport; scores of ships were riding at anchor in the bay ; the wharves were crowded with merchandise, and sailors from all parts of the world wandered to and fro, creating a confusion of tongues, and perhaps a confusion of morals at the same time. All is lonely and deserted now; the wharves are dilapidated, rotting away ; a few broken boats are hauled up on shore, and children play at hide-and-seek amid the ruins of the old dead days.

The fashionable Newportians reside in the upper portion of the town, which grows along the face of the cliff, and is held sacred to themselves. Lodging-houses or " genteel apartments " are things unknown. Only the aristocracy of the surrounding States gather here; people of culture, of refinement, and of wealth. There are no flashily dressed people or Brummagem buildings in Newport, but a solid, substantial dignity greets you everywhere. The road from the lower town winds upwards through a labyrinth of lovely cottages, covered with vines and trailing roses, past an ancient Jewish burial-ground, which has received no silent inmates for many a long year. It is kept in perfect order, and looks like a blooming flower-garden, funds for this purpose having been left by a deceased Rabbi. The old synagogue, gray and hoary, stands in the midst, deserted, haunted only by the echoes of departed days.

By this pretty winding way you reach the high-way, if such a commonplace term can be applied to such a royal road. It is a fashionable thoroughfare and general drive, about two miles and a half long, bordered on either side along the whole route by tasteful villas. Some, indeed, are quite palatial residences; every one is a specimen of architectural beauty; each bears a sort of family resemblance to the other, but no two are exactly alike. Never was such a wealth of architectural attractions gathered on one spot. Along the whole line one beautiful dwelling rises after another, till your mind becomes a jumble of points and arches, cupolas and towers; and you don't know which to admire most. One part of the houses faces seaward, the other fronts the road, which during the season is crowded with handsome, well-appointed equipages, which would do credit to Longchamps or Rotten Row. The ladies sit in their verandahs reading, chatting, or working, as the case may be, and watch their friends " go riding by." The air, laden with the salt sea-breeze, is soft and salubrious; there is generally a sea-wind blowing inland, which tempers the heat of the sun, and renders Newport delightful when the cities are unendurable.

This is our last resting-place in America. Our holiday is over; the time has come when we must turn our faces homeward. No more lingering by the way, no more rolling over prairie lands, or lounging by inland seas. Regretfully, yet not wholly regretful, we say good-bye to Newport, spend half an hour in Boston, then on through Canada, a twenty-four hours' journey to Quebec. We pass through long flat stretches of country, where Nature seems to have exerted herself to show how dull, dreary, and monotonous she could have made the world if she had only tried. Everything is brown, dusty, and parched with the hot thirsty sun, which seems to have drawn every drop of moisture from the poor old earth. Occasionally we catch a glimpse of a lazy, sluggish stream, creeping along as though it was trying to hide itself from the fierce blaze above. We were glad, when the night closed in, to get into our comfortable berth, and shut our eyes on the dreary landscape. At seven next morning we reached Point Levis, and were ferried across to Quebec, where our vessel lay at anchor.

The cathedral bells are ringing, and the sound of their musical chime comes to us pleasantly across the water; we look once more upon the shining roofs and gilded spires pricking the pale morning sky. We should have liked one more ramble through the quaint old streets, but the *Sardinian* lies at the quay, ready to start, the smoke coiling up from her great red funnel, her huge prow rising like the wall of a house from the sluggish water that splashes slowly against her sides. There is bustle on the decks, which are all swept and garnished in readiness for the advent of the coming passengers. Our good captain's genial voice hails us on the gangway; the well-remembered faces of the ship's officers smile a welcome to us as we pass along the deck; last, not least, our kindly stewardess meets and marshals us to our cosy little state-room. In the saloon—which is gay with ferns and flowers and polished plate and shining glass—the ship's canary, the pet alike of officers and passengers, is trilling his loudest and sweetest. All is smiling, bright, and cheery, as we take up our quarters in the little floating world, which was so pleasant a nine-days' home to us a year ago, and is now to be so once more.

An hour afterwards, the shining spires of Quebec have faded from our sight, we are steaming down the mighty St. Lawrence, and our faces are set for England and for Home!

THE END.

PRINTED BY WILLIAM CLOWES AND SONS, LIMITED, LONDON AND BECCLES.

11, *Henrietta Street, Covent Garden, W.C.*
(*Late* 193, *Piccadilly, W.*)

June, 1881.

CATALOGUE OF BOOKS

PUBLISHED BY

CHAPMAN & HALL, LIMITED,

INCLUDING

DRAWING EXAMPLES, DIAGRAMS, MODELS, INSTRUMENTS, ETC.

ISSUED UNDER THE AUTHORITY OF

THE SCIENCE AND ART DEPARTMENT, SOUTH KENSINGTON,

FOR THE USE OF SCHOOLS AND ART AND SCIENCE CLASSES.

NEW NOVELS.

NEW NOVEL BY ANTHONY TROLLOPE.

AYALA'S ANGEL.

By ANTHONY TROLLOPE.   3 vols. crown 8vo.

BLAIR ATHOL: a Novel.

By W. ALISON.   3 vols. crown 8vo.

AMAT: a Novel.

3 vols. crown 8vo.

"'Amat' suggests a love tale, and a love tale it most certainly is. . . . . There is no straining after effect, no obtrusive immorality, no coarseness, and a very slight alloy of slang; of incident of every sort there is an abundance."— *Athenæum.*

BOOKS

PUBLISHED BY

CHAPMAN & HALL, LIMITED.

ABBOTT (EDWIN), formerly Head Master of the Philological School—

A CONCORDANCE OF THE ORIGINAL POETICAL. WORKS OF ALEXANDER POPE. With an Introduction on the English of Pope, by EDWIN A. ABBOTT, D.D., Author of "A Shakespearian Grammar," &c. &c. Medium 8vo, 21s.

AUSTRALIAN MEAT: RECIPES FOR COOKING AUS-TRALIAN MEAT, with Directions for Preparing Sauces suitable for the same. By a Cook. 12mo, sewed, 9d.

BARTLEY (G. C. T.)—

A HANDY BOOK FOR GUARDIANS OF THE POOR : being a Complete Manual of the Duties of the Office, the Treatment of Typical Cases, with Practical Examples, &c. Crown 8vo, cloth, 3s.

THE PARISH NET: HOW IT'S DRAGGED AND WHAT IT CATCHES. Crown 8vo, cloth, 7s. 6d.

THE SEVEN AGES OF A VILLAGE PAUPER. Crown 8vo, cloth, 5s.

BEESLEY (EDWARD SPENCER), Professor of History in University College, London—

CATILINE, CLODIUS, AND TIBERIUS. Large crown 8vo, 6s.

BENNETT (W. C.)—

SEA SONGS. Crown 8vo, 4s.

BENSON (W.)—

MANUAL OF THE SCIENCE OF COLOUR. Coloured Frontispiece and Illustrations. 12mo, cloth, 2s. 6d.

PRINCIPLES OF THE SCIENCE OF COLOUR. Small 4to, cloth, 15s.

BIDDLECOMBE (SIR GEORGE), C.B., Captain R.N.—

AUTOBIOGRAPHY OF SIR GEORGE BIDDLE-COMBE, C.B., Captain R.N. Large crown 8vo, 8s.

BIRDWOOD (C. M.), C.S.I.—

THE INDUSTRIAL ARTS OF INDIA. With Map and 174 Illustrations. 8vo, 14s. New Edition.

BLAKE (EDITH OSBORNE)—

THE REALITIES OF FREEMASONRY. Demy 8vo, 9s.

TWELVE MONTHS IN SOUTHERN EUROPE. With Illustrations. Demy 8vo, 14s.

A 2

BOYLE (F.)—

CHRONICLES OF NO MAN'S LAND. Large crown
8vo, 10s. 6d.

BRADLEY (THOMAS), of the Royal Military Academy, Woolwich—

ELEMENTS OF GEOMETRICAL DRAWING. In Two
Parts, with Sixty Plates. Oblong folio, half bound, each Part 16s.

Selection (from the above) of Twenty Plates for the Use of
the Royal Military Academy, Woolwich. Oblong folio, half-bound, 16s.

BUCKLAND (FRANK)—

LOG-BOOK OF A FISHERMAN AND ZOOLOGIST.
Second Edition. With numerous Illustrations. Large crown 8vo, 12s.

BURCHETT (R.)—

DEFINITIONS OF GEOMETRY: New Edition. 24mo,
cloth, 5d.

LINEAR PERSPECTIVE, for the Use of Schools of Art.
Twenty-first Thousand. With Illustrations. Post 8vo, cloth, 7s.

PRACTICAL GEOMETRY: The Course of Construction
of Plane Geometrical Figures. With 137 Diagrams. Eighteenth Edition. Post 8vo, cloth, 5s.

BURNAND (F. C.), B.A., Trin. Coll. Camb.—

THE "A. D. C.;" being Personal Reminiscences of the
University Amateur Dramatic Club, Cambridge. Second Edition. Demy 8vo, 12s.

CAMPION (J. S.), late Major, Staff, 1st Br. C.N.G., U.S.A.—

ON THE FRONTIER. Reminiscences of Wild Sports,
Personal Adventures, and Strange Scenes. With Illustrations. Second Edition. Demy 8vo, 16s.

ON FOOT IN SPAIN. With Illustrations. Second Edition.
Demy 8vo, 16s.

CARLYLE (THOMAS)—See pages 17 and 18.

CARLYLE BIRTHDAY BOOK (THE). Prepared by
Permission of Mr. THOMAS CARLYLE. Small crown, 3s.

CAVOUR (COUNT)—

THE LIFE OF COUNT CAVOUR. By CHARLES DE
MAZADE. Translated from the French. Demy 8vo, 16s.

CEYLON—

CEYLON: being a General Description of the Island,
Historical, Physical, Statistical. Containing the most Recent Information. With Map. By an Officer, late of the Ceylon Rifles. 2 vols. Demy 8vo, £1 8s.

CHAMPEAUX (ALFRED)—

TAPESTRY. With Woodcuts. 2s. 6d.

CHURCH (A. H.), M.A., Oxon.—

PLAIN WORDS ABOUT WATER. Illustrated. Large
crown 8vo, sewed, 6d.

FOOD: A Short Account of the Sources, Constituents,
and Uses of Food; intended chiefly as a Guide to the Food Collection in the Bethnal Green Museum. Large crown 8vo, 3s.

CLINTON (R.H.)—

A COMPENDIUM OF ENGLISH HISTORY, from the
Earliest Times to A.D. 1872. With Copious Quotations on the Leading Events and the Constitutional History, together with Appendices. Post 8vo, 7s. 6d.

COLENSO (FRANCES E.)—

HISTORY OF THE ZULU WAR AND ITS ORIGIN.
Assisted in those portions of the work which touch upon Military Matters by Lieut.-Colonel EDWARD DURNFORD. Demy 8vo, 18s.

A New and Cheaper Edition. Crown 8vo, 9s.

COOKERY—

OFFICIAL HANDBOOK FOR THE NATIONAL
TRAINING SCHOOL FOR COOKERY. Containing Lessons on Cookery; forming the Course of Instruction in the School. With List of Utensils Necessary, and Lessons on Cleaning Utensils. Compiled by " R. O. C." Sixth Edition, Large crown 8vo, 8s.

CRAIK (GEORGE LILLIE)—

ENGLISH OF SHAKESPEARE. Illustrated in a Philo-
logical Commentary on his Julius Cæsar. Fifth Edition. Post 8vo, cloth, 5s.

OUTLINES OF THE HISTORY OF THE ENGLISH
LANGUAGE. Ninth Edition. Post 8vo, cloth, 2s. 6d.

CRIPPS (WILFRED)—

COLLEGE AND CORPORATION PLATE. [*In the Press*

CURIOSITIES—

CURIOSITIES OF THE SEARCH-ROOM. A Col-
lection of Serious and Whimsical Wills. By the Author of "Flemish Interiors," &c. Demy 8vo, 15s.

DAUBOURG (E.)—

INTERIOR ARCHITECTURE. Doors, Vestibules, Stair-
cases, Anterooms, Drawing, Dining, and Bed Rooms, Libraries, Bank and Newspaper Offices, Shop Fronts and Interiors. With detailed Plans, Sections, and Elevations. A purely practical work, intended for Architects, Joiners, Cabinet Makers, Marble Workers, Decorators; as well as for the owners of houses who wish to have them ornamented by artisans of their own choice. Half-imperial, cloth, £2 12s. 6d.

DAVIDSON (ELLIS A.)—

PRETTY ARTS FOR THE EMPLOYMENT OF
LEISURE HOURS. A Book for Ladies. With Illustrations. Demy 8vo, 6s.

THE AMATEUR HOUSE CARPENTER: a Guide in
Building, Making, and Repairing. With numerous Illustrations, drawn on Wood by the Author. Royal 8vo, 10s. 6d.

DAVIES (ROBERT), F.S.A.—

WALKS THROUGH THE CITY OF YORK. Edited
by his Widow. Demy 8vo, 10s. 6d.

DAVISON (THE MISSES)—

TRIQUETI MARBLES IN THE ALBERT MEMORIAL
CHAPEL, WINDSOR. A Series of Photographs. Dedicated by express permission to Her Majesty the Queen. The Work consists of 117 Photographs, with descriptive Letterpress, mounted on 49 sheets of cardboard, half-imperial. £10 10s.

DAY (WILLIAM)—

THE RACEHORSE IN TRAINING, with some Hints
on Racing and Racing Reform. Third Edition. Demy 8vo, 16s.

DE COIN (COLONEL ROBERT L.)—

HISTORY AND CULTIVATION OF COTTON AND
TOBACCO. Post 8vo, cloth, 9s.

DE KONINCK (L. L.) and DIETZ (E.)—

PRACTICAL MANUAL OF CHEMICAL ASSAYING,
as applied to the Manufacture of Iron from its Ores, and to Cast Iron, Wrought Iron, and Steel, as found in Commerce. Edited, with notes, by ROBERT MALLET. Post 8vo, cloth, 6s.

DE POMAR (THE DUKE)—

FASHION AND PASSION; or, Life in Mayfair. New
Edition. Crown 8vo, 6s.

DE WORMS (BARON HENRY)—

ENGLAND'S POLICY IN THE EAST. An Account of
the Policy and Interest of England in the Eastern Question, as compared with
those of the other European Powers. Sixth Edition. To this Edition has been
added the Tripartite Treaty of 1856, and the Black Sea Treaty of 1871. Sixth
Edition. Demy 8vo, 5s.

THE AUSTRO-HUNGARIAN EMPIRE: A Poli-
tical Sketch of Men and Events since 1868. Revised and Corrected, with an
Additional Chapter on the Present Crisis in the East. With Maps. Second
Edition. Demy 8vo, cloth, 9s.

D'HAUSSONVILLE (MONSIEUR)—

SALON OF MADAME NECKER. 2 vols. Crown 8vo.
[In the Press.

DICEY (EDWARD)—

ENGLAND AND EGYPT. 1 vol. Crown 8vo.
[In the Press.

DICKENS (CHARLES)—See pages 19—23.

THE LETTERS OF CHARLES DICKENS. (Now for
the first time published.) Edited by his SISTER-IN-LAW and ELDEST DAUGHTER.
Second Edition. 2 vols. demy 8vo, 30s.

THE DICKENS DICTIONARY : a Key to the Characters
and Principal Incidents in the Tales of Charles Dickens. By GILBERT A. PIERCE.
With Additions by WILLIAM A. WHEELER. Large crown 8vo, 10s. 6d.

DICKENS (CHARLES) AND ROCHESTER. By
ROBERT LANGTON. With numerous Illustrations. Demy, sewed, 1s.

DIXON (W. HEPWORTH)—

BRITISH CYPRUS. Demy 8vo, with Frontispiece, 15s.

THE HOLY LAND. Fourth Edition. With 2 Steel and
12 Wood Engravings. Post 8vo, 10s. 6d.

DRAYSON (LIEUT.-COL. A. W.)—

THE CAUSE OF THE SUPPOSED PROPER MOTION
OF THE FIXED STARS, with other Geometrical Problems in Astronomy
hitherto unsolved. Demy 8vo, cloth, 10s.

THE CAUSE, DATE, AND DURATION OF THE
LAST GLACIAL EPOCH OF GEOLOGY, with an Investigation of a New
Movement of the Earth. Demy 8vo, cloth, 10s.

PRACTICAL MILITARY SURVEYING AND
SKETCHING. Fifth Edition. Post 8vo, cloth, 4s. 6d.

DYCE'S COLLECTION. A Catalogue of Printed Books and
Manuscripts bequeathed by the REV. ALEXANDER DYCE to the South Kensington
Museum. 2 vols. Royal 8vo, half-morocco, 14s.

A Collection of Paintings, Miniatures, Drawings, Engravings,
Rings, and Miscellaneous Objects, bequeathed by the REV. ALEXANDER DYCE
to the South Kensington Museum. Royal 8vo, half-morocco, 6s. 6d.

DYCE (WILLIAM), R.A.—

DRAWING-BOOK OF THE GOVERNMENT SCHOOL
OF DESIGN; OR, ELEMENTARY OUTLINES OF ORNAMENT. Fifty
selected Plates. Folio, sewed, 5s.; mounted, 18s.

Text to Ditto. Sewed, 6d.

ELLIOT (FRANCES)—
PICTURES OF OLD ROME. New Edition. Post 8vo,
cloth, 6s.

ENGEL (CARL)—
A DESCRIPTIVE and ILLUSTRATED CATALOGUE
OF THE MUSICAL INSTRUMENTS in the SOUTH KENSINGTON MUSEUM, preceded by an Essay on the History of Musical Instruments. Second Edition. Royal 8vo, half-morocco, 12s.

MUSICAL INSTRUMENTS. With numerous Woodcuts.
Large crown 8vo, 2s. 6d.

ESCOTT (T. H. S.)—
PILLARS OF THE EMPIRE: Short Biographical
Sketches. Demy 8vo, 10s. 6d.

EWALD (ALEXANDER CHARLES), F.S.A.—
REPRESENTATIVE STATESMEN: Political Studies.
2 vols. Large crown 8vo, £1 4s.

SIR ROBERT WALPOLE. A Political Biography,
1676-1745. Demy 8vo, 18s.

FALLOUX (COUNT DE), of the French Academy—
AUGUSTIN COCHIN. Translated from the French by
AUGUSTUS CRAVEN. Large crown 8vo, 9s.

FANE (VIOLET)—
QUEEN OF THE FAIRIES (A Village Story), and other
Poems. Crown 8vo, 6s.

ANTHONY BABINGTON: a Drama. Crown 8vo, 6s.

FEARNLEY (W.), late Principal of the Edinburgh Veterinary College—
LESSONS IN HORSE JUDGING, AND THE SUM-
MERING OF HUNTERS. With Illustrations. Crown 8vo, 4s.

FITZGERALD (PERCY)—
BOSWELL AND CROKER'S BOSWELL. Demy 8vo,
12s.

FITZ-PATRICK (W. J.)—
LIFE OF CHARLES LEVER. 2 vols. Demy 8vo, 30s.

FLEMING (GEORGE), F.R.C.S.—
ANIMAL PLAGUES: THEIR HISTORY, NATURE,
AND PREVENTION. 8vo, cloth, 15s.

HORSES AND HORSE-SHOEING: their Origin, History,
Uses, and Abuses. 210 Engravings. 8vo, cloth, £1 1s.

PRACTICAL HORSE-SHOEING: With 37 Illustrations.
Second Edition, enlarged. 8vo, sewed, 2s.

RABIES AND HYDROPHOBIA: THEIR HISTORY,
NATURE, CAUSES, SYMPTOMS, AND PREVENTION. With 8 Illustrations. 8vo, cloth, 15s.

A MANUAL OF VETERINARY SANITARY SCIENCE
AND POLICE. With 33 Illustrations. 2 vols. Demy 8vo, 36s.

FORSTER (JOHN)—
THE LIFE OF CHARLES DICKENS. With Portraits
and other Illustrations. 15th Thousand. 3 vols. 8vo, cloth, £2 2s.

THE LIFE OF CHARLES DICKENS. Uniform with
the Illustrated Library Edition of Dickens's Works. 2 vols. Demy 8vo, £1 8s.

FORSTER (JOHN)—

THE LIFE OF CHARLES DICKENS. Uniform with the Library Edition. Post 8vo, 10s. 6d.

THE LIFE OF CHARLES DICKENS. Uniform with the "C. D." Edition of his Works. With Numerous Illustrations. 2 vols. 7s.

THE LIFE OF CHARLES DICKENS. Uniform with the Household Edition. With Illustrations by F. BARNARD. Crown 4to, cloth, 5s.

WALTER SAVAGE LANDOR: a Biography, 1775–1864. With Portrait. A New and Revised Edition. Demy 8vo, 12s.

FORTNIGHTLY REVIEW—

FORTNIGHTLY REVIEW.—First Series, May, 1865, to Dec., 1866. 6 vols. Cloth, 13s. each.

New Series, 1867 to 1872. In Half-yearly Volumes. Cloth, 13s. each.

From January, 1873, to the present time, in Half-yearly Volumes. Cloth, 16s. each.

FORTNUM (C. D. E.)—

A DESCRIPTIVE AND ILLUSTRATED CATALOGUE OF THE BRONZES OF EUROPEAN ORIGIN in the SOUTH KENSINGTON MUSEUM, with an Introductory Notice. Royal 8vo, half-morocco, £1 10s.

A DESCRIPTIVE AND ILLUSTRATED CATALOGUE OF MAIOLICA, HISPANO-MORESCO, PERSIAN, DAMASCUS, AND RHODIAN WARES in the SOUTH KENSINGTON MUSEUM. Royal 8vo, half-morocco, £2.

MAIOLICA. With numerous Woodcuts. Large crown 8vo, 2s. 6d.

BRONZES. With numerous Woodcuts. Large crown 8vo, 2s. 6d.

FRANCATELLI (C. E.)—

ROYAL CONFECTIONER: English and Foreign. A Practical Treatise. With Coloured Illustrations. Third Edition. Post 8vo, cloth, 7s. 6d.

FRANKS (A. W.)—

JAPANESE POTTERY. Being a Native Report. Numerous Illustrations and Marks. Large crown 8vo, 2s. 6d.

GALLENGA (ANTONIO)—

SOUTH AMERICA. With a Map. 2nd Edition. Demy 8vo, 14s.

GEROLDT (FRITZ)—

NINE COLONIES. 1 vol. Crown 8vo, 4s.

GILMAN (R. J.)—

GUZMAN THE GOOD: a Tragedy; and other Poems. Second Edition. Crown 8vo, 3s. 6d.

HALL (SIDNEY)—

A TRAVELLING ATLAS OF THE ENGLISH COUNTIES. Fifty Maps, coloured. New Edition, including the Railways, corrected up to the present date. Demy 8vo, in roan tuck, 10s. 6d.

HAMILTON (VEREKER M.) and STEWART M. FASSON—

SCENES IN CEYLON. Oblong, with 21 Illustrations.
[*In the Press.*

HANCOCK (E. CAMPBELL)—

THE AMATEUR POTTERY AND GLASS PAINTER
Including Fac-similes from the Sketch-Book of N. H. J. WESTLAKE, F.S.A. With an Appendix. Demy 8vo, 5s.

HARDY (LADY DUFFUS)—

THROUGH CITIES AND PRAIRIE LANDS. 1 vol.
Demy 8vo. [*In the Press.*

HATTON (JOSEPH)—

TO-DAY IN AMERICA. Studies for the Old World and
the New. 2 vols. Crown 8vo. [*In the Press.*

HECTOR (JOHN)—

THE UNDERLYING PRINCIPLES OF INDIAN
FISCAL ADMINISTRATION. Crown 8vo, 4s.

HILL (MISS G.)—

THE PLEASURES AND PROFITS OF OUR LITTLE
POULTRY FARM. Small crown 8vo, 3s.

HITCHMAN (FRANCIS)—

THE PUBLIC LIFE OF THE EARL OF BEACONS-
FIELD. 2 vols. Demy 8vo, £1 12s.

HOLBEIN—

TWELVE HEADS AFTER HOLBEIN. Selected from
Drawings in Her Majesty's Collection at Windsor. Reproduced in Autotype, in portfolio. £1 16s.

HOME LIFE—

HOME LIFE. A Handbook of Elementary Instruction,
containing Practical Suggestions addressed to Managers and Teachers of Schools, intended to show how the underlying principles of Home Duties or Domestic Economy may be the basis of National Primary Instruction. Crown 8vo, 3s.

HOVELACQUE (ABEL)—

THE SCIENCE OF LANGUAGE: LINGUISTICS,
PHILOLOGY, AND ETYMOLOGY. With Maps. Large crown 8vo, cloth, 5s.

HUMPHRIS (H. D.)—

PRINCIPLES OF PERSPECTIVE. Illustrated in a
Series of Examples. Oblong folio, half-bound, and Text 8vo, cloth, £1 1s.

JARRY (GENERAL)—

OUTPOST DUTY. Translated, with TREATISES ON
MILITARY RECONNAISSANCE AND ON ROAD-MAKING. By Major-Gen. W. C. E. NAPIER. Third Edition. Crown 8vo, 5s.

JOHNSON (DR. SAMUEL)—

LIFE AND CONVERSATIONS. By A. MAIN. Crown
8vo, 10s. 6d.

JONES (CAPTAIN DOUGLAS), R.A.—

NOTES ON MILITARY LAW. Crown 8vo, 4s.

KELLEY (E.G.), M.D.—

THE PHILOSOPHY OF EXISTENCE.—The Reality and
Romance of Histories. Demy 8vo, 16s.

KEMPIS (THOMAS À)—

OF THE IMITATION OF CHRIST. Four Books.
Beautifully Illustrated Edition. Demy 8vo, 16s.

KLACZKO (M. JULIAN)—

TWO CHANCELLORS : PRINCE GORTCHAKOF AND
PRINCE BISMARCK. Translated by MRS. TAIT. New and cheaper Edition, 6s.

LEFEVRĒ (ANDRÉ)—

PHILOSOPHY, Historical and Critical. Translated, with an Introduction, by A. W. KEANE, B.A. Large crown 8vo, 7s. 6d.

LETOURNEAU (DR. CHARLES)—

SOCIOLOGY. Based upon Ethnology. Translated by HENRY M. TROLLOPE. Large crown 8vo, 10s.

BIOLOGY. Translated by WILLIAM MACCALL. With Illustrations. Large crown 8vo, 6s.

LOW (C. R.)—

SOLDIERS OF THE VICTORIAN AGE. 2 vols. Demy 8vo, £1 10s.

LUCAS (CAPTAIN)—

THE ZULUS AND THE BRITISH FRONTIER. Demy 8vo, 16s.

CAMP LIFE AND SPORT IN SOUTH AFRICA. With Episodes in Kaffir Warfare. With Illustrations. Demy 8vo, 12s.

LYTTON (ROBERT, EARL)—

POETICAL WORKS—COLLECTED EDITION. Complete in 5 vols.
FABLES IN SONG. 2 vols. Fcap. 8vo, 12s.
LUCILE. Fcap. 8vo, 6s.
THE WANDERER. Fcap. 8vo, 6s.
POEMS, HISTORICAL AND CHARACTERISTIC. Fcap., 6s.

MALLET (DR. J. W.)—

COTTON : THE CHEMICAL, &c., CONDITIONS OF ITS SUCCESSFUL CULTIVATION. Post 8vo, cloth, 7s. 6d.

MALLET (ROBERT)—

GREAT NEAPOLITAN EARTHQUAKE OF 1857. First Principles of Observational Seismology, as developed in the Report to the Royal Society of London, of the Expedition made into the Interior of the Kingdom of Naples, to investigate the circumstances of the great Earthquake of December, 1857. Maps and numerous Illustrations. 2 vols. Royal 8vo, cloth, £3 3s.

MASKELL (WILLIAM)—

A DESCRIPTION OF THE IVORIES, ANCIENT AND MEDIÆVAL, in the SOUTH KENSINGTON MUSEUM, with a Preface. With numerous Photographs and Woodcuts. Royal 8vo, half-morocco, £1 1s.

IVORIES : ANCIENT AND MEDIÆVAL. With numerous Woodcuts. Large crown 8vo, 2s. 6d.

HANDBOOK TO THE DYCE AND FORSTER COL- LECTIONS. With Illustrations. Large crown 8vo, 2s. 6s.

MAXSE (FITZH.)—

PRINCE BISMARCK'S LETTERS. Translated from the German. Second Edition. Small crown 8vo, cloth, 6s.

McCOAN (J. CARLILE)—

OUR NEW PROTECTORATE. TURKEY IN ASIA : ITS GEOGRAPHY, RACES, RESOURCES, AND GOVERNMENT. With a Map showing the Existing and Projected Public Works. 2 vols. Large crown 8vo, £1 4s.

MEREDITH (GEORGE)—

MODERN LOVE, AND POEMS OF THE ENGLISH ROADSIDE. With Poems and Ballads. Fcap. 8vo, cloth, 6s.

MOLESWORTH (W. NASSAU)—

HISTORY OF ENGLAND FROM THE YEAR 1830
TO THE RESIGNATION OF THE GLADSTONE MINISTRY.
A Cheap Edition, carefully revised, and carried up to March, 1874. 3 vols.
crown 8vo, 18s.
A School Edition. Post 8vo, 7s. 6d.

MORLEY (HENRY)—

ENGLISH WRITERS. Vol. I. Part I. THE CELTS
AND ANGLO-SAXONS. With an Introductory Sketch of the Four Periods of
English Literature. Part II. FROM THE CONQUEST TO CHAUCER.
(Making 2 vols.) 8vo, cloth, £1 2s.

Vol. II. Part I. FROM CHAUCER TO DUNBAR.
8vo, cloth, 12s.

TABLES OF ENGLISH LITERATURE. Containing
20 Charts. Second Edition, with Index. Royal 4to, cloth, 12s.
In Three Parts. Parts I. and II., containing Three Charts, each 1s. 6d.
Part III., containing 14 Charts, 7s. Part III. also kept in Sections, 1, 2, and 5,
1s. 6d. each ; 3 and 4 together, 3s. *₊* The Charts sold separately.

MORLEY (JOHN)—

LIFE AND CORRESPONDENCE OF RICHARD
COBDEN. 2 vols. Demy 8vo. *[In the Press.*

DIDEROT AND THE ENCYCLOPÆDISTS. 2 vols.
Demy 8vo, £1 6s.

CRITICAL MISCELLANIES. Second Series. France
in the Eighteenth Century—Robespierre—Turgot—Death of Mr. Mill—Mr. Mill
on Religion—On Popular Culture—Macaulay. Demy 8vo, cloth, 14s.

CRITICAL MISCELLANIES. First Series. Demy 8vo, 14s.

NEW UNIFORM EDITION.

VOLTAIRE. Large crown 8vo, 6s.

ROUSSEAU. Large crown 8vo, 9s.

CRITICAL MISCELLANIES. First Series. Large crown
8vo, 6s.

CRITICAL MISCELLANIES. Second Series. *[In the Press.*

DIDEROT AND THE ENCYCLOPÆDISTS. Large
crown 8vo, 12s.

ON COMPROMISE. New Edition. Large crown 8vo,
3s. 6d.

STRUGGLE FOR NATIONAL EDUCATION. Third
Edition. Demy 8vo, cloth, 3s.

MURPHY (J. M.)—

RAMBLES IN NORTH-WEST AMERICA. With
Frontispiece and Map. 8vo, 16s.

MURRAY (ANDREW), F.L.S.—

ECONOMIC ENTOMOLOGY. APTERA. With nume-
rous Illustrations. Large crown 8vo, 7s. 6d.

NAPIER (MAJ.-GEN. W. C. E.)—

TRANSLATION OF GEN. JARRY'S OUTPOST DUTY.
With TREATISES ON MILITARY RECONNAISSANCE AND ON
ROAD-MAKING. Third Edition. Crown 8vo, 5s.

NESBITT (ALEXANDER)—

GLASS. Illustrated. Large crown 8vo, 2s. 6d.

NEWTON (E. TULLEY), F.G.S., Assistant-Naturalist H.M. Geological Survey—

THE TYPICAL PARTS IN THE SKELETONS OF A CAT, DUCK, AND CODFISH, being a Catalogue with Comparative Description arranged in a Tabular form. Demy 8vo, cloth, 3s.

O'CONNELL (MRS. MORGAN JOHN)—

CHARLES BIANCONI. A Biography. 1786–1875. By his Daughter. With Illustrations. Demy 8vo, 10s. 6d.

OLIVER (PROFESSOR), F.R.S., &c.—

ILLUSTRATIONS OF THE PRINCIPAL NATURAL ORDERS OF THE VEGETABLE KINGDOM, PREPARED FOR THE SCIENCE AND ART DEPARTMENT, SOUTH KENSINGTON. With 109 Plates. Oblong 8vo, plain, 16s. ; coloured, £1 6s.

OZANNE (I. W.)—

THREE YEARS IN ROUMANIA. Large crown 8vo, 7s. 6d.

PAST DAYS IN INDIA ; or, Sporting Reminiscences in the Valley of the Saone and the Basin of Singrowlee. By a late Customs Officer, N.W. Provinces, India. Post 8vo, 10s. 6d.

PIERCE (GILBERT A.)—

THE DICKENS DICTIONARY: a Key to the Characters and Principal Incidents in the Tales of Charles Dickens. With Additions by William A. Wheeler. Large crown 8vo, 10s. 6d.

POLLEN (J. H.)—

ANCIENT AND MODERN FURNITURE AND WOODWORK IN THE SOUTH KENSINGTON MUSEUM. With an Introduction, and Illustrated with numerous Coloured Photographs and Woodcuts. Royal 8vo, half-morocco, £1 1s.

GOLD AND SILVER SMITH'S WORK. With numerous Woodcuts. Large crown 8vo, 2s. 6d.

ANCIENT AND MODERN FURNITURE AND WOODWORK. With numerous Woodcuts. Large crown 8vo, 2s. 6d.

POLLOK (LIEUT.-COLONEL)—

SPORT IN BRITISH BURMAH, ASSAM, AND THE CASSYAH AND JYNTIAH HILLS. With Notes of Sport in the Hilly Districts of the Northern Division, Madras Presidency. 2 vols. Demy 8vo, with Illustrations and 2 Maps.- £1 4s.

POYNTER (E. J.), R.A.—

TEN LECTURES ON ART. Second Edition. Large crown 8vo, 9s.

PRINSEP (VAL), A.R.A.—

IMPERIAL INDIA. Containing numerous Illustrations and Maps made during a Tour to the Courts of the Principal Rajahs and Princes of India. Second Edition. Demy 8vo, £1 1s.

PUCKETT (R. CAMPBELL), Ph.D., Bonn University—

SCIOGRAPHY ; or, Radial Projection of Shadows. New Edition. Crown 8vo, cloth, 6s.

RANKEN (W. H. L.)—

THE DOMINION OF AUSTRALIA. An Account of its Foundation. Post 8vo, cloth, 12s.

REDGRAVE (GILBERT R.)—

MANUAL OF DESIGN, compiled from the Writings and
Addresses of RICHARD REDGRAVE, R.A. With Woodcuts. Large crown 8vo, 2s. 6d.

REDGRAVE (RICHARD)—

MANUAL AND CATECHISM ON COLOUR. 24mo,
cloth, 9d.

REDGRAVE (SAMUEL)—

A DESCRIPTIVE CATALOGUE OF THE HIS-
TORICAL COLLECTION OF WATER-COLOUR PAINTINGS IN THE
SOUTH KENSINGTON MUSEUM. With numerous Chromo-lithographs and
other Illustrations. Published for the Science and Art Department of the Committee of Council on Education. Royal 8vo, £1 1s.

RIAÑO (JUAN F.)—

THE INDUSTRIAL ARTS IN SPAIN. Illustrated. Large
crown 8vo, 4s.

RIDGE (DR. BENJAMIN)—

OURSELVES, OUR FOOD, AND OUR PHYSIC.
Twelfth Edition. Fcap. 8vo, cloth, 1s. 6d.

ROBINSON (C. E.)—

THE CRUISE OF THE *WIDGEON*: 700 Miles in
a Ten-Ton Yawl. With 4 Illustrations, drawn on Wood by the Author. Second
Edition. Large crown 8vo, 9s.

ROBINSON (JAMES F.)—

BRITISH BEE FARMING. Its Profits and Pleasures.
Uniform with the FARMING FOR PLEASURE AND PROFIT Series.
Large crown 8vo, 5s.

ROBINSON (J. C.)—

ITALIAN SCULPTURE OF THE MIDDLE AGES
AND PERIOD OF THE REVIVAL OF ART. With 20 Engravings. Royal
8vo, cloth, 7s. 6d.

ROBSON (GEORGE)—

ELEMENTARY BUILDING CONSTRUCTION. Illus-
trated by a Design for an Entrance Lodge and Gate. 15 Plates. Oblong folio,
sewed, 8s.

ROBSON (REV. J. H.), M.A., LL.M.—

AN ELEMENTARY TREATISE ON ALGEBRA.
Post 8vo, 6s.

ROCK (THE VERY REV. CANON), D.D.—

ON TEXTILE FABRICS. A Descriptive and Illustrated
Catalogue of the Collection of Church Vestments, Dresses, Silk Stuffs, Needlework,
and Tapestries in the South Kensington Museum. Royal 8vo, half-morocco,
£1 11s. 6d.

TEXTILE FABRICS. With numerous Woodcuts. Large
crown 8vo, 2s. 6d.

ROLAND (ARTHUR)—

FARMING FOR PLEASURE AND PROFIT. Edited
by WILLIAM ABLETT. 6 vols. Large crown 8vo, 5s. each.
DAIRY-FARMING, MANAGEMENT OF COWS, &c.
POULTRY-KEEPING.
TREE-PLANTING, FOR ORNAMENTATION OR PROFIT.
STOCK-KEEPING AND CATTLE-REARING.
DRAINAGE OF LAND, IRRIGATION, MANURES, &c.
ROOT-GROWING, HOPS, &c.
MANAGEMENT OF GRASS LANDS. [*In the Press.*

SALUSBURY (PHILIP H. B.), Lieut. 1st Royal Cheshire Light Infantry—
TWO MONTHS WITH TCHERNAIEFF IN SERVIA.
Large crown 8vo, 9s.

SCOTT-STEVENSON (MRS.)—
OUR HOME IN CYPRUS. With a Map and Illustra-
tions. Third Edition. Demy 8vo, 14s.
RIDE THROUGH ASIA MINOR. 1 vol. Demy 8vo.
[*In the Press.*

SHIRREFF (EMILY)—
A SKETCH OF THE LIFE OF FRIEDRICH
FRÖBEL, together with a Notice of MADAME VON MARENHOLTZ BULOW'S
Personal Recollections of F. FRÖBEL. Crown 8vo, sewed, 1s.

SIMMONDS (T. L.)—
ANIMAL PRODUCTS: their Preparation, Commercial
Uses, and Value. With numerous Illustrations. Large crown 8vo, 7s. 6d.

SMITH (GOLDWIN)—
THE POLITICAL DESTINY OF CANADA. Crown
8vo, 5s.

SMITH (MAJOR R. MURDOCK), R.E.—
PERSIAN ART. Second Edition, with additional Illustra-
tions. Large crown 8vo, 2s.

ST. CLAIR (S. G. B.), Captain late 21st Fusiliers, and CHARLES A. BROPHY—
TWELVE YEARS' RESIDENCE IN BULGARIA.
Revised Edition. Crown 8vo, 9s.

STORY (W. W.)—
ROBA DI ROMA. Seventh Edition, with Additions and
Portrait. Crown 8vo, cloth, 10s. 6d.
THE PROPORTIONS OF THE HUMAN FRAME,
ACCORDING TO A NEW CANON. With Plates. Royal 8vo, cloth, 10s.
CASTLE ST. ANGELO. Uniform with "Roba di Roma."
With Illustrations. Crown 8vo, 10s. 6d.

STREETER (E. W.)—
PRECIOUS STONES AND GEMS. Second Edition.
Demy 8vo, cloth, 18s.; calf, 27s.
GOLD; OR, LEGAL REGULATIONS FOR THIS
METAL IN DIFFERENT COUNTRIES OF THE WORLD. Crown 8vo,
cloth, 3s. 6d.

STUART-GLENNIE (JOHN STUART), M.A., Barrister-at-Law—
EUROPE AND ASIA: DISCUSSIONS OF THE
EASTERN QUESTION. In Travels through Independent, Turkish, and
Austrian Illyria. With a Politico-Ethnographical Map. Demy 8vo, 14s.

TANNER (HENRY), F.C.S.—
JACK'S EDUCATION; OR, HOW HE LEARNT
FARMING. Large crown 8vo, 4s.

TOPINARD (DR. PAUL)—
ANTHROPOLOGY. With a Preface by Professor PAUL
BROCA. With numerous Illustrations. Large crown 8vo, 7s. 6d.

TROLLOPE (ANTHONY)—
AYALA'S ANGEL. 3 vols. Crown 8vo.
LIFE OF CICERO. 2 vols. 8vo. £1 4s.

TROLLOPE (ANTHONY)—
THE CHRONICLES OF BARSETSHIRE. A Uniform
Edition, in 8 vols., large crown 8vo, handsomely printed, each vol. containing Frontispiece. 6s. each.

THE WARDEN.	THE SMALL HOUSE AT
BARCHESTER TOWERS.	ALLINGTON. 2 vols.
DR. THORNE.	LAST CHRONICLE OF
FRAMLEY PARSONAGE.	BARSET. 2 vols.

AUSTRALIA AND NEW ZEALAND. A Cheap Edition,
with Maps. 2 vols. Small 8vo, cloth, 7s. 6d.

SOUTH AFRICA. 2 vols. Large crown 8vo, with Maps.
Fourth Edition. £1 10s.

SOUTH AFRICA. Crown 8vo, 3s. 6d.
(For Cheap Editions of other Works, see page 25.)

UNIVERSAL—
UNIVERSAL CATALOGUE OF BOOKS ON ART.
Compiled for the use of the National Art Library, and the Schools of Art in the United Kingdom. In 2 vols. Crown 4to, half-morocco, £2 2s.

Supplemental Volume to Ditto. 8s.

VERON (EUGENE)—
ÆSTHETICS. Translated by W. H. ARMSTRONG. Large
crown 8vo, 7s. 6d.

WALMSLEY (HUGH MULLENEUX)—
THE LIFE OF SIR JOSHUA WALMSLEY. With
Portrait, demy 8vo, 14s.

WATSON (ALFRED E. T.)
SKETCHES IN THE HUNTING FIELD. Illustrated
by JOHN STURGESS. Second Edition. Demy 8vo, 12s.

New and Cheaper Edition. Illustrated by JOHN STURGESS. Crown 8vo, 6s.

WAYLEN (JAMES)—
THE HOUSE OF CROMWELL AND THE STORY
OF DUNKIRK. Royal 8vo, cloth, 12s.

WESTWOOD (J. O.), M.A., F.L.S., &c.—
CATALOGUE OF THE FICTILE IVORIES IN THE
SOUTH KENSINGTON MUSEUM. With an Account of the Continental Collections of Classical and Mediæval Ivories. Royal 8vo, half-morocco, £1 4s.

WHEELER (G. P.)—
VISIT OF THE PRINCE OF WALES. A Chronicle of
H.R.H.'s Journeyings in India, Ceylon, Spain, and Portugal. Large crown 8vo, 12s.

WHITE (WALTER)—
HOLIDAYS IN TYROL : Kufstein, Klobenstein, and
Paneveggio. Large crown 8vo, 14s.

A MONTH IN YORKSHIRE. Post 8vo. With a Map.
Fifth Edition. 4s.

A LONDONER'S WALK TO THE LAND'S END, AND
A TRIP TO THE SCILLY ISLES. Post 8vo. With 4 Maps. Third Edition. 4s.

WILDFOWLER—
SHOOTING, YACHTING, AND SEA-FISHING TRIPS,
at Home and on the Continent. Second Series. By "WILDFOWLER," "SNAP-SHOT." 2 vols. Crown 8vo, £1 1s.

SHOOTING AND FISHING TRIPS IN ENGLAND,
FRANCE, ALSACE, BELGIUM, HOLLAND, AND BAVARIA. By "WILD-FOWLER," "SNAPSHOT." New Edition, with Illustrations. Large crown 8vo, 8s.

WORNUM (R. N.)—

HOLBEIN (HANS)—LIFE. With Portrait and Illustrations. Imp. 8vo, cloth, £1 11s. 6d.

ANALYSIS OF ORNAMENT: THE CHARACTER-
ISTICS OF STYLES. An Introduction to the Study of the History of Ornamental Art. With many Illustrations. Sixth Edition. Royal 8vo, cloth, 8s.

WYLDE (ATHERTON)—

MY CHIEF AND I; OR, SIX MONTHS IN NATAL
AFTER THE LANGALIBALELE OUTBREAK. With Portrait of Colonel
Durnford, and Illustrations. Demy 8vo, 14s.

YOUNGE (C. D.)—

PARALLEL LIVES OF ANCIENT AND MODERN
HEROES. New Edition. 12mo, cloth, 4s. 6d.

SOUTH KENSINGTON MUSEUM DESCRIPTIVE AND ILLUSTRATED CATALOGUES.

Royal 8vo, half-bound.

BRONZES OF EUROPEAN ORIGIN. By C. D. E. Fortnum.
£1 10s.

DYCE'S COLLECTION OF PRINTED BOOKS AND
MANUSCRIPTS. 2 vols. 14s.

DYCE'S COLLECTION OF PAINTINGS, ENGRAVINGS,
&c. 6s. 6d.

FURNITURE AND WOODWORK, ANCIENT AND
MODERN. By J. H. Pollen. £1 1s.

GLASS VESSELS. By A. Nesbitt. 18s.

GOLD AND SILVER SMITH'S WORK. By J. G. Pollen.
£1 6s.

IVORIES, ANCIENT AND MEDIÆVAL. By W. Maskell.
21s.

IVORIES, FICTILE. By J. O. Westwood. £1 4s.

MAIOLICA, HISPANO-MORESCO, PERSIAN, DAMAS-
CUS AND RHODIAN WARES. By C. D. E. Fortnum. £2.

MUSICAL INSTRUMENTS. By C. Engel. 12s.

SCULPTURE, ITALIAN SCULPTURE OF THE MIDDLE
AGES. By J. C. Robinson. Cloth, 7s. 6d.

SWISS COINS. By R. S. Poole. £2 10s.

TEXTILE FABRICS. By Rev. D. Rock. £1 11s. 6d.

WATER-COLOUR PAINTING. By S. Redgrave. £1 1s.

UNIVERSAL CATALOGUE OF WORKS OF ART. 2 vols.
Small 4to. £1 1s. each.

UNIVERSAL CATALOGUE OF WORKS OF ART. Supple-
mentary vol., 8s.

SOUTH KENSINGTON MUSEUM SCIENCE AND ART HANDBOOKS.

Published for the Committee of Council on Education.

THE INDUSTRIAL ARTS OF INDIA. By GEORGE C. M. BIRDWOOD, C.S.I. 8vo, with Map and 174 Illustrations, 14s.

HANDBOOK TO THE DYCE AND FORSTER COLLECTIONS. By W. MASKELL. With Illustrations. Large crown 8vo, 2s. 6d.

THE INDUSTRIAL ARTS IN SPAIN. By JUAN F. RIANO. Illustrated. Large crown 8vo, 4s.

GLASS. By ALEXANDER NESBITT. Illustrated. Large crown 8vo, 2s. 6d.

GOLD AND SILVER SMITH'S WORK. By JOHN HUNGERFORD POLLEN. With numerous Woodcuts. Large crown 8vo, 2s. 6d.

TAPESTRY. By ALFRED CHAMPEAUX. With Woodcuts. 2s. 6d.

BRONZES. By C. DRURY E. FORTNUM, F.S.A. With numerous Woodcuts. Large crown 8vo, 2s. 6d.

PLAIN WORDS ABOUT WATER. By A. H. CHURCH, M.A., Oxon. Illustrated. Large crown 8vo, sewed, 6d.

ANIMAL PRODUCTS: their Preparation, Commercial Uses, and Value. By T. L. SIMMONDS. With numerous Illustrations. Large crown 8vo, 7s. 6d.

FOOD: A Short Account of the Sources, Constituents, and Uses of Food; intended chiefly as a Guide to the Food Collection in the Bethnal Green Museum. By A. H. CHURCH M.A. Oxon. Large crown 8vo 3s.

FOOD, THE ADULTERATION OF. By J. BELL. Large crown 8vo. *[In the Press.*

SCIENCE CONFERENCES. Delivered at the South Kensington Museum. Crown 8vo, 2 vols., 6s. each.
VOL. I.—Physics and Mechanics.
VOL. II.—Chemistry, Biology, Physical Geography, Geology, Mineralogy, and Meteorology.

ECONOMIC ENTOMOLOGY. By ANDREW MURRAY, F.L.S. APTERA. With numerous Illustrations. Large crown 8vo, 7s. 6d.

JAPANESE POTTERY. Being a Native Report. Edited by A. W. FRANKS. Numerous Illustrations and Marks. Large crown 8vo, 2s. 6d.

HANDBOOK TO THE SPECIAL LOAN COLLECTION of Scientific Apparatus. Large crown 8vo, 3s.

THE INDUSTRIAL ARTS: Historical Sketches. With 242 Illustrations. Demy 8vo, 7s. 6d.

THE INDUSTRIAL ARTS: Historical Sketches. With 242 Illustrations. Large crown 8vo, 3s.

TEXTILE FABRICS. By the Very Rev. DANIEL ROCK, D.D. With numerous Woodcuts. Large crown 8vo, 2s. 6d.

IVORIES: ANCIENT AND MEDIÆVAL. By WILLIAM MASKELL. With numerous Woodcuts. Large crown 8vo, 2s. 6d.

ANCIENT AND MODERN FURNITURE AND WOODWORK. By JOHN HUNGERFORD POLLEN. With numerous Woodcuts. Large crown 8vo, 2s. 6d.

MAIOLICA. By C. DRURY E. FORTNUM, F.S.A. With numerous Woodcuts. Large crown 8vo, 2s. 6d.

B

SOUTH KENSINGTON MUSEUM SCIENCE & ART HANDBOOKS—*Continued.*

MUSICAL INSTRUMENTS. By CARL ENGEL. With numerous
Woodcuts. Large crown 8vo, 2s. 6d.

MANUAL OF DESIGN, compiled from the Writings and
Addresses of RICHARD REDGRAVE, R.A. By GILBERT R. REDGRAVE. With
Woodcuts. Large crown 8vo, 2s. 6d.

PERSIAN ART. By MAJOR R. MURDOCK SMITH, R.E. Second
Edition, with additional Illustrations. Large crown 8vo, 2s.

FREE EVENING LECTURES. Delivered in connection with
the Special Loan Collection of Scientific Apparatus, 1876. Large crown 8vo, 8s.

CARLYLE'S (THOMAS) WORKS.

CHEAP AND UNIFORM EDITION.

In 23 vols., Crown 8vo, cloth, £7 5s.

THE FRENCH REVOLUTION :
A History. 2 vols., 12s.

OLIVER CROMWELL'S LET-
TERS AND SPEECHES, with Eluci-
dations, &c. 3 vols., 18s.

LIVES OF SCHILLER AND
JOHN STERLING. 1 vol., 6s.

CRITICAL AND MISCELLA-
NEOUS ESSAYS. 4 vols., £1 4s.

SARTOR RESARTUS AND
LECTURES ON HEROES. 1 vol., 6s.

LATTER-DAY PAMPHLETS.
1 vol., 6s.

CHARTISM AND PAST AND
PRESENT. 1 vol., 6s.

TRANSLATIONS FROM THE
GERMAN OF MUSÆUS, TIECK,
AND RICHTER. 1 vol., 6s.

WILHELM MEISTER, by Göthe.
A Translation 2 vols., 12s.

HISTORY OF FRIEDRICH THE
SECOND, called Frederick the Great.
7 vols., £2 9s.

LIBRARY EDITION COMPLETE.

Handsomely printed in 34 vols., demy 8vo, cloth, £15:

SARTOR RESARTUS. The Life and Opinions of Herr
Teufelsdröckh. With a Portrait, 7s. 6d.

THE FRENCH REVOLUTION. A History. 3 vols., each 9s.

LIFE OF FREDERICK SCHILLER AND EXAMINATION
OF HIS WORKS. With Supplement of 1872. Portrait and Plates, 9s.

CRITICAL AND MISCELLANEOUS ESSAYS. With Portrait.
6 vols., each 9s.

ON HEROES, HERO WORSHIP, AND THE HEROIC
IN HISTORY. 7s. 6d.

PAST AND PRESENT. 9s.

OLIVER CROMWELL'S LETTERS AND SPEECHES. With
Portraits. 5 vols., each 9s.

LATTER-DAY PAMPHLETS. 9s.

LIFE OF JOHN STERLING. With Portrait, 9s.

HISTORY OF FREDERICK THE SECOND. 10 vols.,
each 9s.

TRANSLATIONS FROM THE GERMAN. 3 vols., each 9s.

CARLYLE'S (THOMAS) WORKS—*Continued.*

GENERAL INDEX TO THE LIBRARY EDITION. 8vo,
cloth, 6s.

EARLY KINGS OF NORWAY: also AN ESSAY ON THE
PORTRAITS OF JOHN KNOX. Crown 8vo, with Portrait Illustrations,
7s. 6d.

PEOPLE'S EDITION.

In 37 vols., small Crown 8vo. Price 2s. each vol., bound in cloth; or in sets of 37 vols. in 19, cloth gilt, for £3 14s.

SARTOR RESARTUS.
FRENCH REVOLUTION. 3 vols.
LIFE OF JOHN STERLING.
OLIVER CROMWELL'S LETTERS AND SPEECHES. 5 vols.
ON HEROES AND HERO WORSHIP.
PAST AND PRESENT.
CRITICAL AND MISCELLANEOUS ESSAYS. 7 vols.

LATTER-DAY PAMPHLETS.
LIFE OF SCHILLER.
FREDERICK THE GREAT. 10 vols.
WILHELM MEISTER. 3 vols.
TRANSLATIONS FROM MUSÆUS, TIECK, AND RICHTER. 2 vols.
THE EARLY KINGS OF NORWAY; Essay on the Portraits of Knox; and General Index.

TROLLOPE'S (ANTHONY) WORKS.

CHEAP EDITION.

Boards, 2s. 6d.

THE PRIME MINISTER.
PHINEAS FINN.
ORLEY FARM.
CAN YOU FORGIVE HER?

PHINEAS REDUX.
HE KNEW HE WAS RIGHT.
EUSTACE DIAMONDS.
DUKE'S CHILDREN.

Boards, 2s.

VICAR OF BULLHAMPTON.
RALPH THE HEIR.
THE BERTRAMS.
KELLYS AND O'KELLYS.
McDERMOT OF BALLYCLORAN.
CASTLE RICHMOND.
BELTON ESTATE.
MISS MACKENSIE.
LADY ANNA.

HARRY HOTSPUR.
RACHEL RAY.
TALES OF ALL COUNTRIES.
LA VENDÉE.
DOCTOR THORNE.
IS HE POPENJOY?
EYE FOR AN EYE.
COUSIN HENRY.

B 2

DICKENS'S (CHARLES) WORKS.

ORIGINAL EDITIONS.

In Demy 8vo.

THE MYSTERY OF EDWIN DROOD. With Illustrations
by S. L. Fildes, and a Portrait engraved by Baker. Cloth, 7s. 6d.

OUR MUTUAL FRIEND. With Forty Illustrations by Marcus
Stone. Cloth, £1 1s.

THE PICKWICK PAPERS. With Forty-three Illustrations
by Seymour and Phiz. Cloth, £1 1s.

NICHOLAS NICKLEBY. With Forty Illustrations by Phiz.
Cloth, £1 1s.

SKETCHES BY "BOZ." With Forty Illustrations by George
Cruikshank. Cloth, £1 1s.

MARTIN CHUZZLEWIT. With Forty Illustrations by Phiz.
Cloth, £1 1s.

DOMBEY AND SON. With Forty Illustrations by Phiz.
Cloth, £1 1s.

DAVID COPPERFIELD. With Forty Illustrations by Phiz.
Cloth, £1 1s.

BLEAK HOUSE. With Forty Illustrations by Phiz. Cloth,
£1 1s.

LITTLE DORRIT. With Forty Illustrations by Phiz. Cloth,
£1 1s.

THE OLD CURIOSITY SHOP. With Seventy-five Illus-
trations by George Cattermole and H. K. Browne. A New Edition. Uniform with
the other volumes, £1 1s.

BARNABY RUDGE: a Tale of the Riots of 'Eighty. With
Seventy-eight Illustrations by George Cattermole and H. K. Browne. Uniform with
the other volumes, £1 1s.

CHRISTMAS BOOKS: Containing—The Christmas Carol;
The Cricket on the Hearth; The Chimes; The Battle of Life; The Haunted House.
With all the original Illustrations. Cloth, 12s.

OLIVER TWIST and TALE OF TWO CITIES. In one
volume. Cloth, £1 1s.

OLIVER TWIST. Separately. With Twenty-four Illustrations
by George Cruikshank. Cloth, 11s.

A TALE OF TWO CITIES. Separately. With Sixteen Illustrations by Phiz. Cloth, 9s.

*** *The remainder of Dickens's Works were not originally printed in Demy 8vo.*

DICKENS'S (CHARLES) WORKS—*Continued.*

LIBRARY EDITION.

In Post 8vo. With the Original Illustrations, 30 vols., cloth, £12.

			s.	d.
PICKWICK PAPERS ... ... 43 Illustrns., 2 vols.			16	0
NICHOLAS NICKLEBY ... ... 39 ,, 2 vols.			16	0
MARTIN CHUZZLEWIT ... ... 40 ,, 2 vols.			16	0
OLD CURIOSITY SHOP & REPRINTED PIECES 36 ,, 2 vols.			16	0
BARNABY RUDGE and HARD TIMES ... ... 36 ,, 2 vols.			16	0
BLEAK HOUSE ... ... 40 ,, 2 vols.			16	0
LITTLE DORRIT ... ... 40 ,, 2 vols.			16	0
DOMBEY AND SON ... ... 38 ,, 2 vols.			16	0
DAVID COPPERFIELD ... ... 38 ,, 2 vols.			16	0
OUR MUTUAL FRIEND ... ... 40 ,, 2 vols.			16	0
SKETCHES BY "BOZ" ... ... 39 ,, 1 vol.			8	0
OLIVER TWIST ... ... 24 ,, 1 vol.			8	0
CHRISTMAS BOOKS ... ... 17 ,, 1 vol.			8	0
A TALE OF TWO CITIES ... ... 16 ,, 1 vol.			8	0
GREAT EXPECTATIONS ... ... 8 ,, 1 vol.			8	0
PICTURES FROM ITALY & AMERICAN NOTES 8 ,, 1 vol.			8	0
UNCOMMERCIAL TRAVELLER ... . 8 ,, 1 vol.			8	0
CHILD'S HISTORY OF ENGLAND ... ... 8 ,, 1 vol.			8	0
EDWIN DROOD and MISCELLANIES ... ... 12 ,, 1 vol.			8	0
CHRISTMAS STORIES from "Household Words," &c. 14 ,, 1 vol.			8	0

THE LIFE OF CHARLES DICKENS. By JOHN FORSTER. With Illustrations.
Uniform with this Edition. 1 vol, 10s. 6d.

THE "CHARLES DICKENS" EDITION.

In Crown 8vo. In 21 vols., cloth, with Illustrations, £3 15s. 6d.

		s.	d.
PICKWICK PAPERS ... ... 8 Illustrations ...		4	0
MARTIN CHUZZLEWIT ... ... 8 ,, ...		4	0
DOMBEY AND SON ... ... 8 ,, ...		4	0
NICHOLAS NICKLEBY ... ... 8 ,, ...		4	0
DAVID COPPERFIELD ... ... 8 ,, ...		4	0
BLEAK HOUSE ... ...: 8 ,, ...		4	0
LITTLE DORRIT ... ... 8 ,, ...		4	0
OUR MUTUAL FRIEND ... ... 8 ,, ...		4	0
BARNABY RUDGE ... ... 8 ,, ...		3	6
OLD CURIOSITY SHOP ... ... 8 ,, ...		3	6
A CHILD'S HISTORY OF ENGLAND ... ... 4 ,, ...		3	6
EDWIN DROOD and OTHER STORIES ... ... 8 ,, ...		3	6
CHRISTMAS STORIES, from "Household Words" ... 8 ,, ...		3	6
TALE OF TWO CITIES ... ... ° ... 8 ,, ...		3	0
SKETCHES BY "BOZ" ... ... 8 ,, ...		3	6
AMERICAN NOTES and REPRINTED PIECES ... 8 ,, ...		3	6
CHRISTMAS BOOKS ... ... 8 ,, ...		3	6
OLIVER TWIST ... ... 8 ,, ...		3	6
GREAT EXPECTATIONS... ... ... 8 ,, ...		3	6
HARD TIMES and PICTURES FROM ITALY ... 8 ,, ...		3	0
UNCOMMERCIAL TRAVELLER ... ... 4 ,, ...		3	0

THE LIFE OF CHARLES DICKENS. Uniform with this Edition, with
Numerous Illustrations. 2 vols. 7s.|

DICKENS'S (CHARLES) WORKS—*Continued.*

THE ILLUSTRATED LIBRARY EDITION.

Complete in 30 Volumes. Demy 8vo, 10s. each; or set, £15.

This Edition is printed on a finer paper and in a larger type than has been employed in any previous edition. The type has been cast especially for it, and the page is of a size to admit of the introduction of all the original illustrations.

No such attractive issue has been made of the writings of Mr. Dickens, which, various as have been the forms of publication adapted to the demands of an ever widely-increasing popularity, have never yet been worthily presented in a really handsome library form.

The collection comprises all the minor writings it was Mr. Dickens's wish to preserve.

SKETCHES BY "BOZ." With 40 Illustrations by George Cruikshank.

PICKWICK PAPERS. 2 vols. With 42 Illustrations by Phiz.

OLIVER TWIST. With 24 Illustrations by Cruikshank.

NICHOLAS NICKLEBY. 2 vols. With 40 Illustrations by Phiz.

OLD CURIOSITY SHOP and REPRINTED PIECES. 2 vols. With Illustrations by Cattermole, &c.

BARNABY RUDGE and HARD TIMES. 2 vols. With Illustrations by Cattermole, &c.

MARTIN CHUZZLEWIT. 2 vols. With 4 Illustrations by Phiz.

AMERICAN NOTES and PICTURES FROM ITALY. 1 vol. With 8 Illustrations.

DOMBEY AND SON. 2 vols. With 40 Illustrations by Phiz.

DAVID COPPERFIELD. 2 vols. With 40 Illustrations by Phiz.

BLEAK HOUSE. 2 vols. With 40 Illustrations by Phiz.

LITTLE DORRIT. 2 vols. With 40 Illustrations by Phiz.

A TALE OF TWO CITIES. With 16 Illustrations by Phiz.

THE UNCOMMERCIAL TRAVELLER. With 8 Illustrations by Marcus Stone.

GREAT EXPECTATIONS. With 8 Illustrations by Marcus Stone.

OUR MUTUAL FRIEND. 2 vols. With 40 Illustrations by Marcus Stone.

CHRISTMAS BOOKS. With 17 Illustrations by Sir Edwin Landseer, R.A. Maclise, R.A., &c. &c.

HISTORY OF ENGLAND. With 8 Illustrations by Marcus Stone.

CHRISTMAS STORIES. (From "Household Words" and "All the Year Round.") With 14 Illustrations.

EDWIN DROOD AND OTHER STORIES. With 12 Illustrations by S. L. Fildes.

DICKENS'S (CHARLES) WORKS—*Continued.*

HOUSEHOLD EDITION.

Complete in 22 Volumes.   Crown 4to, cloth, £4 8s. 6d.

MARTIN CHUZZLEWIT, with 59 Illustrations, cloth, 5s.
DAVID COPPERFIELD, with 60 Illustrations and a Portrait, cloth, 5s.
BLEAK HOUSE, with 61 Illustrations, cloth, 5s.
LITTLE DORRIT, with 58 Illustrations, cloth, 5s.
PICKWICK PAPERS, with 56 Illustrations, cloth, 5s.
OUR MUTUAL FRIEND, with 58 Illustrations, cloth, 5s.
NICHOLAS NICKLEBY, with 59 Illustrations, cloth, 5s.
DOMBEY AND SON, with 61 Illustrations, cloth, 5s.
EDWIN DROOD; REPRINTED PIECES; and other Stories, with 30 Illustrations, cloth, 5s.
BARNABY RUDGE, with 46 Illustrations, cloth, 4s.
THE LIFE OF DICKENS. By JOHN FORSTER. With 40 Illustrations. Cloth, 5s.
OLD CURIOSITY SHOP, with 32 Illustrations, cloth, 4s.
CHRISTMAS STORIES, with 23 Illustrations, cloth, 4s.
OLIVER TWIST, with 28 Illustrations, cloth, 3s.
A TALE OF TWO CITIES, with 25 Illustrations, cloth, 3s.
GREAT EXPECTATIONS, with 26 Illustrations, cloth, 3s.
SKETCHES BY "BOZ," with 36 Illustrations, cloth, 3s.
UNCOMMERCIAL TRAVELLER, with 26 Illustrations, cloth, 3s.
CHRISTMAS BOOKS, with 28 Illustrations, cloth, 3s.
THE HISTORY OF ENGLAND, with 15 Illustrations, cloth, 3s.
AMERICAN NOTES and PICTURES FROM ITALY, with 18 Illustrations, cloth, 3s.
HARD TIMES, with 20 Illustrations, cloth, 2s. 6d.

MR. DICKENS'S READINGS.

Fcap. 8vo, sewed.

CHRISTMAS CAROL IN PROSE. 1s.
CRICKET ON THE HEARTH. 1s.
CHIMES: A GOBLIN STORY. 1s.

STORY OF LITTLE DOMBEY. 1s.
POOR TRAVELLER, BOOTS AT THE HOLLY-TREE INN, and MRS. GAMP. 1s.

A CHRISTMAS CAROL, with the Original Coloured Plates; being a reprint of the Original Edition. Small 8vo, red cloth, gilt edges, 5s.

DICKENS'S (CHARLES) WORKS—*Continued.*

THE POPULAR LIBRARY EDITION

OF THE WORKS OF

CHARLES DICKENS,

In 30 Vols., large crown 8vo, price £6; separate Vols. 4s. each.

An Edition printed on good paper, containing Illustrations selected from the Household Edition, on Plate Paper. Each Volume has about 450 pages and 16 full-page Illustrations.

SKETCHES BY "BOZ."

PICKWICK. 2 vols.

OLIVER TWIST.

NICHOLAS NICKLEBY. 2 vols.

MARTIN CHUZZLEWIT. 2 vols.

DOMBEY AND SON. 2 vols.

DAVID COPPERFIELD. 2 vols.

CHRISTMAS BOOKS.

OUR MUTUAL FRIEND. 2 vols.

CHRISTMAS STORIES.

BLEAK HOUSE. 2 vols.

LITTLE DORRIT. 2 vols.

OLD CURIOSITY SHOP AND REPRINTED PIECES. 2 vols.

BARNABY RUDGE. 2 vols.

UNCOMMERCIAL TRAVELLER.

GREAT EXPECTATIONS.

TALE OF TWO CITIES.

CHILD'S HISTORY OF ENGLAND.

EDWIN DROOD AND MISCELLANIES.

PICTURES FROM ITALY AND AMERICAN NOTES.

The Cheapest and Handiest Edition of

THE WORKS OF CHARLES DICKENS.

The Pocket Volume Edition of Charles Dickens's Works.

In 30 Vols., small fcap. 8vo, £2 5s.

LIBRARY
OF
CONTEMPORARY SCIENCE.

SCIENCE OF LANGUAGE. By A. HOVELACQUE. 5s.
BIOLOGY. By DR. C. LETOURNEAU. 6s.
ANTHROPOLOGY. By DR. PAUL TOPINARD. 7s. 6d.
ÆSTHETICS. By EUGENE VERON. 7s. 6d.
PHILOSOPHY. By ANDRE LEFEVRE. 7s. 6d.
SOCIOLOGY. By DR. CHARLES LETOURNEAU. 10s.

LEVER'S (CHARLES) WORKS.
CHEAP EDITION.
Fancy boards, 2s. 6d.

CHARLES O'MALLEY.
TOM BURKE.
THE KNIGHT OF GWYNNE.
MARTINS OF CROMARTIN.
THE DALTONS.
ROLAND CASHEL.
DAVENPORT DUNN.
DODD FAMILY.

Fancy boards, 2s.

THE O'DONOGHUE.
FORTUNES OF GLENCORE.
HARRY LORREQUER.
ONE OF THEM.
A DAY'S RIDE.
JACK HINTON.
BARRINGTON.
TONY BUTLER.
MAURICE TIERNAY.
SIR BROOKE FOSBROOKE.
BRAMLEIGHS OF BISHOP'S FOLLY.
LORD KILGOBBIN.
LUTTRELL OF ARRAN.
RENT IN THE CLOUD and ST. PATRICK'S EVE.
THAT BOY OF NORCOTT'S.
CORNELIUS O'DOWD.
SIR JASPER CAREW.
NUTS AND NUT-CRACKERS.

Also in sets, 27 Vols., cloth, for £4 4s.

WHYTE-MELVILLE'S WORKS.
CHEAP EDITION.
Crown 8vo, fancy boards, 2s. each, or 2s. 6d. in cloth.

UNCLE JOHN.
THE WHITE ROSE.
CERISE.
BROOKES OF BRIDLEMERE.
"BONES AND I."
"M. OR N."
CONTRABAND.
MARKET HARBOROUGH.
SARCHEDON.
SONGS AND VERSES.
SATANELLA.
THE TRUE CROSS.
KATERFELTO.
SISTER LOUISE.
ROSINE.
BLACK BUT COMELY.
RIDING RECOLLECTIONS.
TILBURY NOGO.
ROY'S WIFE.

List of Books, Drawing Examples, Diagrams, Models, Instruments, &c.,

INCLUDING

THOSE ISSUED UNDER THE AUTHORITY OF THE SCIENCE AND ART DEPARTMENT, SOUTH KENSINGTON, FOR THE USE OF SCHOOLS AND ART AND SCIENCE CLASSES.

CATALOGUE OF MODERN WORKS ON SCIENCE AND TECHNOLOGY. 8vo, sewed, 1s.

BENSON (W.)—

PRINCIPLES OF THE SCIENCE OF COLOUR. Small 4to, cloth, 15s.

MANUAL OF THE SCIENCE OF COLOUR. Coloured Frontispiece and Illustrations. 12mo, cloth, 2s. 6d.

BRADLEY (THOMAS), of the Royal Military Academy, Woolwich—

ELEMENTS OF GEOMETRICAL DRAWING. In Two Parts, with 60 Plates. Oblong folio, half-bound, each part 16s. Selections (from the above) of 20 Plates, for the use of the Royal Military Academy, Woolwich. Oblong folio, half-bound, 16s.

BURCHETT—

LINEAR PERSPECTIVE. With Illustrations. Post 8vo, cloth, 7s.

PRACTICAL GEOMETRY. Post 8vo, cloth, 5s.

DEFINITIONS OF GEOMETRY. Third Edition. 24mo, sewed, 5d.

CARROLL (JOHN)—

FREEHAND DRAWING LESSONS FOR THE BLACK BOARD. 6s.

CUBLEY (W. H.)—

A SYSTEM OF ELEMENTARY DRAWING. With Illustrations and Examples. Imperial 4to, sewed, 8s.

DAVISON (ELLIS A.)—

DRAWING FOR ELEMENTARY SCHOOLS. Post 8vo, cloth, 3s.

MODEL DRAWING. 12mo, cloth, 3s.

THE AMATEUR HOUSE-CARPENTER: A Guide in Building, Making, and Repairing. With numerous Illustrations, drawn on Wood by the Author. Demy 8vo, 10s. 6d.

DELAMOTTE (P. H.)—

PROGRESSIVE DRAWING-BOOK FOR BEGINNERS. 12mo, 3s. 6d.

DICKSEE (J. R.)—

SCHOOL PERSPECTIVE. 8vo, cloth, 5s

DYCE—

DRAWING-BOOK OF THE GOVERNMENT SCHOOL
OF DESIGN : ELEMENTARY OUTLINES OF ORNAMENT. 50 Plates.
Small folio, sewed, 5s. ; mounted, 18s.

INTRODUCTION TO DITTO. Fcap. 8vo, 6d.

FOSTER (VERE)—

DRAWING-BOOKS :
(a) Forty-two Numbers, at 1d. each.
(b) Forty-six Numbers, at 3d. each. The set b includes the subjects in a.

DRAWING-CARDS :
Freehand Drawing : First Grade, Sets I., II., III., price 1s. each ; in cloth cases,
1s. 6d. each.
Second Grade, Set I., price 2s. ; in cloth case. 3s.

HENSLOW (PROFESSOR)—

ILLUSTRATIONS TO BE EMPLOYED IN THE
PRACTICAL LESSONS ON BOTANY. Prepared for South Kensington
Museum. Post 8vo, sewed, 6d.

JACOBSTHAL (E.)—

GRAMMATIK DER ORNAMENTE, in 7 Parts of 20
Plates each. Price, unmounted, £3 13s. 6d. ; mounted on cardboard, £11 4s.
The Parts can be had separately.

JEWITT—

HANDBOOK OF PRACTICAL PERSPECTIVE. 18mo,
cloth, 1s. 6d.

KENNEDY (JOHN)—

FIRST GRADE PRACTICAL GEOMETRY. 12mo, 6d.

FREEHAND DRAWING-BOOK. 16mo, cloth, 1s. 6d.

LINDLEY (JOHN)—

SYMMETRY OF VEGETATION : Principles to be
Observed in the Delineation of Plants. 12mo, sewed, 1s.

MARSHALL—

HUMAN BODY. Text and Plates reduced from the large
Diagrams. 2 vols., cloth, £1 1s.

NEWTON (E. TULLEY, F.G.S.)—

THE TYPICAL PARTS IN THE SKELETONS OF A
CAT, DUCK, AND CODFISH, being a Catalogue with Comparative Descriptions arranged in a Tabular Form. Demy 8vo, 3s.

OLIVER (PROFESSOR)—

ILLUSTRATIONS OF THE VEGETABLE KINGDOM.
109 Plates. Oblong 8vo, cloth. Plain, 16s.; coloured, £1 6s.

POYNTER (E. J., R.A.), *issued under the superintendence of*—

ELEMENTARY, FREEHAND, ORNAMENT :
Book I. Simple Geometrical Forms, 6d.
„ II. Conventionalised Floral Forms, &c., 6d.

FREEHAND—FIRST GRADE :
Book I. Simple Objects and Ornament, 6d.
„ II. Various Objects, 6d.
„ III. Objects and Architectural Ornaments, 6d.
„ IV. Architectural Ornament, 6d.
„ V. Objects of Glass and Pottery, 6d.
, VI. Common Objects, 6d.

POYNTER—Continued.

FREEHAND—SECOND GRADE:

Book I. Various Forms of Anthermion, &c., 1s.
„ II. Greek, Roman, and Venetian, 1s.
„ III. Italian Renaissance, 1s.
„ IV. Roman, Italian, Japanese, &c. 1s.

THE SOUTH KENSINGTON DRAWING CARDS,

Containing the same examples as the books:
Elementary Freehand Cards. Four packets, 9d. each.
First Grade Freehand Cards. Six packets, 1s. each.
Second Grade Freehand Cards. Four packets, 1s. 6d. each.

PUCKETT (R. CAMPBELL)—

SCIOGRAPHY, OR RADIAL PROJECTION OF

SHADOWS. Crown 8vo, cloth, 6s.

REDGRAVE—

MANUAL AND CATECHISM ON COLOUR. Fifth

Edition. 24mo, sewed, 9d.

ROBSON (GEORGE)—

ELEMENTARY BUILDING CONSTRUCTION. Oblong

folio, sewed, 8s.

WALLIS (GEORGE)—

DRAWING-BOOK. Oblong, sewed, 3s. 6d.; mounted, 8s.

WORNUM (R. N.)—

THE CHARACTERISTICS OF STYLES: An Intro-

duction to the Study of the History of Ornamental Art. Royal 8vo, cloth, 8s.

DRAWING FOR YOUNG CHILDREN. Containing 150

Copies. 16mo, cloth, 3s. 6d.

EDUCATIONAL DIVISION OF SOUTH KENSINGTON

MUSEUM: CLASSIFIED CATALOGUE OF. Ninth Edition. 8vo, 7s.

ELEMENTARY DRAWING COPY-BOOKS, for the Use of

Children from four years old and upwards, in Schools and Families. Compiled by a Student certificated by the Science and Art Department as an Art Teacher. Seven Books in 4to, sewed:

Book I. Letters, 8d.
„ II. Ditto, 8d.
„ III. Geometrical and Ornamental Forms, 8d.

Book IV. Objects, 8d.
„ V. Leaves, 8d.
„ VI. Birds, Animals, &c., 8d.
„ VII. Leaves, Flowers, and Sprays, 8d.

⁎ Or in Sets of Seven Books, 4s. 6d.

ENGINEER AND MACHINIST DRAWING-BOOK, 16 Parts,

71 Plates. Folio, £1 12s.; mounted, £3 4s.

PRINCIPLES OF DECORATIVE ART. Folio, sewed, 1s.

DIAGRAM OF THE COLOURS OF THE SPECTRUM,

with Explanatory Letterpress, on roller, 10s. 6d.

COPIES FOR OUTLINE DRAWING:

DYCE'S ELEMENTARY OUTLINES OF ORNAMENT, 50 Selected Plates, mounted back and front, 18s. ; unmounted, sewed, 5s.

WEITBRICHT'S OUTLINES OF ORNAMENT, reproduced by Herman, 12 Plates, mounted back and front, 8s. 6d. ; unmounted, 2s.

MORGHEN'S OUTLINES OF THE HUMAN FIGURE reproduced by Herman, 20 Plates, mounted back and front, 15s. ; unmounted, 3s. 4d.

ONE SET OF FOUR PLATES, Outlines of Tarsia, from Gruner, mounted, 3s. 6d.; unmounted, 7d.

ALBERTOLLI'S FOLIAGE, one set of Four Plates, mounted, 3s. 6d.; unmounted, 5d.

OUTLINE OF TRAJAN FRIEZE, mounted, 1s.

WALLIS'S DRAWING-BOOK, mounted, 8s., unmounted, 3s. 6d.

OUTLINE DRAWINGS OF FLOWERS, Eight] Sheets, mounted, 3s. 6d. ; unmounted, 8d.

COPIES FOR SHADED DRAWING:

COURSE OF DESIGN. By CH. BARGUE (French), 20 Selected Sheets, 11 at 2s. and 9 at 3s. each. · £2 9s.

ARCHITECTURAL STUDIES. By J. B. TRIPON. 10 Plates, £1.

MECHANICAL STUDIES. By J. B. TRIPON. 15s. per dozen.

FOLIATED SCROLL FROM THE VATICAN, unmounted, 5d.; mounted, 1s. 3d.

TWELVE HEADS after Holbein, selected from his Drawings in Her Majesty's Collection at Windsor. Reproduced in Autotype. Half imperial, £1 16s.

LESSONS IN SEPIA, 9s. per dozen, or 1s. each.

COLOURED EXAMPLES:

A SMALL DIAGRAM OF COLOUR, mounted, 1s. 6d.; unmounted, 9d.

TWO PLATES OF ELEMENTARY DESIGN, unmounted, 1s.; mounted, 3s. 9d

CAMELLIA, mounted, 3s. 9d.; unmounted, 2s. 9d.

COTMAN'S PENCIL LANDSCAPES (set of 9), mounted, 15s.

    ,,   SEPIA DRAWINGS (set of 5), mounted, £1.

ALLONGE'S LANDSCAPES IN CHARCOAL (Six), at 4s. each, or the set, £1 4s.

SOLID MODELS, &c.:

*Box of Models, £1 4s.

A Stand with a universal joint, to show the solid models, &c., £1 18s.

*One Wire Quadrangle, with a circle and cross within it, and one straight wire. One solid cube. One Skeleton Wire Cube. One Sphere. One Cone. One Cylinder. One Hexagonal Prism. £2 2s.

Skeleton Cube in wood, 3s. 6d.

18-inch Skeleton Cube in wood, 12s.

*Three objects of *form* in Pottery:

    Indian Jar,   ⎫
    Celadon Jar, ⎬ 18s. 6d.
    Bottle,   ⎭

*Five selected Vases in Majolica Ware, £2 11s.

*Three selected Vases in Earthenware, 18s.

Imperial Deal Frames, glazed, without sunk rings, 10s. each.

*Davidson's Smaller Solid Models, in Box, £2, containing—

2 Square Slabs.	Octagon Prism.	Triangular Prism.
9 Oblong Blocks (steps).	Cylinder.	Pyramid, Equilateral.
2 Cubes.	Cone.	Pyramid, Isosceles.
4 Square Blocks.	Jointed Cross.	Square Block.

* Davidson's Advanced Drawing Models, £9.—The following is a brief description of the Models:—An Obelisk—composed of 2 Octagonal Slabs, 26 and 20 inches across, and each 3 inches high; 1 Cube, 12 inches edge; 1 Monolith (forming

    * Models, &c., entered as sets, can only be supplied in sets.

SOLID MODELS, &c.—*Continued.*

the body of the obelisk) 3 feet high; 1 Pyramid, 6 inches base; the complete object is thus nearly 5 feet high. A Market Cross—composed of 3 Slabs, 24, 18, and 12 inches across, and each 3 inches high; 1 Upright, 3 feet high; 2 Cross Arms, united by mortise and tenon joints; complete height, 3 feet 9 inches. A Step-Ladder, 23 inches high. A Kitchen Table, 14½ inches high. A Chair to correspond. A Four-legged Stool, with projecting top and cross rails, height 14 inches. A Tub, with handles and projecting hoops, and the divisions between the staves plainly marked. A strong Trestle, 18 inches high. A Hollow Cylinder, 9 inches in diameter, and 12 inches long, divided lengthwise. A Hollow Sphere, 9 inches in diameter, divided into semi-spheres, one of which is again divided into quarters; the semi-sphere, when placed on the cylinder, gives the form and principles of shading a dome, whilst one of the quarters placed on half the cylinder forms a niche.

*Davidson's Apparatus for Teaching Practical Geometry (22 models), £5.

*Binn's Models for Illustrating the Elementary Principles of Orthographic Projection as applied to Mechanical Drawing, in box, £1 10s.

Miller's Class Drawing Models.—These Models are particularly adapted for teaching large classes; the stand is very strong, and the universal joint will hold the Models in any position. *Wood Models*: Square Prism, 12 inches side, 18 inches high; Hexagonal Prism, 14 inches side, 18 inches high; Cube, 14 inches side Cylinder, 13 inches diameter, 16 inches high; Hexagon Pyramid, 14 inches diameter, 22½ inches side; Square Pyramid, 14 inches side, 22½ inches side; Cone, 13 inches diameter, 22½ inches side; Skeleton Cube, 19 inches solid wood 1¾ inch square; Intersecting Circles, 19 inches solid wood 2¼ by 1¾ inches. *Wire Models*: Triangular Prism, 17 inches side, 22 inches high; Square Prism, 14 inches side, 20 inches high; Hexagonal Prism, 16 inches diameter, 21 inches high; Cylinder, 14 inches diameter, 21 inches high; Hexagon Pyramid, 18 inches diameter, 24 inches high; Square Pyramid, 17 inches side, 24 inches high; Cone, 17 inches side, 24 inches high; Skeleton Cube, 19 inches side; Intersecting Circles, 19 inches side; Plain Circle, 19 inches side; Plain Square, 19 inches side. Table, 27 inches by 21½ inches. Stand. The set complete, £14 13s.

Vulcanite Set Square, 5s.

Large Compasses, with chalk-holder, 5s.

*Slip, two set squares and **T** square, 5s.

*Parkes's Case of Instruments, containing 6-inch compasses with pen and pencil leg, 5s.

*Prize Instrument Case, with 6-inch compasses, pen and pencil leg, 2 small compasses, pen and scale, 18s.

6-inch Compasses, with shifting pen and point, 4s. 6d.

Small Compass, in case, 1s.

* Models, &c., entered as sets, can only be supplied in sets.

LARGE DIAGRAMS.

ASTRONOMICAL:

TWELVE SHEETS. By JOHN DREW, Ph. Dr., F.R.S.A. Prepared for the Committee of Council on Education. Sheets, £2 8s.; on rollers and varnished, £4 4s.

BOTANICAL:

NINE SHEETS. Illustrating a Practical Method of Teaching Botany. By Professor HENSLOW, F.L.S. £2; on rollers and varnished, £3 3s.

CLASS.	DIVISION.	SECTION.	DIAGRAM.
Dicotyledon	{ Angiospermous .. {	Thalamifloral	1
		Calycifloral	2 & 3
		Corollifloral	4
		Incomplete	5
	Gymnospermous		6
Monocotyledons	{ Petaloid .. ..{	Superior ..	7
		Inferior	8
	Glumaceous		9

BUILDING CONSTRUCTION:

TEN SHEETS. By WILLIAM J. GLENNY, Professor of Drawing, King's College. In sets, £1 1s.

LAXTON'S EXAMPLES OF BUILDING CONSTRUCTION IN TWO DIVISIONS, containing 32 Imperial Plates, £1.

BUSBRIDGE'S DRAWINGS OF BUILDING CONSTRUCTION. 11 Sheets. 2s. 9d. Mounted, 5s. 6d.

GEOLOGICAL:

DIAGRAM OF BRITISH STRATA. By H. W. BRISTOW, F.R.S., F.G.S. A Sheet, 4s.; on roller and varnished, 7s. 6d.

MECHANICAL:

DIAGRAMS OF THE MECHANICAL POWERS, AND THEIR APPLICATIONS IN MACHINERY AND THE ARTS GENERALLY. By DR. JOHN ANDERSON.
  8 Diagrams, highly coloured on stout paper, 3 feet 6 inches by 2 feet 6 inches. Sheets £1 per set; mounted on rollers, £2.

DIAGRAMS OF THE STEAM-ENGINE. By Professor GOODEVE and Professor SHELLEY. Stout paper, 40 inches by 27 inches, highly coloured.
  Sets of 41 Diagrams (52½ Sheets), £6 6s.; varnished and mounted on rollers, £11 11s.

MACHINE DETAILS. By Professor UNWIN. 16 Coloured Diagrams. Sheets, £2 2s.; mounted on rollers and varnished, £3 14s.

SELECTED EXAMPLES OF MACHINES, OF IRON AND WOOD (French). By STANISLAS PETTIT. 60 Sheets, £3 5s.; 13s. per dozen.

BUSBRIDGE'S DRAWINGS OF MACHINE CONSTRUCTION. 50 Sheets, 12s. 6d. Mounted, £1 5s.

LESSONS IN MECHANICAL DRAWING. By STANISLAS PETTIT. 1s. per dozen; also larger Sheets, more advanced copies, 2s. per dozen.

LESSONS IN ARCHITECTURAL DRAWING. By STANISLAS PETTIT. 1s. per dozen; also larger Sheets, more advanced copies, 2s. per dozen.

PHYSIOLOGICAL:

ELEVEN SHEETS. Illustrating Human Physiology, Life Size and Coloured from Nature. Prepared under the direction of JOHN MARSHALL, F.R.S., F.R.C.S., &c. Each Sheet, 12s. 6d. On canvas and rollers, varnished, £1 1s.

1. THE SKELETON AND LIGAMENTS.
2. THE MUSCLES, JOINTS, AND ANIMAL MECHANICS.
3. THE VISCERA IN POSITION.—THE STRUCTURE OF THE LUNGS.
4. THE ORGANS OF CIRCULATION.
5. THE LYMPHATICS OR ABSORBENTS.
6. THE ORGANS OF DIGESTION.
7. THE BRAIN AND NERVES.—THE ORGANS OF THE VOICE.
8. THE ORGANS OF THE SENSES.
9. THE ORGANS OF THE SENSES.
10. THE MICROSCOPIC STRUCTURE OF THE TEXTURES AND ORGANS.
11. THE MICROSCOPIC STRUCTURE OF THE TEXTURES AND ORGANS.

HUMAN BODY, LIFE SIZE. By JOHN MARSHALL, F.R.S., F.R.C.S. Each Sheet, 12s. 6d.; on canvas and rollers, varnished, £1 1s. Explanatory Key, 1s.

1. THE SKELETON, Front View.
2. THE MUSCLES, Front View.
3. THE SKELETON, Back View.
4. THE MUSCLES, Back View.
5. THE SKELETON, Side View.
6. THE MUSCLES, Side View.
7. THE FEMALE SKELETON, Front View.

ZOOLOGICAL:

TEN SHEETS. Illustrating the Classification of Animals. By ROBERT PATTERSON. £2; on canvas and rollers, varnished, £3 10s.
  The same, reduced in size on Royal paper, in 9 Sheets, uncoloured, 12s.

THE FORTNIGHTLY REVIEW.

Edited by JOHN MORLEY.

THE FORTNIGHTLY REVIEW is published on the 1st of every month (the issue on the 15th being suspended), and a Volume is completed every Six Months.

The following are among the Contributors:—

SIR RUTHERFORD ALCOCK.
MATHEW ARNOLD.
PROFESSOR BAIN.
PROFESSOR BEESLY.
DR. BRIDGES.
HON. GEORGE C. BRODRICK
SIR GEORGE CAMPBELL, M.P.
J. CHAMBERLAIN, M.P.
PROFESSOR SIDNEY COLVIN.
MONTAGUE COOKSON, Q.C.
L. H. COURTNEY, M.P.
G. H. DARWIN.
F. W. FARRAR.
PROFESSOR FAWCETT, M.P.
EDWARD A. FREEMAN.
MRS. GARRET-ANDERSON.
M. E. GRANT DUFF, M.P.
THOMAS HARE.
F. HARRISON.
LORD HOUGHTON.
PROFESSOR HUXLEY.
PROFESSOR JEVONS.
ÉMILE DE LAVELEYE.
T. E. CLIFFE LESLIE.
RIGHT HON. R. LOWE, M.P.
SIR JOHN LUBBOCK, M.P.

LORD LYTTON.
SIR H. S. MAINE.
DR. MAUDSLEY.
PROFESSOR MAX MÜLLER.
PROFESSOR HENRY MORLEY.
G. OSBORNE MORGAN, Q.C., M.P.
WILLIAM MORRIS.
F. W. NEWMAN.
W. G. PALGRAVE.
WALTER H. PATER.
RT. HON. LYON PLAYFAIR, M.P.
DANTE GABRIEL ROSSETTI.
HERBERT SPENCER.
HON. E. L. STANLEY.
SIR J. FITZJAMES STEPHEN, Q.C.
LESLIE STEPHEN.
J. HUTCHISON STIRLING.
A. C. SWINBURNE.
DR. VON SYBEL.
J. A. SYMONDS.
W. T. THORNTON.
HON. LIONEL A. TOLLEMACHE.
ANTHONY TROLLOPE.
PROFESSOR TYNDALL.
THE EDITOR.
&c. &c. &c.

THE FORTNIGHTLY REVIEW *is published at* 2s. 6d.

CHAPMAN & HALL, LIMITED, 11, HENRIETTA STREET,
COVENT GARDEN, W.C.

CHARLES DICKENS, AND EVANS,]   [CRYSTAL PALACE PRESS.